THE
APOCALYPSE
REVELATIONS

A NOVEL BY
BILL SALUS

First printing: March 2019

Prophecy Depot Publishing
P.O. Box 5612
La Quinta, CA 92248

Customer Service: +1 714-376-5487

www.prophecydepotministries.net

ISBN: 9781797573885

Cover by Matthew Salhus and Mark Conn
Interior by Mark Conn

Printed in the United States of America

Contents

Contents *(continued)*

Acknowledgements

Heartfelt thanks to my wife, children, grandchildren and friends who inspired me to write this book. A further debt of gratitude is extended to Ned and Karol Bankston, Bob and Lynette Holmes, Brad Myers, Ladd Holton, Bill and Beverly Williams, Gordon and Ruth Peterson, Scott and Deborah Bueling, the Gaskin's, Mark Conn, Ellen Traylor, our Prophecy Depot Ministry Partners and all those below who in one way or another, through prayer, encouragement, support, research, or otherwise, genuinely blessed this book.

Introduction to
The Apocalypse Revelations

Ancient biblical prophecies are about to roll off their parchments and pound onto the pavement, and they promise to pack a powerful global punch. Americans are about to be plunged into a perilous period, of which the Bible has more to say about than any other period in mankind's history.

The Apocalypse Revelations takes the readers on a journey through the end times. Follow a family as they experience the prophecies that are destined to change the world forever. It's not enough to simply talk about these predictions, but we need to understand how they will impact our lives when they find their fulfillment. This is the true intent of this novel.

This book merges together the novel sections in the books called, *Revelation Road, Hope Beyond the Horizon* and *Apocalypse Road, Revelation for the Final Generation*. These two books combined a novel with a biblical commentary. Now you can read those two novels as one stand-alone book.

This book chronologically orders the events that will happen soon between now and the start of what the Bible describes as the final 7-year Tribulation Period. These events take you through the Church Age and beyond into the gap the follows it, but precedes the turbulent 7-years of final tribulation.

If you are concerned about what your future holds, then consider The Apocalypse Revelations as your instruction manual for the events of the END TIMES!

Best Reading Regards - Bill Salus

1

Iran Prepares for the Apocalypse!

"The time has come! Islam's messiah has readied for his return," declared the charismatic Shiite cleric Zamani Nikahd. "President Zakiri, we must alert the others without delay, and inform them that their multi-front attack upon the little Jewish Satan is now imminent!"

Nikahd, the mesmerizing spiritual mentor of the Iranian President Muktada Zakiri, claimed to have recently received another compelling night vision from his Islamic Messiah, Muhammad al-Mahdi.

"Zamani, you must be certain! We cannot afford any costly mistakes. Israel has recently completed the deployment of its Iron Dome defenses around Tel Aviv and Jerusalem. They will retaliate hard against us and our friends if they survive," cautioned the apocalyptically-minded president.

"There can be no doubt. The vision was crystal clear," Nikahd insisted.

"What did you see? Was he riding furiously upon his white horse again?" Zakiri anxiously inquired.

"In the night vision, al-Mahdi rode his white horse through the mushroom cloud over northern Israel again, but this time he had his sword in one hand, and the holy Qur'an held high in the other. A multitude of his followers appeared, all lining the streets of Jerusalem and praising him. They all bore the visible marks of prostration on their foreheads, from bowing down five times to pray," Nikahd exclaimed.[1]

"Praise be to Allah," Zakiri replied. "I will persuade the Ayatollah that, at last, the time of the blessed Mahdi's return draws near! I will give him the good news that the Islamic Republic of Iran shall soon reign over our Muslim brothers once and for all!"

"No need for persuasion," the Imam assured him. "I discussed this latest vision with the Ayatollah just prior to coming here. He confirmed the vision's interpretation, and blessed the plan to attack Israel. He instructed me to tell you to visit him secretly upon the completion of our meeting."

"As you know, I have been preparing for al-Mahdi's return ever since I received my divine calling to create the apocalypse that hastens his coming," Zakiri declared. "The Ayatollah's blessings and your night vision serve as my final confirmation to wipe Israel off the pages of time!"

"We must put the multi-front attack against the Jews in motion straight away," Nikahd urged. "Are the Syrians, Hezbollah and Hamas prepared to attack at your command?"

"We possess legitimate war-pacts with them all. They are obligated to act," confirmed Zakiri.

"Those pacts only come into play when one or all of us come under Israeli attack," Nikahd reminded him. "This is entirely different; we are ordering, not receiving the attack. Our proxies may fear Israel's retaliation and ignore their commitment to us."

"Absolutely not!" Zakiri insisted. "Syrian President Tereiri realizes he has no choice. He fears the loss of political power, if not his own life, without our support. Our protection kept him in power during the Syrian Civil War but youth protests in that region have gotten out of hand. He needs us badly. Furthermore, our military cemented relations with his army commanders at that time. The Syrian forces are in our back pockets."

"Hezbollah and Hamas as well? Are they prepared to mobilize upon command?" Nikahd questioned.

"They seek to spill Israeli blood across the Holy Land and to drive the Jew monkeys into the Mediterranean Sea!" Zakiri exclaimed.

Hamas Called to Iran

Sadegh Mousavi was enjoying an early afternoon lunch with his most trusted military leader, Ahmad Al-Masri, when his secretary Neda interrupted on the intercom. Excusing himself momentarily from their daily briefing, he pushed a button on the phone and picked up the receiver. "This had better be important!" he growled.

Apparently enthused by what he was hearing on the other end of the receiver, Mousavi nodded frequently as the secretary relayed a message. He finished the call by simply saying, "Tell Zakiri's office we will be there first thing tomorrow morning."

As he hung up, Mousavi leaned over his desk and boasted to his top General, "Looks like we fly to Tehran tomorrow to meet with Hezbollah and the Syrians. Neda is seeing to our travel arrangements. She will transmit our flight information to your office by the day's end."

Sadegh Mousavi had moved up the ladder to the highest rung of Hamas' organizational hierarchy. He had begun his bid for Hamas' highest post in the aftermath of *Operation Cast Lead*, in early 2009. He was the organization's most skillful diplomat and one of the primary architects behind the recently formed Hamas-Fatah unity government. Many Arabs believed that without Mousavi's political brinksmanship, the two Palestinian factions would still be warring against one another. But they weren't; their civil rivalries had ceased.

Mousavi had also succeeded in gaining the trust of Israel's liberal president, Eliezer Moday. Their strange bedfellows' friendship was creating a schism between Moday and Israel's conservative prime minister, Moshe Kaufman. Kaufman didn't trust that Mousavi's political agenda had Israel's best interest at heart.

Moday had convinced many of the liberal Knesset members that Israel's only chance to avert all-out Mideast war was to give back the land Israel had acquired in 1967. Kaufman believed, like his predecessor, Benjamin Netanyahu, that forfeiting this land would deprive Israel of defensible borders. Political head-butting was beginning to divide the country.

Looking hopefully at Al-Masri, Mousavi asked, "Has the latest weapons shipment been safely smuggled through the Rafah Crossing?"

"Yes sir," Al Masri said with a nod, "it was just confirmed to me this morning."

"Excellent," Mousavi enthused. "Have the weapons deployed immediately to the appropriate munitions locations. Alert your commanders that we are meeting with Zakiri, and that Hamas may soon be called into action against Israel!"

Syrian President Receives Iranian Ultimatum!

Iranian President Muktada Zakiri stood behind his stately desk as Syrian President Hassan Tereiri entered his office. The two men's eyes locked on one another for a brief moment, but Tereiri was quick to lower his head. "Allah be praised," he humbly greeted.

Zakiri waved his hand at the stiff leather chair before his desk and declared, "Hassan, my compatriot, please sit. I have something important to tell you."

Without delay the Syrian complied. Zakiri gazed down on him in a show of power, before slowly settling into his own palatial chair, the mammoth desk between them. Tereiri squirmed.

"Mr. President," Zakiri said, condescendingly, "Do you know why I have asked you to meet with me alone, in advance of our sacred meeting with our Muslim brothers?"

Fidgeting, Tereiri replied, "I am blessed beyond words, Mr. President that you would choose to meet with me personally. To what do I owe this honor?"

Zakiri leaned back and exclaimed, "I have chosen to warn you in advance of the powerful information that will be conveyed, and of the behavior I want you to exhibit throughout! You must do exactly as I command, out of respect for all that Iran has done to keep you in power."

President Tereiri was stunned. "What is this warning, your Grace?"

Zakiri looked sternly at the Syrian. "As you clearly know, if it were not for my protection, the rebel dogs that are after your blood would have already prevailed against you. Iran's funding has provided you with weaponry and personnel to help you remove the Zionist pigs from the sacred land of Palestine. The time has come to put these weapons to task!"

Moving forward and placing both hands firmly on his desk, Zakiri exhorted, "I must address you bluntly regarding certain visions received from Allah by Nikahd. They confirmed that Allah has called all Muslims to this crowning moment. Nikahd's latest vision instructs that the time to multilaterally strike Israel has come!"

As Zakiri had anticipated, Tereiri evinced little enthusiasm at this pronouncement. Rising, Zakiri peered directly into his political puppet's eyes. "Did you hear me, Hassan? The long-awaited moment has arrived. I am counting on you to perform as instructed!"

Tereiri stammered, "Are...are you absolutely certain the time is right, Mr. President?"

Zakiri fumed, "Are you questioning me?"

With mounting courage, Tereiri declared, "Israel is prepared for this, and I fear my country, not yours, will suffer the brunt of the burden. The IDF has promised to destroy me and my entire posterity in the event of such an attack."[2]

"Where is your faith?" Zakiri decried. "Would you put your clan before the wishes of Allah? Certainly, Allah's blessings and protection are bestowed upon us in this war against the Jews!" Then, taking a deep breath, he donned a more subdued demeanor. "Where is your faith, man? Don't disappoint Iran or your fellow countrymen. You will sit quietly, as ordered, at tomorrow's meeting, and you will support the offensive I propose to our united brothers, lest Iran be tempted to cut you off from our blessed protection. There are limits to my patience with you and your country. I warn you, don't test them at tomorrow's meeting!"

Trembling, Tereiri asked, "What, precisely, do you expect from me at this sacred meeting?"

Zakiri sat down with a sigh. "That's a much better response, Hassan. You will not question the moment that we choose to strike the little Satan. You will support the actions that are required of you and your army. This decree is not negotiable and your leadership in the destruction of Israel will garner praise from throughout the Islamic world. Now, I ask you a final time: can I count on you to support what Allah himself has declared to be our finest hour?"

Realizing that he had no choice, Tereiri donned a diplomatic smile and confirmed, "Mr. President, I will do as you propose and act according to Allah's will."

Zakiri offered a benediction, as Tereiri prepared to depart. "May Allah bestow the bounty of his blessings upon you, your family, and your countrymen."

Tereiri bowed respectfully. "As you wish, Mr. President."

Without further utterance, their private meeting was adjourned.

Iran Instructs Proxies, Syria, Hezbollah, and Hamas, to Attack Israel!

It was a cozy group that gathered in Zakiri's chamber the next day. "Gentlemen, Iran greets you all in the blessed name of Allah," Zakiri greeted his Islamic brothers.

Similar salutations echoed back from his illustrious proxy leaders and the top commanders seated at their sides.

"As you all know," Zakiri began, "we have been waiting for that anticipated moment which Allah has appointed to bring about the destruction of Israel. I am pleased to announce that, according to a recent revelation of Muhammad Al-Mahdi to my trusted advisor Zamani Nikahd, that moment has arrived!"

Pausing, Zakiri observed the attendees seated around the oversized oval table. Except for the Syrian, Hassan Tereiri, they all nodded approvingly, and with invigorated interest.

Observing Tereiri's lack of enthusiasm, Zakiri stared him in the eye, causing his colleagues to also turn their attention toward him. Squirming slightly, in his palatial high back chair, Tereiri nodded, just as his peers had done.

Continuing with his rallying speech, Zakiri said, "The last time you all joined me here in Tehran we formed a war-pact against the Zionist regime. At that time, we vowed to fight together against Allah's number one and two enemies, the Jews and their American supporters."

Again, Zakiri paused to observe his comrades' audible responses.

The outspoken Secretary General of Hezbollah, Muhammad Imad Fadlallah, raised his voice above the others and declared, "Death to the Two Satans!"

Satisfied, Zakiri informed the group of the specific details of Nikahd's vision and concluded, "The vision signals that the time to wipe Israel off the map is now!"

At those words, Sadegh Mousavi of Hamas could no longer restrain his enthusiasm. Jumping up, he pounded the table, and blurted out, "Death to Israel! Victory shall be ours!"

His comments evoked a frenzied response from the other leaders. Even Hassan Tereiri expressed delight. The meeting had become a pep rally against the Jewish State, as every man, to the last of them, testified their anti-Semitic sentiment.

Zakiri couldn't have been more pleased, and quickly moved into the war plans. "No weapon can be withheld from attacking Israel. All of your combined firepower must be unleashed promptly and simultaneously! Iran is prepared to follow in a second wave with our mighty arsenal."

This statement took some of the wind out of Tereiri's sails, causing him to exhibit a slightly soured facial expression, which President Zakiri caught out of the corner of his eye. To appease his Syrian cohort, Zakiri added, "Iran guarantees that our second wave will strike Israel early, before they can mount a serious response."

Hezbollah's Fadlallah boasted, "There is nothing to fear, Hezbollah handed Israel its head on a platter in our summer war with the Jews in 2006. Attacking together we can assuredly destroy the Zionist pigs and liberate Palestine for Hamas and our Palestinian brothers."

Continued war plotting and anti-Israel comments characterized the remainder of the four-hour conference. Plans to ambush Israel from all sides were solidified behind closed doors.

When the meeting adjourned, there were no photo shoots or press releases, as the leaders from Syria, Hezbollah, and Hamas left undetected through a side door. The moment they emerged from the palace, they were escorted off in their limousines for the Tehran Imam Khomeini Airport, and their trips back to their respective countries.

Their generals, however, remained behind for secret consultation with the IRGC commanders. When Israeli intelligence picked up on the fact that the IRGC was conducting such a meeting, they perceived something dangerous was brewing, and promptly began alerting key military and political personnel throughout the nation.

Iran had anticipated this response and quickly issued a reverse public relations press release to diffuse Israeli fears. *Iran Prepares Proxies for Israeli Preemptive Strikes*, the *Tehran Times* reported, thus shifting the onus onto Israel. The hope was that Israel and the world would think the commanders were meeting for defensive, rather than offensive military purposes.

The scheme apparently worked, as business in Israel went on as usual.

2

Troublesome Times on Humanity's Horizon

Clearing out his desk that Friday, eleven-year-old Tyler Allen Thompson closed the books on his elementary school experience. Finally, the day had come that he was graduating to Eastside Middle School, a few blocks away. One last bell and a much-anticipated summer vacation was all that separated him from joining his sister Jami and their mutual friends at Eastside in the fall.

Eastside was located directly across the street from the local Frostee Freeze, where all the neighborhood kids hung out after school. Although it would be Jami's final year at Eastside, he looked forward to walking to school with her and benefiting from her "miss teen queen" popularity on campus. At last, no longer would he be the only elementary school kid on their block.

At the sound of the bell, handsome Tyler spruced up his thick brown hair, courteously bid his teacher farewell, and darted out for a weekend of celebration, to be capped off with a Sunday fishing outing with his beloved Grandpa George.

Tyler was very proud of his entertaining and intelligent grandfather, and cherished the quality time they frequently shared. They were like two peas-in-a-pod and it was obvious where Tyler got his good looks. His sixty-eight-year-old grandfather still maintained a good physique, stylish head of silver hair, and sported a well-manicured, mustached goatee.

George Thompson was a much-decorated, retired four-star army general who seized every opportunity, especially fishing, as a tool to train Tyler in the lessons of life. In addition to his healthy lifestyle and hearty resume, George intently studied

Bible prophecy and sincerely believed his grandson could be living in the final generation. Considering this, he felt compelled to prepare his only grandson for the future he believed was beginning to unfold.

Sunday morning arrived and, wishing to get an early start at fishing, George convinced Tyler's parents, Thomas and Lisa, to allow the boy to attend the 8:00 a.m. church service with himself and Grandma Mimi (her real name was Martha, but everyone who knew her simply called her Mimi). Tyler, who usually attended the local Jewish synagogue, had recently converted to Christianity as a result of his grandpa's tutelage. Tyler's conversion would eventually prove problematic with Lisa's side of the family, who came from a highly orthodox Hebrew pedigree. However, for now, the dust was settling on the religious family matter, so with a little brinksmanship George was able to maneuver his grandson into chapel.

It was Tyler's first time attending the adult service at George's non-denominational church. Apart from attending some special outreach youth events and a Christian rock concert, Tyler was basically a newcomer to the church experience. But, having become a recent convert and soon to be a sixth–grader, Tyler felt a sense of maturity sitting next to his grandparents in the sanctuary.

George was unusually energized this particular Sunday in anticipation of a guest speaker, the well-known author and "end times" expert, Jim Linton. George had read every one of Linton's dozen or so books and was eager to familiarize Tyler with one of his favorite teachers. Last week's church bulletin said Linton's topic would be, *The Importance of Bible Prophecy in These Last Days. This is an important message for Tyler's generation*, thought George, when he read his bulletin.

George's enthusiasm was further fueled by the fact that prolonged Arab protests and revolts continued to plague the Middle East region. These protests were causing wide scale governmental collapses and opened the door for radical regimes to emerge in their place. All of the unrest increasingly isolated Israel from the Arab League and opened the door for the

Iranian mullahs to expand their radical Shiite Islamic beliefs throughout the greater Middle East region.

From Lebanon to Iraq, Iran was forming a formidable alliance of Arab proxy states which already included Lebanon, Syria, and Jordan. In the end analysis, the rapid formation of these unexpected alliances between Sunni and Shiite Muslims was forcing Israel into a precarious position. All of these troublesome events served to further George's feelings that mankind had been plunged past the point of no return into the biblical end times.

Linton, a noted Mideast expert who wasn't one to sugar-coat his messages, delivered a sobering sermon that Sunday. Right out of the gate he taught about a coming period of worldwide "tribulation." He warned that troublesome times were on humanity's horizon and listed a flurry of last days' signs supporting his claims. Middle East rumors of war, significant earthquakes, and the ongoing global economic crisis topped his list.

"Prepare yourselves," he said. "All of this protracted Arab unrest, coupled with Iran's recent announcement that it was on the verge of becoming a nuclear nation, will undoubtedly morph into a Mideast conflict that could open up a Pandora's Box in the Holy Land." Frightened by Linton's message, Tyler snuggled close to his grandmother's side, pressing her soft blond hair against her shoulder.

As Grandpa George feverishly penned his notes and the entire congregation sat on the edges of their pews, Jim Linton concluded by reminding them about the importance of putting their faith in Christ "before it's too late." He closed by quoting a passage in the New Testament, Luke 21:36:

"Watch therefore, and pray always that you may be counted worthy to escape all these things that will come to pass, and to stand before the Son of Man."

Dozens accepted his invitation to come forward and accept Christ as their Savior. The message had been so timely and overwhelming; Tyler was hard pressed to find a dry eye in the sanctuary. Even his grandfather, who seldom shed a tear, had trickles running down both cheeks. After the service, Tyler kissed Mimi goodbye, hopped into his grandpa's truck, and the two of them departed for their favorite fishing spot on the picturesque banks of the Colorado River.

Silence marked their travel that Sunday. George sensed that his grandson was finding it difficult to assimilate all the information he had just received. The message exceeded even George's expectations, and so he resigned himself to focusing on fishing and little else for the rest of the day.

Arriving at their destination, they got out the gear and proceeded as planned to catch some fish. However, it wasn't long before Tyler broke the ice and said, "Poppy, I'm confused about what the speaker said. Can you explain to me in kid language what he meant about the terrible times coming?"

Realizing Linton's message had left an indelible impression on young Tyler, the family patriarch pondered the overwhelming implications of the question. Baiting his pole and contemplating his answer, Poppy calmly responded, "Well Ty, remember the teacher talked about the tribulation period?"[3]

"Yes," Tyler's eyes were fear-filled. "My Mom doesn't believe in Jesus. Will she go through that?"

A moment of silence ensued, broken only by the sound of Poppy's line casting into the river.

Oh Lord, George silently prayed, grant me the right words. Although George would typically seize the opportunity to teach Tyler, he was overwhelmed by the magnitude of translating the question into his beloved grandson's level of comprehension. Swallowing hard, he uttered, "Wouldn't you rather talk about, fishing or sports, or something a little less complicated?"

Peering into his grandpa's eyes, Tyler answered, "Not today, Poppy. The tribulation seems much more important!"

Suddenly a fish snagged Tyler's pole causing him to shift his attention to the catch at hand. From that point forward fantastic fishing required their undivided attention, temporarily sparing George a painful discussion.

3

Tribulation Generation

Having emptied the Colorado River of their daily fishing limit, Poppy and Ty loaded back into the truck and headed homeward. Grandpa figured the tribulation topic was destined to resurface during the thirty-minute drive. He had avoided answering Tyler's questions thus far due to spectacular fishing conditions, but during those fish-filled hours he had wisely considered his answer.

Rather than wait, he seized the opportunity to share his answer and began rather awkwardly, "The tribulation is a painful seven-year period for the world, Ty. Both people and God's beautiful creation will experience enormous suffering."

Fumbling to remove his headset and turn off his iPod, Tyler questioned, "What's that Gramps?"

"The *trip- trib*-ulation period; you asked about it earlier," Poppy stuttered. "It will be a terrible time for man and creation. There will be earthquakes, nuclear contamination, and a whole lot of worldwide devastation. The Bible says several oceans, streams, and rivers, maybe even the Colorado, will become polluted, causing many fish to die," he added.[4]

"Are you talking about a lot of major earthquakes all over the world, like the nine-point one in Japan that killed thousands of people?" Tyler asked.

Poppy swallowed. "Yes, like that one."

"We spent a few days studying earthquakes in class when the Japanese earthquake happened," Tyler said. "I remember the teacher said about a quarter-million people died in a huge earthquake in Haiti about a year before, because of their low construction standards."

Tyler's studious response slightly eased Poppy's tension about translating the tribulation into kid's language, and so he replied, "That sounds correct. It never ceases to amaze me how much fifth graders are learning these days. I feel like I can talk to you about almost anything."

Clearing his throat, Tyler corrected, "Excuse me. I'm a sixth grader now."

"Oh, forgive my forgetfulness. It never ceases to amaze me how advanced sixth graders are these days," Poppy humorously rephrased.

Grinning broadly, Tyler replied, "Well you know we are more advanced than you and Mimi were when you were in school. Don't forget we have the Internet now!"

"Oh, I see," Poppy said, holding back his laughter. "Did you know that Jesus predicted 2,000 years ago, that big earthquakes would come someday?"

"Of course, that's what Mr. Linton said in church today," Tyler reminded.

"That's right. I was checking to see if you remembered," chuckled Poppy.

After a momentary interval, Poppy continued, "He also said they have been increasing all over the world."

Reflecting, Tyler questioned, "Do you mean that not only fish, but hundreds of thousands of people are going to die, too?"

"Yes, the Bible book of Revelation warns that *millions* of people will die," Grandpa sadly noted.

"But why does that happen to the world? Can't people make it better so God doesn't have to punish them and the planet?" Tyler inquired.

"Good question," Grandpa mumbled.

Not expecting the conversation to swerve off into the philosophical realm, Poppy had to put on his thinking cap before responding to Tyler's intelligent questions. Collecting his thoughts, he answered, "The Bible says the heart of mankind is desperately wicked and we will continue to make matters worse because we inherited a genetic defect from Adam and Eve called 'sin.' This is why God sent his only Son, Jesus, as a sacrifice for everybody's sins. In other words, Ty, people won't make the planet a better place; it's against their selfish nature."

Since Tyler gave no immediate response, Poppy assumed he had answered Tyler's questions satisfactorily. To his relief, Tyler did not broach the subject of his mother's unsaved status in this round.

However, a few minutes later, the questions got tougher. "What about all the other religions," he asked, "And, how can someone really know if God is real?

Startled by Tyler's spiritual depth, Poppy deflected with, "What all are they teaching you kids in school these days?"

"Don't be silly, Gramps. They can't teach about religion in schools anymore. I learned a little bit about different religions at synagogue, preparing for my Bar Mitzvah."

Collecting his thoughts once again, Poppy answered, "Many false religions wrongly teach that people can become god. You know from synagogue that Satan lied to Adam and Eve in the garden of Eden. The Devil declared that by eating from the forbidden tree in the midst of the garden, they would become like God. After they ate of that fruit, they realized that he had lied to them. That lie has continued on in some of the false religions, like Hinduism and Buddhism."

Tyler replied, "We didn't learn much about those religions."

George continued, "As far as your second question, I believe that somewhere in the first chapter of the book of Romans it teaches that God can be known by observing creation. The passage says that men are to recognize there is a God through His creation."

"Makes sense," Tyler conceded.

Moments later, he inquired, "Poppy, why does this bad stuff have to happen while I'm growing up? I want to enjoy my summer and go to Eastside with my friends. Someday, I want to work with my dad in construction and have a family of my own. Are you sure there will be a tribulation in my lifetime?

"I know it doesn't seem fair," Grandpa said," but from the way the world looks now, with earthquakes increasing, and other big problems in the world, it looks like Jim Linton is right. It pains me to tell you that your generation could be the last one. But remember, Christians escape the tribulation. That is what the rapture is for," Poppy reminded.

Tyler reluctantly commented, "You're right, it's not fair. I sure hope you're right about the rapture. It didn't make sense what Mr. Linton said about it. It sounded crazy, like an episode from a Star Wars movie! Didn't he say Christians are going to disappear into the clouds by being poofed into thin air?"

"The rapture is one of the big events people need to understand," Poppy replied. "The Bible calls it a mystery. Jesus comes by surprise and takes millions of believers to heaven. The Bible says it occurs on a cloudy day and happens faster than you can blink your eyes. The people left behind will be shocked, and wonder where everybody disappeared to. It is described in several connecting Bible Scriptures."

George concluded, "If you like, someday Mimi and I can do a study with you, to help you understand it better."

"I think we should, because it sounds really weird," exclaimed Tyler. With this, Tyler turned on his iPod and put his headset over his ears once again.

4

Israel Comes Under Multi-Front Attack!

Observing that his grandson had checked out of the discussion and into his pre-teen music world, Poppy tuned into his favorite Christian radio station and continued homeward.

Shortly into the program, the radio station interrupted its broadcast, announcing: "This is Allen Smith, station manager at KWBC. We interrupt our regularly scheduled program to bring you an important breaking news alert! We have just been informed that a barrage of rockets has rocked Tel Aviv. Reportedly, scud missiles carrying chemical warheads were included in the assault. Although many missiles were intercepted by Israel's Iron Dome defense system, several apparently got through, hitting Israel's capital city. Unconfirmed reports suggest that hundreds of Israelis are believed injured or dead as a result of these fatal blasts."

"Hysteria fills the city streets, as several hundred thousand tourists and local residents scramble for gas masks and nearby bomb shelters. We have Sheila Abernathy, our correspondent on the ground in Tel Aviv, with us by phone. Sheila, what can you tell us?"

Turning up the volume, Grandpa immediately blurted out, "Turn off your iPod quick, Ty! We have to hear this."

"What is it Poppy?"

"Quiet please! This is important!" Grandpa exclaimed!

"Yes, Allen, this is Sheila. I'm on my cell phone shouting through a gas mask, racing to the nearest bomb shelter. Can you hear me?"

"Barely, Sheila. You're breaking in and out, but go ahead," said Allen.

Sheila frantically reported: "Panic indeed characterizes the scene here in Tel Aviv. Numerous powerful explosions hit the most densely populated portions of the city. Deadly chemical components are spreading rapidly throughout the area. Our crew is being evacuated to safety, so I have only a few moments to report what's happening here."

"In my thirty years of reporting I have never seen anything as dangerous and chaotic as this. Just down the street there are dozens of people without gas masks collapsing on the pavement. Some of the main roads are severely damaged and I fear the emergency first responders will be unable to get to them in time. This is an absolutely horrific site!"

"Sheila, this is extremely troubling! How soon until you and the crew reach safety?"

"We've neared the shelter and I have to sign off for now," Sheila responded.

"We thank the Lord that you and the crew have reached safety!" Allen said. "Dear listeners, Israel has come under serious attack and dangerous developments are occurring right now. Stay tuned to this station and we will give you further news updates on this accelerating situation as soon as we receive them. This is Allen Smith reporting from KWBC."

"Wow!" Grandpa exclaimed as he pounded his dashboard.

"Wow what?" Ty nervously asked.

"Psalm 83, that's what!" Poppy declared. "The final Arab–Israeli war might be happening right now!"

Putting the pedal to the metal in a mad dash to reach home, Poppy scanned through the radio dial, attempting to gain a full assessment of the accelerating events.

Numerous local stations were reporting the breaking Middle East news. One reported Ben Gurion airport had also been severely struck by missile fire, causing the immediate cancellation of all flights in and out of Israel.

Another channel announced Hezbollah and Syria claimed responsibility for the attacks.

As the reports streamed across the airwaves, Poppy flattened the accelerator pedal to the floorboard and darted around cars, hastening homeward as if he were racing the final lap of the Indianapolis 500.

"Slow down Poppy! You're going to get us both killed!" anguished Tyler.

Shushing his grandson, Poppy said, "Don't worry! I know this road like the back of my hand. I could drive it with my eyes closed."

Panic stricken, Tyler made sure his seatbelt was buckled tight and braced for the white-knuckle ride of his life.

It wasn't long before Poppy screeched into his driveway, prompting Tyler to nervously ask, "Aren't you taking me home first?"

"Not right now, Ty. I have to watch the news to find out more about what's going on in the Middle East. Come inside; Grandma Mimi will drive you home shortly," he promised.

Flinging the front door wide open, he scurried past his high school sweetheart's open arms to retrieve his Bible and turn on their big screen TV.

Focusing her aqua-blue eyes upon her grandson, who straggled in slump-shouldered a few minutes afterward, Mimi asked, "What's going on with your grandfather, and why didn't he take you home first?"

"Psalm 83, whatever that is," he whimpered.

Instantly, Mimi's countenance changed, as her compassionate heart dropped deep within her.

Pulling her grandson close to her side, she said, "Calm down. It's nothing you need to worry about. It's something your grandfather is interested in. It has something to do with what was taught in church earlier today and probably got your grandpa overly excited."

Wiping a trickle of tears from his eyes, Tyler asked, "Do you mean it's the tribulation?"

"Oh Lord, no! I don't think it's quite that serious," she replied.

"I'm scared! Why won't Grandpa tell us what's going on?" asked Tyler.

Mimi displayed her grandmotherly grin and jested, "I'm sure he will when he gets done wearing out the remote control," she said, guiding him toward the kitchen. "For now, have a fresh-baked chocolate chip cookie and try to calm down."

Taking in the fresh-baked aroma permeating throughout the kitchen, Tyler succumbed to her request. *Cookies and milk with Mimi is more fun than dealing with Grandpa's freak-out right now*, thought Tyler.

As the two of them sat across from each other at the kitchen table, Tyler asked, "Mimi, do you know about the Psalm war Poppy is concerned about?"

"Oh yes. I'm no expert, but your grandfather reminds me about it every time something gets weird in the Middle East," she sarcastically humored.

"Is it really bad thing? I mean, do you think my cousins in Israel could get hurt?" Tyler inquired.

"Any war is bad, and people often get hurt, but Poppy says according to a book he studied called *Isralestine*,[5] Israel wins the Psalm 83 war, and becomes a safer place for a while." Mimi comforted.

"Does this war have something to do with the problem between the Palestinians and the Jews?" Tyler queried.

"Yes, I guess you could say that; Poppy says something happens and the Arabs and Palestinians have a final war with the Jews. He says the Psalm lists a specific group of Middle East countries and terrorist groups that form a confederacy to wipe Israel off of the map forever." Mimi replied.

"That's terrible! Is Poppy sure that Israel wins?" he nervously asked.

"Yes, Poppy says Israel definitely wins," she replied.

"Ty, please don't get all worked up again. I don't know enough about all this stuff to answer your questions. We'll clean up in here and head into the parlor to see what's going on with Poppy. I'm sure everything will be fine. Your grandfather gets easily excited about Middle East news, so let's keep cool. It's probably nothing major," Mimi said in a comforting tone.

Meanwhile in the parlor, Grandpa had his Bible open to Psalm 83 and was couched closely in front of the TV, as if it were Super Bowl Sunday. Remote in hand, he flipped through the mainstream news channels like there was no tomorrow. As he suspected, they were all covering the Middle East conflict, just like they had during *Operation Desert Storm*. During that period, many Americans were glued to their televisions sets, gleaning all the news they could gather. George believed this conflict would be even more powerful and newsworthy.

Observing out of the corner of his eye that Mimi and Tyler had left the kitchen and entered the parlor, George exclaimed "This has to be it! It's too big to be just another skirmish."

By now, further reports had streamed in, declaring Israel had launched a barrage of retaliatory missiles into Lebanon and Syria, near Damascus, and that a nationwide mobilization of all Israeli military personnel and armor was underway.

Removing her apron and placing it on a nearby chair, Mimi sat on the edge of the sofa next to George. In her characteristic angelic voice, Mimi asked, "Are you prepared to calmly tell us what in the world is going on? You stormed in the house as if it were Armageddon and left your grandson weeping alone in the car."

"Forgive me, Ty. I should have been more considerate. I must have panicked you in my enthusiasm," Poppy apologized.

"You scared me half to death, Grandpa," declared Tyler. "First you have me listen to a speaker talk about the world ending and then you drove like a maniac on the freeway. Speaking about the end of the world, I thought my world was going to end because you were going to get us in a wreck!"

"How serious is this Middle East flare-up you're watching?" Mimi asked. "And please don't blow it out of proportion just because you think it has something to do with the Psalm 83 Bible prophecy."

Having lived with her husband most of her life, Mimi was well acquainted with his tendency to tell tall tales and turn current events into biblical exegesis.

Pulling his glasses down to the tip of his nose and peering above the rims, George retorted, "This is the real Mideast McCoy! No more bad rap for old George! This is the Psalm 83 prophecy many of us have been anticipating. I knew it was just a matter of time before the missiles would be blasting throughout Mideast skies."

"The other day the news reported the Palestinians and Jews were going to resume peace talks," Mimi stated.

"Wishful thinking!" replied George. "I keep telling you the Arabs and Jews probably won't make peace, because most Middle East Arabs hate the Jews and refuse to recognize Israel's right to exist. World leaders have been trying to fix the problem over there for over six-decades, to no avail; now the inevitable war has come!"

"Poppy, do you think my aunts and uncles and cousins living in Israel will be hurt?" Tyler worried.

"The Bible predicts Israel will win this war, but it is hard to know how many Israelis will be harmed while the war is being waged," answered Poppy. "News channels are already reporting serious damage and loss of life inside Tel Aviv. Fortunately, most of your family lives closer to Jerusalem. This could work to their favor, since the Arabs have holy sites there and they won't want to bomb them," Poppy comforted.

Mimi, who was obviously not an entire novice to prophecy, wondered, "I overheard the newscaster report Israel launched missiles at Damascus. Could it be Isaiah 17 has just happened, George?"

Cringing, Tyler asked, "Is that another bad prophecy? What's does that Isaiah thing say?"

"The destruction of Damascus," Grandpa declared. "Isaiah 17 predicts that Damascus will someday cease to be a city, and be reduced to rubble."

"Isn't Damascus an important city?" Tyler questioned.

"Indeed, it is," Poppy replied. "Damascus is the oldest continuously inhabited city in recorded history, dating back four thousand years to the time of father Abraham. It's Syria's capital, with about four million people in and around the metropolitan areas of the city. It's a strategic target for Israel, because every known terrorist organization has either an office or headquarters located there."

"Do you think Israel just destroyed Damascus, like Isaiah predicted?" Tyler marveled.

"This has not been confirmed, yet. All we know so far is that Israel fired missiles in the direction of Damascus. However, Isaiah's prophecy seems to suggest that Israel will be responsible for the destruction of Damascus. Isaiah also suggests the destruction is sudden, as if it happens overnight. So it's possible that's what we're witnessing," Poppy explained.

Together they watched further news reports filter in suggesting Damascus was severely damaged in the fighting, which promptly provoked an emergency meeting of the Arab League. Leaders from Egypt, Jordan, Lebanon, and all the other twenty-two member Arab states were en-route to Saudi Arabia, to convene.

Concurrently, the United Nations immediately issued an official statement condemning Israel's use of excessive force against its Arab neighbors. The statement called for the immediate cessation of all violence between Israel and Syria, Hezbollah, and Hamas, who had simultaneously begun attacking Israel from the southwest out of the Gaza Strip. It was obvious to all that this was a pre-planned, confederate effort to destroy Israel.

Meanwhile, as Mideast matters rapidly deteriorated, Tyler's mother, Lisa, came storming into the house, asking harshly, "What in the world is going on? Jami and I were clear across town at the factory outlets mall when Tyler called me, sobbing. He said his grandfather was acting strange and left him alone in the car, and we stopped what we were doing and raced over to find out why!"

Lisa had been a fashion model before marrying Tyler's father, Thomas, fifteen years ago. Once upon a time, her inviting smile and fit feminine figure adorned the covers of many popular fashion magazines, and her natural beauty epitomized the phrase "drop-dead-gorgeous." She had since become a career mom, but maintained a part-time relationship as an independent consultant for several magazine companies she had formerly modeled for. Possessing her master's degree in marketing, Lisa had standing, high-paying job offers with several companies, should she ever seek to enter the full-time workplace again.

However, she was content with motherhood, and when it came to household and family matters, she ruled the roost like a protective mother hen. Lisa did everything possible to insulate Jami and Tyler from adversity and negativity; so much so, that George often had heated exchanges with her that always began with, "You need to come off the cover, girl, and join the real world."

Suffice it to say, George and Lisa had their share of go-rounds, which Lisa usually won. Through the years, she had discovered all his hot buttons and knew when to push them. On the flip side, she also knew how to sweet talk him into her corner afterward.

"What were you both doing at such a large public place?" George challenged. "Don't you realize the country is nearly on lock down since the Department of Homeland Security elevated the terror threat level to its highest level since September 11th?"

"If you're so worried about terrorism, why did you take my son to a large church and then go fishing at a popular spot?"

Lisa bantered back. "Besides, why did you make Tyler cry and leave him in the car? Did he do something wrong?"

"Calm down, dear," Mimi soothed. "Everything's under control. We are trying to explain to Tyler what is happening in the Middle East right now."

"The Middle East? Mimi, he's only a child!" she argued. "Besides, I watched some of it on the news before Jami and I left for the outlets. What's the big deal? The Arabs have been warring against the Jews from time immemorial. This conflict is nothing new!"

"Nothing new?" George retorted.

Just then Mimi, seeing Tyler's countenance fall, and fearing the conversation would worsen, interrupted. "Where's Jami?" she asked.

"Waiting outside in the car," Lisa replied.

Grabbing Tyler by the hand, Mimi led him toward the door. "I want to go say hello to her. I will get Tyler in the car for you," she offered.

Waiting for Mimi and Tyler to step safely beyond arguing distance, Lisa asked, "George, what were you about to say?"

"You need to come off the cover, girl, and join the real world!" George huffed. "We're talking about chemical warheads, gas masks, bomb shelters, and perhaps even nuclear weapons against Damascus. These aren't disgruntled Palestinians lobbing protest stones at the Jews; these are high-tech arsenals intended to wipe Israel off the map!"

George reiterated, "I have been warning you and Thomas for the past few years that the Middle East is about to go apocalyptic. Bible prophecies calling for the destruction of Damascus and a climactic Arab-Israeli war have been stage-setting since Israel fought against Hamas in *Operation Cast Lead* dating back to the time Barrack Obama was inaugurated president. I think what we are watching now could be the beginning of battles of epic proportion."

"Forgive me, father-in-law," Lisa admonished, "but being Jewish, I don't believe in Jesus! Nor do I believe in Bible prophecy. If you and Mimi want to be born-again Christians and believe in an apocalypse, that's your prerogative. However, I'm warning you not to frighten Tyler with such talk. He has enough problems growing up in this crazy world as it is, not to mention all the teen-age peer pressure he's going to face next year at Eastside Middle."

"Did you mean Eastside Middle, or 'Middle East'"? George taunted. "Because the way things are presently going over there, who knows what Tyler's world will look like by the time school resumes in the fall?"

"Enough already! This conversation is going nowhere," Lisa snapped back. "Is this what Christians want? Do they *want* war and suffering to continue between the Arabs and the Jews?"

Taken aback, George replied, "Of course not! You know I love the Jewish people and serve a God who loves both Arabs and Jews. Tyler and I were expressing our sincere concerns about the safety of your family in Israel before you arrived. But, Lisa, it takes two to make peace, and even the most liberal Jews in Israel are realizing the Arabs don't want peace!"

Frustrated, Lisa sighed, "I know you mean well, but it's getting late and I'm going to take the kids home now."

Driving off in her sporty BMW, Lisa attempted to calm Tyler down by shifting his focus back to his summer vacation plans. She told her son, "You concentrate on being a twelve-year-old and focus on having fun this summer with your sister and friends. Let your father and me deal with your grandparents regarding these grown-up matters."

Sitting shotgun, Jami asked, "What 'matters'? What's Tyler all worked up about?"

"It's not for you to worry about. It's a Christian thing and not open for further discussion."

"But, Mommy," Tyler said, "I'm a Christian! It's important for me to learn about all this Bible stuff."

"For Christ's sake!" Lisa ironically blurted. "You are just a child and unable to make major commitments."

"But, Grandma Naomi and you told me that next year I have my *bar mitzvah*, and that means I'm old enough to understand religion," Tyler argued.

Stunned by her brother's insightfulness, Jami stared at him in amazement.

Observing Jami's countenance, Lisa reminded her, "Don't forget that he's not thirteen, *yet*."

"I'm almost twelve," Tyler rebutted.

Desperately wanting an end to the conversation, Lisa shouted, "I don't care what my mother and I said. You can't make this decision on your own right now!"

Once again, tears began to streak Tyler's cheeks.

"Now look what you've done!" Jami howled. "Why can't you and Grandma Naomi accept Tyler's decision to become a Christian? What's the big deal about Christianity? Why is everyone on your side of the family bothered by it?"

Realizing her comments had struck a sensitive family nerve, Lisa apologetically said, "I'm sorry, Son. I don't mean to lose my temper about this. I know how important being Christian is to you. It's just that my family longs for us all to move to Israel to be near them, and for you to be *bar mitzvahed* there. When I told them you recently converted, they felt betrayed."

"But, what about Dad?" Tyler reminded her. "He's been a Christian since he was my age. Your family has learned to accept him."

Lisa rolled her eyes. "Yes, but your father hasn't been practicing his religion for years! He doesn't really know what faith he is!"

Taking a deep breath, and locking in on Tyler's eyes through the rear-view mirror, Lisa calmly requested, "Look, I'll try to be sensitive to your feelings about religion. For now, let's get home and have a good dinner, and try to have a better day tomorrow."

5

Panic in Damascus

Beginning her expedient evacuation from Damascus, Adara Tereiri cried out to her father, Syrian president Hassan Tereiri, "What have you initiated? Our country is in utter turmoil! Syria has come under serious attack from Israel!"

With tears streaming down her frightened face, Adara continued, "Brother Kamal has warned that we all must flee immediately because Israel is coming to destroy Damascus and our dynasty. He has already prepared a place of refuge for us in Jordan."

The Syrian president replied to his daughter, "I know this situation is escalating and looks like it's spiraling out of control, but don't panic. President Zakiri of Iran has promised his country's full support to our final war with the Jews."

Adara continued to agonize, "What does Kamal mean that the Jews won't stop fighting in Syria until they have destroyed Damascus and eliminated our entire family? What have you done? Why are the Israelis specifically targeting our clan and our capitol city?" To which Hassan caustically replied, "Nonsense, your brother is speaking nonsense! He has chosen to be a coward at this critical time in our history. He is worried about Israeli Prime Minister Kaufman's empty threats to destroy Damascus, and our whole family in the event of war. These are baseless intimidations from Kaufman."

Dragging her father firmly by the arm toward the rear door of the capitol building, Adara beseeched him, "Come with me now; we can't trust Iran, we must all flee to Jordan immediately. The protestors are beginning to revolt against us again. Tens-of-thousands are communicating over Facebook and the Internet calling for fellow Syrians to kill us, and to plead for Israel's Defense Forces to back down. Brother says that protesters are already assembling to overtake the capitol. He said that if the revolutionaries don't succeed in killing us, the Bible says that Israel surely will!"

Adara fell to the floor as her father shook loose from her iron choking grip. She began pleading, "Father please, don't be foolish; come with us before it's too late, and even your grandchildren are killed. The protestors are panicking in the streets. If we don't go now, we will never survive!"

Her father's anger flared, "How dare you quote from the enemy's Bible; and you and your brother are not going anywhere. Zakiri has vowed to employ the use of his nuclear weapons to wipe Israel off of the map. This war will be over before it begins. And, you and your brother are not leaving this country. I will have no show of weakness from my family, or any of my countrymen. The protestors and the Jews will bathe in their own blood for their aggressive actions."

Instructing security close by to seize his daughter, Hassan commanded that his cowardly son Kamal also be captured. "Confine them until I decide what to do with the two of them," Tereiri ordered.

Adding complexity to Hassan Tereiri's circumstances, his son Kamal had betrayed his family's Muslim heritage by recently converting to Christianity. While touring through Bangladesh, Indonesia, and the Sudan, filming his documentary called *Can Muslims be Moderate*, he interviewed Christian missionaries who had convinced him over time that, according to several Surah's inside the Koran, there was no such thing as a moderate Muslim.

Moreover, they also succeeded in persuading him that Jesus Christ was the world's Messiah. Gaining his confidence, they eventually convinced him that Syria was clearly identified in biblical prophecy, in Isaiah 17 and elsewhere.

"Dad, the Bible declares Damascus will someday cease to be a city, it will become a ruinous heap, and I'm concerned that unless you strike peace with Israel, that day will arrive soon" Kamal had pleaded to his father Hassan, upon his return from filming overseas.

Incensed by his son's treasonous comments about Israel, Syria's capitol city, and his conversion to Christianity, Hassan Tereiri had ostracized his infidel son, and extradited him to Amman, Jordan, promptly upon his return.

Hassan Tereiri had hoped that his friend King Hussein of Jordan would be able to deprogram his son's Christian thinking. King Hussein was considered to be the most moderate Middle East Muslim leader, and the most familiar with westernized thinking. Hassan thought, *if anyone could convince his son Kamal that Muslims can be moderate, it would be his close friend Hussein*. But, Kamal was relentless in his pursuit to warn his royal family of their pending peril.

Adara, out of love and compassion for her brother, lent his Christian preaching a sympathetic ear, and this troubled the Syrian president all the more. Although Adara was reluctant to hastily abandon her Islamic roots, she did begin wondering if Kamal was correct, and if the Bible could foretell Syria's future. With the war presently being waged against Israel, she feared Damascus could be destroyed!

Thus, now at the height of Hassan Tereiri's war distress, the thought of his children betraying his destiny with Islamic infamy was intolerable. *Incarcerate them both. How dare they disrupt this momentous moment in time*, he thought to himself.

Nevertheless, somewhere beneath his troubled Islamic-inculcated soul, he wondered if his firstborn son Kamal could be correct. What if Damascus could soon see its doom? Certainly, the news he had received from the Saudi king earlier that morning *weighed heavily upon his heart…*

Departing into his office, he called President Zakiri immediately and promptly pleaded, "Where is your army, and when do you plan to launch your supposed nuclear weapons into Israel? We are under severe attack by the IDF, just as I had feared. My family is betraying me and trying to flee to Jordan, the revolutionaries are charging against my capitol as we speak, and worst of all, my chief commanders are warning that Israel is preparing to fire nuclear weapons against us. We need Iran to get involved now, without delay!"

In arrogant disbelief, the Iranian president Zakiri declared, "That's preposterous! Israel would face international condemnation for such an attack. This is not a possible scenario, and your commanders' assessments should be seriously questioned."

Furiously, Tereiri confirmed, "Israel made it no secret this morning when they informed Saudi King Abdullah of their intentions to deploy their Dolphin Class submarines in the Mediterranean Sea for a nuclear mission against Damascus. King Abdullah called me immediately afterward, and said Israel wanted him to make sure Syria understood IDF's nuclear intentions. Our intelligence reports confirm that Israeli warships are on the move in the Mediterranean. Waiting to see if this is merely a rumor of war is no longer a luxury afforded to Hamas, Hezbollah, Iran, or Syria. Iran must enter, and exercise control over the Middle East war theater immediately as you promised!"

Zakiri lashed back, "How dare you issue orders to me, Hassan! I'm in command here, and I have just ordered the Secretary General of Hezbollah, Muhammad Imad Fadlallah and Sadegh Mousavi of Hamas to initiate the second stage of the war against Israel. I command you, too: follow suit, and keep in stride with our attack schedule. Iran will enter into the fight after you all have inflicted the next round of damage upon Israel, and not before."

Tired of being chastised, and realizing the imminent danger of an IDF nuclear threat, Tereiri replied, "With all due respect Zakiri, you underestimate the battlefield! Israel is already retaliating with excessive force, and they will use their nuclear arsenal. The Israelis are in a fight for their survival, and they won't leave their best weapons on the shelf. First Damascus, and then Tehran will be their targets. The Jews know that you have commanded this attack, and they will seek revenge against Iran, as well. By your own admission, you miscalculated Israel's response. You think the IDF will authorize only a measured response, but I tell you they will nuke both our countries!"

Irately, the Iranian president commanded, "You shall do as I say, or you won't have to worry about the protesters or the Jews; Iran shall have your head! I have instructed the deployment of IRCG troops to our western borders, and intend to shut down the Strait of Hormuz tomorrow, according to our joint military plans. The world will condemn Israel when Iran chokes off its major artery of oil distribution. Israel will not use nuclear weapons against you for fear that doing so will provoke the wrath of the world upon itself!"

Before Tereiri could reply, the dial tone rang in his ear. Zakiri had hung up, leaving the Syrian president no alternative but to stay true to their apocalyptic course. However, now he realized that all the warring parties were in a no-stops final fight for survival, and that Syria was on its own!

6

There's Trouble in Tehran and Destruction in Damascus

Throughout the next few days, George Thompson and his faithful companion of forty-four years, Mimi, remained generally fastened to the sofa and focused upon the TV, watching Mideast matters significantly worsen. Additionally, George entertained a steady stream of phone calls from fellow prophecy buffs interested in comparing notes as to the biblical ramifications of the escalating Mideast mayhem.

Apart from the occasional visit to the latrine, as retired General George often referred to their bathroom, and their daily workout in their garage conversion gym, they hunkered down in the parlor for what they anticipated could be a very long haul. They were quite content remaining indoors because they were fixated upon the mainstream news; but, more importantly, the Department of Homeland Security (DHS) had raised the American terror alert level to its severest condition, as a result of the current Arab-Israeli war.

The alert level began its upward ascent a year earlier, during the widespread protests in the Arab Spring of 2011. But, the escalating multi-front Middle East conflict sent the United States terror level soaring to new heights.

Intensifying matters, Iran was mobilizing its IRGC troops to move westward toward Israel and moving several warships into the Red Sea. Moreover, Iran closed off the Strait of Hormuz, causing oil prices to skyrocket, stock markets to plummet, and great concern within the international community.

If all the above wasn't troubling enough, Iranian president Zakiri vowed to unleash thousands of terror cells deeply imbedded in the United States, in a massive nuclear Jihad against Americans.

Iran's hostile actions and troubling threats prompted many Americans to storm the gas stations to top off their tanks, for fear of further gas shortages and price spikes. Additionally, panicked consumers stampeded grocery and big box stores, emptying shelves of emergency goods like food, water, basic weapons, and first aid kits.

However, George, being an end-time's survivalist, already had his stockpile of gold, guns, and goods in order, and wasn't caught up in the frenzy.

Many Americans were refraining from going to public centers of interest, like sporting events, malls, and movie theaters, for fear of chemical, suicide, and other types of terror attacks. These fears were further nurtured by the fact that the New York City and Los Angeles police departments were utilizing newly developed radiation detector devices on a daily basis, to search for dirty bombs potentially concealed somewhere within their city limits.

Although initially George wasn't overly concerned about all these above developments, his disposition was rapidly changing, now that Israel had come under fire from Iran's proxies. He realized Iranian terror threats against America were equally as credible. He commented to Mimi, "It may not be wise for Lisa and Jami to make their mother-daughter mall visits, anymore."

"How do you propose to stop them, after your recent spat with Lisa?" Mimi asked. "And, if that's the case, then it's not advisable for you and Tyler to go fishing again, until all this Mideast dust settles."

Her fishing comment, reminiscent of Lisa's barb to the same effect, hit below the belt, provoking George to respond, "That's overkill! Terrorists are not going to blow up fishing holes. For Pete's sake, they don't even know where the good ones are located!"

•••••

It was near dusk on the Sunday after the war broke out, when their solitude was interrupted by the sound of the doorbell, announcing a surprise visit from George's old army buddy and best friend, Robert Rasmussen. Robert, always clean shaven and lightly splashed with Old Spice cologne, had shared in several overseas tours of duty with George. But now, like George, he was enjoying the rewards of retirement.

"The Man with the Midas Touch," as George often referred to him, was a man of means. He possessed a portfolio worth millions of dollars, which was partially from inheritance, but mostly from sound investing. Robert had been away on an extended business trip when the war broke out, and was grateful to be back in his home town.

Robert's house was a stone's throw from George's, and having lost his wife, Ruth, to cancer a few months earlier, he spent much time at the Thompson residence. On this occasion, George was especially pleased to see Robert, because he wanted to get his prophetic slant on Mideast events.

Rasmussen was no novice when it came to understanding Bible prophecy. Author of hundreds of widely published prophecy articles and an invited guest of numerous radio and TV shows, he was considered by many to be an end-times expert. The slightly balding Robert, at six-foot-four, maintained a strong physique and keen mind. Sixty-two and retired, he also maintained a well-trafficked prophecy blog/website, which normally received several thousand unique visitors daily.

Razz, short for Razzmatazz (George's nickname for Robert), strongly believed the next Middle East war would fulfill prophecies contained in Ezekiel 38-39. These two chapters, he believed, described a Russian-Iranian led coalition against Israel in the end times.

The moment the Middle East war broke out, George had a hunch Razz would identify it with Ezekiel's war, rather than the Arab-Israeli war predicted in Psalm 83. Finally, with Razz back in town, he could find out if his suspicions were correct!

Upon greeting Razz at the door, George led him toward the parlor, where Razz asked, "George, have you and Mimi been watching the Middle East go apocalyptic this past week?"

"Absolutely! Mimi and I have become dysfunctional couch potatoes since the war broke out. We're afraid to turn off the news for fear we'll miss some late breaking event. And, we hesitate to leave the house for fear of meeting up with an Islamic suicide bomber," George replied.

Razz chuckled at George's half-serious comment. "The latest news warns that Iran is coming into the Mideast fray militarily. Everyone in the military circles we travel, recognizes that Iran has instigated its proxies of Syria, Hezbollah, and Hamas to wage this multi-front war against the Israelis. That is going to force Israel to attack the rogue state, and attempt to destroy their nuclear weapons program. I can see all this leading to the fulfillment of Ezekiel 38 and 39."

"Oh brother, here we go again!" George sighed. He then called out to Mimi, "Dear, will you fire up a pot of coffee, please; and I'll attempt to set Razzmatazz straight about where these Psalm 83 events are headed?"

As if to ignore George's passing Psalm 83 comment, Razz quickly interjected, "The Israel-US covert cyber war, initiated in the summer of 2010, seemed to slow down Iran's nuclear program dramatically, but my sources all confirm Iran is about to become a *bona fide* nuclear nation, and may already be armed and dangerous with several undetected nukes hidden somewhere in their underground nuclear facilities. If so, this is concerning to not only Israel, but America as well." Former UN ambassador John Bolton has been warning us that the world will probably have to accept a nuclear Iran, which will reshape the balance of power in the Mideast.[6]

"That may all be true Razz, but what is going on in the Middle East presently is primarily an Arabs verses Jews conflict, not a Russian, Turkish, and Persian verses Israel event!" George replied. "Besides, some of us are fully expecting Israel to strike Iran's nuclear sites, especially in Bushehr, in fulfillment of Jeremiah 49:34-39."

With a deer in the headlights stare at George, Razz replied, "What in the world are you talking about? Are you referring to the prophecies regarding ancient Elam? I am under the impression Jeremiah's Elamite prophecies were historically fulfilled during the conquest of the Persian Empire."

As Mimi handed him his fresh cup of java, Razz said, "George, refresh my memory about Elam."

George replied, "As you well know, Ezekiel was not the only Old Testament prophet predicting Iran's end-time fate. His contemporary, Jeremiah, prophesied against Elam. Ezekiel 38 identified today's Iran as Persia, which was Iran's former name until it changed in 1935. However, Jeremiah labeled at least part of modern-day Iran as Elam. At that time, about 2,600 years ago, Persia encompassed the majority of modern-day Iran, but Elam, with its capital city of Susa, covered most of what is now west-central Iran, including the area of Iran's main nuclear site at Bushehr."

Realizing his extensive recent research had piqued Razz' curiosity, George continued, "Elam dates back approximately 4,000 years, to when Chedorlaomer was the Elamite king. Abraham conquered him in his quest to free his nephew Lot from captivity.[7] Recently, several end-time scholars, like Dr. Arnold Fruchtenbaum, John McTernan, and Sean Osborne have been teaching that Jeremiah's Elamite prophecies will find fulfillment in the last days.[8] Considering you are one of the experts on Iran in end-time's prophecy, I'm surprised you haven't been apprised of their important studies," George concluded.

While sipping upon Mimi's fresh brew and momentarily reflecting upon George's Elam comments, Razz suddenly sprayed out a mouthful of coffee. "What's that, George? Is that a satellite feed of Damascus?"

Huddling together in front of the TV, the three of them listened intently as the newscaster announced, "We have just received confirmed reports that the city of Damascus and its surrounding metropolitan areas have been destroyed. Repeat, Damascus has been destroyed." The broadcaster went on to say, "The satellite images you are watching right now vividly illustrate the entirety of Damascus reduced to rubble!"

Jumping up, George shouted, "That's it! There you have it! The fulfillment of Isaiah 17:1 has just occurred!"

While his wife sank into a state of shock, he began pacing the parlor.

"Unbelievable!" he cried. "We knew this was coming!"

"But watching it unfold before our very eyes breaks my heart!" sobbed Mimi.

Razz, his voice quaking, groaned, "This is the point where our hearts overtake our heads. We can hypothesize till doomsday, but to realize that hundreds of thousands of people have just been incinerated…"

His words trailed off as George bent over to grip his friend's shoulder. Mimi placed a hand there, as well, and the three wept.

7

Israel Attacks
Iranian Nuclear Sites

"**W**hat went wrong?" Iranian president Muktada Zakiri inquired of his spiritual advisor Zamani Nikahd. "How could Israel use nuclear weapons against our closest allies? Were we not all, including the Syrians, under the divine protection of Allah, and called to hasten the return of messiah Muhammad Al-Mahdi?"

Nikahd replied, "Fear not, my vision of his return was crystal clear. Mahdi is coming! We are only to know when, not necessarily how, Muktada, and his time is near."

Unimpressed with his advisor's vague and cliché-like comment, Zakiri asked, "Then what am I to do, sit around and wait for Hezbollah, and Hamas to be destroyed alongside, before Iran attacks Israel? There is no word from Syrian president Hassan Tereiri, or his chief commanders, so I fear they all died during the blast, and lie buried deep beneath the Damascus rubble."

Nikahd looked upward, as if entering into a trance, and said with a patronizing voice, "You must be patient, Muktada; I'm awaiting another vision to direct us."

"Be patient!" shouted Zakiri, "There is no more time to be patient. Nikahd, if you have ill-advised me, I will have your head on a platter."

Cowering backward a few steps while slightly prostrating, Nikahd muttered, "Allow me to depart from here, my esteemed president, to my holy chambers to pray to Allah for our answer. I'm certain Allah will guide me in this matter."

Zakiri frowned at him and commanded, "You have twenty-four hours and not a minute more to bring me back Allah's message. And, if you fail to return with Allah's guidance I will consider you to be a false prophet and have you killed. Meanwhile, I will put our capitol and nuclear sites on high alert in preparation for an Israeli strike. I fear President Tereiri was right, and the multi-front attack against Israel was premature. Tereiri warned me that if Damascus came under nuclear attack from the Israelis, that Tehran would be targeted, as well."

The Night of the Israeli Air-strike

It was past dusk in the Middle East, and the sun had settled in the western skies, when Israel Prime Minister Kaufman gave the green light to attack Iran's chief nuclear sites, including their main one located in Bushehr.

"We have succeeded in destroying the capitol of our nearest neighbor to the northeast, and now it's time to neutralize our foremost existential threat, the rogue state of Iran. We must send their nuclear program back to the stone age, like we did to Iraq in 1981, and Syria in 2007," Kaufman announced to IDF military chief of staff General Jacob Barak.

Barak replied, "Very well, we will put *Operation Samson's Storm* into overdrive against the Iranians. This command comes not a moment too late, prime minister, because our window of opportunity to strike Iran's nuclear sites was rapidly closing. IDF intelligence suggests the Iranians are merely weeks away from incorporating the Russian S-400 missile defense system into their IRGC arsenal. This state-of-the-art Russian missile defense system would jeopardize all future IAF stealth attack capabilities."

"Those Russian traitors," replied Kaufman in frustration. "They can never be trusted!"

General Barak cautioned, "It will be an extremely dangerous air campaign with unpredictable consequences, because our intelligence suggests Iran may already be expecting our attack. Also, we suspect that President Zakiri of Iran has already acquired, or possibly developed several nuclear weapons devices. If anything goes wrong, Israel should be prepared for a retaliatory nuclear attack within moments afterward. We must prepare all our emergency services beforehand, and you must be isolated to safety."

Kaufman replied, "My administration will take all necessary precautions to protect our citizens and ourselves from potential harm this nightfall."

Barak consoled, "The good news is that we have crippled Syria by destroying Damascus, so Iran will be worried about the similar thing happening to Tehran. This should cause them to think twice before retaliating against us."

"This night will go down in infamy as the night we ensured Israel's national survival. May the blessings of Hashem be upon you and our valiant fighters this night General Barak," Kaufman responded, with praise in his voice.

Early the following morning the presses, airwaves, and Internet social networks like Facebook, YouTube, and Twitter were streaming with unconfirmed reports that Israel had attacked Iran.

"Israel Strikes Iranian Nuclear Sites," read the headline of the *US and World Daily Chronicle*. The article stated that Iran had anticipated an Israeli air-strike, but was unable to prevent it, and in the end suffered great loss at the hands of the Israelis. It appeared as though Israeli sorties struck their nuclear targets with precision, and won an incredible dogfight in the air against the Islamic Republic of Iran Air Force (IRIAF), in the process.

YouTube and television news footage showed a barrage of Iranian anti-aircraft fire streaming through the blackened skies, but not one Israeli Air Force (IAF) plane was reportedly struck down. Additionally, numerous Iranian fighter jets were caught on camera exploding in the skies. For many Americans watching on their TV sets at home, it was reminiscent of the night skies over Baghdad in 1990-1991 during *Operation Desert Storm*, but much more riveting.

Furthermore, the night canvas was splattered with unexplainable events. IAF pilots recounted stories of how a mysterious iridescent cloud cover formed around their fighter jets, providing a protective shield that hid them from view, absorbed the sound of their jets, and seemingly deflected Iranian anti-aircraft fire from harming their crafts.

"The experience was entirely surreal, like being animated in the air. If we weren't involved in a serious aerial conflict with the Iranians, we would have thought we were simply floating silently in the clouds, and suspended in time. We heard and saw the Iranian fighter Jets surround us, but before they could see us we tagged them, and took them down. It was nothing short of a miracle," remarked IAF Lieutenant Jonathan Vitow, shortly after returning back from the battle.

Moreover, some pilots stated the stealthy illumination only seemed to be visible when flying inside the clouds. They sincerely believed the cloud canopy obscured their planes from the vision of the oncoming Iranian fighter jets, which seemed to be expecting the IAF attack.

"No doubt about it; they were expecting us. The element of surprise was non-existent, we became the ambushed, but our forces survived unscathed. This can't be said of the Iranians," confirmed IAF Lieutenant General Binyamin (Benny) Lieberman, assessing the mission.

Oddly, although the night skies over Iran seemed like a Walt Disney World fireworks display on the fourth-of-July, multiplied times ten, no illuminated clouds were caught on camera. However, reports coming out of Iran declaring that their advanced radar systems were unexplainably jammed throughout the night, seemingly added credence to the IAF pilots' eyewitness accounts. Iran's nuclear facilities had been strategically struck, and the damage on the ground was being assessed, but for the time being it appeared as though Israel had dodged the Iranian nuclear bullet for a little while longer.

As news reports streamed in across the TV, George and Razz were astonished at how the IAF had escaped the tactical air-strike unscathed. Razz posed the question: "How does one record such a miraculous war effort in the military journals? Does the author write, 'While narrowing in on their nuclear targets, the IAF was ambushed by protective cloud-cover that enabled them to see, but blinded their enemy?'"

Humoring his friend, George answered, "Sounds good to me Razz. It's just another typical Israeli war story, like when Gideon destroyed the Midianites in Judges 7:16-22."

Razz concluded, "This attack against Iran is going to send Russia through the roof. Russia is heavily invested in Iran's nuclear program and is currently exporting their S-400 missile defense system to the Iranian president Zakiri. This could disrupt the flow of Iranian money desperately needed by the Russian economy. At the very least, we can expect this to cement Russian-Iranian national relations all the more tightly."

George responded, "Let me guess, you think this IAF attack against Iranian nuclear sites will cause Russia to form its Muslim coalition with Iran, Turkey, Libya, and the other in fulfillment of Ezekiel 38 and 39."

"Absolutely, it seems logical to me," answered Razz.

Contemplatively, George responded, "I disagree, and think Psalm 83 will result. But, with all that is happening in the Mideast it appears we will soon see who is correct."

Iranians Flee from Nuclear Fallout

Later that day, news reports were coming in that nuclear fallout from the IAF air-strikes was creating a Chernobyl-type condition in west-central Iran. The Bushehr nuclear reactor was emitting high levels of radiation, necessitating a mass evacuation from the area. Affected populations were fleeing hand-in-hand with their children and any personal belongings they could carry in their cars or on their backs.

Tens of thousands were scattering in differing directions. Reportedly, some were heading up into northern Iran, and some downward toward the south. Iraq and Kuwait were opening their adjoining borders temporarily to those Iranians seeking to flee the country. A humanitarian crisis of epic proportion was developing, amidst the backdrop of all the other Mideast chaos.

George, Mimi, and Razz couldn't believe what they were witnessing.

Teary-eyed, Mimi lamented, "Things just went from bad to horrible in the Middle East."

Embracing his wife, who was visibly shaken by what she was watching, George tried to console her, "Mimi, all we can do is pray for the Iranian people. Most of those precious souls are victims of the Ayatollah's radical regime. They tried to protest their government's actions repeatedly over the past decade, but were either beaten, imprisoned, or executed by President Zakiri's henchmen. The smart Iranians will exit into the neighboring countries until the fallout settles, and the Zakiri regime topples."

Razz sympathized and said, "At least many of the protestors from the Arab Spring had the ability to assemble, but the Iranian protestors were always denied that privilege."

Composing herself slightly, Mimi suggested, "Maybe if there is any silver lining to this tragedy, it will cause many people to consider how crazy and out of control the world has become; and how important it is to trust in God."

8

Arabs Unite to Fight: Is it Psalm 83, Ezekiel 38 or Armageddon?

The world seemed to spin off its axis that apocalyptic summer. It was as if Damascus had become the apex of the universe and its total destruction somehow shifted the earth out of planetary alignment. Oil rich Arab states turned into hardened lava flows overnight, as more OPEC nations retaliated against Israel. Saudi Arabia, Iraq, Kuwait, Bahrain, Qatar, and the United Arab Emirates, coupled with the North African OPEC nations of Libya and Algeria, all played the oil card alongside Iran, attempting to provoke international condemnation against Israel's aggression.

The League of Arab States had scarcely concluded its weeklong meeting before Syrian casualties numbered in the hundreds of thousands, and equally as many refugees from both Syria and Iran flooded the desert sands of Iraq. Syrians crossed over Iraqi borders from the northwest and Iranians from the southeast.

Without delay, Arab armies began to mobilize against Israel. All twenty-two members of the Arab League declared war against the Jews, including Egypt and Jordan, who discarded previous peace accords, and renounced Israel's right to exist. Overnight, Arab skies were filled with the smoke of burning Israeli flags and chants of "Al Mawt Li Israel!" (Death to Israel!)

So much was happening so fast, that Razz all but moved into the Thompson residence. Reflecting on their Desert Storm days, Razz and George encamped in front of the TV 24/7, monitoring war events. With their laptops on and Bibles open, they acted as if they were deployed on a fact-finding mission for the US intelligence community.

It was almost comical, how they compared notes and shared night watch duty to ensure they didn't miss any breaking news. At one point, their military madness crossed the demarcation line of insanity, causing Mimi to chastise them both for arguing about whose turn it was to visit the latrine. "Boys if you don't start behaving, I'm going to turn off the TV and kick you both out of the house! I know you are trying to correlate the war events with Bible prophecy, but frankly, I'm appalled at how insensitive you have both become! Human lives are at stake around the world!"

Humbled by her comments, the two of them retreated, hangdog, to the garage gym. They admittedly had become numb from watching so much devastation. Countless disheartening pictures of charred and contaminated victims bombarded the news channels. In addition, an endless stream of Syrian and Iranian widows and orphans were filmed wandering aimlessly in the barren Mideast deserts.

Concurrently, a large exodus of Syrian Kurds began to migrate toward the north, concerning the Turkish government. The Turks were still recovering from the Kurdish refugee crisis resulting from the Syrian revolts of 2011. At that time, thousands of Kurds crossed the adjoining Turkish-Syrian borders, attempting to flee persecution from the Syrian Alawite regime.

All of these pictures and powerful events were too much for even the most calloused to process. Still, they knew the worst was yet to come, that the destruction of Damascus was only the start of much more disaster to follow.

As they reclaimed their humanity that afternoon, Razz came up with a brilliant idea. "George," he said, "we should start blogging daily about what's going on and field questions that must certainly be developing. You can handle the Psalm

83 questions and I'll tackle the Ezekiel 38 ones. All the while, we should seize this opportunity to further the gospel to the concerned."

Although they were still split as to what prophecy was finding fulfillment, undoubtedly an epic holocaust had begun. Perhaps it was too premature to know whether Psalm 83 or Ezekiel 38 would unfold in the wake of Damascus's destruction, but what mattered was getting the good news about Jesus Christ out to as many people as possible. They both agreed that time was of the essence, because, in their estimation, the rapture could occur at any moment.

They began blogging, and Razz' website hits quadrupled immediately. They began receiving a constant barrage of blogs, emails, and phone calls. It was as if the Lord opened the floodgates to the harvest field.

As they anticipated, people had lots of questions. Many were about Psalm 83 and Ezekiel 38, but mostly folks sought instructions on what to do in the midst of the Mideast peril.

Collectively, the two of them responded to hundreds of questions daily. One blogger was so impressed, he called them the *End-times tag-team extraordinaire.*

They treaded the blog-waters as long as they could, until finally, Razz called in reinforcements. He began forwarding many of the emails and phone calls to his inner circle of trusted eschatologists, who included George's favorite teacher, Jim Linton. These were peers with whom Razz had volleyed emails back and forth through the years. Whenever Razz discovered a new prophetic insight, he sought their professional opinions before going public.

Razz and George needed their support now, more than ever. They were receiving hits and inquiries from scores of believers and unbelievers who had Google-searched fodder phrases like "the rapture," "apocalyptic Middle East," "Magog invasion," "Psalm 83," and "Damascus destroyed," which, in turn, led many to Razz' site, email, and cell phone.

This increased activity reminded Razz of his trip to ground zero, in the immediate aftermath of September 11, 2001. Those terrorist attacks had spawned a harvest field of hungry souls seeking answers to what had occurred on that infamous day. At that impressionable time, he fielded questions like, "Is it Armageddon?" and "Does the Bible have anything to say about terrorism?"

Like then, the bloggers and callers were asking apocalyptic questions in the aftermath of Damascus's destruction and Iran's radiation fallout crisis.

"No, it's not Armageddon; it could be Ezekiel 38," Razz echoed to numerous callers. Similarly, George was directing callers to Psalm 83.

However, more importantly, they and their colleagues seized the opportunity to present the gospel to hundreds, if not thousands, during the latest round of the Middle East conflict.

9

Psalm 83:
The Final Arab–Israeli War

As the war progressed, it became apparent to both George and Razz that Mideast developments resembled the prophetic descriptions detailed in Psalm 83, rather than Ezekiel 38 and 39. Hezbollah to the north, Egyptians and Saudis to the south, Hamas to the southwest, Palestinians and Jordanians to the east, and even Iraqi forces, had assembled alongside the seriously beleaguered Syrian troops, to surround the Israelis.

As specified in the Psalm, the time had arrived wherein the Arabs stood united against Israel. The "Mother of all Mideast Wars" was inevitable. Although the United Nations Assembly was furious with Israel for reducing Damascus to rubble, their hands were tied, and they were becoming increasingly pre-occupied with the burgeoning Iranian refugee crisis. All previous land for peace proposals calling for the Palestinians and Israelis to live securely side by side were discarded. Diplomacy had failed, staining the legacies of several US presidents and leaving all-out war as the only option.

It was bottom-line time; Damascus was destroyed, the Iranian nuclear threat was minimized, and now the Arabs and Jews were going to have to "duke-it-out" on their own terms in the Holy Land. The international forum had proven to be a fruitless dead-end street. Moreover, the weaponry of the imminent clash was certain to make all previous Arab-Israeli wars seem like minor skirmishes.

This time, only one kingdom would be left standing when the final bell rang. George and Razz confidently concluded that according to the Lord's promises to Abraham, Isaac, and Jacob, inscribed inside the Bible, that Israel would be the victor.

The Arab confederacy invoked their god Allah with a mandate to destroy Israel. They boldly announced, almost word-for-word, what had been prophesied in Hebrew 3,000 years before: "Halak Kachad Goy Shem Yisrael Zakar Lo Od" (Come let us (*Arabs*) wipe them (*Jews*) out as a nation that the name of Israel be remembered no more.) The "seer"[9] Asaph saw this world-changing event coming,[10] and warned that the Arabs would confederate to destroy Israel, in order to possess the Promised Land.[11]

Watching satellite shots of the massive mobilization of multinational Arab armies near Israel's borders, George asserted, "They never wanted peace with the Jews; they wanted peace without the Jews!"

"You are absolutely correct! They weren't seeking a two-state solution; they had a one-state solution in mind all along," Razz responded. "They wanted one more Arab state called Palestine."

"Those poor Arab souls," said George.

"What do you mean?" asked Razz.

"The Arabs are about to go toe-to-toe with the 'exceedingly great army' of Ezekiel 37:10, that has already demonstrated its regional superiority against Damascus and Iran," George answered.

Nodding in concession, Razz said, "I know I'm supposed to be an end-times expert, George, but I've been so preoccupied with Ezekiel 38, I apologize for not giving Psalm 83 more attention. I'm familiar with the *whos, whats, whens, wheres,* and *whys* of Psalm 83, but please describe for me *how* you believe this war will play out."

Striving not to gloat over his scholarship, George humbly replied, "Unlike the Ezekiel 38 invasion, wherein the Lord personally destroys the invaders, the Israeli Defense Forces are instrumental in defeating the Arab confederacy of Psalm 83. Several Old Testament passages in Ezekiel 25 and 35, Obadiah,

Jeremiah 49, Zechariah 12, Zephaniah 2, and Isaiah 11 describe an empowered IDF destroying Israel's surrounding Arab enemies. It seems the Lord raises up this mighty army primarily for this purpose, since it plays no vital role in either the Ezekiel invasion or during the events of Armageddon that follow both," George expounded.

"Good point," acknowledged Razz. "Have you discovered any Scriptural clues as to the length of the Psalm 83 battle?"

"Not really; but, we both know Israel doesn't have the luxury of waging a war of attrition. They have to act expeditiously and decisively to counteract formidable Arab arsenals. The recent destruction of Damascus is a good example," reminded George.

General George was continuing to pour out his prophetic insights when Mimi cleared her throat loudly, her notorious way of signaling, "It's a wrap; pack it up; that will be enough for today." She had been twiddling her thumbs, while listening to their laborious conversation. In her you're-boring-me-to-death voice, with which George and Razz were very familiar, she beckoned, "Would you officers mind adjourning to another area of the compound, so I can have some time alone?"

"Mimi, aren't you interested in all this?" George objected.

Sarcastically, she answered, "Dear, for the past fifteen minutes I have been listening to you both flap your gums and entertain your egos. Whenever you get on a roll, talking about this stuff, I know it could be hours before you come up for air."

"We're not entertaining our egos," George rebuffed. "These are important facts!"

Giving him the if-looks-could-kill stare, she replied, "Yes, I'm sure they're important facts to retired Generals and prophecy buffs, but they're boring me to death! In fact, I fully intend to boot you boys out of the room and turn the channel to Home and Garden Television Network (HGTV), if we don't resume some normalcy in this house for the afternoon!"

Before the Mideast war broke out, Mimi would watch HGTV most every night after dinner, to unwind from her day. Her comments to switch the channel to her favorite TV network made it obvious to both George and Razz that Mimi was on information and emotion overload. Suffering from a loss of hope that life would ever be the same again, she wasn't quite ready for the world to fall apart, or for Jesus to whisk her away into the rapture clouds just yet.

She desired to see her grandkids go to college and get married. She wanted to travel and enjoy retirement with her husband. Earthquakes and holy wars were intruding on life, liberty, and the pursuit of her happiness!

Fortunately, after forty-four years of marriage, George knew when it was time to back down and afford Mimi her space. She had been a trooper up 'til now, allowing Razz and he the run of the house. But he clearly recognized she was about to have a meltdown.

"Can I get you anything, or do anything for you, dear?" George gently asked.

Mimi blinked back tears. "When was the last time you got on the phone with your son, or called your sister, or did anything besides go round and round with Razz about Middle East Bible prophecies?" she whimpered.

Realizing rhetorical questions like this weren't intended to be answered, George made eye contact with Razz and gestured for a smooth, but swift departure. "What say we adjourn upstairs for a while, ol' buddy," he suggested, and delicately handed Mimi the remote control.

The two of them decided to empathize with Mimi's frustration for the remainder of the day. They watched some baseball and shot some pool in the bonus room. Instead of fielding prophecy questions, they called some friends and family to bid them well.

Razz even headed home relatively early, to give George and Mimi space to regroup as a couple.

At least for that night, they both took a leave of duty.

10

The Russian – Iranian Nuclear Connection

Stuffing the classified dossier hastily into his brown leather attaché case, Mikhail Trutnev whisked suspiciously toward the back-exit door of his office, startling his secretary. The silver-haired receptionist that seldom donned a smile, Alena Popov, had set nearly every one of his appointments over the past ten years, and was unprepared for his dubious departure.

"Wait a minute. You have a full schedule of appointments today! Where are you going, and when will you return?" She bellowed.

"Clear my calendar for the rest of the day, I have something pressing to go over with Prime Minister Primakov, and don't know when I'll be returning," he called over his shoulder.

Trutnev was the Russian prime minister's closest confidant. Sergei Primakov relied exclusively on him for all of his intelligence on internal and nuclear affairs. Mikhail became a highly-decorated General for his leadership roles in the Soviet-Afghan War, waged between 1979-1989, first and second wars with Chechnya, between 1994-1996 and 1999-2000 respectively, and successes in the Russian invasion of the Democratic Republic of Georgia in August, 2008.

Mikhail maintained extremely close ties to several veteran agents in Spetsnaz GRU (the Special Forces of the Foreign Military Intelligence Directorate), which is staffed by the most experienced and elite of Russia's special operators since its creation in 1949, at the onset of the Cold War against the West. The prime minister depended to a fault upon Mikhail and was about to be confronted nervously by him at his desk.

Prime Minister Primakov instructed his personal secretary to let General Trutnev into his office. Closing the door securely behind his visitor, Prime Minister Primakov calmly said, "Good Morning, General. Have some hot tea; it's my favorite blended brew, just given to me by Chinese Ambassador Li Chin."

Fixated on the pressing matter at hand, Trutnev ignored the invitation and hustled the critical documents out of his briefcase and placed them on Primakov's desk, almost tearing them in his haste.

Puzzled, Sergei gestured to a chair in front of his desk, "Mikhail, what is this about?" Then, looking about the room suspiciously, Primakov jested, "Have you come to warn me of an assassination plot?"

Trutnev swallowed nervously, "I wouldn't say that, at least, not yet," he replied.

Taken aback, Primakov gazed piercingly into his confidant's eyes, and proceeded to pour Mikhail some tea into a rare porcelain cup from the Romanov era.

"Tell me then," Sergei said, "what is so urgent?"

"Sir, you must be briefed immediately about distressing information I recently received. This information is extremely troubling in light of Iran's current nuclear radiation crisis. I have been delivered highly classified information about the missing tactical nuclear devices that I reported to you several months ago."

Prime Minister Primakov's heart sank. Speaking with a hint of annoyance in his voice, he replied, "That report was incomplete and not verifiable, if I remember correctly, Mikhail."

"The investigation was as complete as possible at the time Mr. Prime Minister," Mikhail replied.

"Are you insinuating that I let the matter fall through the cracks?" Primakov challenged.

Taken aback, Mikhail clarified, "No, no, no, Mr. Prime Minister! I just wanted to brief you about the sealed report my secretary delivered to me when I entered my office this morning. Normally, she greets me with my hot coffee when I arrive, but instead she handed me this distressing report. It reveals that several tactical nuclear devices are unaccounted for, at three of our more loosely monitored military installations. I know we lacked information on that, since my last report, and given the dangerous implications of these details, I feel your attention to this matter is of utmost importance."

Realizing he had procured Primakov's undivided attention, Mikhail scooted the report toward the prime minister, who was now seated across from him at his oversized, rectangular oak desk. Shifting to the edge of his high-back leather chair, Primakov promptly picked up the report and began reading silently.

Mikhail stirred restlessly across from him, twiddling his fingers and glancing nervously about the room. The prime minister's eyebrows rose higher with each page. His countenance had changed dramatically since he had poured Mikhail's tea.

Mikhail was increasingly fidgety, and standing, began pacing about the office. The prime minister, deeply engrossed in the documents, failed to notice Mikhail's mounting anxiety.

The communiqué clearly spelled out that several "suitcase" nuclear devices had entered Iranian Revolutionary Guard Corps hands. The report also outlined IRGC plans to use these devices for "strategic" purposes if Israel or the West struck Iranian nuclear facilities, or other specific targets.

As the prime minister completed the report, he looked up sternly into Mikhail's eyes, stopping him in his tracks. "Has President Ziroski been briefed on this?" Primakov snapped. Moving within whisper distance of the prime minister, Mikhail reluctantly answered, "Perhaps, I'm uncertain."

"What do you mean, 'uncertain'?" The prime minister said with a grimace.

Mikhail muttered, "My secretary said the envelope showed up mysteriously on her desk this morning, with no memo or trace of origin. She said she had spotted an aide to President Ziroski in the hallway moments before she stepped out of her office to visit the lounge."

"Hmm," the prime minister grunted. "Please continue."

Mikhail proceeded on. "When she returned, the sealed dossier was sitting in plain view, in the center of her desk. She said that whoever left the folder purposely brushed aside several other papers to make room for it. Her guess was that the confidant strategically positioned the document on her desk, expecting it would be passed to me expeditiously."

Ignoring Mikhail's obvious attempt to speak softly, Primakov blurted out, "This means that the president knows everything!"

The prime minister's harsh tone caused the General to step backward. Visibly shaken, Trutnev, asked meagerly, "What are we to do?"

Primakov let out a deep sigh as he leaned back into his overstuffed chair and reached inside the lapel of his suit coat to extract his handkerchief. Blotting beads of sweat from his brow, he sat eerily still for a few minutes.

Looking for some sort of cue from his superior, Mikhail stood speechless.

Having gathered his thoughts, Primakov at last stood up from behind his desk. Smoothing his suit, and firming up the knot of his tie, he calmly gazed at his closest comrade. By now, Mikhail resembled a deer frozen in the headlights of an oncoming car. Both, he and his untouched cup of tea, had grown cold inside.

With as much professionalism as he could muster, Primakov said, "Mikhail, I thank you for bringing this report to my attention. Apparently, President Ziroski is sending me a message. I will have to meet with him personally to let him know that his message was received. I will let you know if you can be of any further help in this matter." The prime minister gestured toward the door and Mikhail gladly seized the opportunity to exit the office.

Once Mikhail had departed, Primakov calmly reached for his desk phone and pushed the intercom button.

"Yes, Mr. Prime Minister," his secretary answered.

"Please set up an appointment for me to meet with the president, as soon as possible, he ordered."

"Of course, Mr. Prime Minister, what shall I say it's regarding?" she asked

Ignoring her question, the prime minister slouched back down to his chair and braced for the wrath he expected to soon receive, from Russia's cruelest Czar.

President Mad Vlad

Meanwhile, Russia's president was meeting with his UN Ambassador, Anatoly Tarazov, addressing other important classified matters inside of his expansive office.

"Is it true Anatoly, that the cabinet members of the politburo have begun sinisterly calling me the Mad Vlad behind closed doors?" The ruthless Russian inquired.

Accustomed to closely guarding his responses, Tarasov nervously replied, "Such rumors are circulating Mr. President."

Stepping beside his life-size picture of Joseph Stalin, Ziroski asked, "And you, dear comrade, have you ever made such remarks?"

"No," Tarasov insisted, "Absolutely not; perish the thought!"

Ziroski jeered, "Your response pierces me comrade! I am surrounded by spineless fools who feel threatened by me, and I find few to trust anymore. Mother Russia requires the strictest allegiance from her servants in these turbulent times. In the past, you have caused me to question your loyalty; am I to believe things have changed with you now?"

Buckling under scrutiny, the Ambassador whined, "All that you have ever asked of me, I have performed, since that unfortunate episode. I will never let you down again."

Ambassador Tarasov referred to the time he had fumbled a few critical words during an important speech regarding Russia's intentions for Iran's nuclear development program. Russian fuel rods that had been recently loaded into Iran's primary nuclear facility had become a hot button of controversy in the halls of the General Assembly.

Anatoly Tarasov was under strict orders to diffuse the debate. Ziroski had scripted the exact wording to be spoken, and was beyond furious when Anatoly Tarasov deviated from the teleprompter speech. Mad Vlad had said Anatoly's disobedience bordered on treason.

Mad Vlad spoke directly to his point, "The United States continues to antagonize the Iranian President Muktada Zakiri, even after Israel has violated Iranian airspace and caused the Bushehr nuclear reactor crisis. We must persuade them to lift their ongoing sanctions upon Iran swiftly. Zakiri is becoming increasingly desperate and out of control!"

Anatoly agreed, "Anything, Mr. President; what would you have me do?"

Ziroski replied, "China is prepared to criticize America and several European nations severely for still harboring what they are now calling "inhumane sanctions" against Iran. These countries are still suspecting Iran has nuclear devices undetected somewhere that Israel didn't destroy, and as such refuse to lift the sanctions. I have inside information that their assessments are accurate, and Iran does possess nuclear devices."

Anatoly gasped and echoed his earlier comment, "Perish the thought!"

Ziroski then instructed his chief diplomat, "You must lock arms with Chinese Ambassador Chin, and lobby in the assembly against America's charge to maintain and strengthen sanctions. These sanctions are crippling Iran and will provoke Zakiri to lash out!"

Tarasov consented, "I am very close with Ambassador Chin, and we know how to turn the political tables on the American delegation. We have made it extremely difficult through the UN in the past, for America to get broad support for deeper sanctions against the Iranians, and with Iran's radiation fallout crisis, we can humiliate America for certain."

"Ratchet up the pressure to a point of embarrassment," Vlad commanded. "I want the United States isolated in their campaign against Iran. Get the European nations to distance themselves from America on this matter, or else I guarantee Zakiri will take matters into his own apocalyptic hands. He informed me yesterday that his crazy Imam Zamani Nikahd has received another ridiculous vision that their Mahdi won't come unless the Great Satan America is attacked!"

Confused, Tarasov replied, "I thought you, too, were fed up with the Americans?"

"I am," Ziroski answered, "but, I want Iran to focus its aggression toward Israel, rather than attempt to terrorize the United States. Attacking America will awaken a sleeping giant and complicate world matters. The Jewish State is threatening our energy plans for the region. Jewish exploits need to be stopped, before they discover oil, in addition to all their recent natural gas discoveries."

Just then the president's intercom sounded and his secretary announced that the prime minister had arrived for their meeting.

Brushing the Ambassador out the door, as if he were an annoying fly, Mad Vlad barked, "Off with you now, and go take care of our business in the General Assembly."

Mad Vlad's Sinister Plan

President Ziroski had received and reviewed the classified report well in advance of forwarding it strategically to Prime Minister Primakov. Suspecting the missing nukes would soon be utilized against Israel or the West, he needed a high-level scapegoat. Hence, the prime minister had become the fall guy for Mad Vlad's diabolical plan.[12]

Primakov entered the room punctually at 3:00 p.m. As Ziroski's secretary closed the door behind him, Primakov pulled the classified dossier from his satchel and commented, "I thank you Mr. President, for agreeing to meet with me, I have a very pressing matter to discuss with you."

Playing possum, Ziroski questioned, "What pressing matter, Comrade; I'm very busy today?"

Primakov pulled a nearby chair close to Mad Vlad's desk, proceeded to sit down, and held out the document asking, "Sir, are you familiar with this document regarding our missing "baby nukes"?

"What missing nukes?" Ziroski growled, glaring intensely at Primakov.

Primakov placed the report squarely in the center of Ziroski's desk and stammered, "Mr. President, forgive me if I'm mistaken, but I assumed that you had seen this."

Ziroski stood up and leaned over his desk, fists planted on either side of his desk pad and declared, "You assumed right! Do you, for one moment, think that I am not aware of everything that is going on in my administration, long before you read your damaging reports?"

Primakov squirmed, realizing his problems were mushrooming.

Ziroski angrily continued, "You previously assured me that there would be no further fallout from that matter, that you and comrade Trutnev's department had matters well in hand. And now, as Iran undergoes a radiation crisis, I find out this troubling information. If Iran uses our nukes against Israel or American targets, there will be severe consequences!"

Slamming down his fist on the dossier, Mad Vlad thundered, "What can you add to this report?"

Primakov sputtered, "Mr. President, my staff is investigating the accuracy of these findings, as we speak."

Leaning across his desk, as if to bite Primakov's head off, Ziroski bellowed, "What kind of a fool do you take me for? I know for a fact that you just found this information and have had no time to investigate it further. You knew nothing of this major problem until I had my confidant deliver the dossier to your office. I knew about it long before you even got wind of it. I've already conducted my own internal investigation and confirmed these details to be true."

Tongue-tied, the prime minister timidly muttered, "Mr. President, I only meant…"

"You only meant what?" Ziroski interrupted. "You told me Trutnev had matters under control and that this issue was put to rest. Now we learn that some of our "baby nukes" are in rogue Iranian hands! You fool! Zakiri informed me this morning that Israel did not destroy these nuclear devices, and I fear he intends to use them against the United States."

"I will offer Zakiri double their value to repurchase them back," suggested Primakov.

But, Ziroski countered, "I have already made Zakiri a more than generous offer, and he is not interested. He said the IRGC paid top dollar for these nuclear devices and refused to divulge how and when they were procured."

Primakov moved to stand up, stating apologetically, "Mr. President, according to Trutnev, these suitcase nuclear weapons were all accounted for."

"Your lies never cease," Ziroski retorted. "You and Trutnev are setting up Mother Russia for a hard fall. But, as always, I'm way ahead of you Sergei. You will be the one who takes the fall if Iran utilizes these nuclear weapons. As prime minister, you will shoulder sole responsibility for the disappearance of these nukes."

Becoming increasingly unnerved, Primakov replied, "Zakiri would be a fool to launch these weapons against Israel or America. It would be a death wish."

"Let me assure you," Ziroski avowed, "Iman Nikahd has convinced Zakiri that he has been called by Allah to this end. When Zakiri uses these weapons, and I expect he will, the two of you, along with Mikhail Trutnev, and Zamani Nikahd will all be tried and hung by the International Court! Then the Ayatollah and I can rebuild Iran's nuclear program and seize control over all the vast resources of the Fertile Crescent."

11

Terrorists Attack America Again!

Following Mimi's momentary meltdown earlier that week, George thought it would be therapeutic to host a weekend barbeque with some friends and family. So, that following Saturday, he invited Lisa, Jami, Tyler, Razz and a few close friends over for his specialty: seared rib-eye steaks, marinated in a richly seasoned soy-Italian sauce.

Unfortunately, his son Thomas was still out of state working on a commercial construction project and couldn't attend. In light of volatile world events, his prolonged absence from home was causing Lisa many restless nights. Her sleeplessness was beginning to show in her tired eyes and the dulling of her usually vibrant complexion.

Knowing how conscientious Lisa was about her beauty and parenting skills, Mimi commented, "You're holding up quite well in light of playing the role of two parents lately. George and I couldn't be more pleased with you as a daughter-in-law."

Setting down her kitchen utensil and turning toward Mimi, Lisa affectionately replied, "Well, that's very nice of you to say, Mimi. I haven't been sleeping well, while Thomas has been away. Normally, I do okay in his absence, but I'm worried about him, the kids, my job, and my family in Israel. It's almost impossible to get any beauty rest anymore."

"Well, beauty isn't everything, and besides, God made you absolutely adorable," replied Mimi.

Lisa shrugged. "You're being kind," she said, "but I don't feel very adorable these days. My eyes are puffy, my neck aches, and I plucked out my first gray hair this morning!"

"Mimi resembled that remark," George heckled, intruding into their conversation.

"Yeah, about thirty years ago. Thank goodness for make-up and hair-color," Mimi jested.

"Poppy, how long 'til we eat?" asked Tyler, entering the kitchen.

Grandpa knew that Tyler's question was code for, "Can I steal a bite before dinner?" George had spoiled his grandson with taste-testing throughout his childhood. As a result, Tyler had developed an incurable habit of loitering around the grill, expecting his grandpa to sneak him tasty morsels before dinner was served.

Winking, George slyly replied, "Why don't you come out and help me turn the steaks in about ten minutes."

"You got it, Gramps," Tyler laughed, running back to the patio.

While the Thompsons attempted to resume normalcy on the home front, the developing Middle East humanitarian crisis had the international community reeling in shock. The UN pleaded for, and achieved, a brief ceasefire so relief workers could tend to the hordes of dead and wounded in the Middle East. This allowed for a momentary calm before the pending storm of Holy War in the Promised Land.

Unfortunately, this was not the case throughout Muslim communities in Europe and elsewhere around the world. Muslim protestors crowded numerous city streets from Paris to London to Jakarta to Khartoum. Molotov cocktails, tear gas, rubber bullets, and "Death to Israel" signs made much of Europe look like the streets of downtown Cairo, in the days leading up to the resignation of Egyptian president Hosni Mubarak. Worldwide Muslim protests were beginning to make the Arab Mideast protests and revolts of 2011 pale in comparison.

Between the destruction of Damascus, the Iranian radiation crisis, and worldwide Muslim protests, there weren't enough newscasters or news cameras to cover all the breaking news. The major news channels had to pick and choose from a plethora of newsworthy events, the ones they felt deserved special coverage.

The picnic tables were set up, the potatoes were baking, and the barbeque was fired up, when suddenly Razz stormed into the backyard. "Come, quick! America has just been terrorized!" The chatty gathering was stunned to silence. "Yankee stadium is ablaze!" gasped Razz. In an instant, the patio cleared as the party moved into the parlor to catch the breaking news.

It looked like September 11, 2001, all over again: panic-filled streets, blaring sirens, and smoke in the air. "A powerful bomb has just exploded during the middle of the Yankee versus Red Sox game!" one newscaster announced. "Details are sketchy, but traces of radioactive fallout have been detected. As you can see on the screen, HAZMAT teams are already mobilizing on the scene, suited up in full protective gear, as first responders quarantine the area."

News footage of the blast was shocking and evidenced that the explosive was no amateur device. Immediate indicators pointed to the possibility that a tactical nuclear weapon had been detonated. Aerial images of Yankee Stadium made it look like the recent destruction of Damascus had spilled over into New York. Intensifying matters, a decent sized crowd was in attendance to watch both teams battle for first place. Fans that would otherwise refrain from attending, for fear of terrorism, made an exception for this particular game. Initial news assessments all confirmed that the prospects for survivors appeared very grim.

As George feverishly flipped through the news channels, reports streamed in that hundreds of wildfires were blazing throughout various parts of the country. These fires reeked of arson, causing commentators to deduce that a multi-pronged terror attack had been launched against America.

Observing the shock in his guest's faces, George assumed the role of General. He encouraged everyone to remain calm and stay for dinner. "Razz will keep an eye on developing events for us," he volunteered. "Besides, we can't let the terrorists win by ruining a perfectly good barbeque!" Although eating was far from their thinking, they wanly smiled, and agreed to support one another by sharing the meal together, while watching the events unfold.

Unfortunately, the remaining events that unfolded that Saturday evening made the terror of September 11, 2001, pale in comparison. They could only pick at their meals, because the catastrophic events of the day stole their appetites.

Thousands lay dead in and around Yankee Stadium. Meanwhile, first responders throughout the country were mobilizing to put out scores of wildfires. As these developments continued to unfold, more devastating blasts occurred at Wrigley Field in Chicago, and, simultaneously, at Chavez Ravine Stadium in Los Angeles. Although far fewer fans filled these arenas than at Yankee Stadium, those in attendance were all feared dead.

While the country was grappling with the scope of developing events, reports came in that a similar blast had apparently been averted at Tiger Stadium in Detroit. Stadium security officials had been investigating suspicious activity in the docking area, accosted a delivery vehicle, and ended up shooting and killing its driver as he attempted to flee. A detonation device was located inside the vehicle and carefully disarmed. While the stadium was being evacuated, the bomb squad was cautiously searching for the whereabouts of the bomb.

Additionally, several Jewish synagogues across the country were blown up, as suicide bombers, shouting "Allahu Akbar" rushed in during Saturday Shabbat services. Hundreds of Jewish worshippers across America were believed killed or injured.

Viewing these reports, Lisa shuddered. "That could happen in *our* neighborhood," she gasped. "That could be Tyler in one of those buildings!"

George hugged her tightly and said, "Tyler's alright; he's safe right here. We will never let anything bad happen to him." Within their embrace, the centuries old Jewish-Christian divide was temporarily bridged. In that instant, a Jew and a Christian had found common ground by facing the shared enemy of Islamic fundamentalism.

Now both Israel and America were under siege; but in America's case, the specific enemy was difficult to identify.

Initial reports implicated Al-Qaeda. WikiLeaks documents had reported the Pentagon believed that Al-Qaeda possessed one or more nuclear devices. However, intelligence findings were being confounded by the fact Karim Nazari, Al-Qaeda's new leader, had recently relocated from the caves of Afghanistan to protective obscurity inside Iran. His unconfirmed whereabouts complicated matters, causing the Pentagon concern that a concerted terror campaign involving Al-Qaeda and the rogue state of Iran was unfolding.

Was Iran making good on Zakiri's promises to create an apocalyptic condition inside Israel and America, to hasten the coming of the Twelfth Imam? And, was Al-Qaeda running interference for Iran, by igniting widespread wildfires and blowing up Jewish synagogues nationwide?

The Twelfth Imam, also referred to as the Mahdi, is the Shiite Islamic messiah. In recent months, Iranian Shiite Mullahs had boasted that combined attacks on Israel, the "Little Satan," and America, the "Great Satan," would invoke the Mahdi's end-time return. Iranian president Zakiri was echoing similar apocalyptic sentiment through Al-Jazeera television and the Tehran Times newspaper.

Additional concerns were directed toward Hezbollah, headquartered in Lebanon. It was common knowledge that cell groups from this Iranian-backed military organization had entered America by crossing the border of Mexico. Several known members of the terror group, which had recently been detained in Texas, admitted this. Furthermore, they informed authorities that Hezbollah had maintained an operative presence in the countries of Mexico and Venezuela for years.

Despite all the above, no smoking guns were jumping out at investigators and due to Mideast volatility, America had to proceed with the discovery process cautiously. What was certain was that the responsible party would receive the harshest of punishment. Meanwhile, Americans were told to go on lockdown and watch their TVs for further developments and instructions.

From the moment, the stateside terror began, Lisa had been attempting to contact Thomas on his cell phone. Nationwide connectivity was hindered, due to the enormous call volume. Finally, after dozens of attempts, she got through to him and was relieved to hear he was in his car, headed home.

"Hallelujah!" she shouted. "Thomas will be here tomorrow night. They postponed construction temporarily so he and his crewmembers could head home."

Mimi asked anxiously, "How is he, and what did he say?"

"He's in shock" Lisa responded. "The minute they heard about Yankee Stadium, they shut down the construction, and he grabbed his crew and headed home. He was thankful to hear from me because none of them have been able to get through to their loved ones by phone. He wants me to get home and contact all the workers' family members, right now."

"I will follow you home," George offered. "We should take the service streets as a precaution."

"I'm riding with Poppy," Tyler cried.

"Lisa, I think you should grab the address book with worker's phone numbers and an overnight bag for you and the kids. Stay at our house until Thomas gets home," Mimi urged. "We can call everyone from here."

"Thanks, Mimi, but I'll feel more comfortable at home," Lisa replied. "We'll be fine. Hopefully, the worst is about over."

Realizing Lisa was firm in her decision, George asserted, "Let's get you all home, then."

Exchanging farewell embraces with Mimi, Lisa and Jami jumped into the BMW and headed out; George and Tyler shadowed them in the pick-up. Observing his grandfather place a shotgun in the backseat of the truck before departing, Tyler asked, "What is going to happen to America? Are we going to be okay?"

George blinked back some tears and gave a reply he only half believed: "I'm sure Americans will rally together quickly, like we did after September 11th. In no time the country will get back to normal. Until then, everyone will have to make adjustments, like your dad leaving his job and us following the girls home tonight. America is a strong country and we will get even with the terrorists. Afterward, our streets will be safe and you will be hanging out at Frostee Freeze, again."

12

The Arabs Surrender

By the time Thomas and his crew arrived home, American terrorism experts were alternately pointing fingers of blame at Iran, Al-Qaeda, and Hezbollah. Although none of them had claimed responsibility; all were prime suspects. And even though the enemy remained unidentified, the Joint Chiefs of Staff advised US Secretary of Defense Donald Yates and newly elected President John Bachlin to prepare for a multi-front Mideast war.

Pre-scheduled plans for full troop pullout in Afghanistan were promptly postponed, as that war-torn country is strategically located on Iran's eastern border. Ground, air, and naval forces were put on ready alert, and massive amounts of heavy military equipment was being readied for rapid redeployment. Although US President John Bachlin had campaigned against further US military involvement in the Middle East things had changed drastically.

Meanwhile, the Middle East predicament was heating up again. Like a kettle boiling over on the stove, the newly formed Islamic Unified Arab Forces (IUAF) were preparing to face off with the IDF. Some US military analysts suggested the terrorist attacks in America were staged as a diversionary tactic, enabling the IUAF to garner more time to assemble and strategize. These pundits believed the Arabs relied on the terrorists to eliminate America from the Mideast equation, by terrorizing the country from within.

Others disagreed, claiming the concerted terror campaign had to have been months in the making. No matter which side was right, it looked like David and Goliath had been resurrected for a final battle in the Middle East.

Finally, after several failed attempts to reach his father over the crowded land telephone lines, Thomas got through on his cell phone. "Dad, I missed you and mom immensely. How are you both doing?"

Attempting to console his only son, George replied, "Under the circumstances we are doing fine son. We are so relieved that you got back home safely to be with Lisa and the kids."

In a seemingly helpless tone, Thomas said, "I just hate having to leave Lisa and the kids alone, but I have no choice, it's so hard to find good work anymore.

Observing his son felt a sense of guilt about the matter, George praised his son for doing what it takes to be a good family provider. "Son we are so proud of you and know that you have to do what it takes to survive these tough times. And you know your mother and I will always be here for all of you."

Unable to contain his emotions, Thomas said tearfully "What in the world is going on? I am so very concerned for everyone's safety. Do you think things are going to get worse?"

"That's no easy question son?" replied George. "The world's falling apart at home and abroad."

"Is this it? Do you and uncle Razz believe the Bible predicted America would come under siege?" Thomas inquired.

"I don't know about that, but we do believe Middle East events are driving all the chaos, and are about to accelerate into the biblical wars of Psalm 83 followed by Ezekiel 38," George answered.

Composing himself somewhat, Thomas confided, "I'm glad you taught me the fundamentals of survival as a child. I have my gold, guns, and goods in place."

"That's all important under the circumstances, but what's most critical is your faith in God," reminded George.

"I agree," confirmed Thomas. "I'm back on board with the Lord, and when war broke out in the Middle East, I started following uncle Razz' daily blog."

Unfortunately, the call was abruptly disconnected because of over-crowded phone lines, but George was delighted to hear his son was trusting God again. He attempted to reconnect over the phone with Thomas throughout the day, even utilizing his landline as an alternative to his mobile phone. But, the heavily trafficked lines rendered a perpetual busy signal, prohibiting further contact.

That day, the sound of Mideast war drums were quickly drowned out by the sound of Scud missile blasts and advanced rocket explosions. Unfortunately for the Arabs, the advanced rockets were primarily launched from Israel's side. Before America could render a final verdict on whether or not to get involved, the Arab–Israeli war had kicked into highest gear.

The Arabs were taking a shellacking.

Over the next two weeks, as America tarried over what terrorists to fight, her citizens gradually went back to work, and Razz, George, and Mimi watched the capitals of the Psalm 83 nations surrender to Israel one-by-one. Before the radioactive dust from Damascus and Bushehr settled, the kings, princes, prime ministers, and presidents of Amman, Beirut, Cairo, Gaza City, Riyadh, and Ramallah were waving white flags and bowing in defeat toward Jerusalem.

It was obvious the IDF had previously formulated a fool-proof, prison-rules plan for dealing with this multi-front Arab attack. It was as if someone had tipped off the Israeli Defense Minister to Psalm 83 ahead of time.

With extreme precision, Israel's army attacked the jugular vein of the Arab States. Airstrips, munitions sites, military headquarters, capital cities, and more, were hit with sortie upon sortie, loaded with tactical weapons. The Mediterranean Sea could not be quieted, as nuclear-tipped warheads were launched from Israel's Dolphin class submarines upon strategic targets in Egypt, Saudi Arabia, and portions of Northeast Syria near the borders of Iraq. Not even the holy cities and shrines of Islam were off IDF limits.

The Al Aqsa Mosque and the Dome of the Rock in Old Jerusalem had been captured by IDF ground troops. Air strikes had severely damaged Islam's two holiest sites, at Mecca and Medina. Muslims were temporarily stranded without a place to pilgrimage.

But probably most shocking was the way Arab "friendly fire" slaughtered many within IUAF ranks. It was as if a drunken stupor had overtaken their armies, like when Gideon fought against the Midianites, recorded in the biblical book of Judges. Many military analysts believed Israel utilized advanced strategic EMP technologies against IUAF centers of command and military installations, causing Arab attacks to backfire.

In the aftermath, some Middle East Muslims began questioning Allah's "Akbar" (greatness), while others continued to rally worldwide against the Jewish State with intensified violent protests. Before the "fat lady" could sing her closing chorus, Israel was taking prisoners of war and hoisting Israeli flags over many Arab capitals.

Among them was Egypt, Israel's ancient nemesis. Home to about 80 million Egyptians, their homeland was turned into desolation as a result of Israel's retribution. Egypt's cruel leader, Muhammad Al-Barwahi, who had seized military power during the vacuum created by the Egyptian protests, had played the lead role in forming the IUAF. He had armed Hamas to the hilt, and then pointed all of Egypt's firepower at Israel, forcing the Jews to almost wipe Egypt off of the map.

Hundreds of thousands of Egyptians were either dead, injured, or in need of quick deportation. Egypt's desolation made portions west of the Nile almost uninhabitable, due to radiation fallout. Nuclear experts feared it could be forty years before some of the remote parts of Egypt could be repopulated. Miraculously, shifting wind patterns kept the fallout from approaching Israel, enabling the IDF to advance its front lines into areas east of the Nile.

One day, toward the war's end, Razz pointed to the TV and commented, "Look at all these Arab prisoners being escorted to prison camps. It reminds me of the Gulf War images, when thousands of Iraqi prisoners waved white flags and begged for mercy. I can't imagine where they plan to detain them all." George joined in with the speculation, "You just watch, Razz!

POW camps will start popping up in southern Lebanon, and remote parts of the Negev and Sinai deserts. The IDF will choose these locations to keep their enemies isolated."

Razz was reminded of a related prophecy in the book of Obadiah. Opening his "New King Jimmy" Bible to the specific passage, he read: "'...and the *captives of this host* of the children *of Israel* shall possess the land of the Canaanites as far as Zarephath.' Zarephath was a Phoenician town inside ancient Sidon, today's Southern Lebanon," Razz explained.[13] George took his turn, adding, "Obadiah also predicted Israel would possess the Gaza, West Bank, southern Jordan, and most of the desert area of the Negev and Sinai in addition to southern Lebanon. And, Jeremiah 49:1-6 tells us that after Jordan's capital, Amman, is destroyed, along with many surrounding cities and villages in northern Jordan, Israel will take over Jordan. Jeremiah seems to have foretold the surrender of Jordan."

Razz agreed. "After the destruction, we just witnessed, the Israeli Air Force (IAF) hammering upon Cairo, Suez, and Luxor, it appears Isaiah 19:18 will soon find fulfillment, as well."

"What does that say?" asked George.

Flipping his Bible to the pertinent passage, Razz read, "In that day five cities in the land of Egypt will speak the language of Canaan and swear by the LORD of hosts; one will be called the City of Destruction."

"What's the language of Canaan?" George questioned.

"Today it's Hebrew, of course," Razz responded.

Normally, Mimi would have interrupted their bantering back and forth, but on this occasion, she startled them by speculating, "Conditions in the aftermath of Psalm 83 will probably bring more Jews into Israel."

"How do you figure, Mimi?" Razz responded.

George jumped in. "She's right! Israel could become the land of opportunity for Jews around the world. It'll be a safer place, and Arab oil and other commercial industries could be exploited; not to mention the large natural gas and oil deposits recently discovered there."

Clearing her throat, Mimi said, "Excuse me, there is one too many Mimis in this conversation. As I was attempting to say, Muslims are in a mob mentality throughout the world, making it unsafe for Jews living outside of Israel. This is why I think they will now flee to Israel, to escape mounting persecution."

Applauding her insight, Razz responded, "If what you both predict comes to pass, then the stage could rapidly be set up for the fulfillment of Ezekiel 38 and 39. It won't take long for Israel to 'dwell securely' and become the prosperous nation Ezekiel describes. Their new opportunities will require increased manpower. You two might be on to something."

Pleased that Mimi was involved in the conversation, Razz asked her, "Didn't Lisa's siblings recently move to Israel to join their parents and other relatives?"

Delighted by Razz' family-related question, she answered, "That's correct. And some of them live near the war zone. The crowded phone lines have prevented her from communicating with them."

"What about emails?" asked Razz.

"Lisa said they're not getting through, either," Mimi reported.

"Regarding Lisa and Jami, George and I are very concerned about their rejection of Christ. Thomas hasn't exactly bannered his Christianity on his sleeve and Tyler is a newborn babe in Christ; so thus far, neither of them has convinced Lisa or Jami to accept Jesus into their hearts as their personal Lord and Savior. If you and George are correct that Isaiah 17 and Psalm 83 are fulfilled now, I'm frantically concerned the rapture could occur at any moment and they'll be left behind."

Razz asked her, "How soon are you expecting the rapture to occur?"

Carefully choosing her words, Mimi responded, "George and I share in your belief the rapture could occur at any moment.

The fact it didn't happen before this major war means it's nearer now than ever before, don't you think?"

Razz agreed and added, "I also believe it is an imminent event and think it might occur before Russia, Iran, Turkey, and the other Ezekiel 38 invaders confederate against Israel."

Razz' Ezekiel 38 comments piqued George's interest, prompting him to ask, "What makes you say that?"

Razz answered, "Several things; one being that Ezekiel identifies the Jewish people as 'My people Israel' three times during the episode. To me, this means the event is very Jewish centered and raises questions as to the whereabouts of the church by that time."

"Ezekiel 38 and 39 clearly identifies Israel in the last days. I have often used these chapters to refute Replacement theology, which is the belief God is done with the Jews and the church has taken their place. It is impossible to put the church in place of Israel in this prophetic episode."

"Furthermore…" he said, when Mimi interrupted, asking, "Why is there a furthermore? How did we go from family talk about Lisa's and Jami's salvation to discussing Ezekiel 38? Can we agree the rapture is near and we need to pray and plead for their salvation before we vanish? I'm looking for constructive ideas to help them, not details about an event you don't think we will even experience."

Razz apologetically agreed and suggested that they pray for Lisa and Jami. Mimi began, "Beloved Lord, we lift up Lisa and Jami before your throne. Have mercy on their souls. Save them, Lord! By your design they were created. They are your children. Their salvation is your heart's desire. We agree with you that they are precious. Lord, make their salvation assured through the blood of Yeshua, Jesus Christ. Seal them in your hand for eternity. In the name of Jesus, we pray."

Together, the three of them said, "Amen."

13

Israel, the Next Emerging Market

Cleaning up the carnage from *Operation Israeli Freedom*, which became the secular title for Psalm 83, proved to be an enormous task. Undoubtedly, the IDF had earned itself the reputation of becoming an "exceedingly great army,"[14] but there was collateral damage on both sides of the Arab – Israeli fence. Unlike *Desert Storm*, which primarily experienced Arab casualties, *Op Israeli Freedom* was a far cry from being a sanitary war.

Even though the Arabs suffered a sweeping defeat, scores of Israelis were killed or injured during the conflict. Mopping up the mess and restoring Middle East infrastructures could take months, perhaps years, and require more Jews to migrate into Israel to accomplish the herculean task.

In an attempt to replenish its wounded and lost population, Israel's Ministry of the Interior launched a global campaign called *Tzion Levav*, meaning "Zion's Heart" in Hebrew. This campaign promised a "Greater and Safer Israel." It entreated Jews living abroad to migrate back to their ancient homeland and become the heart and soul of a new, expanding Israel. The slogan read, "Escape Anti-Semitism, Experience Religious Freedom, and Enjoy Economic Opportunity; Come Home to the Holy Land!"

The campaign was extremely successful, and without delay Jews worldwide heeded the invitation. One by one, family upon family, community upon community, multitudes of Jews began flocking into the victorious Jewish State. As a result of the IDF victory, Israel was becoming a safer place. The threat of war and Arab terror was subsiding and the Jewish State wholeheartedly welcomed the immigrant manpower.

Meanwhile, the broader Gentile world was thrust into a state of flux, wondering whether to condemn Israel or cooperate with the victorious Jewish State. As George and Razz suspected, humanity had questions, and a harvest field was forming.

America was pleased that, in short order, the IDF had done much of its war business for it. Those responsible for terrorizing America would exact the harshest punishment imaginable, but for now *Op Israeli Freedom* had dealt a lethal blow to Hezbollah and Al-Qaeda. Both terror groups were severely punished by the IDF for their antagonistic participation in the war. Surviving members of both groups were among the first to be processed in the POW camps. According to US assessment, both groups had been involved with Iran in the terror attacks inside America.

For Iran's involvement, the US began deployment of 80,000 additional troops into the region. The troop surge was primarily directed toward Afghanistan, due to its strategic location on Iran's eastern border. Iran feared harsh American retaliation, and quickly called upon Russia to increase its military presence in the region. Reportedly, Russian president Ziroski promised the Ayatollah of Iran his country's full support, and deployed of an equal number of Russian troops into Turkey and Iran. This complicated American military plans and was certain to revive the Cold War.

Meanwhile, back at the Thompsons', George and Razz quickly discovered that many so-called Christian leaders were clueless about the prophetic relevance of *Op Israeli Freedom*. Statements out of the Vatican and the World Council of Churches condemned Israel's action, demanded the return of Arab POWs to their homelands, and called for the formation of a Palestinian State. Thus, the preponderance of the Christian church failed to appropriately associate the Arab – Israeli war with its Psalm 83 counterpart.

While Israel was mopping up in the aftermath of the IDF victory over the Psalm 83 Arab nations, Razz received an urgent phone call from his close friend Nathaniel Severs. Severs was the president of Unistate Global Investments Corporation, one of the largest investment firms in America. UGIC managed more high profile accounts than any other brokerage house in the country. Severs ranked among the nation's top economists and sported a resume more extensive than the presiding Federal Reserve Chairman, Benjamin Bernard.

Razz and Nathan were high school friends, who had played on the varsity football team together. Although their careers subsequently sent them in different directions, they kept in frequent contact, and like a fine wine, their friendship had sweetened with age. Nate, as Razz referred to him, had never married. His successful career had taken him to almost every country on the globe, earning him the respect of many world leaders and a good share of romantic relationships with female celebrities along the way.

Speaking several languages and epitomizing the "tall, dark, and handsome" cliché, Nate didn't limit his options to famous American women only. His lavish lifestyle often prompted Razz to ask, "When are you going to slow down and let one of these starlets catch you, before you go to your grave lonely?" Nate, who possessed an endless repertoire of one-liners, would always volley back with something like, "Marriage is like religion: there are so many to choose from and until you're certain you've identified the right one, it's best to keep on looking."

In return, Razz would warn, "How many failed relationships and brushes with bad religions will it take before you realize Jesus is the way, the truth, and the life, and the only way through to the Heavenly Father?"[15] It pained Razz to realize that Nate was still undecided about Christ, even though he had shared the gospel with him countless times.

"Hello, Nate, and to what do I owe the honor of this call?" answered Razz.

"I was hesitant to make this call," Severs said, "and sincerely wish it was merely a friendly one, Razz. However, world economies are unraveling by the minute, as you can imagine. I personally wanted to encourage you to make immediate major protective moves with your UGIC accounts."

"What do you advise, Nate? I'm already overloaded with futures, commodities, gold, cash, and rare coins," declared Razz."

It's hard to say; things are so unpredictable at present. We just need to stop the bleeding. My staff informed me your investment accounts, like most everyone else's countrywide, have dropped approximately forty-five to fifty percent since all the chaos began," replied Severs.

Visibly disturbed, Razz asked, "What about investing in Middle East oil? Some news channels are saying Israel hopes to quickly contract with several American petroleum companies to get some of the conquered OPEC oil circulating into global economies again."

"Israel is definitely interested in bringing order to the Mideast chaos by flooding world markets with oil," Severs replied. "However, investing in oil futures right now is extremely risky. Before everything blew up, crude oil was closing at $152 per barrel. However, since OPEC shut down production a few weeks ago, the price per barrel shot up to $398 a barrel."

"Yes," groaned Razz. "I'm already feeling it at the pump. Yesterday I paid $11.38 a gallon. It cost me almost $200 to fill up my SUV!"

Overhearing their conversation, George chicken-scratched a quick note and placed it in front of Razz: *Remember Israel – Ez. 38—lotsa $$$ B4 Russia invades.*

Razz nodded, then proceeded to tell Nate, "I sincerely think Israel is the place to invest at this point."

"Really? Explain," Nate urged.

"According to Bible prophecy, Israel is going to become very prosperous someday. It appears that day draws near," replied Razz.

"How can you know that with certainty?" asked Nate.

"If you recall a couple of lunches ago, before all the mayhem, I warned you that Russia was going to hook up with Iran and several other nations to invade a safe and extremely wealthy Israel," Razz reminded.

"Yes, I recall, but why do you feel Israel stands at that point, presently?" Nate questioned.

"Well, Israel decisively defeated its Arab enemies and can now dwell securely and exploit Arab oil, commercial, and agricultural resources," asserted Razz.

Nate warned, "It could take months before Israel gets OPEC drills pumping, and the Suez Canal and Strait of Hormuz open again. Moreover, Iran will certainly attempt to prevent Israel from using the Persian Gulf to export its oil and commerce. Not only that, but it's almost impossible to get phone or internet service in most of the Middle East; no incoming or outgoing mail is being processed throughout most of the area; tourism and commercial travel is at a standstill; and a majority of the oil refineries and Arab infrastructures are severely damaged."

Razz responded, "Then months it is. Besides, it's better to bless Israel and be patient with my investments than to continue losing money in volatile world markets."

"Well, the latter is certainly the case!" Nate agreed. "As you command, we will invest in the wealthy Israel you are anticipating. The UGIC staff will promptly prepare a pro-Israel *pro forma* for your preview."

As soon as Razz hung up, George asked, "Well, what's the economic expert experiencing?"

"World markets are collapsing and all investments are erratic! He's reluctantly going to research investment potentials developing inside Israel," answered Razz.

"Do you think investing is relevant in light of the imminent coming rapture?" George asked. "What?" Razz laughed. "You were the one shoving a post-it about greater Israel under my nose when I was on the phone!"

"Touché," George chuckled. "We can't be utter escapists. We have to occupy the earth and be good stewards of our finances in case the Lord tarries a little while longer."

"Ezekiel 38 teaches that Israel will garner 'great spoil' just before Russia invades," Razz reminded. "It must be referring to spoils of war from the Arab conflict."

"Razz, do you still believe America shows up as merchants wanting to conduct commerce with Israel in the Ezekiel 38 prophecy?" George inquired.

"Certainly, why wouldn't I?" Razz reiterated.

"In light of America's horrible economy and major recent terrorist attacks, America's not the same stable superpower it once was. This has caused me to rethink America's role, if any, in end-time's prophecy. Frankly, I'm not sure anymore that the US is in Bible prophecy," George explained.

Razz reflected, "America needs Israel right now. The roles are reversed; instead of Israel depending on us for their survival, we now depend on them to survive our struggling economy. Israel has already rescued us from Al-Qaeda and Hezbollah, and now America absolutely has to come alongside Israel and help the expanding Jewish State emerge into its full potential."

"I hope you're right Razz. Our country is in dire straits right now," George said with a sigh.

"Stop being such a downer, George. The US is about to bless Israel and be blessed in return,' Razz opined.

14

Greater Israel Makes
Plans for a Third Temple

The following afternoon George was able to get Thomas back on the phone. It was an abbreviated call and upon hanging up, George informed Mimi, "Thomas and Tyler are on their way here." "Oh, that's wonderful!" she replied. "Do you realize we haven't seen our son in over a month?"

"Cherish the remaining moments we have with him," George responded.

"What's that supposed to mean?" Mimi wondered.

"Supposedly, Thomas and Tyler have something extremely important to discuss with us," George added.

"Did he say what it was?" Mimi asked anxiously.

"Something about Lisa wanting them all to move to Israel immediately," George announced.

Mimi's hand flew to her mouth. "My worst nightmare come true," she cried. "I just knew when Lisa's family moved over there they would pressure her to follow!"

Seeing her reaction, George reconsidered. "Let's not jump to any conclusions," he said, "Let's hear what he has to say."

Overhearing, Razz offered, "It's temporarily safe, though in the long haul maybe not smart."

"Why do you say that?" asked Mimi.

"Because the Russians are coming," Razz reminded.[16]

Anxiety began to set in. "Stop beating around the bush," Mimi pleaded. "What's that supposed to mean?"

"The Russian - Iranian led invasion of Israel predicted in Ezekiel 38 and 39 will overshadow this recent Arab – Israeli war," Razz clarified.

"He's right, dear," George echoed. "But, the coming invasion will make this last one look like small potatoes."

Mimi concernedly responded, "I thought you military experts believed we won't be here for the Magog invasion."

Razz reiterated, "We can't be certain, Mimi. The rapture is an imminent event and we are not told anywhere in Scripture about its exact timing. All we are reasonably certain about is that we are not appointed to wrath, as the Bible puts it."[17]

"There are good reasons to believe the church escapes the entire battle, but not all expositors are convinced about this. I don't want to panic you, but it's possible many Israeli residents could die as a result of this massive invasion. If Thomas moves his family to Israel, he could be putting them in harm's way," warned Razz.

Overwhelmed with concern for Thomas and his family, George asked, "Razz, would you please stay and share these concerns with Thomas?" "Don't you think for one second about leaving," Mimi chimed in. "We need you to help us rid our son of this ridiculous notion to move to Israel. This is absolutely absurd. It's a war zone over there. What's he thinking?"

"Certainly, I'll stay! I'm very concerned that he thoughtfully, and prayerfully, considers this major move at such a time as this," replied Razz.

At that point, George felt compelled to share what Thomas told him over the phone the day before. "I neglected to inform you both that Thomas is reading his Bible and frequenting Razz' daily blog-site to keep up with Mideast events."

"Hallelujah! Finally, some comforting news," exclaimed Mimi. "Train your child up in the way he should go, and when he is old he will not depart from it," Mimi quoted Proverbs 22:6, her favorite child-rearing Bible verse.

"If we can't convince him to stay in America, at least he takes Christ with him to Israel," commended George.

Awaiting the arrival of Thomas and young Tyler, the three of them watched further significant Mideast events unfold on the news.

It was indeed an eventful day that saw Israel make several controversial sovereign moves. In the morning, the Israel Land Administration (ILA) was delegated the responsibility of annexing sizable allotments of Arab lands, including the Sinai Peninsula and portions of Egypt, Jordan, and Lebanon. By capturing these additional lands, Israel could increase its size by over 35,000 square miles.

Upon hearing this announcement, Razz said, "Amazing! The Israelis fought for over six decades to maintain control over a meager 8,000 to 9,000 square miles, but after their decisive victory in *Operation Israeli Freedom* they can now call the shots."

Shortly after the ILA announcement was made, the Israeli Minister of Defense called for the 403-mile-long "West Bank Barrier Wall" to be demolished without delay. Reminiscent of President Ronald Reagan's famous "Tear down this (Berlin) wall" challenge to Mikhail Gorbachev, the Israeli leader cried, "Tear down this fence of terror!" This wall had served its purpose by separating Palestinian terrorism from Israel proper. However, in the aftermath of Psalm 83, Israel anticipated that all Arab terrorism would subside, rendering this wall no longer necessary.

Recalling events from the previous day, Razz recounted how significant it was that the Ministry of Religious Affairs granted the Jewish Temple Foundation permission to go forward with the construction of the third Jewish temple, where the Islamic Dome of the Rock had once stood.

At the time of the announcement, Ehud Cohen, the Temple Foundation spokesman, boasted that the Temple Foundation estimated the altar could be set up, temple instruments readied, and Levitical priesthood operational in a matter of days. The temple instruments had been previously prepared, and the

Levite priests already identified, making Cohen's comments a definite possibility. He further declared the actual temple could be constructed within the span of one to two years.

"Well, George and Mimi, to me, the Religious Affairs temple announcement puts the end-times' frosting on the last days' cake," said Razz.

"I totally agree, Razz. We have to make sure Thomas realizes how fast prophetic events are occurring in Israel, right now!" George exclaimed.

Razz further added, "It will be a cold day in Hades before the international community tolerates the construction of this temple. The altar may be erected, a few priests ordained, and subsequently some animals sacrificially slaughtered, but it won't be long before a public outcry is voiced by Muslims, Catholics, Orthodox Christians, and even animal rights activists, worldwide. After all, this site is holy to Christians and Muslims, as well as Jews."

As they were conversing, Thomas and Tyler arrived. Right away Mimi noticed Thomas didn't look like his vibrant self. Normally, his complexion was tanned, muscles toned, and his smile infectious, but this visit he seemed pale, worn-out, and downtrodden.

"What's wrong, Son? You don't look quite like your chipper self today," she commented.

"I'm fine, Mom, just a little stressed by what's happening in the world," he replied.

After exchanging endearing hugs and we missed yous, they adjourned upstairs to the family room for their important meeting. This secluded area of the house was where pressing family matters were traditionally discussed. As they seated themselves, Tyler fastened himself to his favorite place of refuge, at Mimi's side. Mimi realized things were weighing heavily upon her grandson's mind.

"Thomas," George began, "I invited Razz to join us because of his expertise concerning what's transpiring in the Middle East."

"Absolutely," Thomas responded. "I wouldn't have it any other way."

"So, what's up with this talk about moving to Israel?" asked George.

"Lisa's brother, Joseph, who has been living in Israel the longest of all her seven siblings, is a close friend of Israel's Minister of the Interior, Avi Fleishman. Because of Lisa's extensive background in tourism advertising, Joseph has recommended her to Avi, who is seeking experienced Jewish employees for his rapidly expanding agency."

"Fleishman, who is becoming one of Israel's most respected leaders, has offered her a high-ranking government position. He wants her to be an associate director of marketing for the *Tzion Levav* campaign. She will be working alongside Avi and several of his key staff administrators."

"Also, her family has offered to gift us a large down payment toward the purchase of a home in Israel, so we can all live close to each other. They are telling us that the Israeli government is developing an incentive plan to encourage home ownership. They want more Jews to move to Israel right away. Especially, Jews who would like to inhabit the former Arab territories, although the housing incentive applies anywhere in Israel."

"Supposedly, individuals who can prove at least one spouse comes from Jewish descent receive a 0% interest loan for the first ten years, while the nation expands. Her entire family over there is enthusiastic about the prospects of what they are calling a 'Greater Israel.'"

Unable to contain her dismay at this sudden turn of events, Mimi opined, "We were under the impression that Lisa was finding it difficult to communicate with her family over there, and now you're informing us you're packing up, moving abroad, and buying a house!"

"I'm amazed, myself," Thomas answered. "She *was* having trouble connecting with them. These recent plans have developed over the past forty-eight hours and now she has her mind set on accepting the job and making the move. Please don't act so surprised mother. Lisa has previously warned us she wanted to someday move to Israel. Nonetheless, Tyler and I are struggling with the sudden timing of this, and that's why we wanted to tell you what was going on."

"How soon is all this supposed to take place?" questioned Razz.

"Mom was booking her and Jami's flight on our way over here," whimpered Tyler.

Turning her attention toward her grandson, Mimi asked "How do you feel about moving to Israel, Ty?"

Snuggling even closer, he replied, "I'm upset because I was looking forward to going to Eastside Middle School with Jami. And I'm scared because of the war over there. Also, I don't want to move that far away from you and Grandpa."

Puzzled, George asked Thomas, "Son, I'm curious: why is Lisa booking a flight so suddenly, and why are Tyler and you remaining behind?"

Thomas explained, "We have a split decision in our household on this matter. I just returned from a month of seven-day work weeks in Florida and haven't had time to digest all this. Barely arriving through the front door, I was bombarded with Jami's plans to move to Israel and attend a private school with her cousins."

"Tyler and I are uncertain about shipping off to Israel so soon after the major war. I believe it was the war of Psalm 83, according to what I read on Uncle Razz' blog-site. And Tyler confirmed that's what you told him on the way home from fishing, when the war broke out."

Empathizing with Thomas's concerns, Razz chimed in, "I'm in solid agreement with you, Thomas. The dust hasn't settled over there yet. The place is still a dangerous war zone. Your parents and I have been monitoring recent announcements coming from Israel's government. They're making major land acquisitions, tearing down the partition wall, and making preparations to construct their third temple. I'm also concerned that Israel will have trouble incarcerating all the Arab POWs. The makeshift detention camps they set up are temporary facilities, at best."

George added, "Muslims across the globe are sure to unite, to prevent Israel from implementing these plans. The world will be appalled when animal sacrifices commence on a new altar in Jerusalem. Israel needs to be cautious regarding such matters, or they'll provoke worldwide Anti-Semitism. World governments and economies need time to digest what just happened over there."

"Not to mention, it looks like Russia and America are about to go to war in Iran and Afghanistan!" declared Razz.

Drawing a deep breath, Thomas announced, "I appreciate all your concerns, but in the end analysis, I fear that Tyler and I must move with them to Israel."

"But, why, Son?" George pleaded. "You just said you and Lisa were divided on this."

Shrugging, Thomas admitted, "Actually, your own words have convinced me! It seems clear that Bible prophecies are being fulfilled at an accelerated pace. First the destruction of Damascus, followed by Psalm 83, and now they are planning to construct the Jewish temple. This implies Christ could be coming for believers at any moment!"

"That's right, but…" George faltered.

Thomas looked sympathetically at his parents. "Unfortunately, Lisa is clinging to her Jewish roots and is influencing Jami to do the same," he confessed. "Their Jewish heritage is blinding them to the truth about Jesus as the Messiah. It breaks my heart that they continue to reject him as their Lord and savior. I feel a deep sense of guilt for not being a better Christian husband and dad. I'm hoping that, by making this move and sticking by them, I can finally lead them to the Lord. Recent events could create a change in their hearts."

"That's noble, Son; however, you admitted, yourself, that these events are causing them to cling to their Jewishness, instead," his father reminded.

Thomas saw only one alternative. "I'm left with no choice but to follow them to Israel and continue to love and witness to them."

Tyler suddenly stiffened. "Why do I have to go with you? Please don't make me move! I can live with Mimi and Poppy and go to school in America!"

Weeping alongside her grandson, Mimi pleaded, "Thomas, let him stay behind with us. Your father and I will raise and protect him here inside our home. Please don't subject him to the uncertainties over there. It's not safe! Your father and Razz believe that Russia will soon invade Israel. They believe all of you will be in harm's way if you move there."

Leaping to his feet, Thomas pleaded, "Don't do this to me, Mother! We can't have this conversation! My mind is made up and I'm not leaving my son behind. You can't expect me to abandon my family at this critical time. That's all there is to it!"

George raised a hand to calm him.

"No, Dad! Listen! Lisa will have a good job and I will have no problem getting work as a general contractor over there. Her brother informed me this morning that thousands of new homes are in planning stages to be built, to absorb the Jewish influx into Israel. Nobody can predict how soon any invasion will occur. It may not happen for many years, or even decades!"

Breathless, he slumped to his seat again. "The best thing you can do is pray for us!" he insisted. "If anything changes, I will let you know, but for now, this matter is closed."

Huddling together, they wept and prayed. George asked God to protect, preserve, and prosper them in the new Israel.

Thomas struggled to separate his son from Mimi's tearful embrace. "Come, Son," he said, determination ringing in his voice. "Let's get ready to go to the Promised Land."

15

Russia Forms an Evil Plan to Invade Israel

The next several months proved to be extremely fruitful for Israel. Gaining regional superiority, the enlarging Jewish State commanded the attention and respect of many world leaders and global markets. The little nation of Israel, which much of the Muslim world had wanted to wipe off the map, had morphed into Islam's arch nemesis.

Meanwhile, many Muslims no longer made a distinction between Israel and America; they called them singularly the "Great Satan."

As Razz had predicted, America immediately began assisting Israel to acquire and exploit Arab assets by investing and contracting with the "greater and safer" Jewish State. Reciprocally, the struggling US economy received a much-needed shot in the arm, as Israel offered Americans many economic opportunities. Israel required American ingenuity and manpower, and shelled out the shekels to hire the best the United States had to offer.

Russia, on the other hand, began coveting Israel's burgeoning prosperity and plotted a comprehensive campaign to divert Israel's newfound spoils into its own national coffers.

"My dearest friend! How are you? Thank you for coming to my country on this momentous occasion," in humblest salutation, the Russian president Vladimir Ziroski greeted Ayatollah Khomani.

The Ayatollah had just arrived at the request of president Ziroski, to solidify Iran's involvement in the multi-nation coalition Russia was forming in opposition to Israel. Russia's leader proposed that the strictest of sanctions should be imposed upon Israel for plundering the Arab states. His plan intended to enforce the sanctions by preventing Israel to export its commerce into world markets. Ultimately the plan contained war strategies, if Israel failed to comply with the coalition's wishes.

The supreme leader of Iran shook his Russian counterpart's hand and said "The honor is indeed mine, dear president. We have many common interests to discuss these days."

Ziroski conceded, "Most certainly we do, supreme leader of Islam. Iran and Russia must collaborate on a mutual plan to eliminate Israel, and elevate Islam under your exclusive leadership, if the Jews resist our coalition's mandate. The Israelis have made a grave mistake by attacking your country and unleashing its nuclear arsenal against our Arab brothers. Already the nuclear fallout from Bushehr is beginning to clear from Iranian skies, and Israel's glory will soon wane thin if our combined forces invade their soil."

The Ayatollah lamented, "Millions of my people still scatter into the nations for fear of the radio-active fallout, and Israel must not go unpunished! *There is no if; Mr. President we absolutely must invade Israel!*

Ziroski concurred, "We are on the same page of history together on this my friend. Israel will not survive our concerted effort."

"Our foolish president Zakiri and his mystic friend Zamani Nikahd have caused much hardship in my country," the Ayatollah replied, "and they are soon to be exiled and replaced with leaders who will make certain that this time the state of Israel gets wiped off the pages of time forever."

"Praise be to your all-powerful god Allah," said Ziroski, in a most patronizing tone.

Khomani continued, "The three-phased plan you set forth against Israel with our Muslim brothers in Turkey, Libya, the Baltic States and African countries is fool proof. Allah gives his blessings to go forth with *god-speed*. Israel should not be allowed to bask for long in its glory for the killing of our Arab brothers. The Arab possessions and lands should be returned to them, after our coalition takes its just rewards."

Ziroski agreed, "Russia is extremely honored to call Iran our partner, along with the other Muslim countries in this matter. There will be ample spoils of war to share. Our coalition is already mobilizing to blockade all the waterways the Jews want to use to export their plunder. The commercial relationships they are attempting to form with America, Asia, Australia, Canada, and the European countries will never get off the ground. Our coalition will prevent them from making good on their promises to export their newfound booty overseas. Our consortium will see to it that no waterway to their east, north, west, or south will be open to them."

Applauding his comments, the Ayatollah commented further, "Iran is saddened to hear the Saudis have opted to refrain from joining the fight against Israel with us. They would have proven to be a strategic ally. They could prevent the Jews from transporting commerce through the Arabian Peninsula. But after the damage Israel afflicted upon them in their recent war, I guess they have proven to be true Sunni cowards."

With anger in his eyes, Mad Vlad Ziroski replied, "If the Saudis allow the Jews safe passage upon their soil we will invade their kingdom alongside the Jewish kingdom. This was declared to them when they chose not to join our coalition."

"Excellent, no longer will they be a thorn in Iran's side," the Ayatollah concluded.

After the Iranian supreme leader departed homeward, Mad Vlad finished making his international rounds with the coalition countries. One-by-one, about a dozen nations signed on to the cruel Russian leader's foul campaign against Israel. He became obsessed with the desire to stop the burgeoning Israeli economy dead in its tracks. Mad Vlad's thinking was constantly sinister. His thoughts were continuously evil toward Israel.

"When I destroy the Jews, I will thank them for harnessing all the Arab wealth into one coffer, making it easier for Russia to seize. When my hordes bury their dead bodies, I will be sure to spit on their coffins, and pillage their cities and ravish their widows," he inscribed one night in his private journal. Israel's celebration over their surrounding Arab enemies would turn out to be short lived, as Mad Vlad Ziroski had quickly put his evil plan in place.

Ziroski seized every opportunity to harness the hatred of Israel among the Muslim countries that enlisted in his confederate alliance. Skillfully, he solicited the nations that most hated Israel, bordered strategic waterways, and desperately needed economic revival. Most of them housed significant Muslim populations, such as the former Soviet Union republics of Kazakhstan, Tajikistan, Turkmenistan and Kyrgyzstan. Additional key coalition members, which were also predominately Muslim, included Tunisia, Algeria, Sudan, Ethiopia, and Somalia.

Mad Vlad's league had to be strategically located along all the important waterways surrounding Israel. The northernmost African nations of Libya, Tunisia, and Algeria were called upon to patrol the Mediterranean Sea to the south, while Turkey manned the maritime responsibilities on the northern part of Sea. The East African countries of Sudan, Ethiopia, and Somalia were to monitor all commerce commuting via the Suez Canal, down through the Red Sea. Iran was designated exclusive accountability for guarding the Strait of Hormuz and all Israeli export efforts through the Persian Gulf.

Russia even attempted to enlist Yemen, to prevent Israeli commerce from diverting on land through the Arabian Peninsula to the Arabian Sea. But the Yemenites, like the Saudis, opted out of the coalition. These two countries were still recovering from the devastating Psalm 83 war.

It was widely speculated that if it weren't for Israel's desire to capture OPEC oil under Saudi soil, Saudi Arabia would have been destroyed alongside Damascus. Furthermore, it was reported that the Saudis wanted no further part in a campaign against the "God of Israel," whom they believed had empowered the IDF against them and their Arab cohorts.

US President John Bachlin still threatened revenge against Iran for terrorizing America; but meanwhile, Americans were counting their blessings, considering Israel's military victory and economic expansion as the medicine Wall Street needed.

However, Russia's newly forming coalition, bent on preventing Israel from conducting international commerce, caused American war drums to pound loudly. Painful reminders of the Cold War and Mutual Assured Destruction (MAD) were rekindled, as raging rhetoric emanated from Washington and Moscow.

Both countries were heavily deployed throughout the Middle East. Russian troops were stationed in Turkey, Iran, and several Baltic States; the US Navy had deployed a full armada of nuclear-equipped fleets into the Persian Gulf and Mediterranean. US Naval commanders were on strict orders to monitor all maritime activities and assure safe passage of Israeli ships destined for international ports.

A showdown between America and Russia's confederacy seemed imminent, causing President Bachlin's administration to hastily attempt to form its own coalition of allies from Europe. Although this slowed Russian plans, it also aggravated their will to attack Israel.

Russia made no bones about it: Israel faced an existential threat from the north. The Russian-led consortium contested Israel's ownership of conquered Muslim lands and Arab spoils of war. Muslim hordes, assembled by Ziroski, demanded that Israel release all Arab prisoners of war and return their lands to them. Russia promised to help its partners recapture the Arab territories, and line their pockets with plunder and booty in the process.

All of these developments occurred before map makers could redraw atlases of the reshaping region.

Just when Israelis thought the worst was behind them, they stood at the threshold of an even greater danger. It appeared another genocidal attempt was being formulated on a far more formidable front.

Although the IDF had achieved the status of an "exceedingly great army," Israel realized their defense forces were outgunned by Russia's nuclear-equipped confederacy. Israel resigned itself to reliance upon American mediation and muscle, but in this go-round the Jews questioned the trustworthiness of America's resolve and military might. America was still recovering from terror at home and exhaustive military campaigns in Afghanistan, Iraq, Libya, and elsewhere.

Additionally, Israeli leaders were very concerned that, in the process of protecting Israel, America might extract revenge against Iran and ignite further widespread war. One miscalculation could trigger a domino effect, preventing Israel's "great spoil" from reaching Asian and European markets.

Leaders of the European Union were working feverishly to create calm and stability in the Middle East. EU President Hans Vandenberg, was working tirelessly with his parliament to resolve geo-political disputes emanating in the aftermath of *Operation Israeli Freedom.*

He even solicited input from the Pope and other religious leaders, due to the religious underpinnings of the regional volatility. Only a comprehensive plan, addressing all economic, political, geographical, and religious concerns, would stand a chance of bringing peace to the Holy Land.

Meanwhile at home, it was blatantly clear to George and Mimi that their loved ones, now living in Israel, were in harm's way. Thomas and his family were already moved into their new home near Jerusalem, the grandkids were attending local schools close by, and Lisa and Thomas were gainfully employed. As suspected, the events described in Ezekiel 38 and 39 were stage-setting for rapid fulfillment.

"Thank God, you were able to give Thomas and Lisa that video before they departed!" Mimi told George.

"What video was that?" asked Razz.

"Linton's latest DVD, dealing with end-times prophecies," replied George. "It had barely hit the retail shelves before Psalm 83 occurred. It's a masterful work, sequencing prophetic events, including the rapture, on through to Christ's second coming."

"Yes, I've heard about that one," Razz recalled. "Isn't that the one where he predicts the rapture occurs between Psalm 83 and Ezekiel 38?"

"Yes, it is," George confirmed. "And he presents many of the same arguments you teach. In fact, he credits some of your work at the end of the video."

Razz nodded, humbled. "Do you have an extra copy we can watch right now?"

"Unfortunately not, I only purchased one copy from his table when he spoke at our church," George stated in regret. "I got it for Mimi, but felt compelled to give it to Thomas to show to Lisa and the kids when they settled down in Israel."

"Did Linton get into my teachings about Gog's evil plan?" Razz questioned.

"Yes, and he agreed with you whole-heartedly. In fact, Linton devotes about five minutes to Russia's attempt to blockade the waterways."

"So, he agreed with me that Russia's coalition is strategic," Razz mused.

"Yes," George assured him. "He echoed your sentiments exactly. Linton even included footage that mimics what Russia and its coalition are accomplishing at present."

"Has Thomas shared the DVD with the family, yet?" Razz wondered.

"No. He says Lisa and Jami are too up caught in the family's religious crossfire."

Mimi sadly added, "Lisa and her family refuse to consider anything related to Jesus or Bible prophecy. In fact, Thomas told me Lisa's mother recently said, 'It was Jehovah, not Jesus, who protected Israel in the recent war.'"

"Of course she would say that!" Razz replied.

George agreed, "It fits with what Paul says in Romans 11:25. The Jews are hardened to the truth about Jesus until the 'fullness of the Gentiles' is completed."

Mimi bristled. "Of course, it doesn't help that, in the name of Christ, Jews have endured centuries of bigotry and persecution! Why would Christians expect they should be open to the gospel?"

Razz' face reddened. "That's all too true, Mimi. I am sure that factors into the scenario!" Clearing his throat, he added in a conciliatory tone, "Maybe it helps to know that the next verse says after the fullness of the Gentiles is completed, 'all Israel will be saved.' Unfortunately," he said, hesitating and shaking his head, "before Israel acknowledges Christ as Messiah, they go through two more genocidal campaigns."

Mimi groaned, "What do you mean 'two more genocidal campaigns'?"

"The Ezekiel 38 invasion will happen, followed a few years later by the Antichrist's final pogrom. Zechariah 13:8 predicts he will annihilate two-thirds of the Jewish population dwelling in Israel at the time." He went on, "Since Gog is already forming a coalition, these two genocidal attempts will probably occur in Lisa's and Jami's lifespan."

As tears welled in Mimi's eyes, George remarked, "That's why time is of the essence for them to watch that DVD! Thomas informed me he has told them about the video and placed it in their home safe, where they keep their emergency funds. He believes that, should the worst happen, Lisa will rescue the cash from the safe and hopefully watch the video at the same time."

"Good plan!" Razz declared. "And, if Christians are not raptured prior to the battle, Thomas can try one more time to open his family's eyes to the good news about their Messiah!"

16

The Christian Exodus
into the Clouds

"**S**cooting to the edge of his chair, financier Nathaniel Severs suddenly shouted, 'Unbelievable!'"

Severs was celebrating the success of Razz' portfolio with him over lunch, when his attention was abruptly drawn to the restaurant big screen TV.

While quickly turning about in his chair to share in the excitement, Razz asked his host, *"What?* What are you looking at?"

To their collective astonishment, a strange luminous image was flickering brightly on the oversized television. "The Virgin Mary appears above Vatican City," the ticker tape stated, as it streamed across the bottom of the screen.

Instantly, the room went silent as patrons shifted their attention to the event coverage. Hastily, the young hostess grabbed the remote, and maximized the volume just in time to hear, "A Mary apparition is apparently occurring in the heart of Vatican City."

The newscaster, who could barely compose herself, continued, "The large luminescent image you can probably make out on your screen is said to be the Virgin Mary! Our local affiliates tell us that the radiant image is well defined from their vantage point inside Vatican square. They are giving us confirmed reports that an apparition is indeed appearing at this very moment. Please stay with us as we continue to broadcast the image, while attempting to connect with one of our reporters on location."

Squaring around to face his friend, Razz blurted out, "This is huge! I'm getting a very eerie feeling right now, Nate!"

"Me, too! Do you think this apparition has anything to do with the weird atmospheric conditions shrouding the planet," Nate queried?

What Severs was alluding to was a week-long cloud that had enveloped the earth unexplainably. Unprecedented monsoon weather patterns, normally confined to the southern hemisphere that time of the year, overtook the northern hemisphere, as well. West African, Asian, Australian, and North, Central, and South American skies were all overtaken by towering cumulonimbus clouds reaching well into the stratosphere.

Eerily, at the same time, most of Europe became obscured underneath towering ash-clouds emanating out of the Icelandic Eyjafjallajökull volcano. The volcano that briefly brought European air travel to its knees in 2010, had recently erupted again, spewing out volumes of caustic cinder high into the surrounding skies.

Making matters worse, the sun could scarcely be seen, and satellite views pictured skies blanketed in gray. Top meteorologists declared the atmosphere had never experienced such abnormal conditions, causing great concern across the globe. The planetary picture was so portentous it prompted Israeli weather forecaster, Jonathan Levinson, of *Israel Network News* (INN), to label the looming tempest the "Exodus Eclipse," reminiscent of the Hebrew escape from Egyptian bondage approximately 3,600 years before.

To the astonishment of his countrymen, Levinson compared the present weather predicament to the pall of darkness alluded to in Exodus 14. He reported Pharaoh Ramses[18] was plagued by similar bizarre weather patterns, and posed the question, "Where's Moses when you need him to part the gray skies?" Although he intended the comment in jest, it almost cost Levinson his job, in light of the severity of the unprecedented weather phenomenon.

Worldwide gloom quickly spawned feelings of widespread doom, causing conspiracy theorists to speculate that a secret global cloud-seeding experiment had metastasized out of control, threatening humanity's existence. Conversely, New Age spiritualists predicted mankind's alien creators were opening hyper-dimensional atmospheric portals through which to return to recapture the planet. World governments gave no good explanation, leaving people in a dismal emotional state.

Amidst the backdrop of the densely overcast troposphere, Catholics had converged upon Vatican City to discover who would become the newly elected Pontiff. Pope Pius XIII had recently passed away and the Cardinals were deliberating inside the Sistine Chapel with their ballots in hand.

With baited breath, throngs of the faithful waited in the square outside to hear the bells of St. Peter's Basilica sound, and to see the white smoke billow from the chapel's furnace, indicating a new Pope had been decided upon.

It had been over six days, and the multitudes were growing impatient. They had witnessed the summer skies mysteriously darken, and rumors began circulating that the heavenly firmament was transmitting a troublesome sign. Fueling the emotions of the faithful was the increased presence of the Swiss Guard. These Vatican security forces continuously poured into St. Peter's square on heightened alert for potential terrorist attacks.

As the crowds inside the square grew increasingly tense, the Marion apparition suddenly occurred. The enormous luminous figure appeared overhead, hovering close atop the high cross on St. Peter's Basilica. Her radiance was so intense; the worshippers fell to their faces.

Miraculously, beams of sunlight penetrated through the thick cloud-cover, magnifying the pierce marks upon her outstretched hands and majestically illuminating the cross below. In possibly the only place on the planet where sunshine could be seen, the rays were so concentrated that fire appeared to be burning into both her hands, yet they were not consumed.

The prostrate crowd fell silent as the apparition began communicating her message to the minds and hearts of many onlookers. These selected visionaries suddenly rose to their knees and started shouting aloud, "The Lady of All Nations has come to reconcile the world to her immaculate heart!"[19]

Moments later, a host of others cried out, "The time has finally come for the Co-Redemptrix to redeem all of her children."

Apparently, the apparition had anointed a random host of onsite voices. Clearly, they communicated the same messages, and repeated them several times. After the announcements had ceased, the visionaries began chanting, "Hail Mary, full of grace." Their hypnotic incantations mesmerized the rest of the faithful and morphed into a choir echoing throughout St. Peter's Square.

Despite the apparition's near-blinding glow, television crews were able to video the spectacle. Clear images were hard to capture, but, it was clear to all who witnessed the spectacle that something supernatural was occurring.

After telling Severs that there was no way of confirming that the Marian apparition had anything to do with the bizarre weather scenario, Razz turned around to watch further developments at the Vatican.

Camera crews and reporters at the site began broadcasting the chants of the visionaries. Through their voices, the supposed Marian messages resonated throughout the world, as thousands of television and radio networks covered the event. As her messages streamed across the TV ticker, Severs asked, "Do you believe that's a true Marian apparition appearing over the Vatican?"

"It's hard to make out *what* it is from these images," replied Razz. "But, the visionary communications seem credible. My guess is that it is."

"Are you suggesting that Mary, the mother of Jesus, really does appear to the faithful?" Nate marveled.

"Absolutely not!" Razz exclaimed. "I *do not* believe that's the Mary of the Bible presently surfing the skies above Vatican City! Whoever, or whatever, that is, has to be demonic!"

"Demonic?" Nate gasped.

"The biblical Mary would never make such outlandish claims to be a Co-Redemptrix, on even par with Jesus Christ! The book of Luke quotes her as saying she, herself, 'rejoiced in God her Savior.'[20] She can't *be* a savior if she *needs* a Savior!" declared Razz.

Nate sat back in bewilderment. "Well you have to admit this *is* a miraculous event," he argued.

"Don't be fooled by her enchantments," cautioned Razz. "Scripture tells us even Satan can deceptively transform himself into an angel of light."

Nate shook his head and crossed his arms. "Are you suggesting that Satan has duped the Catholics all these years into thinking he's the Virgin Mary?"

"Hardly," Razz replied, trying to reason with Nate. "Let me give you some Scriptural insights about the 'queen of heaven's' apparitions, and their role inside Roman Catholicism. The book of Revelation warns about a coming false world religion identified as 'Mystery Babylon the Great, the Mother of Harlots' and…"

While his words still filled the space between them, in the blink of an eye Razz disappeared inexplicably from sight!

Nathan couldn't believe his eyes. In an instant, his best friend had vanished into thin air without a trace. Frantically, he jumped up and cried out, "Razz, Razz, where did you go?" Pulling closely to his heart Razz' clothing, which had fallen to the floor, Nathan started to weep profusely.

On several previous occasions, Razz had forewarned his worldly friend that the day would come when Christians would be caught up into the clouds in the twinkling of an eye; Nathan came to grips with the fact that this was what had just happened.

Stricken with grief, he dropped to his knees. It wasn't long before he heard the sound of others weeping and noticed more abandoned garments sprinkled about the restaurant floor. Reluctantly pulling himself up to the table, he looked about him, only to view a sea of tears cascading down the cheeks of those left behind.

It was about five minutes later that Nathan realized the television broadcast of the Mary sighting had abruptly shut off. He had no idea what was taking place at Vatican City.

Immediately, he tried to pull up the internet on his cell phone, but no service was available. He darted outside to listen to the radio in his Mercedes and was shocked to see what looked like an apocalyptic episode out of the "Twilight Zone" occurring on the bustling city streets.

Sirens blasting, car alarms blaring, and shouts of "Please help me!" echoed resoundingly throughout the chaotic business district. Cars were wrecked, fire hydrants were gushing, and people were running frantically every which way, like headless chickens.

Nathan felt as though his soul had been ripped out, as he realized that Jesus had just come for the Christians. In that powerful moment, he knew that Razz had been preaching the one true religion to him, all along. He recalled the numerous times Razz had reminded him that Jesus was the Way, the Truth, and the Life, and that he alone was the pathway to heaven.

As he wove in and out of wreckage *en-route* to his home, he remembered Razz' last request, made during their luncheon: "Since I have no children of my own, please promise me that you will make sure Thomas Thompson and his family receive my full inheritance when I die or…get raptured."

Razz informed him during their luncheon that he volunteered him alongside George Thompson as co-executor of his trust, enabling this wish to be accomplished. "I know you can be trusted, and knew you wouldn't mind, so I had my attorney take care of the paperwork."

As recently as that very day, Razz had mentioned the rapture. How sorrowful Nathan felt that, throughout all of the years, Razz' preaching had fallen on his own deaf ears! *How hard could my heart be, that I wouldn't trust the advice of my high school buddy?* He thought. And now, it was too late; the rapture had passed him, and countless others, by.

Once the power came back on and Severs could get internet service again, the Mary apparitions had ended. The world was now asking serious questions about the whereabouts of the Christians, and whether the "Queen of Heaven"[21] would reappear to bring peace to Earth, as she pledged?

17

After the Rapture, the World Gets Religious

The disappearance of Christians profoundly affected America and portions of Europe, whereas in Muslim-dominated countries like Turkey and Iran, life went on relatively unchanged. American forces stationed in the Middle East had become fractured by the heavenly departure of nearly a quarter of their troops and commanders. The rapture had rendered the US military extremely vulnerable against a potential face-off with Russia's coalition in the Holy Land.

Similarly, on the American home front, the country was rapidly deteriorating into a condition of chaos, prompting the US government to enact martial law nationwide. Anarchy plagued much of the country, as utility companies frantically attempted to restore services to municipalities and diminished National Guard forces mobilized in metropolitan areas.

It was the aftermath of Hurricane Katrina, multiplied by ten thousand, all over again. However, in this case, there was no US President to blame for slow response times, since President Bachlin and many members of Congress were numbered among the departed. Unbelievers were left behind to fend for themselves, and America's future remained uncertain.

Unistate Global Investments Corporation, Nathaniel Severs investment firm, was teetering on the verge of collapse, given all that had happened worldwide. It became blatantly clear to Nathan that the "god of money" had made his final exit from America when the Middle East chaos erupted. He recognized Razz had hit the nail on the head about investing in the new Israel, and decided to direct his company's focus on the emerging Jewish State.

Furthermore, Nathan began to grasp the significance of what was occurring worldwide, and spent several days in prayer and fasting, reviewing Razz' website articles and attempting to understand what the post-rapture future held in store. Fortunately, his dear friend had compartmentalized his site, making it easy to find future event time charts, as well as learning how to become a "born again" believer.

Those were the two foremost topics on Nathan's mind: "What's next?" *and* "How can I be saved?" Razz even posted articles about how Mary apparitions could increase after the rapture and mislead the masses into the worldwide worship of Mary.

"Father please forgive me, for I have sinned," Nathan prayed, upon kneeling at the foot of his bed one fateful evening. "Please receive me into your kingdom family through the blood of Jesus Christ. I believe you sent him, your only begotten son, to die for my sins, and I am so grateful for that!"

Nathan pleaded for pardon from the Lord. He patterned his salvation prayer on Razz' website roadmap and began reciting the Lord's Prayer[22] often throughout the ensuing days. He became blessed by an unexplainable peace that comforted and guided him.

Assured that he had his spiritual house in order, Nathan proceeded to explain the rapture event to his unbelieving UGIC staff. Due to the magnitude of world circumstances and their utter admiration for their boss, most were receptive and some accepted Christ as their Savior.

Nathan informed his personnel that he intended to expand UGIC's reach into Israel. He put his right-hand man, Harold Hirsch, in charge of American and Global operations and proceeded to secure his belongings for a permanent move to the emerging Jewish marketplace.

With Razz' burgeoning Israel-centered investment portfolio in hand, Nathaniel Severs boarded up his estate and flew to Israel to locate Thomas Thompson. He had previously attempted to contact George and Mimi Thompson, but after leaving about a dozen unanswered phone messages, he surmised they had both been caught up in the clouds alongside Razz and the rest of the born-again believers.

Leaving instructions for his staff to locate the possible whereabouts of the Thomas Thompson family in Israel, Nathaniel Severs began his pilgrimage to the Holy Land. Uncertain whether Thomas had been raptured, he still intended to uphold his promise to Razz, and hand over his portfolio to him or his family. He suspected Lisa and Jami Thompson were left behind, because Razz informed him during their final luncheon that the girls were Jewish unbelievers.

In addition, he realized from Razz' website that the Jews would eventually need a crop of Oskar Schindler[23] prototypes to comfort and protect them in the last days. According to Razz' article series entitled the "Jew in the Last Days," Nathan understood that the Antichrist would soon attempt a final Jewish genocidal campaign that would make the Hitler holocaust seem like a walk in the park.

"Righteous Gentiles," Razz had called them. He wrote that Jesus would pull them close by his right side, like a shepherd gathers his sheep into their sheepfold, and would say to them, "Come, you blessed of my Father, inherit the kingdom prepared for you from the foundation of the world."

Severs promised the Lord that he would become a righteous Gentile like Schindler, even if it cost him his life in the process. He planned to start with Thomas Thompson's Jewish relatives and subsequently work incognito to set up an underground network through his extensive global connections, that would be ready when called upon to facilitate the exodus of Jews to safe-houses throughout the world.

●●●●●

About one-month passed between the rapture and the rap upon the front door of Thomas' residence in Beit Shemesh, Israel. Not knowing what to expect, Nathaniel Severs stood outside the Thompson family door, briefcase in hand. He had met Thomas and his family on several holiday occasions, but wondered if they would recognize him, since those visits occurred when Tyler was but a small child.

He had refrained from previously contacting the Thompsons to alert them of his visit, because he was preoccupied with battening down his own hatches in America, and getting settled into his new location in Israel. He wanted to have his boots on the ground prior to conveying Razz' good intentions and sizable portfolio to the Thompsons. And, most importantly, he felt it insensitive to break the news about Razz' departure over the phone.

Sizing up the tall, suited, gray-haired businessman standing at her doorstep, Lisa said in surprise, "Is that you, Mr. Severs?"

"It is," replied Nathan.

Escorting him inside to the living room, Lisa inquired, "What a pleasant surprise. What brings you across the pond to our humble abode?"

"Your uncle Razz named Thomas and all of you as the beneficiaries of his sizable trust, so I promised to personally present it to your family," he announced.

Immediately Lisa's eyes started to well up with tears, prompting Nate to ask, "What's wrong, dear?"

"Didn't Razz inform you that Thomas and our son Tyler were Christians?" she asked.

"Yes, Lisa, I figured as much from our last conversation," Nathan acknowledged. "When I was unable to reach Thomas' parents to get your family's whereabouts, I knew they, too, were gone."

"Tyler, Thomas, George and Mimi were all taken away!" Lisa sobbed, clutching at her heart. "Things were finally going well for us. The Arab war had ended. We were moved into our new home and the kids were attending local schools. I came home from work one evening and Thomas and Tyler were gone!"

Nathan recounted to Lisa, "I was eating lunch with your uncle Razz, watching the Marian apparition on the restaurant TV, when, poof! He disappeared without a trace!"

Startling Severs, Lisa retorted, "I'm going to be furious with Jesus if he's got anything to do with the disappearances of Thomas and Tyler!"

"What do you mean, 'furious with Jesus'?" Nate asked.

"I've heard speculations that Jesus came like a 'thief in the night' and took the Christians to heaven! When we realized they were missing, Jami and I scoured the countryside for days looking for the two of them. Every waking moment, we wait for them to show up at our doorstep. If it's true that he's to blame, how could a so-called loving Christian Messiah ruin so many families across the world?"

"So, you understand what happened then?" Nathan asked cautiously.

"No, I don't want to understand! I want my family back!" Lisa said in anguish.

"Lisa, they were taken to heaven to be with the Lord and are in a better place," Nathan offered.

Breaking down, Lisa clutched Nathan and wept on his shoulder. "I'm a wreck. I'm angry, lonely, and my husband and son have been taken from me. Israel's on the brink of a major war again, and Jami and I feel so lost and alone!"

During that sensitive exchange, Jami made a surprise entrance into the room. "What's going on mother?" she asked in a disapproving tone. "Who is this man?"

Releasing herself from their innocent embrace, and trying to compose herself, Lisa introduced Nathan Severs as a longtime friend and business consultant of Uncle Razz. "Uncle Razz asked Mr. Severs to assist us through these difficult times," explained Lisa.

"How is uncle Razz? Jami wondered. "I miss him."

Severs was silent, but Jami realized from his facial expression that there was no more Uncle Razz.

"Don't tell me that he's been stolen away, too!" Jami cried.

"That's why I moved to Israel, to help you and your mother cope with what's happened and about to happen," Nathan conveyed.

Bewildered, Jami sighed, "I don't understand."

Lisa wiped her teary face with her sleeve. "I'm a poor hostess," she sniffled. Taking Nate by the arm, she suggested, "Why don't we all take a seat in the family room. You can explain why you've come, and what you think is going to happen."

Seated comfortably together on the oversized sofa, Nate began, "For starters, I have Razz' Irrevocable Trust and Summary of Assets inside my briefcase. He left you both a sizable fortune worth, approximately 150 million shekels, to survive upon. He requested that I guarantee your family is well provided for, in the event of his death or…disappearance."

Lisa was amazed. "Are you suggesting he anticipated his own disappearance?"

"I am. In fact, he predicted the possibility just before it occurred at our luncheon that fateful day," Nathan replied. "He said in the event I die or get raptured, I want you to…"

Interrupting his sentence in midstream, Lisa blurted out, "'Raptured'…did he really say that?"

"Those were his exact words," Nate confirmed.

Lisa shivered, rubbing her hands up and down her arms.

Nate leaned close. "What's so troubling?" he inquired.

"Raptured is the word circulating in Jerusalem, for what happened to the Christians. An upstart movement of Jews is creating a ruckus in the city, claiming the raptured Christians are evidence that Christ is the Messiah!"

"Are you referring to the 'Royal Jews from the Twelve Tribes of Israel'?" Jami asked.

"Yes, I believe so," Lisa answered. "How did you hear about them?"

"Recently, a lot of teachers at school have been warning their students to beware of false teachings that are spreading across the country," Jami reported. "Supposedly, they number 12,000 from each of the ancient twelve tribes, totaling 144,000, spread out in Israel and other parts of the world. They are teaching Jesus is the Messiah and that he is coming to judge humanity and set up a new kingdom, like the ancient garden of Eden. One of my teachers said their message is extremely dangerous, and is purposely intended to drive people away from Judaism."

"Their movement is already gaining steam in America and parts of Europe," Nathan said. "In fact, your Uncle Razz posted several articles about their end-time's ministry on his website."

"Uncle Razz predicted his own mysterious departure and the arrival of these 144,000 Yeshua-believing witnesses?" marveled Lisa. "How could he have known?"

"He gleaned it from years of Bible study," said Nathan. "I would show you where he writes about these subjects on his website, except his and many other Christian sites have been removed from the Internet over the last two weeks."

"Why's that?" Jami inquired.

"Obviously because the world leaders don't want people to connect the disappearance of millions of Christians with the rapture," Nathan deduced.

"Are you suggesting that some group of global elitists is pulling the strings now?" Lisa gasped.

"Yes, but it's far beyond that; according to Razz' writings it's outright demonic!" warned Nathan.

With a puzzled expression, Jami questioned, "'Demonic!' Doesn't that mean inspired by the devil?"

"That's how I would interpret it," Nate agreed. "Razz often used the word when he described prophecies or powerful events intended to deceive people. For instance, he told me just moments before he disappeared, that he believed the Marian apparition occurring right then was demonic."

"That Marian spectacle was amazing!" Lisa recalled. "It was big news here in Israel, at the time. All the newscasters reported on it, but since the Christian disappearances, or should I say 'rapture,' it has been hard to find any more information about the strange events at the Vatican that day."

"Mr. Severs," Jami said fearfully, "I have been worried about where my father and brother vanished to. Every day, I surf the web and watch the news for clues. I wonder if the Mary appearance had anything to do with the Christians leaving." She swallowed hard. "What do you think?" she asked.

Nate studied her pensive face. "It is very coincidental," he agreed. "But, others are saying the disappearances relate to some bizarre alien scenario. Purportedly, humanity is being prepared to meet its alien creators, who are going to help us evolve to a higher consciousness." His tone betrayed his lack of respect for such notions, and Jami didn't know whether to laugh or cry.

"This doesn't surprise me," she admitted.

"What do you mean?" Lisa wondered.

"People are obsessed with this extra-terrestrial stuff!" he replied. "UFOs, abductions…It's on TV and the internet all the time."

Lisa threw up her hands. "Alien abductions! I thought the rapture argument was over the top. But, this theory is absolutely crazy!" she exclaimed. "Official disclosure about alien creators; I thought the Christian rapture argument sounded like pie-in-the-sky, but this theory is absolutely crazy,"

"Call it what you will, Lisa, but it's certainly no laughing matter, and groups suggesting the Christians were raptured in fulfillment of Bible prophecy are being mocked and persecuted.

These 144,000 you're hearing about are encountering an enormous resistance," Nathan reported.

Lisa shook her head wearily. "Nathan, you're welcome to stay with us until you get settled, but this is too much for us girls to process right now."

"No, Mother!" Jami cried out. "Don't ignore what's going on! I want to watch the DVD Grandpa George gave Dad," she pleaded.

"What DVD is that?" asked Nathan.

"It's about the 'last days.' Dad begged and pleaded with us time and again to watch it, but we ignored him," moaned Jami. "Please, Mother, go get it out of the safe so we can watch it with Mr. Severs. Maybe he can explain it to us."

Nathan saw Lisa's countenance change dramatically at the mention of the DVD. He sensed Lisa feared the content would serve as a haunting reminder of her rebellious attitude.

Nathan gently grasped her hand in both of his and said, "Lisa, I'm no expert on the Bible. If I were, I would probably be having dinner in heaven with Razz and the others, right now. But, I believe with all my heart that your husband would want you to watch this DVD, to prepare you for what's coming. And, I would be honored if you would allow me to watch it with you and your daughter."

Turning pale, Lisa managed, "Very well. There's no sense in postponing the inevitable. I'll go get the DVD."

18

Left Behind, the Heavenly Love Letter

As Nate laid out Razz' portfolio on the dining room table, Jami and her mother made their way through the narrow hallway to the safe. Jami was relieved the time had come to unlock the family vault and retrieve her dad's DVD. Finally, she could fulfill her father's wish that she watch the video and discover its crucial content!

Upon opening the safe, Lisa was surprised to see the video staring back at her atop all the important family records. Only a few months prior she had fumbled through the safe and purposely buried it beneath the cash and papers. She recalled thinking, at the time, *Out of sight, out of mind; maybe if Thomas doesn't see it, he will quit pestering me to watch it.*

Noticing its new strategic location, she realized Thomas had since placed it on top of the stack. *Why?* She couldn't help wondering at the time. *Did he believe his disappearance was near at hand?*

Removing the DVD from its case, she was amazed to see a letter gracefully float out and land face down upon the nearby credenza. Startled to see the letter waist high and scarcely an arm's length away, Jami and she stood breathlessly still for a moment. They wondered which of them would muster up the courage to pick it up.

Finally, Jami asked, "Well aren't you going to read the letter, Mother? It's probably a message from Dad to us."

"Of course," Lisa said, frozen in place.

After another pause, Jami asked, "When?"

"When what?" Lisa said brokenly.

"When are you going to read Dad's letter," Jami queried.

Brushing aside a teardrop, Lisa pressed the letter to her lips and gently Eskimo-kissed it with her nose, receiving a refreshing whiff of her favorite masculine fragrance. Her husband had anointed his love letter with the exotic cologne she given him on their last anniversary.

Sitting side-by-side on the sofa inside their makeshift home office, Lisa opened the letter and said, "You're right; it's from your dad."

She began reading aloud, "'Beloved Lisa and Jami, you and Tyler are the best things that ever happened to me in my life!'" Lisa's heart gave a momentary flutter. Collecting her composure, she continued, "'Oh, how I love you with all my being, and want you, Lisa and Jami, to receive this letter with open hearts and minds.'"

Already, the girls could scarcely see through the wellsprings of tears brimming in their eyes. These were Thomas' final thoughts and most cherished words to them. The letter's significance, in light of his permanent absence, pierced beyond the fabric of their hearts into the depths of their innermost beings.

"Read more," pleaded Jami, "I have to hear Dad's last words."

"'By now, you probably realize that Jesus came for Tyler and me. Please don't worry about us. We are in heaven, united with my parents, uncle Razz, and other loved ones who shared our faith. Oh, how desperately we wish you were both with all of us here!'"

Lisa gulped and went on: "'Although we're apart, please be assured that no distance could ever separate me from the love I have for the two of you. You are both so beautiful, loving, and caring! The Lord truly blessed me with the best his creation had to offer, by allowing me to play such an intimate role in your lives.'"

"'As I pen these final thoughts, I'm swept up in a sea of emotions. The possibility that I may never see either of you again, if you remain obstinate toward Jesus, is more than my heart can handle. I'm weeping right now, as our lives together are memorialized forever in my mind.'"

Her heart swelling, she continued, "'I recall seeing Jami take her first breath on the delivery table, as if it were yesterday. Never before had I experienced such a wonderful and powerful moment. I remember her first word, step, birthday, bicycle, braces, braids, and pesky puppy.'"

"'Jami, honey, words can't explain how proud you make me. You are all that a father could have ever hoped for. I pray from the bottom of my heart that you have many wonderful remaining days upon the earth; but, above all else I beg you to accept Jesus into your heart as Savior. Please don't delay! Do it even now as you read this letter and watch this video. I promise you, that you will be with us in heaven, forever.'"

Lisa set the letter down to hug her daughter who was now weeping uncontrollably.

"What is this, Mother? What has happened? What are we waiting for with Jesus? I want to be with my dad and brother. I can't take it any longer!" she sobbed grievously.

The power of the moment was overwhelming, prompting Lisa to say, "I know, honey. It is all going to work out. We still have each other."

"Don't you get it, Mother?" Jami complained. "It's not going to all work out, without Jesus! Don't you understand what Dad's trying to tell us?"

"Certainly, I do," Lisa replied. "I, too, long to be with your father and brother."

Sponging Jami's tears with her sleeve, Lisa picked up the letter and read further.

"'Lisa, the beloved wife of my youth and best friend in life, forgive me for leaving you alone at such a critical time. Please don't be upset at God. Even though our departure may not make sense right now, this is all part of His perfect plan.'"

Clutching the letter next to her broken heart, she looked toward the high heavens and anguished, "How? How can this be a perfect plan?"

Turning her face aside in frustration, she continued to read her husband's final words.

"'Please, as hard as it is for you to consider, remember that I told you that someday Tyler and I could disappear into thin air, with millions of other Christians. If you experience this, please realize that Jesus has come for His church!

"'I plead with you, don't shut out the significance of what has happened, because it will lead you to Jesus, and ultimately here to be with us someday, soon. I wouldn't tell you this if I didn't believe it with every ounce of my heart; and you will also need to share this good news with your family someday.'"

Lisa tossed the letter aside and grabbed her chest gasping for breath. She was turning white and seemed to be hyperventilating.

"Mother, what are you doing? Are you okay?" asked Jami.

"I… I… I can't… I can't take it anymore," stuttered Lisa. "I have to st…st…stop, before I f…f…faint!"

Jami began feverishly fanning her mother's face with a magazine.

"I have done this to us!" Lisa wailed. "My stubbornness has caused us both to be left behind! Sobbing and crying out at the top of her lungs, she pleaded, "Forgive me, Jami! Forgive me, Jami!"

Jami had never seen her mother so distraught, nor held her so tight, as she did in that gripping moment.

Lisa's cries were so loud, Nathan rushed down the hallway to look in on them. "What's happened?" he bellowed anxiously.

"I have ruined my daughter's life! It's my fault she can't be with her father!" Lisa wept.

"Lisa, she can…you both can!" comforted Nathan. "I felt the same way when Razz left me alone that day in the restaurant. I felt so guilty and ashamed for not trusting what he tried to warn me about. Razz tried to teach me about Jesus whenever he could."

"I know. So did my beloved husband," Lisa wailed.

"Mother, you're not completely responsible. Dad and Tyler kept trying to warn me also. I made up my own mind not to trust what they were saying," Jami confessed.

"Look, girls," Nathan intervened, "I recently accepted Christ as my Savior, and if you ever want to see Thomas and Tyler again you need to do the same. But, salvation is much more than a ticket to Thomas; it is the promise of eternal peace, love, and happiness. It is God's gift to us through Jesus Christ. Receiving His gift is the most important thing we can ever do. Your beloved Thomas realized that his sin soon stood between him and his Savior, so he repented and committed his life to the Lord Jesus. So please… do as Thomas instructs, and don't put it off any longer!" he implored.

Regaining some composure, Lisa said, "Thank you, Nathan. What a wonderful friend you are! Undoubtedly, the Lord has sent you to Jami and me."

After Nathan assisted Lisa to her feet, Jami picked up the letter and the DVD and said, "Let's go into the TV room and calm ourselves down, so we can watch Dad's video together."

●●●●●

After a refreshing beverage and snack, Jami gazed into her mother's eyes. "Are you ready for this?" she asked, holding up the DVD.

"I am," Lisa replied.

"Are you sure you want to view Linton's video before meeting Jesus?" Jami asked.

"Yes, your father told me that it would convince me that Jesus is the Jewish Messiah," Lisa hedged.

"As you wish, Mother." Jami consented.

As Jami inserted the disc into the DVD player, Nathan asked, "Is this a recent picture of Thomas and Tyler?"

He had innocently grabbed the video case from the coffee

table and turned it over to the backside to preview Jim Linton's content comments. In the process, he noticed the picture inserted between the outside plastic and the disc sleeve.

Grabbing for the video case, Lisa gasped, "What picture? What did we miss?"

There it was, in plain view, a picture of the two most important men in her life taken just days before their disappearance. Caught up in the sweeping emotions of the love letter, she and Jami had failed to notice the picture inside the DVD housing.

"There was no picture here, before!" Lisa gasped. "I remember looking at both sides of the DVD last time I was in the safe, and this picture wasn't there!"

Leaning against her mother's shoulder to glimpse the photo, Jami surmised, "This is a new picture. It must have been taken right after Dad shaved off his mustache, about a month ago."

"You're absolutely right. I distinctly remember that he shaved the morning Tyler and he took their father-son field trip to the Jordan River," Lisa recalled. "I asked why he was shaving, and with foam all over his face, he said, 'It's time for a change. I had no mustache until after we were married and I want to remind you of our first dates.' Then, he immediately bear-hugged and Eskimo-kissed me, making sure to get half of his shaving cream all over my face," she laughed. Then, soberly, "His exact words that followed our messy embrace were, 'Remember, we used to bear-hug and Eskimo-kiss, back then? That stopped around the time I grew my mustache.'"

"They must have taken the picture during their trip to the Jordan. That's the actual river in the background," Jami commented.

"Wow, you're absolutely right!" Lisa confirmed.

Tears began flowing down the girls' cheeks when Nathan said, "This certainly can't be easy for the two of you."

"No, it's not that," Lisa commented. "It's just that the way they took the picture is a message to us."

"How so?" Nathan inquired.

"See how they embrace with one arm, but their free arms are extended outward, motioning toward the camera, rather than resting naturally by their sides?" Lisa pointed out.

"Yes, that does seem staged," Nathan acknowledged.

Jami explained, "They are reaching out to mother and me for our daily group hug. Every waking morning Dad would huddle us together for a group hug and prayer before he allowed us to step into the new day. He started this family ritual when we moved here to Israel."

"It became my favorite part of every day," Lisa reflected. "I even learned not to cringe every time they closed the prayer in the name of Jesus."

Lisa handed the DVD case to Jami and requested she use her long-manicured fingernails to navigate the photo out of the slipcover.

"Hurry! Let's see if the boys wrote anything on the back," she instructed.

Noticing abbreviated comments on the photo's reverse, Nathan politely asked, "Would you prefer I leave the room, while you read the boys' message?"

Holding his hand, Lisa answered, "No stay here with us, Nathan. You are part of our family, now."

She read the inscription:

"'Group hugs anyone? We are only a salvation prayer away from you right now. We are waiting for you on the shores of heaven with Jesus and our open arms, longing for our family group hug. Believe and be-living with us, now, before it's too late.'"

"'PLEASE, WE BEG OF YOU, DO WHAT OUR LETTER SAYS!!!'"

"'Love, your favorite two boys…T n T'"

Lisa clutched the photo fondly to her bosom, choking back tears.

"Well, that settles it for me, Mother," Jami announced. "I'm taking my leap of faith for Jesus, right now. Tyler told me that when he received Jesus into his life, that his sins were forgiven and that he was a new creation. I saw the change in him, from that point forward. He was more kind and loving toward me as his sister. Jesus changed him. I want to become a Christian and then watch the video, with the comfort of knowing my future is secure with Jesus Christ. I want to live a changed life like Tyler, from this point forward. This is what Dad and Tyler always prayed that we would do."

"Yes, Daughter, I agree 100%," Lisa consented. "I have a peace in my heart about this. It's time for me to stop hiding from the truth, and to receive God's gift of salvation through Jesus Christ. I can almost hear Grandpa George telegraphing me from the shores of heaven: 'Come off the cover girl, and jump on board the Jesus train.'"

Turning to Nathan, she said, "Mr. Severs, we would be honored to have you pray with us to receive Jesus Christ."

Upon hearing her invitation, Nathan could hardly contain his joy. God had honored his prayer to become a righteous Gentile, starting with the Thompson family. "Lord, great is thy faithfulness," he declared. As he wrapped his strong arms around the girls, he said, "Let the group hugs and prayers continue now and forever!"

Leading them in the sinner's prayer, which he had seen on Razz' website, Nate introduced Lisa and Jami, descendants of Abraham, Isaac, and Jacob, to their Lord and Savior, Jesus Christ!

●●●●●

Tears drying on their faces, the three sat down to watch the DVD together. Preparing to insert the disc in the player, Jami switched on the TV. Suddenly, they we're shocked to hear a newscaster announce, **"We repeat, Russia has invaded Israel."**

With a gasp, Lisa cried out, *"OH MY LORD!"*

19

The Message Left Behind

Turning the television volume up, Lisa spoke urgently to her daughter. "Jami, wait a moment before inserting dad's DVD," she said. "Let's watch this breaking news alert!"

Lisa and Jami Thompson had been preparing to watch an important end times video in their home with their friend Nathan Severs, who had arrived shortly after the girls finished reading the love letter, when their plans were abruptly interrupted by the news that Russia had recently launched several missiles into northern Israel. Seated together on the living room sofa, they listened intently as the newscaster announced,

> "This just in: three Russian Kalibr missiles have been fired at Israel from the Black Sea. Although two were successfully intercepted by Iron Dome defense systems, the third has struck in the center of Haifa."

Gasping, Lisa shrieked, "Your uncle Tovia lives in the heart of Haifa. I hope he's OK!"

Placing his arm around Lisa's shoulders, Nathan said, "Don't panic. Let's hear more."

> "Serious casualties are being reported," the newscaster continued.

"My brother's hurt; I have a gut feeling that Tovia has been hurt!" Lisa cried.

Grabbing her mother's cell phone from the coffee table, Jami shoved it at her. "Mother hurry! Call Uncle Tovia right now!"

Handing Lisa his handkerchief, Nathan consoled, "Try to calm yourselves, girls. Let's get the details before jumping to conclusions."

Unable to contain her emotions, Lisa leaped off the sofa, and raced into the parlor to call her brother, while Nathan and Jami listened to the newscaster conclude:

> "It's being reported that Russian President Vladimir Ziroski is giving Israel 24 hours to comply with his recently imposed economic demands, or face a full-scale invasion from his coalition forces. The Russian President declared that the recent missile attack was merely a warning of catastrophic events to come if Israel continues to export its energy resources abroad at unacceptably low prices!"

Terrified, Jami turned to Nathan, asking, "Mr. Severs, does this mean that Israel is going to war with Russia?"

Nathan nodded sadly. "I fear so dear," he replied, "but not just Russia."

"What do you mean?" Jami asked.

"Russia has joined forces with several Muslim countries that include Iran, Turkey, and Libya," he explained.

Rejoining them, Lisa clasped her hands together anxiously. "All the phone lines are busy, and I can't get through to Tovia," she said. "What else did the reporter say?"

"It's not good, Lisa," Nathan replied. "Russia has issued an ultimatum to your government that they must comply with all coalition requests or face all-out war."

Watching her mother sink to the sofa, an anguished Jami cried out, "Not again, Mother! We just fought with the Arabs. Why can't all these Muslim countries leave Israel alone?"

Realizing she needed to be strong for her daughter, Lisa embraced her sobbing teen-ager.

Shaking his head, Nathan said, "It's highly doubtful that Israel will comply with Russia's demands."

Rocking her daughter in her arms, Lisa objected, "What choice does Israel have? Winning a war against the

Arab confederacy was one thing, but Russia's coalition is far more powerful."

Nathan clarified, "Russia's commands are only a smokescreen to their true intent. They are determined to wage war against Israel!

"No!" Lisa insisted. "We can comply with Russia's requests and avert a crisis."

"Not according to your Uncle Razz," Nathan replied.

With the mention of Razz's name, Jami's ears perked up. "What about uncle Razz?" she asked.

Razz, short for Robert Rasmussen, had been Nathan's longtime friend. He had also been Jami's grandfather's best friend. Because of his close relationship with her grandfather, Jami thought of him as her uncle. Razz, along with her grandparents, George and Martha Thompson, her dad, Thomas, and brother, Tyler, had all disappeared instantly with millions of other Christians a few months prior. The mere mention of Razz's name evoked fond memories of Jami's departed loved ones.

Nathan replied, "Razz warned me before he … left us… that Russia would form a predominately Muslim coalition to plunder Israel. He called it the Gog of Magog invasion, and said the event was described in Ezekiel 38. If he was correct, Russia's demands are only the start of far worse things to come."

Lisa rolled her eyes toward Jami, silently imploring Nathan to temper his statement. "That's very interesting, Nathan," she said, "but Israel must concede to the coalition demands."

"Don't you understand, Lisa?" Nathan argued. "Capitulating to Russia's requests would be national suicide. It would only serve to fortify Russia's intent to destroy Israel. Mad Vlad Ziroski would quickly coordinate its coalition members to wage war against the Jewish state. Don't you recognize that Russia's ultimatum is no ultimatum at all? They will wage war against the Jews no matter what your government decides."

Jami sat back and tugged on Lisa's sleeve. "Mother, let's watch Dad's video right now!" she begged. "Maybe Mr. Severs is right. Maybe the Bible predicted what's occurring between Russia and Israel presently, and the video can help us understand what's going on."

Lisa sighed, "You could be right. Your father did say that this DVD contains revelations about what will happen to Israel in the future."

The Message Left Behind

Having recently become a Jewish believer in Jesus, Jami was no longer fearful of watching the apocalyptic video left behind by her father Thomas. While waiting for the DVD to boot up, she propped up the picture on the coffee table of her dad and brother Tyler that they had purposely inserted in the video case prior to their heavenly departure.

"Dad would be proud of us, Mother," Jami said.

Nodding, Lisa replied, "I'm sure he would. After resisting Christianity for so long, we're about to watch the video we were so afraid of."

> *"Welcome. I'm your host, Jim Linton,"* the narrator began. *"What you are about to watch is a chronological ordering of powerful last days events. The Bible, the only holy book with a proven track record of accurately predicting future events, provides invaluable insights intended to navigate mankind through these treacherous end times. As you watch this program, I fear that you may be living out some of its content."*

With that introduction, the trio scooted to the edge of the sofa, devoting their undivided attention to the remainder of the DVD. They were astounded to hear the host begin his predictions with the Arab-Israeli war of Psalm 83, which they had just lived through. The fact that the DVD had been produced before the war added additional credibility to the remaining content. Linton suggested that this war would trigger a period of worldwide sorrows.

> *"After this climactic concluding Arab-Israeli war, powerful prophecies begin to unfold with greater intensity and frequency, like the birth pains of a mother in labor."*

Tears swelled from their eyes as eschatologist Linton proceeded to forecast the worldwide disappearance of Christians.

> *"If not before the Psalm 83 war, probably shortly afterwards, Jesus Christ will come in the twinkling of an eye to catch up His followers into the clouds in an event commonly called the Rapture."*

Lisa paused the program. "If only we had watched this DVD beforehand! We would all be in heaven right now with our family!" she wept.

Taking the remote control gently from her hand, Jami soothed, "Mother, you have to let the guilt go, once-and-for-all. There is no way of telling if this video would have convinced us that Christ was the Messiah. Our Jewish heritage inhibited us from accepting what Dad was trying to teach us."

Nathan, himself a recent Gentile convert, confirmed; "Jami's right Lisa. What might have been is water under the bridge. At least now we can learn what the Bible says about our future."

Jami added, "It's going to be up to us to convince Grandma Naomi, Uncle Tovia, and the rest of our family in Israel that Jesus is the Messiah."

Lisa sighed. "Assuming they're still alive," she whispered,

Nestling in and taking notes, the three of them gleaned all the information they could from the video. Future prophetic events discussed in the DVD included:

1. The mystery of "Babylon the Great," the coming world religion of Revelation 17,
2. The future global government,
3. The cashless society of the one-world banking system,
4. The impending world leader called the Antichrist,
5. The coming strong delusion intended to deceive humankind,
6. The false covenant confirmed by the Antichrist with Israel,
7. Daniel's "Seventieth Week," also called the Tribulation Period,
8. The post-rapture / pre-tribulation gap prophecies,
9. The construction of the third Jewish temple,
10. The "Abomination of Desolation" occurring inside the third Jewish temple,
11. The evangelizing ministry of the 144,000 Jews for Jesus,
12. The twenty-one judgments of the book of Revelation,
13. The ten-kingdom break-up of the global government,
14. The "Patience of the Saints" prophecies,
15. The coming Christian martyrdom,
16. The Armageddon campaign of the Antichrist,
17. The False Prophet,
18. The "Mark of the Beast" and the identity of the number "666,"
19. The faithful Jewish remnant of the tribulation,
20. The war in heaven between Michael the archangel and Satan,
21. The casting out of Satan and his fallen angels from heaven to torment the earth,
22. The Second Coming of Christ,
23. The millennial Messianic Kingdom period.

These and many more prophecies were explored in Linton's comprehensive end times production. However, the one event they kept pausing the video to discuss was the

Russian-Iranian invasion, foretold in Ezekiel 38, which was unfolding before their very eyes.

Fortunately, the host went into elaborate detail about this prophecy. The little audience was relieved to hear that Jehovah had promised to supernaturally defeat the Ezekiel invaders, and to show His power on behalf of Israel in the process.

When they were finished watching the video, Nathan gathered the girls into his arms and said, "Girls, we need to come to grips with the fact, that this is the FINAL GENERATION. From this point forward, life won't be easy. But, we have the Lord and we have each other. I have made some preparations for us. We can do this, don't give up hope."

20

Rabbis Warn of the
Future Russian Invasion

"**G**entlemen," said the haggard Israeli Prime Minister, "as we speak, Russia's coalition is launching missiles into Northern Israel, and mobilizing to wipe us off the map!" Moshe Kaufman pounded a fist onto the table top to emphasize his distress.

The private audience, composed of members of Israel's Chief Rabbinate Council, listened in horror as Kaufman relayed that Russian President Vladimir Ziroski and his Iranian counterpart, Ayatollah Khomani, had issued the command to attack the Jewish state in retaliation for the recent Arab-Israeli war.

Chief Rabbi Joseph Levin spoke out, "Mr. Prime Minister, you stand corrected. It is not the Israelis, but the invaders who will be wiped out, according to the prophet Ezekiel!"

The esteemed Rabbi's confident statement garnered the unanimous support of his half-dozen peers, prompting Rabbi Aaron Edelstein to quote Ezekiel 39:8: *"Surely it is coming, and it shall be done."*

Rabbi Levin nodded approvingly.

"Well," said Rabbi Edelstein, "preparations to cleanse the land of the soon to be dead Russian invaders should be made in advance."

Prime Minister Kaufman had considered it politically expedient to convene this council meeting because in the aftermath of the IDF victory over the Arabs, the political landscape of Israel was becoming vastly more religious. The Chief Rabbinate Council was gaining an enormous amount of clout among the populous, because Rabbi Levin had pointed out the prophecies that had been fulfilled, with great specificity, in the Arab – Israeli war. They explained that the destruction of Damascus was a direct fulfillment of Isaiah 17, and the annexation of Jordan a fulfillment of Jeremiah 49:1-6.

Rabbi Joseph Levin's ability to interpret such prophecies elevated his rabbinical status to an unprecedented level, so much so that there was a saying circulating throughout the land: "If Rabbi Levin proclaimed it, then Jehovah has declared it to be so!"

Prime Minister Kaufman's eyebrows rose with the prophetic utterances of the Rabbis. Skeptically, Kaufman retorted, "Certainly you don't expect me to entrust Israel's national security to the teachings of ancient Hebrew texts! These may have been excellent teaching for their time, but they don't apply to our present circumstances!"

Ignoring Kaufman's comment, Rabbi Edelstein quoted further from the book of Ezekiel:

> *"It will come to pass in that day that I will give Gog a burial place there in Israel, the valley of those who pass by east of the sea; and it will obstruct travelers, because there they will bury Gog and all his multitude. Therefore, they will call it the Valley of Hamon Gog. For seven months the house of Israel will be burying them, in order to cleanse the land. Indeed, all the people of the land will be burying, and they will gain renown for it on the day that I am glorified," says the Lord GOD. "They will set apart men regularly employed, with the help of a search party, to pass through the land and bury those bodies remaining on the ground, in order to cleanse it. At the end of seven months they will make a search. The search party will pass through the land; and when anyone sees*

a man's bone, he shall set up a marker by it, till
the buriers have buried it in the Valley of Hamon
Gog. The name of the city will also be Hamonah.
Thus, they shall cleanse the land." (Ezekiel 39:11-
16, NKJV)

Prime Minister Kaufman scoffed, "What Valley of Hamon Gog and city of Hamonah? That's *Hamo-nonsense.* There is no such place in Israel. Esteemed Rabbis, with all due respect, you put too much stock in the ancient prophecies. We must first defeat the Russians before we can bury them!"

Raising his right hand high in the air, Rabbi Levin jumped to his feet and declared, "The prophecy does not predict any IDF military engagement. We presiding here today all concur. It is the official position of the Chief Rabbinate Council of Israel that Ezekiel's prophecies regarding Gog are to be interpreted literally! Russia's coalition is presently assembling to invade the Jewish state. They will come like an unstoppable storm, and cover the land of Israel with a cloud of jet fighters. *Hashem*…He is the power that will wage war against them supernaturally and singlehandedly. The IDF will bury the invaders, not fight them. It has been written with great specificity, and it shall be fulfilled as foretold. All glory for the victory is to be reserved for Jehovah, the Holy One in Israel!"

At the conclusion of Rabbi Levin's announcement, the other Rabbis called out, "Hear! Hear!" and pounded the table with their fists.

Angrily, Kaufman replied, "The IDF is exceedingly great, and our only defense against Russia's forces. They have proven their fighting skills against the Arabs. The Rabbinate Council admitted this when it declared Psalm 83 had been fulfilled through their recent victory in *"Operation Israeli Freedom.""*

"We still stand behind our Psalm 83 proclamation," insisted Rabbi Levin, to the unanimous vocal approval of the council members presiding alongside.

"Then why do you oppose my plan to mobilize the IDF against Russia's coalition?" Kaufman asked.

Rabbi Edelstein countered, "Why do you pick-and-choose what prophecies to base your executive decisions upon?"

Offended, the Prime Minister barked, "Be reasonable, Rabbis! Israel's existence is at stake! Are you insinuating that, at this crucial juncture, I should whimsically govern my people?"

Rabbi Edelstein shook his head. "Our interpretation of Psalm 83 you do not question, but our interpretation of Ezekiel 38 and 39 you discard. Where is the logic behind your reasoning?"

In frustration, Kaufman issued his final response: "There is no time for philosophical debate with you people. You may have accurately assessed the prophecies of Psalm 83 *after* our IDF victory, but Russia presents a far more formidable coalition. Pray your interpretations are correct, but I must rely on our IDF commanders rather than your scholarly advice in this matter. Israel faces an unprecedented existential threat and the margin for error is too great for rabbinical deliberation. Israelis must take matters into their own hands, and you all had better hope that your ancient prophecies are, indeed, correct!"

Ezekiel's Exceedingly Great Army Prepares to Fight Again

Meanwhile, IDF chief of staff General Jacob Barak had begun a massive mobilization of Israel's air, land, and naval forces. They had been preparing for a face-off with Russia's coalition ever since the consortium placed its unreasonable demands upon the Jewish state and blockaded the vital waterways against Israel a few months prior. The rapid IDF mobilization, coupled with the outcry of the United Nations, had temporarily deterred the Russian invasion.

In a closed-door meeting with the general, a few hours after the Rabbinate conference, Prime Minister Kaufman inquired, "How much longer will the Russians stall their attack?"

Barak insisted, "Not for long. They won't wait for the militaries of the western nations to recover from the disappearances of some of their soldiers to ally alongside us. America is already hastily refilling their ranks in anticipation of this imminent invasion. The western world fears what Ziroski and his cohorts are capable of if they eliminate Israel. There is no doubt that the Russian coalition is poised to strike while the iron is hot!"

Exasperated, Kaufman sighed, "We can no longer rely on the Americans since their Christians have unexplainably vanished. Their military is fragmented and presently all their interim government can do is protest Russian intentions from the sidelines. Western armies will take too long to regroup, and they may never fully recover. We will have to fight the *Ezekiel invaders* singlehandedly like we fought against the Arabs."

"The *Ezekiel invaders*," General Barak echoed. "Don't tell me you have adopted the Rabbis antiquated beliefs!"

Kaufman reluctantly responded, "They were right when they identified Op Israeli Freedom with Psalm 83."

Grasping the prime minister's shoulder, the general argued, "The verdict is still out on their statement about that prophecy. Besides, they didn't predict the war in advance. They only issued their rabbinical interpretation after the fact."

"In this go-round, this is not the case," Kaufman responded. "Their official interpretation is out in front of this pending invasion. They have instructed me to have you and your IDF forces stand down in this battle. According to their understanding of Ezekiel's prophecy, Hashem alone will do our fighting for us."

"Preposterous!" Barak huffed. "Surely you can't take them seriously! Do you expect our countrymen to shout "Shalom" while their women and children are being ravished by the Russians and their enjoining Muslim hordes?"

Kaufman gritted his teeth and shook his head. "You are right, General! We must defend our country! Position all our forces immediately, and brace for the Mother of all Middle East Wars!"

21

The European Union
Consoles Israel

Alone in his office, after his critical meetings with the Rabbinate Council and IDF commander, Prime Minister Kaufman was exhausted. He barely possessed enough energy to tidy up his desk and head home to Tamar, his wife of fifty-four years. Before he could retrieve his overcoat from the office rack, he had to field an after-hours phone call from European Union President Hans Vandenberg.

"Prime Minister Kaufman, thank you for accepting my call at this late hour," came the troubled voice through the handset.

"No hour is too late to speak with you, Mr. President," replied Kaufman.

Hans Vandenberg was a charismatic politician, rapidly emerging onto the world stage as one of its premier leaders. His support toward Israel during the recent Arab – Israeli war had elevated him to the top of the nation's list of allies. Moreover, Vandenberg's ability to stave off the collapse of the Eurozone in the aftermath of that war, by forming a "stability union" amongst the strongest pocket of European countries, had helped him get elected as the President of the EU Parliament.

Hans Vandenberg, not one to beat around the bush, dived directly into the point of his call: "Moshe, I want you to know that the European Union is vehemently opposed to Russia's recent threats against your country. As you know, the proper confederation of EU nations has formally opposed all of the coalition's demands imposed upon Israel, and we have called an emergency meeting, scheduled for tomorrow, to formulate an official EU response to Russia's recent attack upon Haifa."

Encouraged by what he was hearing, Prime Minister Kaufman got his second wind from the grueling day. "President Vandenberg," he enthused, "thank you for your support! I have been conducting key meetings throughout the day with Israel's military and religious leaders, and I assure you that Russia's aggression will be met with an expeditious and decisive response from Israel."

"I expected nothing less; such great courage is characteristic of Israel," commended Vandenberg.

"However," Kaufman continued. "As you can appreciate, the Russian Confederation is far too formidable for the IDF to fight single-handedly. Their demands against Israel, and the missile attack upon Haifa, are unwarranted, and it is impossible for Israel to comply with their unreasonable requests. No sovereign nation possessing legal littoral rights over its ports and waterways, and that operates in full compliance with established international commercial law, like Israel does, should be dictated to by another nation as to how to conduct its commerce. The western world should be outraged by Russia's preposterous demands and unruly behavior!"

Vandenberg agreed. "Prime Minister Kaufman, you are absolutely correct! President Ziroski's coalition gravely concerns the EU. At our emergency meeting we intend to raise all the legal issues and their geo-political ramifications, in an attempt to gain international support for Israel's cause in this matter. I assure you that Russia and its coalition will be ostracized from the global community for their unwarranted aggression if it persists."

Concerned about the potential lack of effectiveness of such a stance, Prime Minister Kaufmann replied, "It is important to Israel that military pacts are made between the EU and the Jewish state. Without such pacts in place, Russia will remain unwavering in its aggression toward my country."

President Vandenberg answered diplomatically, "I intend to bring this important point up at the meeting tomorrow. But I am convinced that strong international resolve should impose sufficient pressure upon the coalition to bring about at least a temporary cessation of aggression. Moshe, we have to get Russia to sit down at the table with us; otherwise, we risk World War III!"

Sensing uncharacteristic political cowardice on Vandenberg's part, Kaufman sternly replied, "With all due respect, sir, I strongly disagree! Russia and its coalition covet Israel's newfound prosperity, and mere political pressure is insufficient. They are committed against us militarily, hoping to confiscate our recently discovered bounties of oil and natural gas, and they want the spoil from the Arab war!"

Vandenberg concurred. "Yes, Prime Minister, the EU intends to condemn this aggression promptly, and in the harshest of terms!"

"But, harsh EU rhetoric is not the solution to the problem!" Kaufman insisted. "It should be obvious to the world that Russia intends to seize control of our primary natural energy resources. If successful, they could monopolize energy exports and become the dominant world power! Their current aspirations are not only an existential threat to Israel, but severely problematic for the EU and the West as well. They don't want to negotiate with the western world…they want to *rule* the *whole* world! And they are convinced that Israel is the primary obstacle standing in their way." Taking a deep breath, he tried to calm his racing pulse. "I can appreciate your concerns Mr. President, but war may not be avoidable in this instance!"

Backpedaling slightly, Vandenberg pleaded, "Be reasonable, Mr. Prime Minister! Western armies, especially the USA and UK, are still in a state of disarray, from the massive unexplained disappearances. But Russia's coalition, comprised mainly of Muslim countries, experienced very few disappearances, leaving their armies virtually intact. Moreover, the Muslim populations residing inside Europe are mostly supportive of the Russian coalition, and are crowding our streets in large numbers in protests against Israel."

"*You* be reasonable!" retorted Kaufman. "Who can negotiate with mad Vlad Ziroski and his cohort Khomani? In these unreasonable times, only Israel provides the voice of reason. The Jews are trying to get world markets back on track, but the Russian coalition intends to block our every move. The only way to quiet Muslim protests is to put Europeans back to work, and that's what Israel proposes to do with our commerce campaign."

Sensing Kaufman's frustration Vandenberg patronized, "I understand, Moshe. These are troubling times for you and your people, and we want to partner commercially with Israel. Believe me the EU is on Israel's side in this matter, but this is not the only important issue the EU is grappling with presently. In light of the recent Mideast war with the Arabs, unexplained disappearances, and the supernatural sighting of the Virgin Mary at St. Peter's Square, the EU is doing all it can to resurrect order. We must give diplomacy a chance! This world cannot absorb another major Mideast war! I believe we can engage in diplomacy with President Ziroski and get him to back down."

Realizing that President Vandenberg, the consummate politician, might actually abandon Israel on behalf of "diplomacy," the Israeli Prime Minister declared, "President Vandenberg, the days of negotiations have departed! The western world is reeling and Islam is spiraling out of control worldwide! If that's not enough, the Pope is predicting that the Virgin Mary will win the world to Catholicism! The EU appears to be subtly endorsing this position, so where does that leave my people?"

Vandenberg cleared his throat. "This is not yet the official EU position," he said. "We are presently conducting roundtable discussions with the Pope and the Holy See. Until those meetings are concluded, the EU remains undecided on this matter."

Kaufman drew his handkerchief and blotted the sweat from his brow while commenting, "At the same time that you have your conversations with the Vatican, the Rabbinic Council of Israel is advocating that the temple be rebuilt and the Law of Moses officially reinstated as the constitution of the Jewish state. The nations have gone insane!"

Hearing only silence on the phone line, the prime minister continued, "Ziroski dances to an entirely different drummer than you and I. He is a Communist atheist! As far as he is concerned, the Jewish Jehovah, apparitions of Mary, and Muslim al-Mahdi are all figments of human imagination. To him, they are useful mechanisms that enable him to achieve world dominance. While the western world attempts to restore order, Mad Vlad tips his missiles with nuclear warheads. There is no negotiating with this madman. The sooner the world realizes this, the better! In fact, it is my firm belief that the reason the Russian missile sent into Haifa was non- nuclear, was because Ziroski merely wanted to send your people a warning. The next time Israel may not be so lucky!"

Recognizing that Kaufman wanted more than the EU was prepared to offer, President Vandenberg concluded, "Prime Minister Kaufman, you have clearly articulated Israel's needs, and I will voice your concerns to my ministers at our cabinet meeting tomorrow. I don't believe it is realistic to expect the EU or the west to offer military support to Israel until all political options have been exhausted. The EU will undoubtedly advise that Israel put a moratorium on annexing more Arab lands, and temporarily abandon all plans to construct a Jewish temple. These issues are not constructive to the peace process, and will inhibit our ability to negotiate with Muslim factions inside the Russian coalition."

"As you will, President Vandenberg," Kaufman conceded. "But the EU does the free world a great disservice by failing to recognize that war with Russia is the inevitable option. You surely understand that it will be impossible for me to get full support from the Knesset for such moratoriums."

22

The EU Condemnation and Vatican Consecration of Russia

It was a dismal day in Brussels when the cabinet members assembled at the EU consulate for their emergency meeting. Thunderous clouds accompanied by severe rains caused airport delays for several dignitaries arriving from neighboring nations. So loud were the thunder-clapped skies, that it seemed as though the high heavens had heard about the meeting and voiced divine disapproval.

In addition to the EU member-states, representatives from the United Nations, UK and the Vatican City State, were also in attendance.

President Vandenberg began the meeting by announcing that he had conducted phone conversations with President Moshe Kaufman of Israel, President Harold Redding of America, and President Hu Jintao of China. President Redding had been the US Vice President at the time of the rapture, when President John Bachlin vanished, leaving Redding as his successor.

"As you know, grave events are escalating again in the Middle East," began Vandenberg. "Israel fears war with Russia and its coalition is imminent, and the United States agrees. I informed both Prime Minister Kaufman, and President Redding, that the EU favors diplomacy rather than war to resolve this dangerous impasse."

Those in attendance nodded and murmured their approval of his stated position.

Vandenberg continued, "I expressed to our Israeli and American friends our harshest disapproval of Russia and its coalition, and reminded them that the EU stands firmly by Israel's side in this matter. I told both leaders that we would do everything in our power, short of offering military assistance, to influence the Russian coalition to refrain from further attacks against the Jewish state. It was important to issue this disclaimer in order to alert both countries that any retaliatory military responses against Russia would be at their own risk, and not supported by the EU."

Cardinal Gabriel Vitalia, representing the Vatican, questioned, "What was the response of China's president Hu Jintao to Russia's formation of a Muslim coalition and recent aggression against Israel?"

Vandenberg reluctantly responded, "President Jintao was neutral. He said his country opts to stay out of this matter, and refuses to issue or endorse any official responses concerning the present Middle East conflict. Frankly, he said China was upset with the Israeli occupation of Arab lands after their recent war victory, and equally disturbed by Russia's formation of a Muslim coalition that is obviously planning to seize control of Israel's gas and oil resources. He said China would wait for current Middle East events to play out, to see which direction the balance of power shifts, before determining his country's course of action."

"That's it?" A high ranking female member from the Italian delegation asked.

Nodding "yes," Vandenberg confirmed, "Not surprisingly, that was President Jintao's response."

"Moreover," he continued, "On your desks, you will find my suggestion for the official EU statement condemning Russia's actions, for your collective review and approval. It outlines the steps the EU and its allies are prepared to take in the event Russian aggression persists. This statement harshly condemns the aggression, but also encourages the Russian confederation to come to the negotiating table. This is why no mention of military consequence has been included in the EU statement.

In light of volatile world events, the EU must be careful not to alienate Israel, Russia or the Muslim nations."

Voicing disapproval, UK Prime Minister Tony Brown stood up and stated, "The international community needs to send Russia a strong military warning that it will not tolerate its aggression! It is blatantly obvious that Russia plans to steal Israel's prosperity. They cannot be allowed to get away with such scandalous behavior!"

President Vandenberg raised his right hand, rebuffing his British colleague. Looking sternly into Brown's eyes the EU president stated, "Excuse me, Honorable Prime Minister, but you can't even control Muslim protests in London, let alone engage in a world war with Russia, Turkey, Iran, and the others! Since Brexit, your country's voice is less influential than it was when it was an EU member, and like America's military, Her Majesty's British forces are in a state of disarray from the disappearances. This is not the time for any of us, especially the UK, to abandon diplomacy. We must carefully calculate the consequences of our actions as the leader of the international community. What if Russia wars against Israel and wins? Then what? Do you want the UK to be the coalition's next target?"

Infuriated, the British Prime Minister stormed out of the meeting, setting the stage for what turned out to be a dictatorial conclusion. Vandenberg managed to keep the podium to himself, and in so doing shut out all dissenting voices; only Cardinal Vitalia was given the opportunity to share the platform. Vandenberg had been forewarned that Pope Vicente Romano was about to make an important announcement to the faithful, and that it was imperative that the EU be informed of his pending declaration.

The Vatican spokesman made it clear that the Pope thoroughly disapproved of EU military intervention on the behalf of Israel. Cardinal Vitalia declared, "Pope Vicente is certain that the recent glorious appearance of the Blessed Mother Mary over St. Peter's Square, and the messages imparted through her visionaries, signal that a time of worldwide peace is forthcoming."

These comments opened the door for Vandenberg to say, "Cardinal Vitalia, it has been brought to my attention that the Pope is about to make an important announcement to the faithful. Can you reveal the content of his forthcoming statement?"

Seizing the opportunity, Cardinal Vitalia continued, "Pope Romano wanted me to remind all of you that the apparition of Our Lady of Fatima in 1917 had a message about Russia.[24] Our Lady prophesied that Russia will be the scourge of all nations, but she promised that if the Holy Father along with the Bishops of the world would consecrate Russia to her Immaculate Heart, then a period of peace will be granted to the world. I have been given direct authority by the Holy See to inform you that the prophecies of Our Lady serve as a direct warning to all of you. We are not to battle this confederacy with weapons, but with prayer to the Blessed Virgin Mary. Russia is not to be politically or militarily provoked, but rather to be spiritually consecrated. Pope Romano is feeling a sense of urgency to fulfill the wishes of Our Lady at Fatima in this matter. He plans on consecrating Russia to her Immaculate Heart soon. However today, shortly after the adjournment of this very EU assembly, Pope Romano will infallibly declare a new Marian dogma naming Mary as Co-Redemptrix, Mediatrix of all graces and Advocate. You are all hereby given advance knowledge of these announcements as of today."

Gasps arose from the audience. "Why now? What are the broader implications of this dogma," they asked among themselves?

Without hesitation, the Cardinal concluded, "Advance knowledge of Pope Romano's intention was given to you today in order to ensure that the EU adopts only a non-violent course of action regarding the Russian Confederation. The EU must not provoke the Russian bear to awaken any further out from its Cold War slumber. The EU must pursue the path of peace, and wait upon the Blessed Mother to reconcile the world to her Immaculate Heart."

With these words still echoing in the chamber, Vandenberg declared that the path of diplomacy would be the EU's official position. They would support Israel only up to the point that such support did not provoke Russian aggression. The Pope's pending announcement would draw a line in the Middle East sand, and would seal the EU's decision.

As promised, later that same day Pope Romano consecrated Russia to Mary and declared the Virgin Mary is Co-Redemptrix, Mediatrix of all graces and Advocate for the People of God. Moreover, the EU announced its official statement condemning Russia for boycotting and attacking Israel, but posing no retaliatory threat to the coalition.

23

144,000 Jewish Evangelists

It was about noon the day after the Russian missile attack in Haifa, when the phone rang, "Hello, Thompson residence," Lisa answered.

"Tovia and his family are all safe!" Naomi exclaimed.

Lisa had just risen from a restless sleep when her mother sounded the good news. She had slept in far later than normal because Jami, Nathan Severs and she had stayed up deep into the wee hours of the night, repeatedly replaying the end times DVD.

Excitedly Lisa responded, "That's fantastic news! Did you talk to Tovia? I haven't been able to get through to him."

"Yes," Naomi confirmed. "Tovia called and said that he and the children made it into the neighborhood bomb shelter moments before the strike. Apparently, the missile exploded several miles away, not causing any damage to their home."

Hearing her mother's voice, Jami entered the room, rubbing sleep from her eyes. "What is it, Mother?" she asked. "What's going on?"

Cradling the receiver next to her heart, Lisa said, "Tovia and your cousins are fine! They weren't near the blast!"

"Is that Grandma Naomi?" Jami asked.

"It is," Lisa replied. "Grandma Naomi just got off the phone with your uncle. Go get ready for school. I will fill you in on what happened after I hang up."

"School," Jami grumbled. "I don't think schools are even going to be open after what Russia did."

"Hold on a moment, Mother," Lisa spoke into the phone.

Covering the mouthpiece, Lisa said, "Jami, go check out your school's website and find out if school is cancelled, while I finish talking to your grandmother, I don't want you to miss school. We have to go about our normal lives."

"Normal lives?" Jami echoed, "How can you say that after watching dad's DVD all night?"

Lisa shushed her daughter and said, "Just do what I say."

Turning her undivided attention back to her mother, it was only a few seconds into the conversation, when Naomi's disposition changed from excitement to concern. "Tovia said something very unsettling to me," she complained.

"What do you mean? What did he say? Lisa asked.

Naomi elaborated, "Tovia and the family were in the bomb shelter with some of those Jesus Jews, you know the ones that supposedly number 144,000 and parade around Israel claiming to be spoken of in the Christian Bible."

Lisa replied, "Yes, I'm very familiar with them. Some people are calling them the *Royal Jews from the Twelve Tribes of Israel*, and they are predicted in the Bible. What are they saying?"

Naomi gasped, "Oh my goodness! Don't tell me you believe them, too!"

Realizing she had shocked her Jewish mother by her comment, she tried to shift the subject back to Tovia. "Go on, Mother. Tell me what Tovia said."

Naomi composed herself and commented, "Fine, but don't tell me you are falling for these Jesus royal nut-cakes."

Waiting in vain to hear Lisa respond, Naomi grumbled, "I don't like this, Lisa. Your lack of response troubles me. So, okay then, apparently, the Jesus Freaks had the *chutzpa* to say that the prophet Ezekiel predicted the Russian confederacy in ancient times. They warned Tovia that there is a massive invasion coming, and that he and all of his family should leave Israel, already! Can you believe the nerve?"

To Lisa's surprise, Jami, who had been listening in on the receiver, inquired, "Did they say there could be Israeli casualties?"

Dumbfounded that Jami was overhearing, Naomi was silent.

"Jami!" Lisa cried, "You shouldn't be hearing this!"

"Maybe we should all leave," Jami wept.

To Naomi's astonishment, Lisa did not correct the girl. "Where would we go?" Lisa replied. "And how would be get there? Flights out of Israel are undoubtedly selling out as we speak!"

"Have you lost your mind?" Naomi blurted out. "Didn't you just tell Jami that Israelis have to live normal lives? What's gotten into you? What are you NOT TELLING me?"

Lisa confirmed, "Ezekiel did predict this war!"

"Oy Vey," gasped Naomi, clapping the palm of her free hand to her forehead. "When did you start reading the Bible? I don't know whether to be proud of you, or furious!"

"Mother," Lisa began, "I was up all last night…watching Thomas' Christian video."

Lisa had no more than spoken the word's "Christian video" before Naomi held the phone in front of her face and began shouting what Lisa took to be Hebrew expletives."

"Stop cussing, Mother!" Lisa cried. "Let me continue!"

Putting the receiver to her ear, Naomi replied, "I'm not cussing! You should know your Hebrew better, so you would understand my words. I am saying this can't be happening! My own daughter turning into a Jesus Jew! My heart is breaking! But who should care?"

"Mother, please," Lisa begged. "Just let me speak."

"I don't know if I can bear to hear what you say!" Naomi fretted.

"Mother, you don't have to believe me, or the Jesus Jews. Just turn on the morning news."

Naomi echoed back, "The morning news? Stop evading my question!"

"It's all over the news!" Lisa replied. "Before you called, Rabbi Joseph Levin of the Chief Rabbinate Council warned that the Ezekiel prophecy could be coming, and that Israelis should prepare for the possibility of another major war."

"Chief Rabbi Levin said that?" Naomi marveled.

"Yes, your *favorite* Rabbi!" Lisa answered, feeling somewhat vindicated.

Naomi muttered, "Hold on. Let me turn on the TV."

As Naomi began to pick up the television remote, she caught herself and said, "Wait a minute, Lisa. You still haven't answered my question. Are you, or are you NOT, telling me that you believe in…Jesus?" The last word caught on her stubborn tongue.

Lisa took a calming breath and replied. "Mother, just watch the news, then do me a favor and read Ezekiel, chapters 38 and 39. Then come over to my house so we can discuss this, face-to-face."

Silence ensued, broken only by a series of deep breaths on Naomi's end.

"Mother, are you still there?" Lisa worried.

"Yes, Lisa, I'm still with you," Naomi begrudgingly confirmed. "Close to fainting, I am. But who should care? I am beside myself! I don't know what to say, already."

Lovingly Lisa replied, "Mother, that's why I want to meet with you. We are living in incredibly treacherous times. As the family matriarch, you need to help us make enormous decisions about how to face the days ahead."

Lisa's diplomacy was intended to soothe Naomi, but the woman only commented, "*Oy Vey!* Now my Christian daughter is a prophetess, would you believe?"

Lisa sighed, "Please, Mother; set aside your prejudice long enough to see what's happening in the world right now. Things have gone absolutely crazy since the Christians vanished, and Israel defeated the Arabs! Even Rabbi Levin is searching ancient Hebrew prophecies for answers."

The mention, again, of Naomi's "favorite" rabbi was hard to fight.

"Very well, Lisa, I will see if I can find your father's Tanakh[25] in his library, and read about Ezekiel's war."

●●●●●

After talking with her mother, Lisa began to phone her brother Tovia, when Jami stopped her in mid-dial. "Mom, as I suspected, there's no school today."

Caught by surprise Lisa stammered, "Oh, uh, alright honey, then go have some breakfast."

Feeling somewhat put-off, Jami asked, "Wait! What did Grandma say? Was she open to talking about dad's DVD?"

"No, she's extremely troubled that I've become a Christian," Lisa answered.

Jami's mouth dropped open. "Oh, no!" she snickered. "You're in big trouble now!"

Lisa smiled. "You'd better brace yourself," she warned, "I invited your grandmother over to talk about things."

Jami perked up as she said, "I'm going to organize my notes from Dad's DVD, in case we can convince Grandma to watch the video."

"Good idea, honey," agreed Lisa.

●●●●●

Scrambling to get his phone, Tovia answered, "Hello, Tovia speaking."

"It's me, Lisa," his sister replied.

"Hi, Sis! I got off the phone with mother a few minutes ago, letting her know we were all OK."

"I know," Lisa replied. "She called me right after. How did things happen yesterday with the missile attack?"

"It was dreadfully scary," Tovia began. "It was more frightening than the Hezbollah conflict in 2006, and our recent war with the Arabs."

"In what way?" asked Lisa.

"For starters, we didn't know if these missiles were equipped with nuclear warheads," Tovia explained, "and second, we were entirely ambushed, having only a moment's notice to gather the kids and rush to the shelter."

Lisa sighed, "I'm so sorry, Tovia. It must have been horrific for you and the children."

Tovia replied, "I'm so proud of the way Amber rounded up Isabella and her baby brother Jaxon, while I grabbed our gas masks and bug-out bags. After the last war, we are prepared for almost anything."

"Tell me more," Lisa requested. "What was it like inside the shelter? Mother said you spoke with some of the Jews claiming to be from the 144,000 of the Bible."

"Are you referring to the so-called Royal Jews of the Twelve Tribes?" asked Tovia.

"Yes," Lisa confirmed, "Mother said they suggested that you should leave Israel because Russia is going to wage a massive war against us."

"Yes, wow!" said Tovia. "These two guys were incredible. They were the only ones in our shelter with laptops. I couldn't believe how prepared they were. By the time we all got there they were picking up Internet Wi-Fi news about events above ground in Haifa. They were also communicating with other Jesus Jews, finding out if other cities in Israel had come under attack. We were blessed that they kept us apprised of what was transpiring on the outside."

Putting her phone on speaker at maximum volume, she gestured to Jami to come listen. "What else did they say?" Lisa inquired. "Did they actually call themselves the Royal Jews from the Twelve Tribes of Israel?"

"No," Tovia laughed. "They said that was a label the Rabbinate Council had come up with to mock their claims of being the 144,000 Hebrew witnesses of the Christian Bible."

"So, they did claim to be spoken about in the Bible?" Lisa asked.

"Yes, they did," said Tovia. "Lisa, these guys were very smart, and extremely kind. There were about forty of us in the shelter with them, and by the time they were done quoting from the Tanakh and their Christian Bible, they had most of us convinced that they really were who they claimed to be."

Tovia confessed, "Sis, I have to be honest with you: Amber, the kids, and I were so impressed with these two men, that we, along with about a dozen others in the shelter, received Jesus as our Lord and Savior."

Tovia was stunned to hear both Lisa and Jami cry out, "Hallelujah!"

"What's up?" Tovia laughed. "Am I picking up room noise, or did someone just say 'hallelujah'?"

"Yes," Lisa responded. "Jami and I are elated by this news! We both received Jesus yesterday, also!

Tovia was delighted to hear about their conversions. "Does Mother know?" he asked.

"Yes and no," said Lisa. "I'm pretty sure she realizes this from our conversation, which happened right after you spoke with her. She is supposed to come over to our house today to discuss Ezekiel's prophecy about Russia."

Tovia was overwhelmed. "Wow!" he cried out. "This is all happening so suddenly! I don't know what to say!"

"Don't worry about mother," Lisa replied. "Jami and I know what to say to her when she arrives. Fortunately, Thomas left behind a DVD that outlines end times events, including the Psalm 38 prophecy."

Tovia corrected her, "Don't you mean Ezekiel 38?"

Jami jumped into the conversation and confirmed, "Yes, Uncle, Mother keeps confusing Psalm 83 with Ezekiel 38. Both events were on the video."

"I understand the confusion," acknowledged Tovia. "Are you sure you know what to say to mother about Jesus, Ezekiel, and the 144,000 Jews?"

Lisa replied, "Well, we wish you were here to help explain things, but we will do our best. Also, do you remember Robert Rasmussen...we use to call him Razz? He was my father-in-law's best friend."

"Vaguely," Tovia said.

"Razz was raptured with Thomas, Tyler, and the other Christians, but before he left he willed his sizeable portfolio to us. His dear friend and financial advisor, Nathaniel Severs, delivered the good news to us personally. Nathan got saved recently also, and he was the one who led Jami and me in a prayer to receive Jesus Christ. I am going to ask Nathan to be with us when Mother arrives. He knows more about these matters than we do."

Tovia was delighted to hear this, but cautioned, "I told Mom that we received Jesus when we were in the shelter, and she immediately resisted the news. If she struggles with what you tell her, I advise that you try to locate one of these 144,000 witnesses in your area to assist you. Apparently, they have a special anointing for leading Jews to accept Jesus as their Messiah. I know that the Holy Spirit used Gershom and Simeon to convince Amber, me, and the children about Jesus. I doubt that we would have converted if they weren't in the shelter with us yesterday."

"That's good advice." Lisa agreed.

"I know there are some in town," Jami chimed in, "because my girlfriend Amy said she saw some Yeshiva students hassling two of them by the high school the other day. I will contact her to see if she knows where to find them."

"I think that would be a great idea," Tovia said.

Lisa heaved a sigh. "Jami and I are delighted that you are all safe," she said. "Oh, by the way, I forgot to ask...are you planning to leave Israel temporarily like the witnesses advised?"

"We're talking about it," said Tovia. "Right now, we are researching where we would go, and watching the news for breaking events. Please call me after you speak to Mother and we will know more. If the topic comes up, tell Mom that we are seriously considering taking the advice of the two witnesses in the shelter."

"Will do," promised Lisa. "We will sign off for now and call you after we talk to Mom."

"Please do," Tovia said. "I will anxiously await your call. Remember to have your gas masks and other preparations in order in case another Russian attack comes upon Israel and you have to rush to your local bomb shelter."

"We are prepared for anything, Brother," Lisa assured him. "We love you. Give Amber and the kids a hug from us."

24

Hooked in the Jaws - Russia Covets Israeli Contracts with the West

"Israel to Export Gas and Oil to the West," read the top front page headline of the *Moscow Times*. The article reported that Israel had signed multi-billion dollar contracts with America and the UK to export significant quantities of natural gas and crude oil directly to them. Furthermore, the article said:

> "In addition to The UK and US, Israel is also courting the EU for natural gas and oil export contracts."

Israeli Prime Minister Moshe Kaufman was quoted as saying,

> "'The EU is also Israel's strong ally and should be rewarded for imposing stiff demands against the Russian coalition. Presently, Israel can supply the EU with an abundance of natural gas and oil resources, which minimizes the need for European reliance upon Russia and Iran for these critical commodities.'"

Having advance knowledge of the outcome of the EU general assembly meeting, Prime Minister Kaufman had spoken out of turn in telling the press about EU sanctions against Russia. The presumptuous announcement galled the Russian president. Slamming his newspaper down on his desk, Vladimir Ziroski shouted at his councilors, "What EU demands? These were only rumors until now. Have any of you heard the details about these "stiff demands" Kaufman is alluding to?

Calming himself, Ziroski continued, "So be it! It doesn't matter what the EU plans. Israel has sealed its own coffin with these western contracts. Mother Russia refuses to compete with the Jews! The time has come to defeat and plunder the Jewish state!"

These egregious comments stunned his cabinet members, including Prime Minister Sergei Primakov, and UN Ambassador Anatoly Tarasov. Mad Vlad Ziroski had just convened his cabinet to discuss a potential future invasion of Israel, when his secretary side-swiped him with the *Moscow Times* and suggested that he read the troubling headline and related article first.

"What western contracts?" Prime Minister Primakov asked.

Thrusting the newspaper across the desk, Ziroski snarled, "Israel plans to export oil and gas to the west!"

Ambassador Tarasov, who had recently attempted to dissuade the EU from considering sanctions said, "Those western traitors! Their ambassadors all promised me that they would not execute those export contracts with Israel without Russia's consent."

"If they want an official response, I'll give them an official response!" Ziroski retorted. "War with Israel, that's Russia's official response!"

Motioning toward his secretary, Mad Vlad ordered, "As soon as this meeting adjourns get Ayatollah Khomani on the phone!"

Prime Minister Primakov, already in trouble with Ziroski for the missing suitcase nuclear weapons that terrorists used to strike American ballparks, patronizingly said, "I vote 'yes' on that Mr. President. This way you can accomplish two important feats at once: dispossess Israel of its energy resources, making the EU solely reliant upon us; and eliminate any threat of sanctions against us. We shall become the superpower that determines the future of the world!"

Ziroski confirmed, "Precisely! My thoughts exactly!"

Mad Vlad informed his cabinet that Russia was fast-forwarding coalition plans to launch a massive attack against the Jewish state, beginning with the northernmost parts of Israel.

Ziroski pledged, "Our confederacy will not allow Israel any further export access through the surrounding regional waterways. Iran will close off the Strait of Hormuz, and our other coalition commanders will police the Mediterranean and Red Seas."

Ambassador Tarasov objected "In light of today's headlines, these maritime measures will undoubtedly upset the Americans and the British."

Pounding his desk, Mad Vlad declared, "The Americans and British have the Russian bear in an uproar! Their armies are weakened and disoriented due to the disappearances. They are no match for our coalition forces and weapons. Our troops have not vanished into thin air like many of theirs. They will protest our invasion from the sidelines, but they won't draw us into a multi-front war. If they do, we will take the battle into their lands. The same applies to the EU. They have Muslim insurgents causing severe unrest internally. If the EU decides to come against us, they will have to fight with the Muslims from within and without!"

●●●●●

Russia Commands Iran to Attack Israel

As the last of Ziroski's cabinet departed, his secretary handed him the phone.

"President Ziroski, I was expecting your call," announced Iran's supreme leader, the Ayatollah Khomani.

Mad Vlad replied, "So you have also read the reports about Israel's contracts with the west?"

The Khomani declared, "Indeed, I have already told President Muktada Zakiri to prepare his commanders for battle! He is awaiting my final order. IRGC generals are probably already coordinating attack details with your generals."

"Prime Minister Primakov is communicating with our military Chief of Staff as we speak," Ziroski boasted.

"Israel has defiantly crossed our final red line in the Middle East sand," the Ayatollah proclaimed. "We Muslims rejoice to send the Jews to their appointment in Jahannam."[26]

President Ziroski smiled. "So be it Supreme Ayatollah!" he agreed. "The Jews will have their rendezvous with death. Assemble your forces for battle. Muslim world leaders await your command."

25

Jews Flee Israel as the Russian Invasion Begins

Rushing to the nearby bomb-shelter, Naomi stumbled and fell to the ground, spraining an ankle. Grasping her leg in agony, she moaned.

Fortunately, this round of sirens in Jerusalem turned out to be a false alarm, allowing Naomi time to calm herself down and slowly get up to test her footing. As she limped back toward home, she called Lisa on her cell phone.

"Hello, Thompson residence," Lisa answered.

"Honey," Naomi sadly said, "I'm sorry to say that I won't be able to come over this afternoon."

"Oh Mother, not again! It's critical that we watch that DVD. It explains what the Bible says Russia is about to do to Israel!"

Naomi apologized. "I know this makes two afternoons in a row that I have cancelled, but I have a legitimate reason today. My excuse yesterday may have been lame, but…" she shuddered. "…Speaking of 'lame,' I think I just sprained my ankle racing to the bomb shelter. I think the Thirty-mile drive to your home in Bet Shemesh will aggravate the sprain. *Oy Vey!* All these sirens and trips to shelters are wearing me out. I'm so stressed I hardly sleep anymore."

"Are you going to be okay"? Lisa asked.

"Yes, of course," Naomi replied. "I'm almost home and plan to ice down the swelling. I'm sure I will be able to get around better after I nurse the ankle a bit."

"I'm going to grab Jami and Nathan Severs, and head to your house. I'll bring the DVD with me," Lisa insisted.

"No, no, no," Naomi argued. "Don't bother! That won't be necessary. I'm not up for it today. Let me rest my ankle and my mind, and I will see how I feel in the morning."

"The morning may be too late!" Lisa responded, "Did you get a chance to read Ezekiel 38, like you promised?"

"Comments like that are not helping me to calm down," Naomi rebuffed. "And, no, I didn't get a chance to comb through the Ezekiel predictions. I was going to start reading the verses when the sirens started sounding. Let me take the rest of the day to rest my ankle and study his writings. I have your father's Tanakh sitting beside my reading chair."

Conceding to her mother's wishes, Lisa replied, "Alright, Mother, but promise me you *will* read Ezekiel 38, and that you will call me if you have any questions. If you need me to come over to nurse your ankle sprain, I will. But, tomorrow we must for sure meet to discuss what's taking place between Israel and Russia. I spoke with Tovia, and he said that he, Amber, Bella, and Jaxon may leave Israel until the Russian threat subsides."

"Oy Vey!" Naomi cried. "I'm losing my mind with you kids. I can't tell your father that you are all Christians! This is not the time for Jews to become Christians! This is the time for Jews to be Jews!"

Forfeiting another phone fight, Lisa consented, "Okay, Mother. Have it your way for now, but as you will see on the news, time *is* of the utmost essence."

Hanging up, Lisa greeted Nathan Severs at the front door. He had come in response to Lisa's request that he be present to talk to Naomi about Ezekiel 38 and the other prophecies on the DVD.

"Greetings, Lisa," said Nathan. "Thanks for inviting me over. Is your mother here yet?"

Reluctantly, Lisa replied, "No, she hurt herself while fleeing to the bomb shelter. She may have sprained her ankle. She wants to rest and nurse it for the rest of the day. She won't be coming over after all."

Handing Lisa a bag of sandwiches and desserts from her favorite neighborhood deli, Nathan said, "I am sorry to hear that. I brought along these goodies to pave the way for our discussion. You told me how much she loves to eat Kosher foods."

Lisa gratefully received the treats. "Please, come in," she welcomed him. "I assure you that these delicious morsels won't go to waste."

Nathan took off his coat and followed Lisa to the kitchen, "This is the second time your mother has stood us up," he said. "I appreciate that an ankle sprain is a serious issue, but we are running out of time to warn her about the impending Russian invasion."

Lisa moaned, "I know, Nathan! I am beside myself concerning her indifference. I sincerely believe that the DVD will lead her to Christ like it did for Jami and me."

Moving into the parlor while Lisa prepared the food, Nathan saw Jami watching the breaking news. "What's going on now?" he asked.

"Not good," Jami anguished. "They're showing satellite shots of troops assembling in Russia, Iran, and Turkey and a couple of other countries that are Russia's allies. These must be the hordes of Gog that the DVD spoke about. The newscaster says that Israelis should brace for an im-immena, um, I can't say the word, but it means like for an immediate attack."

"You mean an 'imminent' attack," Nathan offered.

"Yes, that's the word he used." Jami agreed.

"Lisa, hurry up! You'd better get in here right away," Nathan hollered toward the kitchen.

Scurrying into the parlor, Lisa asked, "What now?"

"Ezekiel 38 seems to be setting up quicker than we thought," Nathan alerted.

Hand-in-hand the trio sat on the sofa's edge as *Israel Network News* (INN) issued an alarming alert:

"We are getting reports from credible Israeli military sources that a massive deployment of Russian, Turkish, and Iranian troops is underway. These reports indicate that the Syrian port city of Tartus, due north of Israel, is their rendezvous destination. Only about 150 miles lies between Tartus and Haifa. As we have been reporting over the past few weeks, Russia, in cooperation with Turkey, has sent large quantities of missiles, tank and heavy artillery into Tartus. Furthermore, our sources warn that the IDF is expeditiously mobilizing for war, and that Israelis should prepare immediately for an imminent large-scale attack from Russia and its coalition."

Frantic, Jami cried, "Didn't Dad's DVD say that Ezekiel talked about Russia attacking from the 'uttermost parts of the north'?"

"Yep, that sounds correct" Nathan replied.

"Mother what are we going to do?" Jami implored.

"I don't know." Lisa said, tears in her eyes. "I don't have the answers. This is all too overwhelming for me."

As the two girls wept together, Nathan stood up and took charge. "We have to get out of here," he ordered. "I have an escape plan prepared. I have kept my private plane and personal pilot on ready standby, just in case things began to escalate."

Startled, Lisa stammered, "Right now? Leave now?"

Pulling her to her feet, Nathan insisted, "We three are getting out of here right now, before Russia attacks!"

White-faced, Jami croaked, "But, how, where, when, what are you talking about?"

Nathan went for his jacket, calling over his shoulder, "You told me what the two Jesus Jews said to Tovia. They warned that people might need to flee, scat, vamoose, get out of Dodge."

"B-but," Lisa resisted, "we can't just pick-up and leave!"

"Oh, yes we can, and we will!" Nathan commanded, grabbing the girls' coats from the hall closet." If you don't, I'm going to pick you both up over my shoulders and strap you into the plane personally! It's not safe for any of us to be in Israel right now. The video said Israel wins the war, but it didn't promise zero Israeli casualties!"

Lisa balked. "What about my mother?" she groaned.

Nathan stopped short, hands on hips. "Look girls," he barked, "I have a private twin engine Cessna jet gassed and ready to go. It will seat up to a dozen passengers with ample luggage space. It is already in a berth by the airport runway. That makes room for you two girls, my pilot, me, your parents and several of your family members. I have made arrangements for us to travel to my villa in Rome. If you have more people, we might have time to make a second flight."

Nathan Severs had paid cash for this home in Rome prior to moving to Israel, in preparation for just such a time as this. He still owned his mansion in America, and was in the process of purchasing additional properties located in several other strategic parts of the world, as part of his plan to set up a network of safe-haven locations for Jews coming under persecution. All of this was to honor his personal promise to Christ to become a last days Oskar Schindler of sorts.

Lisa tried to compose herself... "What do we pack? What about my job? I fill an important position for the Ministry of Interior. I can't just pick-up and leave. What would I tell my boss?"

Firmly grabbing her by the shoulders and staring squarely into her eyes, Nathan replied, "Pack some clothes, personal photos, and banking and portfolio information. Keep it light; I have everything else we need: food, water, gold, and plenty of cash stockpiled in Rome. Regarding your boss, just request a short sabbatical. Tell him you are concerned about a pending Russian invasion and want to move your daughter to safer ground for the time being. Inform him that you will work from your laptop and return after the dust settles. Let him know that you will stay in close contact with him. If he doesn't like it, then don't worry about it. Your uncle Razz bequeathed you a sizeable fortune. You don't have to work another day in your life if you don't want to."

Facing reality, Lisa looked at Jami. "Honey," she said, "Mr. Severs is right. I have to get you out of harm's way and we have to go right now."

"Whoa!" Jami requested. "What about all my BFF's? I don't want them to suffer."

"I understand, honey," Lisa replied, embracing her daughter. "but family first, *best friends forever* are second. If there is time and if they are willing, I'm sure Nathan will do the best he can to help the others."

"Pack your bags and make the calls," Nathan said firmly, "In light of what's transpiring we are definitely leaving before midnight. I'm going to get my gear loaded, contact my housekeeping staff in Italy, and make sure my pilot has the plane readied for several potential flights back and forth to Israel. Call me and let me know who wants to depart with us, and I will be back at 10:00 P.M. to pick all of you up. Remember, the Lord wins this war for Israel according to Ezekiel, so the odds are that you should be able to return home when it's all over. Don't pack the kitchen sink, only the essentials."

Lisa asked, "What if Tovia and his family want to go with us on the first flight? Can we pick them up in Haifa?"

"I hope so" said Nathan. "That's a question for my pilot. He will have to schedule everything through flight control. I need to know as soon as you know about Tovia."

"Certainly," Lisa replied, "I understand. I will call him and my mother right away! Oh, Nathan," she said, looking at him fondly, "thank you so much for being here for us all; you are a life saver!"

Hugging the girls' goodbye, Severs headed home to make preparations for their midnight departure.

Several hours had passed from the time Nathan left Lisa's home, when an urgent call came in.

"Tovia and his family are coming Nathan," Lisa's breathless voice came through. "Can you please inform your pilot to make arrangements with air traffic control to pick them up in Haifa?"

"Arrangements to pick up your brother and his family have already been made," Nathan informed her. "I expected he would want to leave with you, so I had my pilot schedule a flight in advance. Setting this up on such short notice was no easy undertaking, so, please make sure they arrive at the Haifa airport no later than 1:15 A.M."

"Absolutely!" Lisa confirmed. "The family and the two Jesus Jews will arrive on time to leave with you and Jami."

"Me and Jami? And what's this about Jesus Jews?" Nathan balked.

Lisa responded, "I'm not going with you, at least not on the first flight. I can't convince my father and mother or the rest of my family to leave Israel. They think that the US and EU can smooth things over with Russia, and they are accusing me of panicking prematurely. I need another day or two to persuade them. Please take Jami to safety and then come back for me in a few days when I have the other members of my family prepared."

"Yeah?" Nathan quipped. "Well, that's not going to happen, girl!"

"What do you mean?" Lisa argued.

"It's very admirable of you to want to help the family," Nathan replied. "But, you don't have the luxury of a few days. The Russian confederacy has declared war with Israel, and has already given Prime Minister Kaufman a twenty-four-hour ultimatum to surrender unconditionally, or else! We leave now, or we won't leave at all! You'll have to convince the stragglers by phone from Rome, providing subsequent flights are even possible."

A silent interlude passed as Lisa digested the news.

"Okay," Nathan proceeded, "what about these Jesus Jews? What's up with that?"

Grappling with her emotions, Lisa reluctantly explained, "The two gentlemen in the bomb shelter that led my brother and his family to Jesus visited him at his house today. Tovia told them the family was leaving, as they had advised." Lisa took a stuttering breath. "When he told them about your plane, they asked if there might be room for them."

Nathan rolled his eyes. "And…?"

Lisa continued, "My brother called me and I told him I thought there would be enough room on the plane, since I knew Mother and Daddy and the others weren't ready to come." There was a heady pause." I hope I didn't overstep my boundaries, but I believed you would want to help a couple of the Lord's servants."

Nathan cleared his throat, and gave a thoughtful reply. "First let me tell you I'm sorry your parents and siblings are reluctant to leave. If there is any way to return for them down the road, I will personally come back for them all. Second, we should be able to squeeze these two Messianics into the plane, but it's going to be tight. It is probably not a coincidence that they called on Tovia today. Perhaps, they are meant to leave with us. Last, we are still on schedule to pick you and Jami up at 10:00 sharp tonight, so please be ready."

He could hear Lisa's tearful sigh of relief. "Can you contact Tovia and tell him to have everyone ready at the Haifa airport on time?" Nathan directed. "Also, please give me his phone number in case I need to make direct contact with him."

●●●●●

Fleeing for Safety

It was 2:00 A.M. and things were going according to plans. All the passengers and cargo were loaded on board, including the two Jesus Jews, and the plane was ready to take off from Haifa airport. Patiently waiting for the airport tower to grant permission for their departure, they heard the Haifa air raid sirens begin to sound. In a matter of moments, they heard a loud explosion that rocked the plane violently on the runway. Looking through the jet windows they saw a flashing light flaring close by the airport.

"Holy smoke! I think that was a missile explosion!" shouted the pilot. "We need to fly out of here immediately. We can't wait for the traffic tower's permission; we have to take our chances and depart!"

Accustomed to making executive spot decisions, Severs hollered, "Go for it! I don't see any planes arriving or departing. The runway is ours for the taking!"

They safely lifted off and flew into the dangerous skies. The jet was scarcely off the tarmac, when they witnessed several more fiery explosions through the plane's windows. Plumes of smoke were emanating into the charred night skies above Haifa.

Although the two Jesus Jews remained calm, everyone else in the cockpit and cabin were horrified. Amber and Bella began to weep profusely for their hometown family and friends below.

Simeon Abrams, the younger of the two Jesus Jews, startled everyone when he called out, "Don't look down at the destruction; look up for Israel's deliverance. The Lord will make an abrupt end of this battle!"

As they all turned their attention toward the two saintly passengers, Gershom Gold, Simeon's elder clarified, "Simeon speaks correctly. The Lord has prepared a snare for Israel's enemies. Ezekiel declares that the enemies will descend upon Israel from the uttermost parts of the north like a storm, covering the land like a cloud. This process has now begun."

Simeon spoke in turn and declared, "Ages ago the Lord prophesied through Ezekiel in His jealousy and wrath, declaring that when Gog comes against the land of Israel, His fury will show upon His face. This night under the camouflage of darkness, the hordes of Gog will begin their ascent upon the mountains of Israel. A great company will come with their bucklers and shields and they will fill the land with their innumerable troops and spectacular arsenals."

Gershom interjected, "And when they all have arrived and set their arsenals in place, there will be a great earthquake that will shake the entire Holy Land. It will be felt well into the expanded territories Israel recently annexed after their war with the Arabs. Mountain tops will topple and hordes of enemy soldiers will be cast down to their deaths in steep crevices and ravines. The valleys will be filled with the slain hordes of Gog. The magnitude of the event will be an astonishment to all those dwelling upon the face of the earth."

Simeon looked soberly at his companion, "Those that survive will draw their weapons upon each other from fear and panic. They won't know where to launch their missiles. Their rockets will backfire, killing many of their own."

As the two of them took turns speaking, their proclamations became increasingly passionate, the volume of their voices increasing with each declaration. It was as if they were speaking from pulpits in the center of a village announcing the oracles decreed by a powerful king.

Gershom spoke again, raising his right hand for emphasis, "And then the Lord will enter into final judgment with pestilence and bloodshed. He will rain down on Gog and his troops, and on the many peoples who are with him, flooding rain, great hailstones, fire, and brimstone. The carnage will be so widespread that even the birds of the air and the beasts of the earth will have their fill. And the Lord will be magnified in His victory before the watchful eyes of the nations."

Simeon concluded, his tone ominous, "The destruction will extend even to the coastal areas and beyond, as the Lord sends fire from heaven into the enemy's homelands, so that even those who thought they were secure will experience the judgment. The advanced weapons that they have fashioned against Israel will be knocked out of their hands, and Israel will use them as sources of fuel and energy."

Gershom bowed his head, exhausted from the oration, and implored, "Let us pray that the Lord will be merciful to Israel in all of this, and let us invoke the peace of Jerusalem."

•••••

Throughout the duration of the flight to Rome, Simeon and Gershom were peppered with questions from Nathan, Lisa, Jami, Tovia, and Amber. Meanwhile, Tovia's children could hardly keep their eyes open, dozing in an out of slumber. Although eight-year-old *Bella* tried to keep up with the adult conversation, both she and her three-year-old curly haired brother Jaxon, succumbed to the need for sleep.

Tovia's wife, beautiful and inquisitive Amber, began the first round of questioning. Amber was a devoted reader of religious writings, and possessed a better than basic understanding of the New Testament. She asked, "What did you both do before you became members of the 144,000 witnesses of the book of Revelation?"

Simeon, at age twenty-nine, closely resembled the American movie star Ryan Gosling. In fact, young Jami asked him, somewhat flirtatiously, if he was any relation to the actor. Shaking his head, Simeon answered, "I was a tour guide in Israel for Christian pilgrims touring the Holy Land. I started giving tours when I was twenty-two years old. I was required to have expertise in both the Old and New Testaments of the Bible for this job. Although I wasn't a believer in Christ at the time, my photographic memory enabled me to nearly memorize the entire New Testament."

Impressed by Simeon's resume, everyone turned toward forty-eight-year-old, short and pudgy Gershom, who announced that he was a Hebrew scholar that had been a professor at Hebrew University of Jerusalem for the past twenty-years. What Gershom, with his round and jovial face, lacked in appearance, he made up for with his deep, eloquent voice. "Unlike Simeon," he said, "I spent most of my time reading, memorizing, and teaching the Tanakh, the Old Testament of the Bible."

Tovia asked, "When you met us in the Haifa bomb shelter you mentioned that most of you travel in pairs. Why is that?"

"We follow the biblical model of discipling," Simeon explained. Examples are given in Matthew 21:1, Mark 14:9 and elsewhere evidencing that Jesus often sent out his disciples in pairs. Moreover, we have come to recognize that the pairs among us have complimentary skill sets that work well in tandem. Take Gershom and myself, for example. Understanding he may lack in the New Testament, I compensate for, and vice versa with the Old Testament, which is his area of expertise."

Amber had her Bible open to Revelation chapter 14, where she read aloud: *The hundred and forty-four-thousand who were redeemed from the earth. These are the ones who were not defiled with women, for they are virgins."*

Jami blushed, and her mother winked at her. Looking up from the Bible, Amber inquired, "Does this mean that neither of you have been married before, or does it mean that you won't get married from this point forward?"

Young Jami, who was finding it hard to keep her eyes off handsome Simeon, found this question of particular interest, and she leaned in to hear Simeon's response.

Since this question was based on the New Testament, Simeon responded, "That's an excellent question and being an eligible bachelor, one of particular interest to me. Certainly, on the surface it suggests that we are all virgins and in that condition, we can devote 100% of our attention toward serving the Lord. I have looked closely at the original Greek language of the biblical text and I have compared it to the teachings of Paul about married life in 1 Corinthians 7. In some ways, we members of the 144,000 wear the similar shoes of the apostle Paul. Before his Damascus Road experience, which was when he received his calling to serve the Lord, he had unknowingly been prepared for his apostolic ministry beforehand. Paul was an expert on the interpretation of the Law of Moses, which equipped him for his ministry. The 144,000 have also unsuspectingly been prepared in advance for our important call of duty in the end times. In 1 Corinthians 7:6-9, Paul makes an interesting comment after having laid down the groundwork for a successful marriage. He says, *'But I say this as a concession, not as a commandment. For I wish that all men were even as I myself. But each one has his own gift from God, one in this manner and another in that. But I say to the unmarried and to the widows: It is good for them if they remain even as I am; but if they cannot exercise self-control, let them marry. For it is better to marry than to burn with passion.'* I understand that to mean that Paul was unmarried and preferred to carry out his ministry in that capacity."

"What are you saying, that you are never getting married?" Jami blurted out. Then, having embarrassed herself, she sunk back into her seat.

Simeon smiled and wisely dodging her question, he went on: "Amber, you only read part of Revelation 14:4, about the *defiled by woman* and us being *virgins*, would you kindly read the rest of the verse?"

Revisiting the verse, Amber read, *"These are the ones who follow the Lamb wherever He goes. These were redeemed from among men, being firstfruits to God and to the Lamb."*

Now, let me explain the problems I have with simply saying we are virgins. First, the verse implies that women are defiling and that's why we remain as virgins. It's as if we don't want to become contaminated by a woman. That's utter nonsense! God didn't create Eve to defile Adam. In fact, a good woman can serve a vital role in a man's ministry. In my estimation, the apostle Paul didn't remain single out of a fear that he would become corrupted by a woman. He calculated that he could better devote his undivided attention to his calling in an unmarried capacity. He traveled extensively, was often beaten severely, and he spent many of his days impoverished and imprisoned. He recognized that these are not suitable conditions to sustain a healthy and vibrant marriage. This realization alone caused me to look deeper into the true meaning of this verse."

Pausing momentarily, he asked, "Does that make sense so far?"

Jami responded giddishly, "Yes, especially the part about *a good woman can serve a vital role in a man's ministry.*"

Chuckling for a moment, Simeon continued: "I had Amber read the rest of the verse because it emphasizing that we are the ones who follow the *'Lamb wherever He goes.'* This is in stark contrast to, we are the ones who follow the Harlot, wherever she goes. This may be difficult to explain until you learn about the coming global religion, which is represented in Revelation 17 and elsewhere as a harlot. It appears that these verses may teach that the 144,000 witnesses remain chaste solely to the Lord, and are not stained, soiled, or defiled by the coming false world religion represented by the Harlot. One of the distinguishing characteristics of our 144,000 witnesses will definitely be that we will not be defiled by the harlot religion. Or another way of explaining it would be that we are considered virgins because we won't partake of the pagan idolatries that come out of the harlot global religion."

"Oh. I think I understand," Amber muttered, still obviously mystified.

"Wow, that's pretty deep," acknowledged Jami, who was now infatuated with both Simeon's good looks, and obvious intellect. Jami, the Miss Teen Beauty Queen of her old American school, had no idea what Simeon meant, but realized this handsome guy was the full package.

Gershom, sensing Jami's puppy love adoration of his partner, smiled and said, "Amber's question was deep, and deep questions require deep answers." Gershom continued, "Whatever the interpretation will prove to be, it is doubtful that marriage is in the cards for handsome young Simeon. He will be preoccupied serving the Lord."

Tovia took his turn and asked, "How did you both recognize your calling as members of the 144,000 witnesses?"

Gershom decided to answer this question. "What we have been able to ascertain through our communications with the others is that on the day the rapture took place each of us had either a celestial dream or vision. I had a dream, but Simeon had a similar vision. This seems to be universal across the boards. The older among us dreamed dreams, but the younger saw visions."[27]

"What did you dream?" Amber asked.

Gershom elaborated: "First let me say that it appears we all shared miraculously in the same experience. We saw four angels standing at the four corners of the earth. A peaceful calm permeated throughout the entire earth. No wind blew upon the earth, sea, or on any tree. Then we saw another angel ascending from the east, holding a seal in his hand that had been given to him by God. This fifth angel said loudly to the other four angels, *Do not harm the earth, the sea, or the trees till we have sealed the servants of our God on their foreheads.* Then we heard the number One-hundred-and-forty-four-thousand shouted out, after which the names of the twelve Israelite tribes were called out in Hebrew."

"Did it happen that identical way in your vision Simeon?" Jami asked.

"Yes, but there was more," Simeon clarified. "After these things, all 144,000 of us were standing with Christ on Mount Zion. He was clearly recognized by all of us as the Messiah. At that time, we received a seal upon our foreheads, and were given our tribal identities. I found out that my ancestors were from the tribe of Judah, and Gershom discovered that he descended from the tribe of Levi. Then there was a thunderous sound and suddenly we heard harps playing and voices singing. They sang a new song that was specifically sung for us."

Amber asked, "How did you know it was a new song?"

Simeon revealed, "The lyrics were very specific to us. For instance, one stanza announced that we were the undefiled that follow the Lamb of God wherever He goes. Then the chorus declared that we were redeemed as first-fruits to God and to the Lamb. And that there was no deceitfulness coming out from our mouths, or faults counted against us before the throne of God."

Lisa commented, "Wow! That sounds more like a proclamation than a song."

Gershom agreed. "You could say it was both," he confirmed.

Nathan chimed in, "Speaking as a newbie Christian, it is indeed a blessing to learn more from you about Christ, heavenly worship, the importance of our faith, and the coming Bible prophecies. With that said, I am wondering: Does your service to God make you both invincible to the coming dangers predicted in the Bible? And, if you are protected from harm because of your calling, then why did you flee Israel at this time?"

Gershom looked to Simeon and suggested, "Why don't you answer the first question, and I will tackle the second one."

"Certainly," responded Simeon. "First, let me say the honor is ours to be among all of you. The apostle Peter said in his first epistle that a believer's faith is more precious than gold that perishes. Peter added, 'Jesus Christ, whom having not seen you love. Though now you do not see *Him*, yet believing, you rejoice with joy inexpressible and full of glory, receiving the end of your faith—the salvation of *your* souls.'[28] The fact that you all have become born again believers at a time when true Christianity is being severely mocked bodes extremely well for you. To answer your first question, yes, although I prefer the word *protected* over *invincible*. It does appear that the Lord's protection was bestowed upon us during the Mt. Zion experience."

Gershom answered the next question saying, "We are not traveling with you to flee danger in Israel, but to spread the gospel abroad. This is our calling. Simeon and I are clear that we are called to witness to all nations, tribes, peoples, and tongues."[29]

With authority and great command of the scriptures, Gershom Gold and Simeon Abrams answered dozens of questions that night. By the time Nathan's jet landed in Rome, the passengers could comfortably claim that they had completed courses in Christianity and Bible Prophecy 101.

26

The Antichrist and the Coming Global Religion

Upon landing safely in Rome, the group established their temporary headquarters in Nathan Severs' luxurious residence near the center of the city. His lavishly decorated, 9500 square foot palatial home made them feel more like tourists than refugees. The mansion came complete with a four-member housekeeping and cooking staff that promptly attended to all the guests' needs.

In short order, events in the Middle East began to resemble the prophetic descriptions given in Ezekiel 38. The Russian invaders were positioned to pounce upon Israel at any moment just as Gershom and Simeon had warned. Everyone in Nathan's house was nestled in and watching news reports with bated breath. They eagerly expected the Lord to deliver Israel in the manner foretold.

Meanwhile, Lisa repeatedly attempted to contact her family in Israel. Overloaded phone lines kept her from establishing communication. Even though she believed that Israel would survive, she feared for her family, and wanted them to flee somewhere safe.

Seated on Nathan's expansive veranda, which overlooked picturesque Vatican City, Simeon Abrams asked, "Nathan, what prompted you to purchase this spacious home with this priceless view? This property would be perfect for a bed and breakfast business. Is that something you were considering at the time of purchase?"

Nathan responded, "No, not necessarily. But you are correct about this home's investment potential. The primary reason for purchasing this property is because I made a commitment to Christ when I recently received Him as my Lord and Savior that I would become an Oskar Schindler type person in the "Tribulational Period." I believe Rome might serve as strategic escape locations for persecuted Christians and Jews. I hope to someday use this residence as part of an underground network to that end."

Seated alongside them was Tovia, who asked, "What do you mean by persecuted Jews?"

Nathan looked at the Messianics. "I'm no prophecy expert, but I read in Zechariah 13:8, the Antichrist is going to attempt the final genocide of the Jews. Some Gentiles are going to stand up for them in the last days, like Oskar Shindler did during the Nazi era. In Matthew's twenty-fifth chapter, Jesus called them righteous Gentiles and compared them to obedient sheep rather than indignant goats."

Tovia looked toward Simeon and asked, "Do you know anything about this?"

"Yes," Simeon replied. "The prophet Zechariah declared that two-thirds of the Jewish population will be killed in the land of Israel as part of this Antichrist campaign."

Concerned for his unsaved Israeli relatives, Tovia asked, "So what happens to the other one-third that survives? Do they hide out at the Vatican and elsewhere in Rome?"

Nathan responded, "I am uncertain about that. Frankly, I don't know where the surviving Jews will end up, but I do believe that Rome plays a significant role in the end times. I think Scripture is quite clear about that. That's why I decided to prepare a safe house near the Vatican."

Turning to Simeon, Tovia inquired, "Do you know the final destination of this Jewish remnant, according to Bible prophecy?"

"You are right about Rome figuring in Bible Prophecy," the Messianic answered, "but Rome is not the final destination of the faithful Jewish remnant. They end up in ancient Edom according to Isaiah 63 and elsewhere. Edom was located in modern-day Southern Jordan. Just recently, as a result of the IDF victory in the predicted Arab-Israeli war of Psalm 83, Israel annexed this territory as part of its bid for a greater Israel. Presently Edom exists as part of the Jewish state."

Nathan scratched his head and commented, "The end times video Lisa, Jami, and I watched a few days ago made this similar prediction. My close friend Robert Rasmussen was a prophecy expert and he informed me that Rome was a key city in the end times, I bought this property before moving to Israel. Perhaps I purchased this home under misguided assumptions."

Simeon was thoughtful. "Nathan, your house is presently serving a vital function for Jewish refugees," he said. "In fact, apart from you, your pilot, and house staff, the rest of us here are all presently persecuted Jews taking refuge as we await the final fulfillment of Ezekiel 38."

Nathan marveled. "Simeon, you make a good point, but if I am not mistaken, this group isn't the final remnant of Jews that Zechariah predicted would be persecuted by the Antichrist."

Simeon cautioned, "Not yet, anyway."

Simeon's comment caused Tovia to ask, "Are you suggesting that Lisa, Jami, Amber, Isabella, Jaxon, and I will someday be persecuted by the Antichrist?"

Looking Tovia squarely in the eyes, Simeon sympathetically asked, "Do you want my honest answer?"

Taken aback, Tovia gulped. "I…I don't know, now. Then, pondering the staggering possibility, he sighed, "For the sake of my loved ones; please give me the truth."

Simeon replied, "I am not trying to be evasive, but, truthfully, it depends."

"Depends on what?" Tovia urged.

"It depends on your family's ability to survive the dangerous prophecies that come between now and then," Simeon said.

Tovia's face grew pale. "Wh-what should we do in case we face this persecution?" he asked.

"Be informed and obedient," Simeon instructed. "Learn all that you can about this period before it comes. And also, follow Christ's instructions in Matthew 24:15-20 to depart from Israel before the genocidal campaign commences at the midpoint of the Tribulation Period. In these Matthew verses Jesus warned that the Antichrist would enter the third Jewish Temple and fulfill the *'abomination of desolation,'* which was spoken of by Daniel the prophet. This pivotal prophecy is when the Antichrist initiates his killing campaign that Zechariah predicted. Gershom and I will familiarize all of you with the pertinent prophetic scriptures before you head back home."

Humbled by Simeon's comments, Nathan confessed, "Now more than ever, I am committed to becoming an end times Oskar Schindler."

Simeon reached out and patted the host's knee. "Nathan, this house can be used for surveillance of future Vatican events, and to safely house persecuted saints, be they Christians or Jews. So, don't fret over the soundness of your investment."

"Please elaborate about the 'persecutions'," Nathan requested.

Simeon sat back and studied Nathan's pensive face. "The Bible speaks about a perilous time called the *Patience of the Saints,*" he explained. "This period is characterized by Christian martyrdom, which can include both Jewish and Gentile believers. A related verse in Revelation 14 actually declares; *Blessed are the dead who die in the Lord from now on.* This alludes to the fact that people who become believers after the Rapture will be blessed with their eternal salvation, but for many of them it will come at the cost of a martyr's price. They will need to exhibit patience in their faith until Jesus returns in His Second Coming. After which, Christ will establish His Messianic Kingdom."

Nathan beseeched, "Please tell me how my Rome residence could prove useful at such a time."

Simeon expounded, "The final Jewish genocidal attempt mostly occurs in the last half of the Tribulation period, otherwise known as the Great Tribulation. This final three-and-one-half-year time span will be the worst period of Jewish persecution in history. It will not only be characterized by Jewish persecution, but also many Gentiles will be executed for refusing to take the Mark of the Beast in their right hand or forehead. However, several prophecies occur before the Antichrist attempts to extirpate the Jews and execute those refusing his mark."

Nathan inquired, "In Rome? Does this martyrdom occur nearby?"

Simeon clarified, "No, this round of martyrdom in the Great Tribulation is worldwide, but there is a prior group of last days martyred saints. These persecuted saints appear to be distinct from those I just mentioned, and their executions appear to be associated with a global religion headquartered in Rome. Revelation 17:6 says, *'I saw the woman, drunk with the blood of the saints and with the blood of the martyrs of Jesus.'* Many believe that this woman represents the harlot world religion and, in my estimation, you can see her headquarters at the Vatican from your veranda."

This jaw-dropping statement caused Tovia to ask, "Are you suggesting that my family has to survive the coming pogroms[30] of some harlot religion in addition to the extermination attempts of the Antichrist?"

"I expect that you and your family need to be primarily concerned with the genocidal campaign of the Antichrist. The leadership of Israel will soon participate in a seven-year covenant with the Antichrist that affords Jews residing in Israel temporary safety, a form of pseudo peace. But at the midpoint of the seven years, the Antichrist will go into the Jewish Temple and exalt himself above all gods, then promptly commence his campaign of extermination!"

Nathan pushed his glasses, which had dropped down on his nose, back in place, then referred to his notes: "Simeon, you said that the Harlot is drunk with the blood of the saints and the martyrs of Jesus, but you just suggested that you think Tovia and his family will escape this first blood bath. Why do you believe this?"

"This gets tricky," Simeon admitted. "But Gershom and I believe Revelation 17:6 identifies four primary things: the blood, the woman drunk with the blood, the martyred saints, and the martyrs of Jesus."

Nathan's glasses began to slip back down his nose as he attempted to take more copious notes. "I see," he said. "Don't stop, please interpret the meaning of these four things."

"The woman is clearly the Harlot and I believe she represents the false global religion which will be headquartered in Rome. The latest Catholic dogma, which was executed through papal infallibility, elevated Mary as Co-Redemptrix. The global threat to peace posed by the Russian coalition provoked Pope Romano to exercise papal authority in this matter. The world clamors for peace and the Pope believes that the Blessed Mary will bring in this peace."

"How so?" asked Nathan.

Simeon explained, "With the help of supernatural signs and lying wonders this woman will attempt to unite all religions under the canopy of the Roman Catholic Church. She will also usher in the worship and adoration of Jesus in the Catholic communion wafer."

Nathan was astonished, breaking his pencil lead as he struck his notepad. Turning to Tovia, he gasped, "Do you realize what this implies?"

"I have no idea," Tovia answered.

Pointing to the Vatican, Nathan said, "I watched the Marian apparition that occurred right over yonder from a live feed on TV. I was in an American restaurant, and everyone there was absolutely stupefied. I believe this supernatural event was a game-changer, because it has convinced multitudes in the world that the Roman Catholic Church is really the only true church established by Jesus Christ for all the people. While we watched, millions of Christians disappeared in the rapture without warning. These paranormal episodes have left the whole world in a quandary, susceptible to religious deception.

Simeon agreed, "That's what I sincerely believe is happening. Consider the following; Islam is crumbling and will be essentially decapitated after the Lord defeats the Russian coalition. Christianity, apart from people like us, is apostate because the true believers have been raptured. Once the Jews witness their Jehovah defeat the Russian coalition they will reinstate Judaism and construct the third temple. Most Eastern and New Age religions like Hinduism already embrace female goddesses, so the Catholic Queen of Heaven already fits right into their religious framework. I could go on but you get my drift."

Tovia interjected, "Not really. I can understand how Jews will embrace Judaism nationally after Ezekiel 38 concludes, but why will the others jump on the Marian bandwagon?"

Looking at Simeon, Nathan said, "Allow me?"

Simeon nodded.

Nathan went on: "Tovia, mankind has never been more primed in all of its history to be influenced by the supernatural. Everything that is happening defies scientific logic. Add everything up: first there was the unexplained disappearance of millions. Second a miraculous sighting of Mary was witnessed worldwide at the same time. Third was the improbable victory of tiny Israel over the Arabs. And last but not least, soon the Russian coalition will be destroyed by an earthquake, and fire and brimstone cast down from heaven. When you factor all the above you have a formula for enchantment, for an unearthly figure to mysteriously appear out of nowhere and say, "Look to me. I will usher in true peace, prosperity and a benevolent global transformation. Consecrate your lives to your queen who can comfort and prosper you." And why will they follow her? Because she will perform great signs and wonders and have all the right answers."

With that explanation, Simeon nodded approvingly, and Tovia folded his hands and bowed his head in astonishment.

Pushing his glasses back in place, Nathan reviewed his notes and said, "Simeon, how do you interpret the other three things in the Revelation passage?

Simeon pondered this and cleared his throat. "Appreciating the aspect of the *blood* is important in that, it was the sacrificial blood of Christ shed upon the cross that saves sinners. But in Revelation 17:6 we see that the woman is drunk with the blood of two groups of saved souls. This is an utter perversion of the true intent of the blood. When Christians take communion they commonly consume a bread wafer and drink a red liquid resembling the blood of Christ, like wine or grape juice. Luke 22:17-20 teaches that the elements of the Passover, the bread and the wine, represented the body and blood of Christ in the crucifixion. When Christians partake of the wafer and the liquid they are to do so in remembrance of Christ's sacrifice for sin. However, in the Catholic Mass the communion wafer and red liquid supposedly become miraculously transformed into the literal body, blood, soul and divinity of Christ. This is commonly referred to as the Eucharist. I believe this Eucharistic Christ becomes the centerpiece of the global religion."

Nathan spoke up, "Please, indulge me. Let me see if I comprehend the gist of what you are suggesting. My notes say that you believe that the Eucharistic Christ of Roman Catholicism could become the theological centerpiece of the harlot world religion. Therefore, the Catholic teachings will dictate that the sacrificial blood of Jesus needs a continuous ceremonial outpouring through the sacrament of the Eucharist of Christ's blood. This implies that the blood of Christ shed upon the cross two-thousand years ago was insufficient. Because if it was sufficient it would not be necessary for it to be poured out time and time again for the sake of one's salvation. Therefore, the salvation of one's soul is only as secure as his or her last partaking of the Eucharist. Does that sound right?"

Simeon nodded in agreement.

Nathan continued, "This implies that the balance of power over the individual soul shifts to whoever controls the authority over the Eucharist. In essence, the Harlot can say, if you want redemption from Hell you must become a member of my Son's True Church and partake of the Holy Eucharist."

Simeon confirmed, "I think you westerners say, 'By Jove,' I think he's got it, or something of the sort. Nathan, one of the problems with elevating the status of Mary to Co-Redemptrix is that she becomes Christ's co-equal in the eyes of the faithful. As such, this empowers her to sway the faithful in the direction she wishes. In other words, whatever the Co-Redemptrix says goes, even if it contradicts the Bible. Concerning the other two things, which were the *blood of the saints*, and the *martyrs of Jesus*, I believe this is another reason to suspect that the present Catholicism of these last days represents the harlot world religion."

"How so?" Asked Nathan.

Simeon added, "The Catholic Church killed many Christians during the inquisitions dating back as far as the 12th century. Some Protestant estimates range from 50 million to 150 million. The estimates are so vague because the numbers are hard to trace and Roman Catholics typically give much smaller numbers. Many of those identified and killed as heretics were true believers. Thus, from a biblical perspective these were true *saints* and their *blood* was shed by the Catholics. Shockingly, in far too many cases they were martyred because of their refusal to embrace the sacrament of the Eucharist. This explanation would account for why the woman of Revelation 17:6, i.e. historical papal Rome, is guilty of being drunk with the *blood of the saints*. However, the *martyrs of Jesus* that follows in that same verse probably represents a different generation of Christians. I suspect these *martyrs* embody the true believers of today! They are those that accept Christ as their Savior after the rapture. The historical precedent for their martyrdom probably finds connection with the past Catholic inquisition period of persecution. If they rebel from the present teachings of the Catholic Church, especially at this critically chaotic point in time, they run the risk of likewise being killed. Thus, with all that said, the prophecy to be on the lookout for next, besides Ezekiel 38, is regarding the coming false religion, which is headquartered in Rome. And this is why, my beloved friend Nathan, your residence in Rome may prove to be an important investment."

Clearly overwhelmed by Simeon's comments, Tovia stood up, stretched and said, "I need a smoke after all that."

Grinning, Nathan commented, "I didn't know you smoked cigarettes."

Tovia soberly replied, "I don't smoke nor drink, but after learning that you and I are apparently identified in Bible prophecy as the *martyrs of Jesus*, I need something to settle my nerves."

After about five minutes of deep contemplation ensued, Nathan broke the silence with a personal experience. "Razz, which is the nickname given to my friend Robert Rasmussen, was speaking about this harlot religion as 'Mystery Babylon' just before he was raptured. Razz and I were watching the Mary apparition – or as he would say the 'Queen of Heaven' apparition - taking place above the Vatican at the time of his departure. Razz was connecting Rome with Mystery Babylon and this harlot system at the time. His disappearance, the apparition, and the Vatican left such an indelible impression on me that day. I guess this is the other reason, in addition to wanting to be like Oskar Schindler in the end times, that I felt drawn to Rome as an important location in the end times."

Simeon explained, "Your friend Razz was correct. There appear to be prophecies concerning this divine demonic feminine that allures a majority of mankind into the global religion. Revelation 17 identifies her as a harlot, but additional possible prophetic references may allude to her as the "Queen of Heaven." But it is Revelation 17:9 and 18 that tips us off that the city of Rome appears to be the central location of her earthly headquarters."

Nathan reflected. "Right," he said. "That adds credence to why the apparition happened at the Vatican on the day of the rapture."

Simeon nodded in agreement.

Dumbfounded Tovia commented, "I'm confused. Does this mean I have a lot of time after the Ezekiel war to prepare for the great tribulation and also witness to my Jewish parents and siblings in Israel, providing they survive the coming invasion?"

Simeon shook his head. "No, there will probably not be *a lot* of time to accomplish this."

"Then, how much time is there until the Antichrist shows up?" Tovia asked.

"The Antichrist is already here," Simeon announced, to the shock of his listeners. "He hasn't been entirely revealed yet, and he won't dominate until the mid-point of the seven-year tribulation period. But, as prophesied, he comes out of the revived Roman Empire, which corresponds with the European Union. Present indications suggest that it could be Hans Vandenberg, the current EU President, because Revelation 6 informs that he arrives on the world scene promptly after the rapture of the Church, as the first horseman of the apocalypse. Developing ties between the new EU President and Pope Romano also indicate that Vandenberg may be the Antichrist because Revelation 17:3 informs that the Harlot uses the Antichrist's political platform as her religious pedestal.

"According to the apostle Paul, in Second Thessalonians, he went on, "the Antichrist rises to power according to the workings of Satan, with all power, signs, and lying wonders. We have not yet witnessed his great signs, but we will in the coming years. According to Daniel 9 and Isaiah 28, he will be recognized when he confirms a covenant between Israel and Death, which Isaiah says is an agreement with Sheol. This means it is a deceptive covenant that originates from the depths of Hell! When we see EU President Vandenberg confirm this covenant with Israel, then we will know beyond a shadow of doubt that he is the Antichrist. We must watch for the confirmation of the false covenant because it could precede the signs and lying wonders as the first clue to the identity of the Antichrist."

Giving Nathan a deer-in-the-headlights look, Tovia scratched his head in bewilderment.

"Nathan, did you know all this?" he gasped.

"No," Nathan admitted. "Now *I* need a smoke! I'm verging on information overload. Which reminds me: I need to record these critical discussions from now on. I'm kicking myself for not recording all along."

Simeon agreed. "Do you have a recorder handy?" he asked.

"Absolutely," Nathan confirmed, rising from his chair. "I have a pocket size digital recorder. I'll go get it."

Returning moments later with his recorder, Nathan set it, along with a mysteriously sealed box, on the table between them.

Bewildered by the heading on Nathan's glass faced box, which read, *"The Post Rapture Survival Kit,"* Simeon inquired, "Where did you get this?"

"It looked important so I grabbed it off the fireplace mantle of my best friend Razz's house," Nathan replied. "I totally forgot that I had it shipped here along with a few other personal items that he left behind. The movers had placed it next to my recorder, so I grabbed it for you guys to see."

"We need to break open the opaque glass now so that we can see what's inside it," exclaimed Tovia!

"Absolutely!" Simeon agreed.

Gesturing his hand to pause, "Wait, let's record the remainder of this conversation while it's still fresh on our minds; then we'll gather everyone together afterward to join us to break open the glass," requested Nathan.

*"Hmm…*Alright," Tovia reluctantly agreed.

Turning on his recorder Nathan assessed, "If I understand you, Simeon, you are suggesting that a global religion based out of the Vatican emerges, followed by the Antichrist's rise to power."

"That's partially correct," Simeon said, "but there will be some overlap period. The simple way to organize end time is as follows: two distinctly different global religions are forthcoming. The first is headed by a queen who will head the Catholic Church; she will have an outward Christian veneer and encourage the worship of the Eucharistic Christ. Although she masquerades as Mary, in reality she is nothing more than a demonic imposter. The second, and last, is the compulsory worship of the Antichrist. The last false religion standing is that of the Antichrist. He will claim to be God and usher in a New Age type of religion – promising his adherents that they too can evolve to some form of a godhood consciousness. Both religious systems are rooted in satanic deception, which means that mankind experiences a double religious jeopardy after the rapture."

Assuming the role of an interviewer, Nathan formatted the discussion so that the information could someday be transmitted through radio, social networks and other media venues.

"What causes the schism between the Vatican-based religion and the geo-political goals of the Antichrist?" he asked.

Amused by Nathan's talk-show approach, Simeon smiled and replied, "The ultimate aim of the Antichrist is to achieve exclusive worldwide worship. This is why the two systems cannot coexist indefinitely. The Antichrist does not want to share the allegiance of humankind with any other religious system or entity. As his religious platform gains credibility, the popularity of the Harlot will become extremely problematic. This is because the harlot religious system will advocate that Jesus Christ mystically indwells the Eucharist. Although this is an unbiblical spiritual deception, it does indirectly identify Christ in a Messianic role. Any allusions to Jesus Christ as the Messiah will be strictly forbidden by the Antichrist. In fact, during the reign of both religious systems, many who come to a genuine faith in Jesus Christ, through our witness or otherwise, will be martyred."

Nathan requested, "Please, tell us more about the fate of the harlot religion."

Simeon elaborated, "After the harlot religious system has overstayed its usefulness, the Antichrist will have it removed from power by ten kings. After which, the worship of the

Antichrist will be imposed upon the preponderance of humanity. Revelation 13 teaches that no one will even be able to buy or sell unless they receive a mark that identifies their allegiance to the Antichrist."

Nathan inquired, "Is this the prophecy concerning the Mark of the Beast, and the infamous number 666?"

"Yes," Simeon answered.

Nathan apologized, "I am sorry to be so slow Simeon, but I need more clarification. Please continue speaking about the fate of the harlot system."

"The desolation of the Harlot is prophesied in Revelation 17:16," Simeon explained. "These ten kings will receive their authority from the Antichrist according to Revelation 17:12. Although these ten political leaders are probably alive presently, they are not yet positioned in their places. However, when they come into their respective powers, the prophecy predicts that they will grow to hate the Harlot. From the perspective of these kings, the Harlot's abundant wealth and worldwide religious and political power threatens their autocratic authority. This is probably why they eagerly comply with the Antichrist's wishes to eradicate her system."

As Nathan continued to interview Simeon, Tovia got a burst of energy and began note- taking as quickly as he could scribble.

"What then?" asked Nathan.

Simeon informed, "After the Queen of Heaven is dethroned from power, the Antichrist abruptly promotes his religious agenda to the apparent dismay of three of the ten kings. The Antichrist subdues these three adversaries leaving eight kings.

Nathan corrected, "You mean leaving seven kings remaining, don't you?"

Simeon clarified, "No, eight is the correct number, because the Antichrist becomes the eighth king. He will preside in addition to the seven left from the original ten, but he will become their superior. After the remaining seven experience the manner in which the Antichrist eliminates the other three kings, they will probably fear a similar fate as their comrades, if they do not comply with the Antichrist's final system. Remember that the Antichrist rises to power through supernatural means, which suggests the seven subservient kings are either enamored or intimidated by him."

Tovia motioned to Nathan to hit pause on the recorder, and Nathan obliged.

"All of this could take many years Simeon," Tovia reasoned. "Why do you believe time is so short?"

Turning on the digital device, again, Nathan motioned to Tovia to restate his question.

Tovia cleared his throat, and rephrased the matter: "Simeon, in light of what you describe, it seems like the establishment of these two religious systems could require decades or longer to organize. Why do you think these prophecies are fulfilled in a short time span?"

Simeon explained: "I know it seems that what I am suggesting should take decades to fulfill, but in Matthew 24:8, Jesus stated that end times events happen in rapid succession. He likened it to the birth pains of a woman. When a woman is about to give birth, her contractions become more frequent and intense. From this analogy, we presume this will be the case with end time events. Once they begin, they happen one upon another with increased frequency and intensity."

"I was wondering about those birth pains. I was under the impression that was mainly dealing with the rise of earthquakes in various places in the verse prior," Nathan commented. Opening his Bible to Matthew 24:7, he read "And there will be famines, pestilences, and earthquakes in various places."

Simeon replied, "Nathan, you could be right, but I think it's best to look at the birth pains analogy in the overall context of the second coming of Christ. In other words, as the time of His return decreases, the frequency of calamities and world judgments increases. I base this on the questions the disciples asked in Matthew 24:3. They asked Him, "Tell us, when will these things be? And what *will be* the sign of Your coming, and of the end of the age?"

Nathan inquired, "What about the order and timing of the other prophecies, like the building of the Jewish Temple, the two witnesses in Jerusalem, and Armageddon?"

Simeon expounded, "Very astute, Nathan. There will be many prophecies happening while these world religions are operational. Some will find fulfillment during the harlot religious period, while the others don't occur until the worship of the Antichrist takes place."

Simeon had barely finished his final sentence when Amber, who had been glued to the television for hours, frantically cried out, "Come quickly, Tovia! I think a massive earthquake has struck the Middle East!"

Quickly turning off his recorder, Nathan motioned the trio to hurry up and join the group inside who were watching the breaking news. Razz's mysterious box was again left behind.

The seismic rumblings lasted nearly five minutes and it was apparent that a massive amount of devastation had occurred in the Holy Land.

Gershom, who was watching the television with Amber, wiped his brow with a handkerchief. "That must have been the earthquake Ezekiel predicted against the Russian forces," he reasoned.

In a matter of a few minutes the entire household was watching the devastating images come across the television set. It was far too early to estimate the overall extent of the damage, but according to early indications, the death toll was expected to be in the tens of thousands.

Initial reports said the epicenter was north of Israel in Lebanon. The magnitude was registered above 12-plus, exceeding the Richter scale maximum measurement capability.

One seismologist suggested it would be a miracle if any structures remained standing in the most affected areas. Oddly enough though, the quake did not produce a Tsunami in the

Mediterranean Sea. One thing was certain: the earthquake was responsible for killing many Russian coalition troops. This became abundantly evident from helicopter images that displayed hordes of dead soldiers strewn all over the surrounding mountains and ravines. If the earthquake didn't abruptly end the Russian invasion of Israel, it most certainly postponed it until the death and carnage could be addressed.

Gershom announced, "The worst is not over for the coalition invaders. The other calamities we discussed on the flight over here will now occur. It won't be until the world witnesses every sort of bird in the air and beast from the field eating the flesh and drinking the blood of the invaders that the battle-zone will be safe to survey."

Tovia rubbed his arms nervously. "When will it be safe for us to return to Israel?" he asked.

Gershom explained, "Ezekiel 39 informs that manpower will be in great demand in Israel in order to help cleanse the land of the dead and mop-up the mess. I don't suspect it will be much longer until it is safe to return, perhaps a few weeks."

27

The Collapse of the Russian Coalition

"What you are witnessing on your TV screens is an unexplainable phenomenon; satellite zoom shots show multitudes of vultures hovering in the sky above the warzone, in tandem with a convergence of assorted carnivorous animals on the ground," reported meteorologist Jonathan Levinson of *Israel Network News* (INN).

"Simeon," Lisa asked, "could this be the fulfillment of Ezekiel's bird and beast predictions which you were explaining?"

Tuning up the television volume on the remote, Simeon nodded and put his index finger gently to his lips, requesting silence. "Let's hear the entire report to be certain," he said.

"Our correspondents in the field can only feed us limited information about what is transpiring on the ground," Levinson continued. "Contamination from the coalition's weapons of mass destruction, combined with treacherous weather conditions, is restricting their access into the warzone. We are relying heavily on IDF reports and satellite feeds to find out what is happening on the battlefield. We have Dr. Ori Weizman, a spokesperson from the Israel Zoological Society, in the studio with us. Dr. Weizman, welcome to INN."

"It's my pleasure to be with you, Jonathan," the dignified guest replied.

Levinson was quizzical. "The IDF reports that flocks of birds and hordes of animals are converging upon the fallen coalition troops. Supposedly there is such a multitude of creatures that clear satellite surveillance of the battleground is nearly impossible. Can you explain what is causing this strange phenomenon?"

Weizman shrugged. "I wish I could," he answered, "but there is no precedent for this bizarre behavior to be found anywhere. In the past, we have witnessed unexplainable deaths of large flocks of birds, as they fell randomly from the skies, and there have been occurrences of multitudes of fish floating dead upon the ocean's surface; but this episode, we have no history to compare."

Levinson shook his head. "Can you give us an educated guess as to what could be causing this peculiar spectacle?"

"Our best educated guess at the IMS is that the unnatural events occurring in the natural order of creation is provoking these creatures to behave abnormally."

"Could you elaborate on what you mean by that statement?" Levinson asked.

Dr. Weizman rubbed his chin. "The enormous earthquake and its powerful aftershocks have toppled mountaintops and created deep crevasses on the earth's surface. Simultaneous flooding rains, huge hailstones and lightning bursts have convulsed the localized order of things. This alone could impact the behavior of birds and beasts."

Levinson turned to the audience and, in uncharacteristic editorializing, offered, "These unexplainable weather patterns cause one to wonder if the Russian coalition is warring against Israel, or the God of Israel. Whichever is the case; all indicators suggest that Israel is miraculously winning the war." Then, looking at his guest again, he said, "Please continue with your hypothesis about the birds and animals."

Weizman cleared his throat. "Concurrent cataclysmic conditions are sweeping hordes of dead coalition soldiers off mountain slopes and into torrential wadis, creating stockpiles of carrion for the beasts of the earth and the fowls of the air. Chaos and opportunity have spurred into a feeding frenzy, as they have converged upon the fallen human prey. After saying this, he took a handkerchief from his pocket and mopped his brow. "Quite simply, we have never seen anything like this!" he croaked.

"It sounds like a replay of Alfred Hitchcock's horror film, called *"The Birds."* It appears as though Hashem has served up some old-fashioned fire and brimstone for Israel's enemies."

Scarcely grinning at Levinson's remark, Weizman added, "What we are finding highly unusual is that the vultures and animals are preying upon those upturned from the wadis rather than those remaining on the hilltops and mountainsides."

"Why do you suppose that is?" Levinson questioned.

Dr. Weizman speculated, "It is too soon to tell, because contamination, rain, and hailstorms have prevented IDF teams from deploying deep into the battlefield to make a full assessment. Early reports are that those remaining on the hillsides are contaminated from the coalition's WMD's, which in many cases, backfired against their own forces. If this is the case, somehow the creatures have detected this and avoided preying upon them. It makes no sense at all, but this is the only explanation that we have been able to put forth."

Jonathan Levinson's jaw dropped in astonishment. Then, as though a light had gone on in his head, he deduced, "This would imply that the rushing waters of the wadis are cleansing the contamination from the deceased, making them safe for the birds and animals to eat."

Nodding, Dr. Weizman replied, "What other answer could there be?"

Levinson concluded the interview by reporting that the Israelis had seemingly escaped the natural disasters that had struck the Russian hordes. He drew a comparison to the biblical accounts of the Hebrews miraculously escaping the plagues of Egypt.

Fittingly, he quoted Exodus 9:26 to end his report: *"Only in the land of Goshen, where the children of Israel were, there was no hail."*

"Holy smoke!" Nathan expressed after hearing the news report. "Or should I say holy waters! Did Ezekiel predict rushing waters would decontaminate the Russian invaders?"

Gershom piped up, "Yes and no. Yes, there would be dead soldiers for the birds and animals to devour, but no, he didn't specify how the deceased would become edible.

Handing her father's Bible to Gershom, Jami asked, "Could you read to me what Ezekiel said?"

Opening to Ezekiel 39, Gershom read verse 4:

> *"You shall fall upon the mountains of Israel, you and all your troops and the peoples who are with you; I will give you to birds of prey of every sort and to the beasts of the field to be devoured."*

Then he followed with a supporting scripture in verse 19,

> *"And as for you, son of man, thus says the Lord GOD, 'Speak to every sort of bird and to every beast of the field: "Assemble yourselves and come; Gather together from all sides to My sacrificial meal Which I am sacrificing for you, A great sacrificial meal on the mountains of Israel, That you may eat flesh and drink blood."*

Amber inquired, "How can there be human sacrifices for animals? Isn't it supposed to be the other way around?"

Gershom marveled at her insight, and responded, "Very astute, Amber. The Mosaic Law did prescribe animal sacrifices for the sins of the people. However, Jesus the Messiah provided the final sacrifice for all sins at the time He was crucified upon the cross. What Ezekiel appears to be proclaiming is a sort of biblical irony: Gog of Magog invaders sought to sacrifice the blood of the Jews, but the Lord intervened on Israel's behalf and turned the invaders' blood into a sacrifice throughout the land."

Simeon Abrams interjected, "Let me elevate everyone's understanding of the magnitude of what is taking place right now with the convergence of all these birds and beasts. As a tour guide in Israel I have been announcing over the past several years how birds and animals have been migrating and populating in Israel unexplainably. For instance, vultures non-indigenous to Israel, like the Griffon vultures that normally breed in mountain crags in southern Europe, north Africa, and Asia, have been colonizing in northern Israel, the Golan Heights, and areas of the Negev desert."[31] Also, Israel is home to several species of carnivorous animals like badgers, cheetahs, jackals, hyenas, leopards, wolves, foxes and more."[32]

Lisa asked the two witnesses, "Does this mean we can all return to Israel soon?"

Gershom consoled, "Yes, it won't be long, but it could be a few more weeks until the IDF quarantines the unsafe areas and restores order throughout the land."

Looking at Nathan, Lisa responded, "Since I work for the Ministry of the Interior, I must get back immediately to assist with the national restoration process. With your permission, Jami and the others can stay behind until the government informs me that it is safe for their return."

Nathan confirmed, "Permission granted; that is what this home in Rome is for. However, not all of us will be returning to Israel with the group."

Puzzled, Lisa asked for clarification.

Gershom interjected, "Simeon and I have asked Nathan to take us to America with him when he goes soon to visit his Unistate Global Investments Corporation (UGIC) headquarters."

Nathan confirmed, "I have been in contact with my staff in the states and they need me to come back to our main office headquarters for some important meetings."

Jami, who had attached herself to Nathan as a father figure, hugged him and worried, "You're not leaving us alone here in Rome are you? I'm only a teen-ager. What if my mother says we can't come back to Israel for several months?"

Nathan, who had never had a daughter of his own, became choked up by her affections and comforted, "No, never Honey! Your mother and I would never let anything happen to you."

Tovia, came close and put his hand firmly upon Jami's shoulder. He motioned to Lisa, Amber, Bella, and Jaxon to huddle together for a group hug, "Jami, as your uncle and the father of your two favorite cousins, I say we are all in this together. None of us will be left alone throughout all of this. From now on we all stick together!"

After Jami's nerves were quieted, Amber asked Gershom, "Why are Simeon and you not returning to Israel with the rest of us? Don't you think your understanding of Bible prophecy is needed in Israel?"

Gershom explained, "We have been summoned by some of the other 144,000 residing in America to come disciple them. They realize who they are, but feel their teaching needs some fine tuning. They informed us that throngs of Americans are responding to their messages of hope in Christ, but they can't keep up with all the questions they are encountering. When Nathan told us he was departing to his corporate office we asked to join him."

"When will you all be leaving?" Lisa asked.

Nathan alerted, "We leave at 3:00 P.M. tomorrow. We will be traveling Air France so as not to tie up my jet, in case you and the others need transportation to and from Israel."

With that announcement, Nathan's chef beckoned everyone into the dining room for a gourmet Italian dinner. Not certain as to how long he would be detained in America, Nathan made certain that his last night with his friends from Israel was festive. No expense was spared on the meal and the assortment of desserts his chef prepared.

When the night was through, everyone had unwound from the stress of the day and was ready for a good night's sleep. Nathan, however, decided to stay up a little longer and search the Internet to see how the news media was reporting on the supernatural defeat of Russia and the large coalition of Muslim nations. He also spent some time visiting some Christian news and blogsites to get their take on this incredible event. To his utter amazement, he was shocked to see that several top Catholic websites were attributing this incredible victory over Russia and its coalition to the intercession of the "Lady of Fatima" and not exclusively to the Lord, Himself, as described in Ezekiel 38 and 39!

One article went on to explain that the consecration of Russia to the Immaculate Heart of Mary by Pope Romano, and the prayers of millions of Catholics worldwide, proves to have led to the miraculous intervention of "Our Lady" in this invasion of Israel.

After reaching the point where he couldn't make any sense of what he was reading on the Catholic websites, he prayed to calm his nerves and quiet his spirit. Then he retired from the overwhelming day.

28

Letter to the
Saints Left Behind

It was about 8:00 a.m. the next morning when Tovia awoke from his slumber. With cup of coffee in hand, he made his way to the veranda where he saw his sister and niece weeping in Nathan's arms. As he approached them, he felt the crunching of glass beneath his shoes. Looking down, he realized that it was fragments of the opaque glass from the mysterious sealed box. In all of the media mayhem from his motherland the day prior, he had completely forgotten about this curious container.

"Good morning Tovia," greeted Nathan.

Cautiously sidestepping more broken glass Tovia replied, "Good morning. Is it ok if I ask, what's happening here? Why all the early morning emotions?"

"Tovia, when the girls heard that this box that I showed Simeon and you yesterday came from Razz's house, they couldn't wait to break it open to view what was inside," Nathan explained.

Brushing back tears, Lisa handed her brother a folded letter and said, "Here read this. It came out of this *Post Rapture Survival Kit*. We couldn't see what was inside because of the opaque glass on the front so we followed the instructions on the box, which said to, "BREAK THIS GLASS WINDOW IF YOU HAVE BEEN LEFT BEHIND!"

Nathan explained, "Among other things, the contents of this box included a Bible with a couple of letters that were signed by Razz and strategically inserted inside it."

Holding up the first letter, Nathan continued, "This letter concerns the Rapture."

Lifting up another letter in his other hand he said, "This one was in Romans 10 and explains how a person gets saved through receiving Christ. The letter Lisa gave you was in the book of Revelation, and when the girls read it, they were deeply moved."

Pulling up a chair, Tovia silently read the letter addressed to the Saints of the 5th Seal.

A Personal Message of Hope to the Saints of the 5th Seal

To the Saints of the 5th Seal; greetings in the name of our Lord and Savior, Jesus Christ. He is Risen!

This letter is intended to inform you about your fate and to comfort you therein. As I author this letter of hope to you, you are yet unaware of your future. The good news is that your souls are saved and your brave testimonies adorn the precious passages in the New Testament of the Bible. Read below what the book of Revelation says about you.

> When He (*Jesus Christ*) opened the fifth seal, I saw under the altar the souls of those who had been slain for the word of God and for the testimony which they held. And they cried with a loud voice, saying, "How long, O Lord, holy and true, until You judge and avenge our blood on those who dwell on the earth?" Then a white robe was given to each of them; and it was said to them that they should rest a little while longer, until both *the number of* their fellow servants and their brethren, who would be killed as they *were*, was completed. (Revelation 6:9-11)

Many of you could be among those that will be slain for the word of God and your testimonies as believers in Christ. By the time you understand your placement on the prophetic timeline and the important role you fulfill for the Lord, many Christians will have instantly vanished in a supernatural event called the

Rapture. This major promise and miracle of Christ was predicted in John 14:1-5. The details were further explained by the apostle Paul in 1 Corinthians 15:51-55 and 1 Thessalonians 4:15-18. You became a believer after this supernatural spectacle happened.

You now exist in a post Rapture world that is experiencing extremely turbulent times. Soon a charismatic world leader known as the Antichrist will confirm a seven-year covenant between Israel and the governing body that is perpetrating a global agenda, which is contrary to what you realize is the truth. You know that Jesus Christ is the "way, the truth and the life!"

Christ is your Savior and this is your testimony from the word of God. However, your message is unpopular among the masses and you will be caused to count the cost of following Christ. You will rise to the occasion and your courage will inspire many others to follow in your footsteps. These are your *"fellow servants and their brethren"* spoken of above.

Your testimonies, alongside the teachings of 144,000 Jewish evangelists, who are identified in Revelation 7:1-8, will inspire "a great multitude which no one could number, of all nations, tribes, peoples, and tongues." (Revelation 7:9). They will follow your great examples and when you, and your *"fellow servants and their brethren"* arrive together in heaven you all will shout "Salvation belongs to our God who sits on the throne, and to the Lamb!" (Revelation 7:10). At that time the angels along with you and all the rest of us in heaven will worship God saying:

> "Amen! Blessing and glory and wisdom, Thanksgiving and honor and power and might, Be to our God forever and ever. Amen." (Revelation 7:12)

You ask *"How long, O Lord, holy and true, until You judge and avenge our blood on those who dwell on the earth?"* The response you receive is to *"rest a little while longer."*

After the Rapture, there are three periods of Christian martyrdom that follows. You are in the first phase, which occurs after the Rapture, but before the confirmation of the false covenant of Daniel 9:27. You reside in the gap period between these two powerful events. Some of you will survive this gap period, but regardless of whether or not you do, all of your souls are saved. The *"white robe"* alluded to above is the assurance of your eternal salvation.

The Post-Rapture / Pre-Tribulation gap is an unspecified period of time and this is the reason why you don't know the length of time until your blood will be avenged upon those that dwell upon the earth. Your *"fellow servants and their brethren"* will not ask this question because they will know their placement on the prophetic timeline. They will know this because they will be martyred after the confirmation of the seven-year false covenant. They will be able to calendar the days until the second coming of Christ.

Your *"fellow servants"* are the ones persecuted and martyred in the first three and one-half years of the seven-years of Tribulation. They will be martyred by the same source that presently persecutes you. This is described in Revelation 17:6.

> "I saw the woman, drunk with the blood of
> the saints and with the blood of the martyrs
> of Jesus. And when I saw her, I marveled with
> great amazement."

You know why the apostle John *"marveled with great amazement."* You are these *"martyrs of Jesus!"* It is your blood that is stained upon her hands. You are preaching the true gospel of Christ, the literal interpretation of the Bible and the valid explanation of the Christian disappearances. The Harlot is prostituting the word of God for world control and global gain. She is preaching a counterfeit gospel, a different Jesus.

John says in Revelation 17:4-5 that her sacrament is a *"golden cup full of abominations and the filthiness of her fornication. And on her forehead a name was written: MYSTERY, BABYLON THE GREAT, THE MOTHER OF HARLOTS AND OF THE*

ABOMINATIONS OF THE EARTH. You have received the true Lord, but Satan is using the Virgin Mary as a demonic imposter, and now your teachings are in direct opposition to hers.

Because she embodies the overpowering religious system that is backed by the one world order, you are identified as dissidents and marked for martyrdom. She represents part one of the *"overflowing scourge"* that Isaiah 28:15 identifies. The Antichrist will confirm a covenant between Israel and her for seven years. Some of you won't be alive when this happens, but your *"fellow servants and their brethren"* will witness this marquee event.

The global government will view this religious system as the temporary opiate of the unruly masses, but they will ultimately dethrone this violent harlot in Revelation 17:16 when the Antichrist is ready to rise to ultimate power. This lawless charismatic character will instruct ten powerful world leaders to desolate this false religious system. This will occur at the midpoint of the seven years of tribulation.

Then the *brethren of your fellow servants* will face off with the final three and one-half years of the Tribulation Period. This will be a time of Great Tribulation and the Antichrist and his False Prophet will be deceiving mankind to believe in *"the Lie"* described in 2 Thessalonians 2. They will force people to worship the Antichrist, and in order to buy or sell they must receive a mark on their right hand or on their foreheads. This is all predicted in Revelation 13. The *brethren of your fellow servants* will not participate in their system, and they will refuse to take the "Mark of the Beast." This will cause them great persecution and many will be martyred like you, the FIFTH SEAL SAINTS.

Be patient in your plight for the Lord, dear saints.

> "If anyone has an ear, let him hear. He who leads into captivity shall go into captivity; he who kills with the sword must be killed with the sword. Here is the patience and the faith of the saints." (Revelation 13:9-10)

> "Here is the patience of the saints; here are
> those who keep the commandments of God
> and the faith of Jesus. Then I heard a voice
> from heaven saying to me, "Write: 'Blessed are
> the dead who die in the Lord from now on.'"
> "Yes," says the Spirit, "that they may rest from
> their labors, and their works follow them.""
> (Revelation 14:12-13)

After reading the letter Tovia said, "Wow, I'm going to need Simeon to explain this letter to me."

"Come on Uncle, even I understand it. We all missed the Rapture and now we are going to be martyred for becoming believers," Jami sobbed.

"Wait honey," replied Tovia. "I'm not so sure this letter applies to all of us because we are Jewish believers. Simeon informed me yesterday, right here where we are all seated, that we may be part of a remnant that survives until the return of Jesus Christ."

"Really Uncle, is it true? Are we going to stay alive until Jesus comes back to Israel?" Jami asked.

Biting his tongue, Tovia said, "Well umm… Well, yes that's what Simeon said. Isn't that right Nathan?"

Realizing that Tovia was telling only the partial truth of the matter to comfort Jami, Nathan nodded his head in agreement.

Thinking for a moment, it dawned on Jami that Nathan was not Jewish. Tears began to roll down upon her face again. "Oh no! Nathan," she began.

Before she could finish, Nathan gently put his fingers upon her lips and said, "Jami, don't worry about me. Simeon had some comforting words for us Gentiles also. He said that some of us survive until the return of Christ. The Bible calls us the "Sheep Gentiles." When Jesus returns, He gathers the Jewish remnant and the Sheep Gentiles to be together forever. So, see honey this is encouraging news for all of us."

29

The Queen of Heaven
Appears Globally

By the time a break in the Mideast storm arrived, it had become abundantly clear to all that the unprecedented poor weather had won the war for Israel. Like many of Israel's ancient victories, it was obvious that their God was behind the scenes making certain that His chosen people survived another Goliath battle.

While the IDF mopped up the battlefield, the world wondered what had happened to the Blessed Mother. Where was the Queen of Heaven when the world needed her most? Pope Romano had made a number of predictive comments in the media that he felt strongly that the Virgin Mary would soon bring a period of peace to the world. He reminded the press on more than one occasion, that in her apparition messages the Blessed Mother had made promises to that effect. What better time than now to prove that she would keep her commitments?

With the clearing of the weather a few days after the Russian coalition was defeated, Lisa was instructed to return to her post with the Ministry of the Interior. She gave a round of hugs to Jami, Tovia, Amber, Bella, and Jaxon, and boarded Nathan's jet for home. As the jet was returning to Israel, Nathan, Gershom, and Simeon were busily conducting their affairs in America.

•••••

Meanwhile, Pope Romano prayerfully pleaded, "Blessed Mother, come quickly, the faithful long for your guidance."

As the Pope prayed inside his chamber, an unexplainable luminous figure appeared over the partial ruins of Mecca. It descended downward gracefully until it hovered a few feet above the sacred Kaaba stone. The Saudis had recently reinstated worship around the black megalith, which had narrowly escaped damage during the Arab-Israeli war. As fate would have it, the Russian coalition invasion of Israel and the horrendous weather patterns had coincided with the Muslim month of Ramadan, stranding a multitude of pilgrims inside Islam's holiest city.

Upon witnessing the strange apparition, the worshippers fell prostrate. Within moments the light took a Marian shape that could be seen motioning to a respected Muslim cleric nearby. Spellbound, he rose and walked to the base of the Kaaba. After kissing the black stone, he turned and began shouting a message to the large Muslim crowd,

> *"Mary, God has chosen you. He has made you*
> *pure and exalted you above all women."*[33]

While the crowd began chanting these same words from the cleric, the apparition suddenly disappeared.

By the time word of the sighting reached Vatican City, Pope Romano was receiving the Rock Star treatment from his peers and the press. News of the Pope's dogma of Mary, which elevated her to be Co-Redemptrix, Mediatrix and Advocate, began to spread rapidly to even the remotest parts of the world. Even Muslims, who were in a state of disarray from their two Mideast war defeats, began embracing his teachings.

Subsequently, to worldwide amazement, the apparition of "Mary" made several surprise supernatural appearances at other key world locations repeating her universal message of love, peace, and global unity. In addition, miracles and healings were occurring at these multiple apparition sites, which prompted many conversions to the Catholic Faith.

After Mecca, she arrived in the clear skies above India's Taj Mahal, which rallied many Hindus to her side. Then she visited Zeitoun, Egypt, where she had been previously witnessed by millions during 1968-1971. Doubling back, she made additional appearances at former notable apparition sites in Fatima, (Portugal) Lourdes, (France) and Guadalupe, (Mexico).

Her sightings became so commonplace, that one late night television talk show host humored in his monologue, the "Queen of Heaven appears to have hit the political campaign trail hard in order to recruit some faithful followers. Who travels to caucuses in an RV anymore? Nowadays you just soar through the heavens with no TSA or other travel restrictions." He further jested, "The Blessed Mother sightings have become so commonplace that the network producers are trying to get her to make a guest appearance on my show."

As a result of her various impactful appearances, multitudes from other religions began streaming into Catholic Churches worldwide. Both new and old members of the "Faithful" began flocking to Rome in anticipation that the Queen might arrive there as well.

And then it happened! Her crowning moment came. She arrived over the Eternal City in all her splendor.

Hovering quietly over Vatican City in what appeared to be brightly lit luminescent figure, she caused an eerie silence to fill the square for about half an hour. Only the prayerful whispers of the multitude penetrated the stillness. Then she revealed herself to the throng assembled beneath.

Her radiant beauty shown so brightly that she could scarcely be looked upon. Her splendor epitomized the essence of serenity. Overwhelming feelings of love, peace, charity, and joy wove together the hearts of the faithful, without a word yet spoken.

No longer able to contain their joy, they began crying out at the top of their lungs, praises to their Queen.

She lifted her hands high toward the heavens and, after several minutes of ecstasy had subsided, she slowly lowered them in front of her in a call for silence.

Meanwhile, Pope Romano and Cardinal Vitalia had made their anticipated appearance on the balcony of the Pope's study. Mimicking his Queen, Pope Romano also lowered his hands in a call for calm.

When not even a whisper could be heard, the majestic woman, suspended high above, turned her full attention toward Pope Vicente Romano. All eyes followed her gaze, and then an enchanting, ethereal voice emanated from the apparition.

Uncharacteristically, the Blessed Mother spoke audibly during the apparition. Her serene voice could be heard throughout the assembly and a local news crew in attendance was able to broadcast her message to its local audience. It so happened that this live program was being watched at Nathan's house at the time of the telecast, which enabled everyone there to hear these words:

> *"Dear Children, thank you for your loyal presence here. Behold my servant, the Vicar of Christ. He will speak my words and carry out my earthly instructions. And through My Son's Church in Rome, the waters of world peace will flow. This is already happening before your eyes. As I warned in my secret message at Fatima, the day would come when Russia would spread its errors throughout the world, but in the end, my Immaculate Heart would triumph. With the collapse of the Russian invasion, the world has witnessed my supernatural powers. Now I will use those powers for the spread of world peace."*[34]

The news cameras shifted their focus to the Pope as a brief pause followed this shocking announcement. Placing his right hand upon his heart, the Pope nodded toward the apparition in solemn approval, which prompted the Queen of Heaven to continue her divine discourse.

"Blessed are the faithful who heed my calls for peace. Therefore, my peace I present to them and I urge the entire world to diligently seek my Son in the Eucharist. The Eucharist can protect you from penalty of mortal sin and provide reparation for your sins against my Immaculate Heart. When you partake of this Holy Sacrament, all will be well with your souls. This is because my Son's holy body and blood is present in the Eucharist. His sacrifice is perpetuated in this holy sacrament. Now my beloved children, the Reformation has ended and you must come to full unity in the faith."

And with those closing words she departed into the blue skies, leaving the cheers and chants of the faithful echoing behind her.

•••••

"That counterfeit imposter," Amber shouted from the veranda of Nathan's home in Rome.

"Sssssh, Auntie! You are going to get us in serious trouble with the neighbors outside on the balcony across from us," Jami pleaded.

The entire clan, still residing in Nathan's home in Rome, had been watching the events at the Vatican from the bird's eye view of his veranda.

Lowering his binoculars to his chest, Tovia asked, "Did you hear everything that the apparition said?"

Unable to control her anger, Amber retorted, "We certainly did! We turned the TV up to almost full volume the whole time she spoke. The apparition tried to steal the Lord's thunder by claiming that she interceded in the defeat of the Russian invaders. I heard those words resonate loud and clear," she bellowed at the top of her lungs.

Quickly placing his hand over her mouth, Tovia ordered, "Quiet! Have you gone mad, Wife? Jami's right; we have to be careful. We are treading on dangerous waters by staying here in Rome!"

Amber calmed herself and said "We need to get Gershom and Simeon on the phone immediately to discuss this."

"Please, before you call them, we need to pack our suitcases and board Nathan's jet!" exclaimed Jami. "I'm frightened by all of this; we need to get out of Rome right now!"

Pushing her father's binoculars back up to his eyes, Bella pleaded, "She's right, Daddy! I'm scared! Look! Those Catholics are acting crazy! We need to go home now!"

Tovia reached into his pocket and pulled out his cell phone. "I know Nathan's plane has returned from Israel, so I'll call the pilot to make sure we are clear to leave immediately," he said. "You all go get packed, because once the pilot gives us the thumbs up, we are all getting out of here."

30

The Harlot Rides the
Beast to Peace and Prosperity

"Holy Father, EU President Hans Vandenberg has requested a private audience with us," Cardinal Vitalia informed his Marian Pope.

"And, where does he propose such a high-level meeting should take place?" Pope Romano inquired.

"In Frankfurt," Vitalia replied.

Donning a curious expression, Romano questioned, "Why Frankfurt of all places, and what concerns our charismatic colleague?"

Vitalia explained, "He has meetings throughout the week with the European Central Bank (ECB) to discuss the faltering Eurozone monetary matters. Vandenberg is fretting over a global economic collapse and believes it can be forestalled by capitalizing on the developing fervor for the Queen of Heaven. He is gravely concerned that the fall of the Russian coalition will result in the utter collapse of their respective governments and economies. Moreover, he fears the mop-up of the Middle East warzone will take months, maybe years. Vandenberg wants to tackle these urgent matters promptly, before the flow of energy resources to the world in general, and Europe specifically, is disrupted.

"Vandenberg's concerns are warranted," Pope Romano agreed. "The Israelis have pledged the bulk of their energy exports to the US and the UK, making it difficult for them to meet European needs. It will be up to the EU to garnish these resources from the defeated lands, and for that they will need the Vatican network."

Cardinal Vitalia reluctantly reminded, "Yes, Most Holy Father, but remember that our influence is not as extensive as it once was, since some people who were known to be Catholics seem to have been taken during the worldwide disappearances. In places like America, Mexico, and Brazil, we are still recovering from the loss."

"I disagree," Romano retorted. "Those who disappeared are being replaced by multitudes of new believers. The Catholic Church has never been in a better position than now to lead the world into a millennial period of peace, prosperity, and unity. And, by no means make mention of this in front of President Vandenberg!"

Acquiescing to the Holy Father's wishes, Romano confirmed, "Travel plans to Frankfurt have already been arranged. We depart early tomorrow."

●●●●●

Accompanied by their heavily armed motorcade, the duo arrived safely at the ECB headquarters the next morning. Adorned head-to-toe in lavish priestly garb, they were swiftly escorted into an extravagant secluded office. Indicating a meeting shrouded in secrecy, the tall thick doors were promptly shut behind them.

Graciously cupping and kissing the Pope's right hand, Vandenberg issued his salutation: "Dear Holy Father and my favorite cardinal, thank you both for interrupting your busy schedules, and coming to Frankfurt on such short notice."

Seating themselves across from Vandenberg, with the mammoth conference table between them, Cardinal Vitalia began, "The Holy Father has already been apprised of your concerns, and agrees that time is of the essence to form a unity pact between the EU and the Vatican."

Turning his gaze to Romano, Vandenberg sought confirmation.

Romano nodded and boasted, "The Queen of Heaven's blessings are upon us."

At this acknowledgment, Vandenberg swiftly spoke: "Excellent! I need you to host a Vatican Council meeting immediately in order to unite all the world's religions under the Catholic canopy for our mutual benefit! We will call it "Vatican Global Council." I wish it to be broadcast live throughout the world!"

Protective of his Pope, and provoked by Vandenberg's abrupt dictates, Cardinal Vitalia complained, "We scarcely just arrive as your guests, and immediately you impose your will upon the Holy Father. Excuse yourself for this irreverent behavior!"

Vandenberg took a sharp breath, faked a smile, and calmly apologized, "Yes, you're absolutely right Cardinal Vitalia. How insensitive of me! In my haste, I took for granted that his holiness and I were on the same political page. Please forgive my thoughtlessness."

Turning his attention back to Pope Romano, Vandenberg, an expert at using the Socratic method of reasoning, restructured his comment: "Your Holiness, in light of the overwhelming favor shown to you by the Queen of Heaven; how should we implement our pact to unite the world and stave off imminent economic calamity?"

"We are on the same page," the Pope replied, smiling wanly at the Cardinal. "Vatican Global Council hosted in Vatican City is a good start, but I am uncertain of both the logic and the logistics of a hastily held live global broadcast. Such a high-level meeting must be conducted behind closed doors. A shroud of secrecy will whet the world's appetite, and provide time to formulate the official Vatican dogma. Additionally, the Vatican dare not subject Our Lady's authority to an uncensored assembly of snake charmers, New-Age mystics, and Hindus that have more deities than there are days on the calendar. Moreover, achieving the full attention of a global audience requires more than just a single broadcast; it will require a universal awareness of the Blessed Mother's benevolent intentions toward all religions."

Scooting closer to the table's edge, the EU president raised one eyebrow and slyly said, "Fascinating plan. Please tell me more."

"We will invite the foremost leaders from every world religion to Vatican City, especially the influential Protestants and Muslims. I have been in contact with many of them, along with our cardinals and bishops over the past few days, and most of them are already pledging solidarity to the Catholic Church and faithfulness to Our Lady. Her miraculous appearances, and supernatural signs and wonders have persuaded most of them to ally with us. We will convene ecumenically and then, through a global satellite broadcast, highlight some of the historical miracles associated with the Eucharist and the apparitions of our Blessed Mother, along with those presently occurring again through her. This will emphasize the importance of worshipping our Eucharistic Lord in the Blessed Sacrament. We will conclude with a joint statement that most religious leaders have presently pledged allegiance to the will of the Queen, the dogmas of the Catholic Church, and the supremacy of the Eucharist."

Somewhat bewildered, Vandenberg inquired, "'Most' of them? Is dissension developing among the Catholic clergy regarding the Queen, the Church or the Eucharist?"

Realizing he had said too much, Romano reflexively grabbed the large crucifix adorning his necklace, and fumbled for the right response.

The pontiff's awkward silence spoke loudly to Vandenberg's suspicions that discord existed within Roman Catholic ranks. "Rumors are currently circulating," Vandenberg noted, "that some US bishops and cardinals, along with several prominent Protestant ministers, openly advocate the apparition's messages are unbiblical…even demonically inspired. Is there truth to these claims?"

Vitalia quickly interjected, "The Holy Father has matters in America well in hand. Such rumors are unfounded."

"Even Archbishop Patrick Dolan? Is he well in hand, Cardinal Vitalia?" Vandenberg queried dubiously.

"He has been ostracized from the ranks of the clergy by his own choice," Vitalia replied, "No longer are his dissenting views about the disappearances and the apparitions given a platform in our churches."

Unconvinced, Vandenberg predicted, "I foresee this scenario as extremely problematic for the greater good of our goals. More serious measures must be taken by the Vatican to prevent these influential leaders from standing in the way of our global unity plans."

Upset by the challenge, Romano countered, "The former Archbishop and his Protestant cohorts serve no threat whatsoever to our unity plans. We have already put harsh measures in place to counteract their schemes. They will be duly warned that Vatican Global Council will have zero tolerance for their blasphemous teachings. Should they challenge our authority, they will realize there are limitations to my patience!"

With that assurance, the trio adjourned, agreeing to enact their unity plans promptly.

31

Israel Cleanses the Holy Land

Mopping up the carnage from the Magog war proved to be no minor undertaking. Hordes of dead and contaminated coalition soldiers lay strewn over vast expanses of Israel. The Israeli government feared a pandemic contagion was inevitable unless a national effort to rid the land of the deceased took place quickly. Wisely, Prime Minister Moshe Kaufman convened with Rabbi Joseph Levin and the Chief Rabbinate Council, seeking support to cleanse the land by whatever methods necessary.

"Rabbi Levin," Kaufman inquired, "disposing of the deceased enemy soldiers expeditiously presents our country with a huge challenge. What does the Torah teach about unclean corpses polluting the holy land? Certainly, Moses must have laid down laws regarding catastrophic conditions that threaten the safety and fertility of the land."

Israel's leading religious figure stood before the council and replied, "The Law of Moses is clear on this matter! There is a prescribed process for handling dead bodies, and a ceremonial purification process that must take place. Numbers 19:11-22 and Deuteronomy 21:1-9 determine that the dead must be buried immediately because exposed corpses are a source of contamination.[35] The land must therefore be completely cleansed and purged of all physical and spiritual defilement. Neither the enemies, their encampments, nor any of their belongings can be left to pollute the land!"

"Agreed," Kaufman replied. "There is no way to comb through the fallen hordes to retrieve their personal effects. We are facing a logistical nightmare in dealing with the burial of the dead. We will need to locate a valley suitable to establish the region's largest mass gravesite. Meanwhile, our military will need to work feverishly to stockpile the enemy's weapons into IDF arsenals. Efforts to accomplish this are...."

Interrupting the Prime Minister in mid-sentence Rabbi Levin informed, "The Rabbinate Council interprets the Torah to teach that all of the enemy's belongings, including their weapons, must be destroyed."

Prime Minister Kaufman pleaded, "Be reasonable, Rabbi. We can agree that the dead must be buried without delay, but the government must be allowed to harness the enemy's weapons to benefit the Israeli people and their military. These high-tech weapons are now the property of the Jewish State."

"Reasonable?" repeated Levin. "Israel's victory was accomplished entirely by the hand of Hashem, the Almighty. All aspects of Levitical Law must be followed in this matter."

Kaufman was aghast. "Show me historical precedent for this in the wars fought by our forefathers, I know of none," he quipped. "Surely such a vast arsenal must not be squandered. Besides, no such talk arose in the aftermath of the IDF victory over the Arabs in what you believe was the Psalm 83 war. Why do you make it a point of legal contention now?"

Kaufman's abrupt remarks sent shudders throughout the rabbis assembled in the room. They murmured amongst each other and cast disgruntled glances at the Prime Minister.

Rabbi Aaron Edelstein reasoned that perhaps the government could be convinced to convert the weapons into sources of fuel and energy to serve Israel. Speaking over the murmurs, Edelstein suggested that since the Torah is speaking about unclean open vessels, and not weapons, that the council could accept the weapons conversion.

Growing increasingly impatient, Kaufman questioned. "Do we have a deal?"

The Rabbis spoke amongst themselves for several more minutes before Levin announced, "We concur that the cleansing of the land is of utmost urgency at this time, so we will keep quiet about the government's treatment of the weapons, and its choice of location for the mass graves. However, our silence must not be construed as approval regarding this weapons matter. Soon, we will propose a suitable plan for the disposal of the weapons that we believe will be mutually acceptable to the Israeli government and the demands of the Law."

Kaufman replied, "That works for me. The Rabbinate Council can perform the ceremonial ritual that un-defiles the land, and the government will use the occasion to reach out to Israelis to purge the land from the dead and collect their weapons. The mammoth task before us requires a nationalized effort. The sooner we begin, the sooner your temple can be constructed. Let's put our people to work to accomplish all of this so that we can get this war-torn country back on its feet!"

Comfortable that his mission had been accomplished with the chief rabbis, Prime Minister convened the members of the Knesset to inform them of the good news. They heaved a collective sigh of relief that the religious and political communities were united for the good of the nation. During the assembly, Kaufman called upon his minister of the Interior, Avi Fleishman, to orchestrate a national campaign to accomplish the monumental feat of cleansing the land of the deceased.

●●●●●

After returning from the parliament meeting that afternoon, the first order of business for Fleishman was to contact his most trusted staff member, Lisa Thompson. "The Ministry of the Interior has been instructed to unite the country in a nationalized campaign intended to cleanse the land of the dead bodies," he told her. "I am putting you in full charge of this operation. Let me know what staff and resources you will need to accomplish this."

"Why me?' Lisa marveled.

"I can't think of anybody on staff that I trust more than you," Fleishman complimented. "The way you have handled affairs from day one on the job is unparalleled, and especially praiseworthy is your faithful service in the days following the disappearances of your husband and son. I don't know how you held up."

Lisa graciously replied, "Thank you for your trust; it means the world to me. Losing Thomas and Tyler in the rapture was gut wrenching, but…"

Suddenly, Fleishman interrupted. "We will have no more mention of the word 'rapture' inside this government department! I caution you; do not embrace the Christian jargon that some are associating with the vanishings!"

Understanding the centuries-old divide between Christians and Jews firsthand, Lisa diplomatically questioned, "Avi, don't you find it curious that Thomas, Tyler, and all the others unaccounted for were Christians? Isn't this slightly suspicious? Don't you have to admit that there may be some truth to what the so-called 144,000 Jews for Jesus are saying about the rapture?"

Putting his index finger to his lips, Fleishman rebuked, "*Sssh!* That's the second time you've used the "R" word!" Smiling, Lisa bartered, "Look, Avi, if I roll up my sleeves and get busy with the blueprints of Israel's national unity campaign, then the least you can do is let me believe my family disappeared to a better place. After all, why are the Jews still waiting for the Messiah to show? In light of what just happened, don't you think he would have shown up by now?"

"The rabbis are predicting he will come soon," Avi replied, "now that the Ezekiel prophecy has just been fulfilled."

"Well, I think our dear rabbis need to read Daniel 9, Psalm 22, and Isaiah 53 again," Lisa argued.

"Why's that?" Avi asked.

"Because they evidence that the Messiah already came about 2000 years ago as a sacrifice for our sins," Lisa explained, "in fulfillment of those prophecies and many more."

Lisa, having gotten the last word in edgewise, bid her boss goodbye as his secretary informed him that Prime Minister Kaufman was on the phone. But before answering the call, he looked sternly at Lisa and cautioned, "I'm warning you Thompson, keep your private beliefs to yourself. There is no place for them inside this workplace!"

Exiting back to her corner office, Lisa silently prayed the Serenity Prayer:

"God, grant me the serenity to accept the things I cannot change, Courage to change the things I can, and wisdom to know the difference."

Lisa realized that she had been called to her high-level post in the Ministry of the Interior for such a time as this. It reminded her of her favorite female Bible character, Hadassah, later renamed Queen Esther; who had to reveal her Hebrew identity to the Persian King Ahasuerus at the risk of being killed. She thought: *If Esther was willing to die to save the Israelites from Persian genocide, then the least I can do is stand up for Jesus so that Jewish souls can be saved by their Messiah.*

Sitting down at her desk, she humored herself: *How Ironic? Jesus was a Jew. He was one of us. How hard can it be to tell fellow Jews that Jesus is the Jewish Messiah?*

● ● ● ● ●

Suddenly Lisa's cell phone vibrated and she noticed that Jami's caller ID was on the lit screen. The phone had been silenced throughout her important morning meetings so she didn't realize that her daughter had left several important messages. Hastily, she answered the phone and greeted, "Hello honey, how are you?"

"I'm upset!" Jami replied. "Why haven't you responded to any of my messages?"

"I'm sorry, dear. I have been in important meetings all morning at work," Lisa apologized.

"I'm at uncle Tovia's and aunt Amber's house," Jami informed. "We had Mr. Severs' pilot fly us home on his private jet because of all that supernatural stuff going on at the Vatican. We arrived in Haifa a few hours ago. This town looks like a war zone and I don't feel safe. Mother, I need you to come get me right away!"

Calm down, honey. Everything will be alright," Lisa comforted.

Jami began crying. "Mommy I miss you," she wept. "I'm so scared!"

"I will make sure you get home soon, dear," Lisa said. "Please let me speak to your uncle."

"Tovia is out surveying the city," Jami replied, "and checking out if he still has an office to work from. But Aunt Amber is next to me."

"Please put her on the phone."

"Hi Lisa. Jami is quite unnerved right now," said Amber.

Lisa acknowledged, "I know, I need to figure out the best way to get her back home immediately."

"What does your schedule look like today," Amber inquired. "Can you come for her?"

"I just got promoted to chief of staff of the Ministry of Interior," Lisa replied, "and Fleishman wants me to lock myself indoors to draft a national campaign to mop up the Magog war mess. He wants it on his desk yesterday, so there is no way I can get up north to your neck of the woods."

"What do you want me to do?" Amber asked.

Lisa instructed, "Please have Nathan's pilot fly her down to Ben Gurion airport and I'll have her escorted to me in a government vehicle."

"No can do," Amber responded. "Nathan instructed him to fly back to Rome for important business. He departed moments after we arrived home."

"What important business?" Lisa questioned.

"You're asking the wrong person," Amber replied. "Tovia can tell you more. Apparently, there is some underground network of former Catholics who are trying to flee from the Vatican to America, or something of the sort. I guess there is an opposition group of left-behind Catholics and Protestants forming in the US."

"Opposition to what?" Lisa asked,

"Again, I'm not the person to ask. It's all Latin to me," Amber quipped. "I can have Tovia call you when he returns."

Lisa sighed, "Amber, for the good of Israel, I need you do to an important favor for me. Please would you consider bringing Jami home to me? It is utterly impossible for me to make the trip to Haifa right now."

"I think that will work," Amber said, "because Tovia wants to witness to his mother about Jesus. He was talking about bringing Jami home and then explaining to Naomi and your father about what the Bible says is happening right now. Frankly, he doesn't think he has a job anymore, after what just happened in Israel. He mentioned that we might have to pack up the family and move closer to all of you."

"I think that's a wonderful idea!" Lisa exclaimed. "It would be such a blessing to have you all near. I'm going to be so busy with this national campaign and I'm sure I can keep you all busy. Besides, my father-in-law's friend Razz left Jami and me more money before he was raptured than we will ever be able to spend in the short time remaining on earth. We will all be taken care of."

Amber confessed, "Lisa you're the best sister-in-law a woman could ever want. I will make sure that Tovia gets Jami home sometime on Monday."

With those words, both Jami and Lisa were comfortable to conclude the call and get prepared to rendezvous on Monday a couple of days after the Sabbath. Jami got back on the phone and said, "Mother, I will be okay those couple of days with my cousins, so don't worry. I know that you are busy at work, but please work through the weekend so we can spend time together. I need a time with you when I get home."

Lisa confirmed, "I will burn the midnight oil. I'll take my work home because the department closes down on the Sabbath. Gershom told me that when Christ fulfilled the law at His first coming, observance of the Sabbath is optional for believers, I'll work all weekend. I love you, Jami! Goodbye 'til Monday."

32

Doomsday Conference Erupts Into Deadly Chaos

It was a seasonally sunny Saturday morning, and astonishingly, all seven-thousand seats in the Grand Canyon University Arena in Phoenix, Arizona were filled. The symposium entitled "SOSC - *Save Our Souls Christ,*" was a kick-off Christian conference primarily designed as a platform to christen a recently conceived organization. It was hosted by the newly formed religious group called "The Society of Second-Chancers, (SOSC)."

The SOSC had been organized by a remorseful group of religious leaders who realized they had missed out on the Rapture. Even though many of their fellow congregants were caught up to be with Christ in the clouds, these men and women had been left behind. Subsequently, they had all repented and received Christ, being born again into a right relationship with Jesus as their personal Lord and Savior.

The group included former Catholics, Protestants, Evangelicals, and Emergents (*members of the post – modern "Emergent Church"*). Importantly, they realized the biblical significance of the 144,000 Jewish Witnesses, and as such, they offered the select group their unconditional support.

The primary purpose of the SOSC was to broadcast the gospel of Christ to the others left behind, credibly explain the Rapture phenomena, proclaim that Christ was returning to judge unrighteousness and ultimately establish His messianic kingdom. Additionally, their mission was to warn the world about the powerful Bible prophecies that would find fulfillment between the Rapture and Christ's Second Advent. The SOSC leaders realized from scripture that the world would eventually experience the emergence of the Antichrist, Armageddon, and the seven-year Tribulation Period. Their hope was to work closely with the 144,000 to lead as many people as possible to Christ in the short span of time remaining.

The event title was actually selected to serve as a play on words. In addition to pronouncing that the Lord gives second chances, the SOSC acronym was cleverly chosen to be reminiscent of the World War I and II encoded telegraph message S.O.S.,[36] or in this post-rapture case, Save Our Souls Christ. It signaled that Christ was the Savior; that He gives second chances, and that a spiritual World War was underway for souls.

The SOSC conference was hosted by Unistate Global Investment Corporation (UGIC) based in Scottsdale, Arizona, whose longstanding president was Nathan Severs. Featured on the platform was a panel of six speakers, which included Gershom Gold and Simeon Abrams of the 144,000 Jews for Jesus, Archbishop Dolan, formerly of the Roman Catholic Diocese of Phoenix, and three well known US Protestant pastors, Ladd Bitterman, Brad Walters and Gary Hanah.

The audience included all of the members from the American chapter of the 144,000 Jews for Jesus, scores of former Catholic and Protestant leaders, a handful of Muslim clerics, and thousands of the general public. To the delight of the SOSC, this conference quickly burgeoned into a mega-event before the doors had even opened. This was because the cable and mainstream news media made it a point to live stream portions of the occasion globally through satellite networks. Additionally, all the primary social networks, including Facebook, Twitter, and YouTube were buzzing with blogs and streaming with homemade videos.

As a result, millions worldwide took an interest in this conference. Individuals from diverse nations, tribes, peoples, and tongues were still seeking answers about the Christian disappearances, the apocalyptic Middle East, and the horrendous economic hardships confronting their respective homelands. Many hoped that this conference could make sense out of the chaos that had so quickly turned their lives upside down. Their governments were failing them, their various religions were short on answers and the apparition's messages about peace, love, unity and the Eucharist still required scrutiny. On the chance that the SOSC could bring them hope and answers, they observed the happening in whichever way they could, with bated breath and expectant hearts.

The event program read as follows:

Speakers	Topics
Simeon Abrams	The Confirmation of the False Covenant Causes Tribulation.
Archbishop Dolan	Are the Apparitions Divine or Demonic?
Gershom Gold	Israel is the Woman of Revelation 12, Not the Queen of Heaven!
Ladd Bitterman	The Five Horses and Six Horseman of the Apocalypse.
Brad Walters	Does God Give Second Chances After the Rapture?
Gary Hanah	True Christians; Prepare to Be Martyred.

Meanwhile, as the Phoenix event was getting underway, EU President Hans Vandenberg, who had just been briefed by confidants of the SOSC conference, frantically attempted to make contact with Pope Romano and Cardinal Vitalia…

"Holy Father, President Vandenberg seeks to conduct an emergency conference call with us," informed Cardinal Vitalia.

"Not again!" Pope Romano replied, "What a nuisance he has become!"

Vitalia warned, "Vandenberg is on the line right now and says an urgent matter in America requires our undivided attention."

"Is it about the Arizona conference?" the Pope guessed.

Joining his vicar in front of the big conference call screen and preparing to initiate the call, Vitalia said, "I don't know. Let's find out first hand."

Receiving a visual and audio feed on his end, Vandenberg greeted, "Hello gentlemen. Can you hear me?"

"Loud and clear Mr. President," Vitalia reported. "You're coming in just fine."

Vandenberg spoke directly to his concern: "Are you both aware of this SOSC conference going on as we speak in the US?

While Pope Romano nodded yes, Cardinal Vitalia confirmed, "Absolutely; we have people planted inside the assembly instructed to sabotage the entire event."

"And, how do you plan to accomplish that from your headquarters at the Vatican?" asked Vandenberg.

Pope Romano boasted, "We have a full-proof strategy in place. First, when a speaker says something controversial about the Vatican or the apparition messages, our people will protest loudly to interrupt the flow of the teaching. Second, they will seize the question and answer sessions to ask pointed theological questions the Vatican has prepared that are specifically intended to outsmart and embarrass the panel of experts. These inquiries are intentionally designed to initiate a non-violent ruckus among those we have purposely planted inside the auditorium. We assure you that the SOSC will not conclude successfully, and the blasphemous conference organizers will have serious reservations about ever hosting a similar conference."

Vandenberg echoed, "A non-violent ruckus; I don't care if the parishioners come out DEAD or ALIVE; these meetings cannot continue. Nothing can be allowed in America, or anywhere else in the world, to obstruct our plans for global political and religious governance."

Cardinal Vitalia cautioned, "President Vandenberg, please, the Holy Father encourages patience concerning such matters. You are privy to know that, incredibly, several miraculous signs have been given to him privately during his daily devotions before the Blessed Sacrament that have caused him to believe that there will soon be incomparable Eucharistic miracles occurring on an unprecedented global scale. The Holy Father believes the overwhelming magnitude of these Eucharistic wonders will unite world religions under the umbrella of Roman Catholicism, which will ultimately create the global stability the EU seeks."

Vandenberg clarified, "Patience is not a luxury we presently possess. Let the miracles of the Eucharist come, but we need an alternative plan in place. In light of the turmoil in the Middle East and global economic crisis, Pakistan has its nukes pointed at India, China is ready to overtake Taiwan and Japan, and North Korea is mobilizing troops along the border of South Korea. There is a global power struggle underway. Nations are fearful for their survival. In an instant, and without warning, another nuclear crisis could occur anywhere in the world. We must maintain strict control of global scenarios and do everything in our power to prevent all future religious gatherings like this SOSC conference. If these US dissenters aren't already convinced by the multiple supernatural appearances of the apparition, then there are no guarantees that Eucharistic miracles will persuade them either!"

"We have our boots on the ground," Cardinal Vitalia insisted, "We are prepared to do whatever it takes to disrupt the event proceedings. Our insurgents include many former Muslims who have come on board as a result of the Marian apparitions. Among them are radicals who hate this upstart so-called Christian group, and they appear willing to die for their faith. In fact, they seem to be looking for religious license to go after these guys. From the Vatican's perspective, their fundamentalist Muslim backgrounds could come in handy when dealing with all non-compliant religious and secular groups."

Vandenberg questioned, "What do you mean 'boots on the ground'? Are you suggesting your accomplices inside the auditorium are armed and dangerous?"

"Of course not," Cardinal Vitalia clarified, "All of America is on high alert for terrorism. Nobody is able to smuggle a weapon into the conference."

Pausing for a moment, Cardinal Vitalia requested, "President Vandenberg, please allow Pope Romano to depart to his holy chambers; he has other pressing matters to attend to. Meanwhile, you and I can iron out the details of our mutual concerns."

Staring skeptically into the video camera, Vandenberg consented, "As you wish Holy Father, but remember, there are no guarantees that your expected Eucharistic miracles will transform these troublemakers into faithful Catholics."

Unappreciative of Vandenberg's piercing comments; Pope Romano retreated to his private quarters. Once he had departed, Vitalia explained, "What I was revealing, President Vandenberg, is that I have a peripheral plan in place in the conference parking lot."

"What do you mean by this?" asked Vandenberg.

Donning a smug look, Vitalia confidentially replied, "Let's just say that for many of the SOSC attendees it will be a long and arduous journey back to the safety of their cars, if you get my drift."

Upon hearing this, Vandenberg's concerns were temporarily mollified. He was content being on a need to know basis about the cardinal's contingency plan, and, at least for the present, he had heard enough. "Very well, dear cardinal, I'm adjourning to my office to monitor the live streaming of the SOSC conference." he said, "I entrust this matter to your competent hands."

"Rest assured, we are watching the event here also, and we are in constant communications with our people inside and outside of the event," the cardinal concluded.

●●●●●

Meanwhile, the SOSC conference was underway and the first speaker, Simeon Abrams was nearing the end of his teaching about the true content of the Antichrist's false covenant, when he speculated that one component of the deal would concern itself with Israel's rights to worship freely according to their ancient Mosaic Law. "The Jews will want to construct their temple and reinstate their animal sacrificial system, and they will refuse to participate in the required sacraments of the Vatican-ruled world religion," he proclaimed.

These comments sparked a murmur among many of the Vatican implants imbedded within the crowd. The disturbance was short-lived, but set the tone for what could follow if the subsequent speakers spoke adversely about the resurging Catholic Church. In fact, it prompted the conference host, Nathan Severs, to change the order of the speakers. Brad Walters was moved into the second slot, because the speakers originally scheduled before him were certain to throw daggers at the Vatican's authority and the messages of the apparitions.

Walters taught primarily from 2 Thessalonians in the New Testament, he warned that the Antichrist could be the charismatic EU President, Hans Vandenberg. However, Walters reminded, "Presently, we can't be certain. But we do know that this coming lawless one's rise to power will be characterized by deceptive displays of signs and wonders unimaginable. In my estimation, these supernatural exhibitions could include spectacular UFO sightings and much more. These miracles will probably be far greater than the demonic Marian apparitions the world has been witnessing. These paranormal events will cause many to believe in a counterfeit gospel, or what the Bible calls 'THE LIE.' Moreover, the Antichrist will be the one that confirms the false covenant with Israel, which Simeon Abrams just preached about."

He reserved his closing comments to say, "Even though unrighteous deception will deceive the masses into believing in the counterfeit gospel, multitudes from all nations, tribes, peoples, and tongues will become born again believers, like those recently raptured. God gives second chances; this is what The Society of the Second-Chancers stands for, and now is your opportunity to accept Christ as your Savior. Trust me, I speak to you first-hand about this merciful attribute of God's character. Even though I pastored a mega-church, I never truly became born again through a genuine faith in Christ."

Walter's then gave an altar call and throngs in attendance made their way up the aisles of the arena toward the prayer teams in front of the podium. The Lord multiplied his Church by about four-thousand that day.

The antagonists amongst the crowd were silenced by this overwhelming display of faith. What could they do? They were essentially handcuffed by the pervasive power and grace of Christ that was obviously controlling the moment. They kept quiet and waited for a more opportune time to execute Cardinal Vitalia's sinister plan. And after the short lunch break, that time arrived.

Archbishop Dolan, who was one of the first high ranking Catholic members to depart from Catholicism after the rapture, was called to the podium as the third speaker. He began by saying, "The Lord clearly has end times plans for Israel. Zechariah the prophet tells us that Israel is the apple of God's eye."

These comments moved Vitalia's spies to the edges of their seats. They quickly recognized what the Archbishop was leading up to.

Dolan continued, "Down through the centuries the Roman Catholic Church lorded its Replacement theology over the faithful. The church fathers began to teach that when the Jews rejected Jesus, the Lord rejected the Jews. This paved the way for the Catholic Church to become Israel's replacement, and heir by default to the promises given to Abraham, Isaac, and Jacob. It was a diabolical scheme that even Martin Luther ultimately embraced at the time of the Reformation. Throughout past centuries, the faithful sitting in the pews became inculcated regarding the sacraments and generally failed to realize that the clergy were hijacking the Lord's promises to Israel. They attended the Mass, prayed the Hail Marys, and went to confession faithfully, but usually never questioned the dogmas and papal edicts that followed."

These remarks created a stir amongst the Vatican infiltrators. Murmurs filled the auditorium, like the sound of an approaching swarm of Africanized bees.[37]

Hearing this, the Archbishop raised his voice and pounded the pulpit declaring, "This is why Pope Romano, Pope Benedict, and most of their predecessors erroneously believed that the Catholic Church, led by the Queen of Heaven, is the mysterious woman of Revelation 12. And, most troubling of all, brothers and sisters, this is why the Vatican appears to be identified in Revelation 17's MYSTERY, BABYLON THE GREAT, THE MOTHER OF HARLOTS AND OF THE ABOMINATIONS OF THE EARTH!"

"Blasphemers, Jew lovers, heretics!" the infiltrators cried out. Many of them began lunging toward the stage, fists held high. The crowd became so unruly that security had to escort the speakers and media camera crews to secluded areas for safety, while simultaneously attempting to restore order. Creating an atmosphere akin to a barroom brawl, the enraged protestors lashed out in every direction. The auditorium was becoming a bloody mess, causing many worshippers to flee for the safety of their cars and charter buses in the parking lot.

Awaiting the masses attempting to flee was an even worse fate, the second wave of protestors. But, this unruly bunch was armed and dangerous. Vitalia's plan B was intended to make a lethal statement to those attending the SOSC event. Several dozen stick-toting radicals, some with concealed weapons, had dispersed unnoticed around the perimeter of the arena parking lot, shortly after the conference began. Upon command, they put on bandanas to disguise their identities, brandished their weapons, and set off Molotov cocktails and tear gas to create confusion. In addition to these militants, several hundred more angry activists from the nearby vicinity had arrived unexpectedly to participate in the ruckus. These were locals who had become furious from watching the live streamed Christian messages from the conference. They infiltrated the parking lot to violently protest the event.

Those conference attendees rushing for safety found themselves immediately in harm's way. The flood of worshippers exiting the auditorium made it impossible for those already outside to retreat back indoors. Fists began flailing, sticks began smacking, knives began stabbing. People were frantically huddling behind cars, and many wounded or killed were dropping in the parking lot all around.

A patrol unit promptly radioed for backup: "90L requests assistance for a large unruly crowd at the Grand Canyon University Arena. Hundreds of people are fighting inside the auditorium and the adjacent parking lot. Several thousand more are storming the doors out of the auditorium, attempting to exit into the lot. We have numerous wounded, and possible fatalities occurring. Please dispatch emergency assistance to the entrance and exit sides of the University Arena immediately."

Lieutenant Paul Jordan, the Watch Commander in charge, was offsite when the urgent call came in. Immediately he instructed, "I need all available units, and emergency response teams, equipped with crowd control gear to dispatch to 3300 Camelback Road east of the arena to clear the parking lot. COME NOW! We have a riot on our hands!"

By the time the squads began to arrive, several gun shots had been fired into the crowd from the northern and southern ends of the parking lot. The scene had rapidly degenerated into a battle zone. The rebel ambush was extremely well planned, and when the emergency backup arrived on site, the aggressors discarded their camouflage, hid their weapons under nearby cars, and blended into the crowd. The prevailing hysteria provided cover and a means of escape.

The scene was so chaotic; the police were mostly unable to identify the assailants. The emergency first responders were overwhelmed at the sheer number of casualties on location.

They did their best to triage the wounded – while overloaded ambulances and rescue vehicles shuttled the injured to nearby hospitals.

At the end of the day, several hundred wounded were listed, dozens critically, and about thirty were pronounced dead at the scene.

The whole world watched in shock as the assault and the rescue took place, including EU President Hans Vandenberg. With mixed emotions, he approved of Cardinal Vitalia's covert chaotic campaign, but seethed at the news coverage by the mainstream media.

"How dare they report the preposterous rumor that I'm the Antichrist?" He raged inwardly. *"Pastor Walters should be shot for making such an accusation before the eyes of the world!"*

33

Jews Return Home as Rumors of Nuclear Wars Abound

After Sunday Mass at St. Peter's Basilica, Pope Romano called Cardinal Vitalia into his office for an urgent confidential meeting.

"Vitalia, I'm appalled at how you let matters get so out of hand at the American conference!" Pope Vicente rebuked.

With a nonchalant shrug, the cardinal snickered, "You know what they say about a mob, Vicente. It has a mind of its own!"

Pope Vicente groaned, "Vitalia, have you no regard for the dead and injured? Bishop Arturo Amanti was in attendance, and is feared to be among the wounded."

Vitalia responded unremorsefully, "Holy Father, with all due respect; please come to terms with the enormity of the present situation. It is past time that you recognize your responsibilities to the unity pact between the Vatican and the EU. The world is on the verge of nuclear war, and the Pakistanis and North Koreans are not standing on the side lines praying Hail Marys, while you plead for miracles. Vandenberg swears that they have their fingers on nuclear triggers as we speak! The miraculous healings and signs and wonders throughout the world thus far are sufficient to justify Vatican authority over all religions!"

Appalled by Vitalia's attitude, Romano reminded, "The Eucharistic miracles will come in God's, not man's time; much in the way the apparitions have appeared at perfect and precise times heretofore."

Rolling his eyes, Vitalia rudely recounted, "The SOSC conference was unruly. You heard how Archbishop Dolan and the other speakers blasphemed against God with their hate speech against the Church and the Blessed Mother. Both he and Bishop Amanti are attempting to lead people away from Catholicism. Even though our numbers grow daily, this venomous rhetoric is being preached from pulpits, it has gone viral over the Internet, and it is spreading like wildfires throughout the world. It must be stopped! The faithful are looking to you for leadership, and frankly, they are not seeing it! You must take total charge before it's too late!"

"How dare you speak to me in this fashion!" Romano exclaimed.

"Better me," Vitalia warned, "than Hans Vandenberg and his political establishment. We need the EU leader to fully support our global plans. He is obviously not supporting our efforts. He is engrossed in soon becoming the world's most powerful leader, and he will try to accomplish this at the Vatican's expense if we are not careful."

Romano glared at the cardinal. "How do you propose to counteract the SOSC?" he growled.

Donning a more sensitive countenance, Vitalia softed his tone and stated, "It's really quite simple. We can kill two birds with one stone. We can appease the EU president and stop the SOSC at the same time."

Romano clenched his fists. "I don't have time for guessing games, Vitalia! Get to the point!" he spat.

The cardinal lowered his head reverently. "As you wish, my dear Pope." Then, taking a deep breath, he declared, "The time to host Vatican Global Council is now! We cannot put it off any longer, waiting for Eucharistic miracles. We must display solidarity with all world religions in support of the Blessed

Mother. Vandenberg will commend you for uniting the faithful, but if you delay, he will grow contemptuous of you."

Romano was stunned. "Enough! Depart from me now! I need to consult with the Blessed Mother!"

•••••

Later, during his evening Hail Marys, the Pope prayed feverishly for Eucharistic miracles to commence:

"I urge you Blessed Mother: tell your beloved Son to esteem His holy Eucharist before the eyes of the world. Let signs and wonders draw the world to your Sacred Heart. Come quickly! Nuclear wars and apostates threaten to deter your benevolent plans for this earth. Humanity cries out for love, peace, and unity, but spiritual turmoil runs rampant. How long, my Queen, until you command full unity among the faiths?"

After hours of beseeching, Romano retired, completely exhausted.

Early the following morning, he proceeded to go before the Blessed Sacraments for his daily devotions. While he was there something miraculous occurred, a direct confirmation from Christ, about the significance of the Eucharist.

"I Am truly present in the consecrated bread and wine," revealed the Eucharistic Christ. *"I have provided many miracles in the past and present of my real blood coming forth from the host as evidence to the unbelievers, and even far greater ones are forthcoming!"*

Falling prostrate, Pope Romano replied, *"I know dear Lord, salvation is in the Eucharist. Thank you, this was the word from you that I sought, and now I have it. I will move forward to unite the world with you through your holy Eucharist."*

•••••

Meanwhile, in her home in Bet Shemesh, Israel that following Monday, Lisa was tidying up her home in preparation for Jami's return. Breaking briefly from her housekeeping duties, she called Nathan Severs, in America.

"Hello, Severs speaking," Nathan answered.

"Nathan, how are you?" Lisa asked.

"Lisa? Your caller ID said 'restricted.' How good to hear your voice!"

"Yes indeed it's me," Lisa confirmed. "I'm calling from Israel about an important matter."

"An important matter?" Nathan repeated, "Does it have anything to do with your new role as the architect of Israel's restoration campaign?"

"It does," said, Lisa, humbled. "How did you hear about that?"

"I spoke with Tovia and Jami on Sunday," Nathan answered, "the day after the Phoenix riot. Did you hear about that tragedy?"

"Absolutely," Lisa replied. "The SOSC event was well covered here. The media was outraged to the point of anger against the event and portrayed it as a divisive Christian fundamentalist attempt to proselytize Jews, condemn Catholics, and frighten Israelis with scare tactics. Were you there?" Lisa inquired.

"Oh yes," Nathan revealed, "My company, Unistate Global Investment Corporation, was the main sponsor. I have fifteen stitches in my right arm, as a result!"

"Oh my Lord!" Lisa exclaimed. "What happened? Are you okay?"

"I'm okay," Nathan assured her, "and so are Gershom and Simeon, who were featured speakers at the event. I had the misfortune of being among those that got attacked by the mob. While attempting to bring calm to the outburst, I was overpowered and beaten by several assailants. One of them brandished a long sharp dagger, which he jabbed into my arm."

"You realize," Lisa interrupted, "that the Israeli government frowns upon the SOSC. They fear that they are orchestrating a campaign of hysteria, intended to convert mankind to Christianity."

Nathan clarified, "Well, Lisa, they are true believers working with the 144,000 to preach Jesus, and to warn about the Bible's end times prophecies. The violence was initiated intentionally, by those opposed to the teaching of the true gospel message."

Lisa guessed, "The Catholics?"

"We believe they are primarily responsible," Nathan replied.

"So…" Lisa reflected, "What Simeon and Gershom predicted is already happening. The harlot world religion is beginning to persecute post-rapture believers."

"You're probably right Lisa," Nathan concurred, "but what happened in Phoenix was a mob that metastasized out of control. It is difficult to know the extent of the Vatican's culpability just yet."

"But, Nathan," Lisa reasoned, "You are describing born again believers being martyred for their faith, by supporters of Rome. I can't remember everything Simeon said, but I do remember that the harlot religion would be headquartered in Rome and would be drunk with the blood of the saints, and the MARTYR'S OF JESUS! Remember? He repeated himself about these martyrs, and was convinced they represented people who became believers after the rapture."

Nathan conceded, "Yes, I do remember those words. Well," he sighed, "we *are* living in the last days, Lisa. You and I both know, things will get a whole lot worse before they get better, from this point forward. A brief silence ensued as they both digested the truth. Then Nathan resumed, "Speaking of the last days, Lisa, your new job description is right out of the end times playbook. You are at the helm of fulfilling the cleanup described in Ezekiel 38 and 39."

Lisa nodded. "Yes, I'm aware of that. That's why I'm calling. My boss wants me to formulate a full-proof campaign that orchestrates the immigration of millions of American Jews, with their financial portfolios in hand, to Israel. We need manpower and capital to get this country back on track. I figured that your Unistate Global company could become one of Israel's most trusted American business resources. This would be the perfect way for you to become the Oskar Schindler you long to be!"

Nathan applauded, "Outstanding! UGIC has invested a lot of research and money into plans to help the coming Greater Israel. Your uncle Razz set me on this course. Besides, many American Jews probably compose a sizeable contingent of the faithful who will escape to Petra when the Antichrist attempts a final genocide."

Lisa shivered at the thought, but managed, "I knew I could count on you, Nathan. I'm going to email you contact information of key individuals within the American Jewish Congress, and about thirty other US Jewish organizations. I have to hang up for now, because Jami should be here any moment. I will instruct my secretary to get that list off to you immediately. I expect you will be received with open arms by these agencies. Be discreet about your Christianity, but always on the lookout to share the gospel."

"Lisa, you make me proud," Nathan saluted. Then, quoting the story of Esther, he proclaimed, "The Lord has lifted you up 'for such a time as this.'"

●●●●●

It was midmorning on that Monday when Lisa peered out her window to see Jami rushing to her doorstep. It seemed forever since she had seen her. Opening the door, Lisa noticed that Tovia, Amber, Bella and Jaxon accompanied her precious teen.

"What a wonderful surprise!" Lisa enthused, exchanging embraces all around. "I didn't expect the whole family! What's the occasion?"

Amber replied, "Remember when we last spoke, I told you Tovia was out checking to see if he still had a job?"

Noting Tovia's sad expression, Lisa groaned, "Don't tell me…"

Tovia confirmed, "I'm officially unemployed, Sis."

"I'm so sorry!" Lisa sympathized.

But Jami broke in, "Wipe off those sad droopy faces, guys! This is all for the best."

"How so?" asked Lisa.

"Mother, you told Auntie Amber about uncle Razz's inheritance. You said the family could come live by us, because you have enough money for everyone! I have already promised that you and I would take Bella to the shopping mall to buy her some Barbie dolls and princess outfits."

At that introduction, Bella grabbed Lisa's hand and snuggled close, "Can we go shopping now, Auntie Lisa?" she pleaded.

Grinning from ear to ear, Lisa said, "Hold your horses, Bella! You all just got here. We need to figure out where your bedroom's going to be before we buy lots of dolls and princess outfits. But, I promise, we will go shopping real soon."

"Me, too?" pleaded young Jaxon. "I need some new toys!

Picking up her handsome little nephew, Lisa assured, "Yes, Jax, you," and kissing his smiling face, "too! When we take Bella shopping, we will take you, too! Your Auntie Lisa wants to spoil both of you. I missed you both so much."

While the adults meandered into the living room, Jami escorted her cousins to her bedroom. Sitting alongside his sister, Tovia told them that his workplace had been leveled from the initial barrage of Russian missiles. "They actually struck in the center of my work complex," he said. "The entire plaza was reduced to rubble. Suffice it to say the company is closed indefinitely."

Grabbing her brother's hand and cupping it in hers, Lisa said, "Not to worry! Jami was right: this is all for the best. I have been promoted to a senior director of the Ministry of Interior, and I will be tripling my staff immediately to accomplish the increased responsibilities I have been given."

"Do you mean…you might have a job for your dear brother?" Tovia marveled.

"Not just a job," Lisa replied. "Your supervisory skills will come in handy. We need a field person to roll up his sleeves and serve as liaison between the I.D.F. and the Ministry of Interior. We are working closely with the military to restore and beautify the country. We are implementing a worldwide campaign to encourage the return of Jews into a safer, greater Israel!"

Tovia rejoiced, "That's outstanding, Lisa! It's good to know that twenty-five years of supervising commercial construction projects can still be put to good use for our country. By the way, Amber shared Romans 8:28 with me before we left Haifa this morning. This verse teaches that all things work together for good for believers. Man-oh-man! That certainly rings true right now. This new job opportunity is music to my ears, and it will be wonderful to work alongside my sister on such an important campaign!"

After intentionally clearing her throat, Amber asked, "What about your dear sister-in-law? Do you have any part time work, or tasking that could be done from a home workstation for a former Sales and Marketing Director?

"Why only part time?" Lisa questioned.

Amber answered, "I still have to be a fulltime mom, and also I want to spend a lot of quality time with your mother, Naomi. I want her to enjoy the company of her grandkids, including Jami. As you know, this time of peace will be short, and I'm hoping to witness to her about Jesus."

Lisa thanked Amber from the bottom of her heart. "I can have my staff customize a workload for you that will fit with your schedule. Your skills will be a great asset. And, there is nothing more important to all of us than to get the rest of our family to receive Christ."

Tovia promised, "Come tomorrow morning I'll look into finding us a home nearby, so that we can all live close to each other. Fortunately, mother is not too far away either, so Amber and the kids can visit her often."

Lisa was ecstatic. "The Lord is so great!" she praised. "He works things together for our good. He has obviously united us in these difficult times to serve Him and help with the restoration of Israel."

They all fellowshipped over hot tea, while in the background from Jami's room, they could hear Bella trying to teach Jaxon the "Jesus Loves Me" song."

"Yes Jeesa wubs me," Jaxon mimicked. "Yes Jeesa wubs me, the Biba tell me so."

"That's so darn cute! Lisa laughed. "I have to get this on video."

As she grabbed her IPhone and headed down the hallway to Jami's room,

Tovia and Amber shadowed close behind, to enjoy the precious moment with her.

A Few Weeks Later...

Everything went well for Tovia's family over the next few weeks. They found a home, moved in, and Tovia began working for the Israeli Ministry of Interior. Even Nathan Severs was making inroads with the American Jewish organizations on Lisa's list. Lisa's campaign to attract Jews from the US to a "safer and greater Israel" was working, and her boss, Avi Fleishman, was ecstatic about the progress.

Surprisingly, tens of thousands of American Jews put their homes on the market, influenced by Lisa's *Aliyah* campaign. Many of them tendered job resignations, and began packing for the Promised Land.

Contributing to this overwhelming response was the fact that the Rapture and Middle East wars had adversely affected US and global stock markets. World-changing events had spiraled the American economy into a tailspin.

Further fueling the Zionistic inclination to leave the US was the fact that anti-Semitism was burgeoning in America. The

Rapture had removed Pro-Israel Christian Zionists from the US population, leaving behind many Americans who now blamed Israel's for their economic hardships. Persecution of the Jews was smoldering, threatening to rise to fever pitch inside the US.

Highlighting this growing trend, a prominent Jewish historian said, *"What's occurring inside the United States of America today is reminiscent of the days leading up to the formation of the Nazi regime in Europe."*

On the flipside, the SOSC working alongside the 144,000 Jewish evangelists was proactively spreading the gospel of Jesus Christ far and wide. A harvest field of searching souls was being cultivated by a world filled with chaos, uncertainty, and supernatural events like the Rapture and the Marian apparitions.

The Rapture of the born-again believers became a witnessing tool that the SOSC and company wisely used to further the Good News. The unsolicited publicity associated with the infamous "Doomsday Conference" never subsided. In fact, millions worldwide stayed plugged into the flood of blogs streaming constantly over social networks concerning the SOSC.

A Vatican Conference Call….

"Cardinal Vitalia, I need to confer with you and Pope Romano, immediately," insisted President Vandenberg.

Receiving Vandenberg's call in the video conference room, Vitalia activated the speaker phone and greeted the EU president on the video screen. "I know, we desperately need to communicate," agreed Vitalia. "I have been warning the Pope that the world is on the brink of nuclear wars between Pakistan and India, and North and South Korea."

"And what has been the Pope's response?" Vandenberg asked.

" 'I need to pray to the Blessed Mother for direction,' " quoted Vitalia. "The Pope believes prayer is the solution right now. He tells me to be patient, that the Blessed Mother will work everything out in her perfect timing. He truly believes that she is about to unify all faiths, and usher in world peace. But I have been warning him that the Pakistanis and North Koreans aren't praying Hail Marys. Rather, they are dusting off their nuclear warheads!"

"Look!" Vandenberg responded, "I know how much you love Pope Vicente…we all do, But the time for prayer is over, and the hour for power has arrived. I'm certain the Blessed Mother would approve of us taking matters into our own hands under the present circumstances. There is no peace or solidarity among world faiths. The Vatican underestimated the SOSC and Jews for Jesus movements. These subversive cults are burgeoning and posing a genuine threat to the necessary cohesion between Catholicism and other world religions."

This last statement rankled the Cardinal. *"Rivaling?"* he spat. "With all due respect, dear president, let's not give them more credit than they deserve. Yes, the SOSC is getting a lot of publicity, but they are shooting themselves in the feet by claiming the Blessed Mother's appearances are part of a great satanic deception! Besides, their narrow minded dogmatic teachings are alienating many devotees of other religions and encouraging them to accept our Catholic teachings. Throughout the world, many are converting to Catholicism, and even the Israelis are calling the SOSC a fanatical group of religious zealots!"

Vandenberg quickly responded, "Yes, what about the Israelis? They are brazenly pressing for full Jewish sovereignty over Jerusalem, with the explicit intent of rebuilding their temple on its ancient site. Considering your real estate holdings in Israel, how does the Vatican feel about that? Aren't Catholics and Muslims appalled by Israeli plans to take over the holy city? The Jews will never accept your form of Christianity, and Prime Minister Kaufman made this abundantly clear to me in a recent phone conversation."

"What phone conversation?" asked Pope Romano; who had just entered the room.

"Good day, Your Holiness," Vandenberg greeted. "Prime Minister Kaufman called me yesterday in response to the threats of nuclear exchange between Pakistan and India, which I warned you was coming, and he stated that Israel would not choose sides on this war and didn't want to get drawn into this conflict. He said the Israelis were still recovering from the Arab – Israeli war, and their struggle against the Russian coalition."

Pope Romano replied, "That's understandable, but what did the Prime Minister have to say about the Catholic Church?"

"To be precise," Vandenberg answered, "Kaufman cautioned that your belief in Christ as the Messiah, your worship of Mary, partaking of the Eucharist and subscription to all the other sacraments are all forbidden in the Torah. According to recent rulings of the Chief Rabbinical Council, which is restoring Israel to historical roots dating back to Moses, your religion and theology is idolatrous. In fact, they concur with the SOSC that the apparition's messages are demonic."

Vitalia jumped up, pounded the table, and angrily blurted out, "What do you mean they agree with the SOSC? That's preposterous! They have publicly denounced the SOSC as radical fundamentalists attempting to subvert the world to their religious dogmas. They can't have it both ways!"

The Pope, who had slumped into a chair, tugged on Vitalia's robe, pulling him back to his seat. "Mr. President," he said, "Israel's push to possess all of Jerusalem is as intolerable as the false teachings of the SOSC and the 144,000 witnesses. Although the Vatican cannot intervene in the religious affairs of Israel, we forbid the Jewish State from eradicating our real estate holdings, and religious claims within Jerusalem. Since they have won their war with the Arabs, they will move swiftly to construct their temple, but we must prohibit them from restricting rightful access to our holy sites inside the Old City."

Displeased with the religious direction of the conversation, Vandenberg objected, "I didn't call to incite a holy war between Catholics and Jews. I have more pressing matters to contend with. Pakistan and India are certain to engage in a nuclear conflict very soon. North and South Korea will undoubtedly follow suit. The world at large is in a free fall, with nations coveting each other's land and resources. Global economies are dying on the vine and political leaders believe the quick fix to their financial woes is the acquisition of spoils from another nation. They want to emulate the model set by Israel that plundered surrounding Arab countries. As you know, Russia formed its coalition to capture spoils from Israel. I warned you both that more outbreaks of wars were my worst nightmare scenario, and you failed to use the Vatican network to prevent this from occurring."

Cardinal Vitalia jumped up again, raising both hands in rebuttal. "Whoa, now!" he cried. "Don't go blaming us for all the world's problems. If anything, the Catholic Church is the cure. You are familiar with the messages of the apparition. Planetary peace will come! We have this assurance from the Blessed Mother."

Vandenberg could see that Pope Romano nodded in agreement with his colleague.

These belated self-assurances agitated Vandenberg to no end, prompting him to complain, "What cure? If you had hosted Vatican Global Council by now, you might be qualified to speak about remedy. Your procrastination has allowed the SOSC to beat you to the punch, and the world has plunged back into all-out war!"

Vitalia looked at his Pope and shrugged. "See, dear Pontiff," he snapped. "I told you so."

"What is that supposed to mean?" Vandenberg asked.

Glaring at Vitalia, the Pope answered, "He doesn't mean anything by it. Look, Mr. President, we can still accomplish our mutual goals. You need us to host a unity conference, and we need you to make the Israelis promise not to infringe upon our rights in Jerusalem. You scratch our back, and we will scratch yours. Israel is concerned about restoring their economy and gathering Jews back into the nation, correct?"

Vandenberg nodded affirmatively.

"Israelis want world markets to welcome them, and not world wars to come against them, correct?" Romano asked.

Vandenberg nodded again. "Yes, I'm following you. Now get to your point."

Pope Romano clearly stated his case: "Israelis need peace and safety in order to continue their campaign of getting world Jewry to relocate to the Jewish state. The Vatican assembly can create religious unity, and encourage world peace and love, but the EU must commit to Israel's peace and security. Israelis need assurance that foreign powers have to go through western armies in order to attack the new Jewish state. What if Pakistan wins against India? Won't Israelis fret that they may become their next target? You, Mr. President, must use your position to ensure Israel that they waged their last war when the Russian coalition was defeated."

Vandenberg exclaimed, "This is precisely what I have been conveying to the EU assembly! Western militaries must unite as a global peace-keeping force, to stabilize world governments and economies. The world can no longer tolerate rogue nations attempting to war their way into weaker nations. Vast arsenals are being confiscated by dictatorial regimes, and they are meeting with little to no resistance in the process. This must be stopped immediately!"

Pope Romano concurred, "And, what better means to accomplish this than through a united EU military force? Israel toppled Arab armies, and the Russian coalition has met with its bitter defeat as well. With the stoppage of Russia's evil confederacy, most every Muslim army that has been standing in your way is removed. The hour has come for the Vatican to usher in peace, and for you to conquer any remaining aggressors standing in the way."

Vandenberg sat back, a satisfied smile on his face. "So, we are in agreement. Arrange for your great council and let me muster up military support."

Pope Romano signed off, saying, "Done. We will stay in close contact and keep you apprised of the forthcoming Vatican meeting."

34

The Vatican Global
Council Meeting

The Announcement of the Meeting

It was a momentous occasion witnessed by thousands assembled in St. Peter's Square. The throngs were experiencing a picture perfect, postcard day, as they watched the church's most elite cardinals and bishops parade into the Sistine Chapel for an emergency assembly. This special session was no ordinary conclave. Since the election of a new Pope was not on the agenda, the crowd and media could only speculate as to the nature of this mysterious meeting. All that was known was what had been provided to the press a few days earlier by Cardinal Vitalia's office.

The press release read that the Pope would convene an emergency ecclesiastical conference at the Vatican. The only reported details were the time, date, and place, and that the top ranking Catholic cardinals and bishops from around the world were required to be in attendance. This shroud of secrecy, coupled with the fact that only the most esteemed Catholic clergy were invited, caused the faithful to flock into Vatican City by the droves to see what the Pope was up to.

Once the elite group was seated inside the chapel, Cardinal Vitalia greeted them: "Welcome, my brothers! His Excellency Pope Vicente Romano has summoned you here today to discuss a world conference that is to be hosted in Vatican City next month. You represent the voice of Roman Catholicism worldwide, and for this reason the Pontiff requests your unconditional cooperation as we attempt to bring all unbelievers to the Catholic Faith through the Immaculate Heart of the Blessed Mother. As you know, this is Our Lady's wish as expressed through her miraculous appearances, both recently, and down through the ages. This was evidenced in the past when our glorious Queen in 1722 dictated to Venerable Mary of Agreda[38] what would take place in the last times. I quote, "Before the Second Coming of Christ, Mary must, more than ever, shine in mercy, might and grace in order to bring unbelievers into the Catholic Faith. The powers of Mary in the last times over demons will be very conspicuous. Mary will extend the reign of Christ over the heathens and Mohammedans, and it will be a time of great joy when Mary, as Mistress and Queen of Hearts is enthroned."[39] The time for total consecration to the Blessed Virgin Mary has now arrived, and it is your collective responsibility to serve the Queen's wishes to the best of your God-given abilities."

With this introduction, the Pope entered the chamber and took his customary seat at the head of the assembly. A reverent silence filled the room as Vitalia ceased speaking long enough for the Pontiff's entry.

Cardinal Vitalia announced, "As you are all aware, people from every world religion have been flocking to Catholic Churches in record numbers, and at an unprecedented pace. Never before throughout history has the world experienced such a spiritual phenomenon. Those desiring to become members of the Catholic Faithful are increasing by tens of thousands every day. The global appearances of the Blessed Virgin, coupled with her compelling messages, have broken down all barriers that once divided dozens of diverse faiths. The Blessed Mother has ushered in a new era, the unity of all humankind. When the world needed her most, our Lady arrived to bless our union with all other religions. The time for human disparity has ended. The message of the Blessed Mother is that we are all, including what remains of Russia, to be consecrated unto her Immaculate

Heart. What the world is presently witnessing is the fulfillment of a remarkable prediction made in 1878 by Pope Pius IX, who predicted, *"We expect the Immaculate Virgin and Mother of God, Mary, through her most powerful intercession, will bring it about that our Holy Mother the Catholic Church…will gain an influence from day to day among all nations and in all places, prosper and rule from ocean to ocean, from the great stream to the ends of the earth; that she will enjoy peace and liberty…and there will then be one fold and one shepherd."*[40]

At that pronouncement, the entire assembly, except the Pope, stood up, applauded and rejoiced. The ovation lasted nearly five minutes, until the Pontiff finally raised both hands for silence. It was as an ecstatic experience, and as the exclusive group sat down, some commented that they were certain they had felt the Blessed Mother's presence in the room.

An eerie silence filled the chapel as the aged Pope hunched over the microphone in front of him. Without referencing the source, he quoted:

> "In our time, when day by day mankind is being drawn closer together, and the ties between different peoples are becoming stronger, the Church examines more closely her relationship to non-Christian religions. In her task of promoting unity and love among men, indeed among nations, she considers above all in this declaration what men have in common and what draws them to fellowship."[41]

Pausing, the Pope was interrupted by some murmuring amongst the assembly. Some were whispering, "I've heard these words before." Other's recognized the source and quietly shared this source with others.

Looking up at the cardinals and bishops, Pope Romano spoke: "I'm pleased that some of you recognize that I'm quoting from the Nostra Aetate of Pope Paul VI, given on October

28, 1965. In light of the mass conversions from formerly non-Christian religions that the Church is presently experiencing, these inspired words are truly fitting."

Pope Romano continued to quote Pope Paul's poignant words:

> "From ancient times down to the present, there is found among various peoples a certain perception of that hidden power which hovers over the course of things and over the events of human history; at times some indeed have come to the recognition of a Supreme Being, or even of a Father. This perception and recognition penetrates their lives with a profound religious sense... Thus, in Hinduism, men contemplate the divine mystery and express it through an inexhaustible abundance of myths and through searching philosophical inquiry. They seek freedom from the anguish of our human condition either through ascetical practices or profound meditation or a flight to God with love and trust. Again, Buddhism, in its various forms, realizes the radical insufficiency of this changeable world; it teaches a way by which men, in a devout and confident spirit, may be able either to acquire the state of perfect liberation, or attain, by their own efforts or through higher help, supreme illumination. Likewise, other religions found everywhere try to counter the restlessness of the human heart, each in its own manner, by proposing "ways," comprising teachings, rules of life, and sacred rites. The Catholic Church rejects nothing that is true and holy in these religions. She regards with sincere reverence those ways of conduct and of life, those precepts and teachings

which, though differing in many aspects from the ones she holds and sets forth, nonetheless often reflect a ray of that Truth which enlightens all men."

Pausing again to peer into the gathering, the Pontiff was delighted to see that the entire group was listening intently to his every word. So he continued:

"The Church regards with esteem also the Muslims. They adore the one God, living and subsisting in Himself; merciful and all-powerful, the Creator of heaven and earth, who has spoken to men; they take pains to submit wholeheartedly to even His inscrutable decrees, just as Abraham, with whom the faith of Islam takes pleasure in linking itself, submitted to God. Though they do not acknowledge Jesus as God, they revere Him as a prophet. They also honor Mary, His virgin Mother; at times they even call on her with devotion. In addition, they await the day of judgment when God will render their deserts to all those who have been raised up from the dead. Finally, they value the moral life and worship God especially through prayer, almsgiving and fasting."

Ending the quote at that point, Pope Romano repeated, "Prayer, almsgiving and fasting; qualities that we can all learn from our Muslim brothers and sisters."

Observing from the gestures amongst the conclave that his mild reprimands were taken to heart, he stated his case in his own words:

"All of you have been divinely appointed for such a time as this to follow the commands of the Blessed Virgin Mary, and to receive the multitudes that she is gathering into the open arms and doors of the Catholic Church. Protestants, Hindus, Buddhists, Muslims and other religions throughout the world are blending their faiths with ours, because the Blessed Mother has captivated them all with her overwhelming grace. Her undeniable appearances and accompanying miraculous events at a number of apparition sites, have served to fill all of your churches with new members, and your treasuries with increased tithes and offerings. At a time when world economies are faltering, your churches experience the blessings of prosperity. For this much-appreciated increase, we are forever indebted to the Blessed Mother. Undoubtedly, other world religious leaders are threatened by this unprecedented turn of events."

Pausing momentarily to peer again into the attentive eyes of his audience, Pope Romano instructed,

"Therefore, the time has come for all of you, the esteemed clergy of the Catholic Church, to reach out to all religious leaders and demonstrate that Roman Catholicism embraces the commonalities of their unique faiths. Muslim clerics from Mecca, gurus from Kolkata, witch doctors from Nairobi, and every other influential spiritual leader worldwide are invited to attend the Vatican Global Council. This super summit is designed to arrest their fears, address their concerns, and answer their abundance of questions about the Blessed Virgin Mary, and her inseparable supernatural connection with the Catholic Church."

With those concluding remarks, the conclave stood in applause as Pope Romano adjourned. At the Pontiff's departure, all eyes turned back to Cardinal Vitalia, who had packages of information containing the event details distributed to everyone. The packets included a list of key names of the non-Catholic religious leaders who were invited, and the curriculum of scheduled events. Additionally, media kits with press releases were included that required each Cardinal and Bishop to see to it that the momentous occasion was announced worldwide, and that all mainstream media and social networks covered this Vatican conference.

Upon explaining the importance of the materials inside the information kits, Cardinal Vitalia updated his peers:

> "The Pontiff and I have been in close contact with E.U. President Vandenberg, who agrees with us that this conference is of critical importance to catalyze world peace through the ecumenical consecration of the faiths to the Immaculate Heart of the Blessed Mother. Unquestionably, we have the full support of the European Union for this endeavor. Working in tandem with the Vatican, the EU will concurrently be introducing a move towards global governance. This comprehensive plan divides the world into ten distinct regions and takes into consideration the diverse cultural and geo-political needs of each province; including the emerging Jewish state of Israel."

With his mention of Israel, Vitalia could hear some grumbling amongst the audience. Israel's religious leadership had become increasingly vocal in their disdain toward the Catholic idolization of the Virgin Mary. Vitalia raised his hands for calm, and clarified,

"I share in your disgust over Israel's Rabbinate Council's outspoken statements condemning the apparitions of Our Lady and referring to our Catholic devotion to the Virgin Mary as idolatry. But this was to be expected of the Jews. Their rejection of our Lord Jesus Christ rendered their hearts hardened toward His Blessed Mother as well. Presently, they do not recognize her redemptory role in the Lord's divine plan. I counsel you to remember what our beloved apostle Paul wrote about this stiff-necked people centuries ago, from a prison cell right here in Rome. In the book of Romans, chapter 11, verses 25 and 26, he writes:

'For I do not desire, brethren, that you should be ignorant of this mystery, lest you should be wise in your own opinion, that blindness in part has happened to Israel until the fullness of the Gentiles has come in. And so all Israel will be saved…'"

This quote caused the preponderance of the conclave to acquiesce to Cardinal Vitalia's reasoning, which calmed the crowd and enabled him to continue:

"As the apostle forewarned, the Jews are blinded to the significance of the Catholic Church. They still don't recognize that the Catholic Church has become the "Fulfillment of the Promises" that were given to the Jews by God. But even still, for yet a little while longer, the Catholic Church must be patient with Israel for the time being and allow President Vandenberg time to implement the E.U.'s plan for world peace and safety. Vandenberg has assured the Vatican that he will impress upon the Israeli government the importance of the Catholic Church in the grand scheme of the E.U.'s overall world political plan. President Vandenberg and Israeli Prime Minister Kaufmann are presently discussing a strategic seven-year plan that ensures the Jewish state certain religious, economic, military, and political protections. We cannot interfere with these E.U. efforts."

Shortly after Vitalia's exhortation, the assembly adjourned, returning to their various countries to make preparations for the upcoming Vatican super summit.

•••••

The Arrival of the Meeting

The weekend of the Vatican Global Council had finally arrived, and the streets of the ancient city of seven hills were bustling with the throngs that had poured in from the four corners of the earth. The atmosphere resonated melodically with the babbling sounds of diverse languages, and the spectacle had become the multi-cultural event of the millennia.

Spectators included nuns dressed in formal black and white habits, Buddhist monks clothed in customary orange robes, Imams draped in sleek white *dishdashas*, foreign diplomats in expensive Armani suits, Eastern Orthodox priests in well-pressed cassocks, and even gothic attired New Agers who were tattooed from top to toe.

Just outside the venue, reporters from all mainstream media gathered hoping to catch interviews with invited guests, or just maybe even a surprise showing of the Blessed Virgin Mary to supernaturally sanction the star-studded event. So many pre-summit interviews were being conducted, that many of the elitist invitees were having trouble gaining entrance through the Basilica's doors. The Swiss Guard had policed many major Vatican events before, but on this specific occasion, their typical quadrant procedures were vastly ineffective. Fortunately, a few of the newscasters were able to seclude some interviewees from the hustle and bustle, to achieve clear audible answers as to why they had come for this convention.

"I have come at the special request of the Vatican to show my support for the unity of the faiths," said a bishop from the Greek Orthodox Metropolis of San Francisco.

A respected Muslim cleric from Saudi Arabia commented, "The Blessed Mary is highly venerated within Islam, and her appearance in Mecca and elsewhere around the world have convinced me and many of my fellow Imams that the teachings of the Holy Koran can be congruent with those of the Catholic Church. We are certain that Allah is commandeering a global campaign of religious unity that will extend far and wide throughout the world."

An Egyptian Muslim leader, who was standing alongside the Saudi cleric, nodded and added, "We have come to learn about the commonalities between Islam and Catholicism. I was one of the fortunate Egyptians who, along with President Anwar Sadat, witnessed Mary apparitions in Zeitoun, between 1968 and 1971. Although I was merely a teen ager at the time, I now realize that her appearances pointed to a future time when all Muslims and Catholics would join faiths together as brothers and sisters. I have primarily come to learn more about the similarities of our respective religions, in order to break down barriers that stand between us."

The newscaster asked a nearby guru from Kolkata, India, several questions: "Why have you come to the Vatican's super summit? Don't Hindus believe there are multiple gods? Why would you come to an event that will obviously be emphasizing that there is only one God?"

The widely-respected sage said;

> "We Hindus can appreciate the divinity of Jesus; this is really no big problem for us. Everyone is on the same pathway to enlightenment. Christ-consciousness is the ultimate state of bliss in Hinduism. We consider Jesus Christ to be another guru that received the "Supreme Personality of Godhead," and the Blessed Mother to be like the "Divine Mother," in our religion. Jesus achieved the highest level of god-consciousness that anyone can strive for; this is undeniable. As far as acknowledging the Blessed Virgin Mary, she is no different than Shakti, Vishnu, Durga, and all the other goddesses Hindus worship. Her apparitions have certainly qualified her as a goddess like the others. In fact, I spent significant amounts of time with Mother Theresa when she selflessly served in my home city, and we always greeted each other with praises of the Blessed Mother together. It was something that bound us together spiritually."

The overall consensus of the many interviews was that the selected guests primarily came to learn about the commonalities of their faiths with Catholicism, and in most instances to demonstrate their support for religious tolerance among the diverse faiths. Even a delegation of Jewish Rabbis commented that they hoped the outcome would be positive for the dramatic spread of Judaism underway in Israel.

One of the Rabbis commented, "We believe it is important that the other spiritual leaders recognize that Israelis should be free to conduct their political and religious affairs in the manner that they see fit.

Not every newscaster onsite was enamored with the Vatican's super summit. One tabloid reporter, with an established reputation for being controversial, cornered a widely-respected cardinal who had arrived late and was racing to get into the Basilica before the ceremonies began. Rudely pushing his microphone into the cardinal's face, the reporter questioned,

> "What do you have to say to the millions of skeptics around the world who are concerned that the Catholic Church might be fabricating a religious hoax with all the Mary apparitions that is intended to indoctrinate the masses into religious dependency at a time when world events make humanity most vulnerable?"

Caught off guard by the insulting question, the cardinal frowned at the reporter and, pointing to his watch, said, "I apologize, but, I have no time for interviews. I'm running late for the summit."

But, the reporter was relentless in his pursuit for an official Vatican comment and rephrased the question more directly: "According to some, religion is the opiate of the masses, the crutch of the crippled mind. And it is an established fact that when the world grows darker, Catholics cling to their belief in the Virgin Mary. How can the world be assured that the apparitions are genuine and not some high tech holographic campaign of Catholic deception?"

Pushing back the reporter, as the cardinal headed toward the closing Basilica doors, the security guard reprimanded, "Stand back! The cardinal has already stated that he's running late and has no comment for you!"

Summit Ceremonies Commence

Inside St. Peter's Basilica, the Vatican Global Council was beginning and all the doors were officially shut to all outside spectators, and press and media sources except for Al-Jazeera TV, and the ETWN Global Catholic Television Network. Cardinal

Vitalia greeted the attendees, made several brief announcements about the theme of the summit, and then began outlining the event agenda.

> "Welcome! Welcome!" he greeted the crowd. "Those assembled here truly represent the world's foremost religious leaders. Additionally, in attendance are many heads of states. All of you have been invited to the Vatican at this most crucial time in human history to share in the Catholic Church's vision of creating world peace through religious unity. Today Pope Vicente Romano will speak directly to the heart of humankind's present predicament. The pontiff will conclude by conducting the traditional mass, aided by the Catholic clergy amongst you, and you who are not Catholic will have the opportunity to remain as observers. Furthermore, over the course of the next two days you are all invited to the various workshops being presented by several of our leading cardinals and bishops. These meetings are designed to deepen your understanding of Pope Romano's benevolent plan for interfaith unity. So now, without further delay, will you all please rise to honor His Holiness Pope Vicente Romano?"

As those in the packed cathedral stood on their feet, the processional of Pope Romano began. Entering in with his usual entourage, surrounded by altar boys bearing incense, and protected by Swiss Guards, the Pontiff moved along the center aisle, waving his hand and blessing the crowd. *A capella* choirs positioned about the nave sang melodically in Latin, the sound reverberating through the mammoth building like the voices of angelic hosts, until the Pope made his breathtaking ascent to the ornate throne behind his altar.

Once the audience was seated, the Pope began delivering his message in Latin. As he spoke, his words were translated into key languages on big screens, recently installed for this special summit:

> "Greetings to you all, my beloved brothers and sisters of the world. The barriers that once existed between all of our diverse cultures, languages, and faiths have been replaced by a greater calling; an irrevocable mission which we all must heed. Mankind, left to its own depraved devices, finally faces the eve of its destruction. Our continued survival necessitates that we must all become more united. Longstanding divisions over race, sexuality and religion must not continue to divide us from one another. Undeniably, the challenges facing our present time make all past problems pale in comparison. Together we stand at the final crossroads: on one side lies death and destruction; on the other exists life and liberation. We have only one reasonable choice: we must collectively tackle humanity's strife headlong together. But how? Which man or woman among us has determined the solution that resolves our numerous conflicts, the potential for nuclear war, economic collapse, plagues and pestilences which currently threaten the continuance of human life?"

Hanging on every profound utterance, the Pope's audience, both inside the Basilica and throughout the television world, sat on the edges of their seats. After a brief pause the Pontiff continued:

> "The solution is self-evident, that it is impossible for any created thing to sustain itself indefinitely and function in accordance

with its design apart from its eternal source of supply. The timepiece's hour hand cannot turn clockwise when the minute hand spins counter-clockwise. The sun cannot rise in the west and set in the east without fatally altering earth's stability. The moon cannot shine apart from the sun's reflection. And, humankind cannot exist without the divine guidance and blessings of their Creator!"

Pausing to peer directly into the lens of the main television camera, Pope Romano appealed to his worldwide audience:

"Wars cannot exist where love abounds, poverty cannot prosper when charity prevails, darkness hides not where the light shines forth, desperation cowers in the face of hope, and evil has no focus apart from the wickedness in the hearts of men. Many religious leaders throughout time have dogmatically declared exclusive allegiance to the Creator, and in so doing provoked the harshest hatred that humanity can experience. Muslims and Christians have warred, Shiites have killed Sunnis, Hindus have killed Muslims, Christians and Jews have massacred each other. These are history lessons that must not be repeated."

His speech was temporarily interrupted by a minor rolling tremor, lasting about twelve seconds, that was clearly felt by all in attendance. Some gripped the seat backs in front of them, while others jumped to their feet. But Pope Romano was unflinching. Reports soon surfaced outside the closed cathedral doors that a 4.8 earthquake had hit in the heart of Rome. Fortunately, only minor damage was done to a few storefront windows and no injuries were reported, but most assembled inside the Basilica drew a correlation between the quake and the warnings of the Pope.

Believing the minor tremor was a divine sign, Pope Vicente capitalized on the moment, becoming even more authoritative in his tone:

> "Again, I ask, who among you can remedy the world's woes and right the course of mankind's misdirection? If there be anyone who can profess, with absolute certainty, that his or her way has the blessings of the Almighty, then please come and take my seat upon this world stage. Which of you has the Blessed Mother singled out as her anointed hand within humanity?"

With those pointed questions, the auditorium lights were instantly dimmed and footage of the apparition's previous Vatican appearance, when she had specifically acknowledged Pope Romano as her "servant," was played on all the big screens.

Dear Children, thank you for your presence here. Behold my servant, the Vicar of Christ. He will speak my words and carry out my earthly instructions.

The Blessed Mother's very words broadcast over the basilica sound system loudly and clearly, as the audience viewed her glorious image on the surrounding screens. Never before seen footage, caught on camera by the Vatican, was being shown, not only to the attendees inside the great hall, but also to the world through ETWN and Al-Jazeera. This film was especially powerful because it captured one of the rare instances that the Blessed Mother had spoken directly to the world without intermediaries. Because she spoke audibly, in her own voice, it seemed a double miracle.

This footage caught the entire event from every angle, because Pope Romano had informed Cardinal Vitalia of a premonition that an apparition might come on that eventful day. As a result, the cardinal had instructed ETWN to position its cameras at strategic locations within St. Peter's Square and surrounding elevated sites.

●●●●●

"Wow! What a trump card!" said EU President Vandenberg, as he watched the footage his office TV. He confided to his closest associate, watching beside him, "I had no idea the Vatican had this surprise up their sleeves. If this broadcast doesn't convince the interfaithers to coalesce with our benevolent global program, then I don't know what will!"

35

Millions Witness Eucharistic Miracles from Rome

With the big screen showing the never before seen footage of the Marian apparition at the Vatican, it was clear that the full attention of everyone inside the Basilica had been captivated. "What does this all mean?" "What will the Pope expect from us now?" "Can he really unite the faiths and bring world peace?" "Where do we go from here?" These were just a few of the questions on the minds of those in attendance.

As the video ended, the lights were restored in the basilica, and the Pope declared:

> "So, as you see, beloved brothers and sisters, it is not merely my wish, but my obligation, at the personal bequest of the Blessed Mother, to unite all faiths to her Immaculate Heart. Born without sin, she lived free from sin all of her life and was assumed into heaven. I quote these words spoken in the 13th century by the esteemed St. Thomas Aquinas, *'God has entrusted the keys and treasures of Heaven to Mary.'*"[42]

Raising up his voice another decibel the pontiff continued,

> "Indeed, the Queen of Heaven, alone, holds the keys to heaven's benevolent future plan for mankind. The time has arrived for all of you, and the members of your respective religions,

to submit your allegiances to her. Our Lady of Fatima, the woman clothed with the sun, has chosen this extraordinary time to reveal herself to the whole world. This is described vividly in the pages of Holy Scripture in the twelfth chapter of the Apocalypse. Only through your submissions to the Blessed Mother can the peace the world so desperately needs be obtained. She has made the evidence abundantly clear, you have seen it with your own eyes, that the dawn of this blessed new era has arrived. The apparitions, miracles, healings and massive Catholic conversions are a testimony, along with Our Lady's supernatural intervention against Russia and its multinational armies, that the Blessed Mother is preparing the way for world peace."

Taking a momentary pause to shift his focus upon a large Muslim contingency from Mecca that had been intentionally seated in front of him, Pope Romano said,

"Long before Mohammed the prophet of Islam ever lived, St. Peter Chyrsologus, our infamous 'Doctor of Homilies' from the fifth-century announced unequivocally that, *'God wills that Mary exact from His goodness peace for the earth, glory for Heaven, life for the dead, and salvation for all who are lost.'*[43]

Lifting his gaze back to the broader audience without interrupting the flow of his homily, he further stated,

"Those nations that persist in waging wars, will face the same undesirable fate as Russia. If rogue states, with their dictatorial leaders, do not cease their spread of evil, they will also be destroyed. Bloodshed and violence are at odds with the sovereign wishes of the Queen of Heaven. But you, the religious leaders of the free world, must not resort to such behavior. United we will stand strong and enable the Blessed Mother's peace to flow through us like a river of life unto the nations. I proclaim to you her sincere promise that, through the guidance of the Catholic Church, all of you can lead the people of every tribe, tongue, and nation into life, liberty, love, and the noble pursuit of world peace and to the salvation of their souls."

Standing up slowly and opening his arms to the crowd and the worldwide audience, Pope Romano issued this benediction,

"Come to her, all my brothers and sisters, come one and all into the open arms of our Blessed Mother, and be fully accepted by her true Church. Do not doubt, but believe when I say that the salvation of every soul can and must be obtained through Our Lady and her Roman Catholic Church. I quote this undeniable truth from Gregory XVI, who presided as our Pope between 1831-1846 A.D., *"It is not possible to worship God truly except in Her; all who are outside Her will not be saved."*[44] Over seven-centuries ago, one of our greatest saints of all times, St. Bonaventure, declared this truth about Our Lady when he admonished, *"No one can enter into Heaven except through Mary, as entering through a gate… He who neglects the service of the Blessed Virgin will die in his sins . . . He who does not invoke thee, O Lady, will never get to Heaven . . . Not only will those from whom*

*Mary turns her countenance not be saved, but
there will be no hope of their salvation . . . No one
can be saved without the protection of Mary.*[45]

Scanning the room, the television cameras captured the faces of the faithful and the newly convinced, whose countenances clearly displayed adoration and allegiance to the Pope. This scene reinforced before the watchful world that the Pope deserved the titles of the Vicar of Christ and the Chosen One of the Blessed Virgin Mary.

Having spoken his final words, the Pontiff made his way to the altar, where the Eucharistic elements were prepared for him to distribute.

Meanwhile, Cardinal Vitalia extended an invitation to the assembly seated inside the Basilica. "You are all invited to witness the Catholic Faithful assembled among you as they partake of the Holy Mass. Although the ceremony is restricted to them alone, we would like to share this sacred observance with all of you who would like to experience how salvation occurs by the partaking of the Eucharist by our Faithful members of the Catholic Church. You are free to remain inside or depart if you prefer."

Only a handful of skeptics left the cathedral. Among the majority who remained, there appeared to be an anxious expectation that something miraculous would occur.

With the Pontiff in place at the altar, the deacon sang the traditional offering of the sign of peace.[46] The Holy Father turned to the cardinals arrayed to receive the sacrament, and offered them the ritual sign of peace, then all the Catholic people turned to each other and passed the peace among themselves. As this transpired, the big screens flashed: *We offer you the peace that the world cannot offer, but that only Christ can give.*

As the Catholics lined up for the partaking of the Eucharist, the choirs, accompanied by the mammoth pipe organ, began singing the familiar song "Lamb of God, take away the sins of the world."

Afterward, Pope Romano began the proceedings by passing out the first few elements to some of the deacons who had lined up. Alongside were about eighty priests assisting the Pontiff, due to the oversized crowd hoping to receive the Holy Communion. Shortly after the proceedings commenced, the Holy Father, with his golden chalice in hand, slowly made his way to a group of about fifty guests of honor among the faithful, who were to receive the elements of the Eucharist personally from the Pope. These included select cardinals, bishops, nuns, deacons, priests, and a few visionaries.

With his departure to the VIP area, the cameras shifted their coverage to Pope Romano's serving of the Holy Eucharist. The Mass was proceeding smoothly as planned, as both the Pope and the priests were distributing the elements in a coordinated fashion.

But curiously, while performing the Intinction[47] of dipping the wafer into the wine filled golden chalice for a respected female visionary standing before him, the Pope paused. It was as if he instinctively sensed that something mystical was about to occur. Fixing his full focus upon the communicant, the Pontiff extracted the Sacred Wafer and delicately lifted it toward her when suddenly something spectacular occurred!

The Miracle of the Eucharist...

When the consecrated element was only inches away from being inserted into her opened mouth, human blood began to exude out of the wafer and swiftly stream down the Pope's robe and drip to the floor. A few seconds into this miracle the Pope experienced a burning sensation in his hand that caused him to drop the wafer back into the chalice from whence it had been dipped. As he quickly peered down into his cup, he was astonished to see that the communion Host had altered its form into flesh.

By now all eyes and TV cameras in the hall directed their undivided attention to the Eucharistic miracle taking place with the Pope. The big screens in the Basilica were all synchronized and live streaming the supernatural events taking place.

"It's turned into flesh," the Pope enthusiastically exclaimed!

Lifting the golden goblet for all to see, he repeated, "The Holy Host has become the bloody flesh of our Lord!"

At that moment, things took a new turn as the blood in the chalice began spurting upward toward the Cathedral's ceiling causing people nearby to step back. It was as though the ceremonial vessel had tapped into a wellspring and converted into a fountain source for this life sustaining substance. To everyone's surprise, the phenomenon defied gravity as the blood did not splash back down upon the ornate marble floors. Rather, it resembled a radiant red tower of plasma.

Pope Romano ecstatically cried out, "HE IS ALIVE! HE IS RISEN!"

With these words echoing throughout the auditorium, another supernatural metamorphosis took place. The towering lifeblood transformed from red liquid into white light. It slowly began to swirl and spiral upward from the cup and sparkle like a luminescent holograph.

The scene was so surreal, a cameraman filming inside the Basilica blurted out to his TV host nearby, "This only happens in animated movies! Tell me this isn't really happening!"

The TV newscaster enthusiastically replied, "I hope you're catching this on camera. We're capturing a live miracle at the *Vatic…!*"

Before she could complete the word *Vatican*, her mouth dropped open at the sight of a semi-transparent male image floating above her. Appearing to be in his early thirties, he was levitating with his arms stretched wide open as though hanging upon a cross. His visage included a crown of thorns reflecting in the light like a halo and His face, though hard to make out, resembled the one from the Shroud of Turin.

While the Eucharistic Jesus was still suspended in mid-air, the renowned female visionary who had been deprived of her wafer began speaking aloud in Latin. Quickly a microphone was whisked over and held in front of her. Anxiously her voice bellowed throughout the auditorium asking for quiet, the Pope and priests began lifting their hands calling for calm. It wasn't long until the apparition's message was piercing through the deafening silence and being translated upon the screens all about the basilica. These powerful words were displayed,

> *"This is My body that was broken and My blood that was shed for you. They are always present in the Eucharist. I have been troubled with many doubters among you, who in the past, have questioned My promise to be present in every Eucharist offering. Who am I, that I would ever fail to fulfill my commitments in this Holy Communion? Am I not the Savior of the world?"*

There was a momentary pause in the message, which allowed the audience to take a gulp of humble pride. Then, the visionary continued channeling and speaking the Lord's message.

> *"Now learn this; In this miracle of the Eucharist, you were privileged to experience My gospel supernaturally through the elements. The wafer is My body in* **Death***. It became My blood that ran down My Beloved Pope's robe where it now stains the floor. Likewise, My blood still cries out from Jerusalem where I was crucified. My Vicar's hands burned as I conferred upon him the agony I felt when the nails were hammered into my hands! The blood touching the floor was my* **Burial***. The transformation of My blood into the white light is My* **Resurrection** *and its upward reach to the cathedral ceiling is My* **Ascension** *into heaven. For, I Am the Resurrection! I alone hold the keys to Heaven and Hell. Redemption is in My Holy Eucharist. It is the Blessed Sacrament that cleanses you from sin and saves your soul!"*

With this interpretation of the miracle, the Pontiff raised up and displayed the chalice before the throngs. As he did, all the Catholic Faithful in attendance folded their hands and fell to their knees in reverence. Then, the audience gasped as the apparition's eyes turned into a flame of fire. The visionary ratcheted up her voice and continued.

> *"I know your works, love, service, faith, and your patience; and as for your works, the last are more than the first. Nevertheless, I have this against some of you in My Church. You allow the sacrilege of My Holy Eucharist to occur. You tolerate, rather than excommunicate, those among you who boldly deny My Presence in the Eucharist."*

With these piercing words, the fiery eyes of the apparition became even brighter and their focus shifted noticeably to several rows filled with affluent Cardinals. The visionary's message paused momentarily in synchronization. As an eerie silence fell upon the audience, it became obvious to everyone that this portion of the message was an admonishment specifically intended for their hearing.

> *"Many of My Eucharistic miracles have been proven to be real blood by the scientists. Even in the face of reality and technical proof, there are still many who do not believe in My Real Presence. This denial of My Presence is the worst of insults and a disrespect for My Gift of the Eucharist. This is why those same people, who reject My Presence, do not feel it necessary to confess their sins. Those, who teach against My Real Presence, and put down these miracles, are the real blasphemers. Those, who do not love My Blessed Sacrament, are the lukewarm that I will vomit from My mouth."*[48]

Tears started flooding the faces of many Cardinals and Bishops who realized that the Eucharistic Christ was speaking directly to a problem that they were struggling with in their congregations. Some of them beseeched aloud repeatedly to the apparition, "Forgive us. Help us our Lord."

As if to acknowledge approval to their requests, the apparition returned to its original form, and as the visionary presented the Lord's final words, a feeling of peaceful bliss permeated the room.

> *"I speak to all of you here now. I have provided this miracle today so that the world will truly know Who I Am. I Am the universal truth and the Giver of eternal life! I wish for all to have Holy Communion with me. I will continue to come into this world faithfully through the petitions of My anointed priests on the appointed days of obligation, now you come devotedly to Me, all of my children. Greet Me through the doors of My "True Church," entreat Me in the extended embrace of My "Blessed Mother" and meet Me in My Holy Eucharist!"*

About twenty seconds lapsed after these final words before the image disappeared. Immediately, a kaleidoscope of emotions - fear, joy, disbelief, awe - overcame the interfaith assembly. Most of them started transmitting emails and texts to their friends, families and associates worldwide. In a matter of minutes, blogs and social networks began buzzing with posted photos and reports of the Eucharistic miracle.

It wasn't long before a stir of amazement spread outside the basilica throughout St. Peter's Square. Most everyone began praising the Blessed Mother and the Pope, but a few others seriously suspected that charlatanism had occurred. One Protestant contingent embedded in the center of the large crowd started shouting, "This is demonic! Pure idolatry! That's not Jesus!"

The people around them started calling them "heretics" and "blasphemers!" Before the Swiss Guard could get there to arrest the matter, the crowd had pounced on the Protestants dropping them to the ground. Then, they began brutally beating them to a pulp. When paramedics arrived on the scene, three were dead and the other six were rushed to the hospital in critical condition.

Meanwhile, inside the Basilica, the apparition's message remained displayed upon the big screens long after the visionary stopped speaking. The Eucharistic miracle became the top news story throughout the mainstream medias of every country. This widely publicized supernatural event served to validate Roman Catholicism as the premier world religion. It also helped to esteem the Pope as the arbiter of moral values and all spiritual truths.

36

Two Witnesses
Prepare for the
Tribulational Period

It was the Tuesday evening following the Vatican super summit event, when Lisa received an alarming message on her home answering machine.

She, along with Naomi, Jami, Amber, and little Bella, had just returned from a short girls' vacation at the recently renovated 5-Star Hilton Eilat Queen Sheba Resort. The lavish hotel, located at the northern tip of the Red Sea, had suffered severe structural damage during the Arab-Israeli war, and was having its grand reopening. Due to Lisa's prestigious position in the government, the fivesome had received the VIP treatment throughout their stay. Having just dropped everyone off at their homes, she and Jami proceeded to check their missed messages.

It was a frantic call from Nathan Severs: "Lisa, where are you? Gershom, Simeon, and I came by your house yesterday to warn you of some very troubling developments! We have all returned to Israel, and we have some critical information to share with you and your family! Please, you must call me immediately, and let me know that the two of you are safe."

Instantly, Jami locked onto her mother's arm and cried, "Oh, no, Mother! Not again! What now?"

Patting her daughter's white-knuckled hand, Lisa comforted, "We're home safe, Jami. Calm down and take a deep breath. Look, the pictures are still hung in place, the furniture's not turned upside down, and our house is still standing. It's going to be okay, honey."

Then, more seriously, she admitted, "But something is definitely troubling Uncle Nathan. Perhaps something serious happened while we were away."

Giving her mother a puzzled look, Jami asked, "Didn't you talk to Uncle Nathan about a week before we left on vacation?"

Lisa confirmed, "Yes, but he didn't say anything about coming back to Israel. In fact, when I asked when we might see him again, he said probably not for a while. He said he was making solid inroads with the Jewish organizations in the U.S. I asked him to contact, and promote the return of American Jews to Israel. I was thrilled that he was having so much success with the project, but I felt disheartened that we might not see him anytime soon."

After dead bolting the front door for extra security, the two of them sat down at the kitchen table and Jami proceeded to return Nathan's urgent call. With the speaker phone turned up to maximum volume, they could both hear it ringing repeatedly.

"Come on, Uncle Nathan! Pick up the phone, already!" Jami moaned.

Finally, after what seemed a month of Sabbaths, the girls heard his voice. "Hello, this is Nathan….."

Not realizing that it was only his recording, Jami bellowed, "Uncle Nathan, it's us! We are…."

Disappointment overtook them when they realized it was only his answering machine. Pausing, Lisa quieted herself and waited for his recorded message to play out. At the sound of the beep, Lisa started to let him know they were safe at home. She had scarcely begun leaving her message, however, when suddenly there was a loud rapping upon her front door.

Stunned, the two girls looked into each other's eyes. "What do we do, Mother?" Jami squeaked.

Lisa gingerly hung up the phone, and with a lump in her throat, softly said, "Here's what we do: you go get our two biggest butcher knives, one for each of us, while I peek through the blinds to see who's knocking down the front door."

Grabbing her mother by the arm again, Jami pleaded, "Wait a minute! Don't peek yet! Knives won't do us any good if someone has a gun!"

Shocked, Lisa swept Jami into her arms. Together they shivered, until a familiar voice beyond the door shouted, "Lisa! Jami! Are you in there? Open up! It's me, Nathan."

Instantly, they ran for the door, unlocked it and threw it open.

Standing at the threshold, Uncle Nathan said, "What took you so long? I saw your car in the driveway and heard you both talking in …"

Before he could finish, the girls held him in a group bear hug.

"You'll never know how good it is to see you!" Lisa exclaimed.

"And I missed my two favorite girls so much!" Nathan echoed. "It's great to hug you both again."

Jami pulled away and looked at him with troubled eyes. "So, what did your message mean, 'troubling developments'?"

Caressing their hands, Nathan replied, "I have some good and some bad news. According to Gershom and Simeon, Moses and Elijah have returned to earth and are in Jerusalem about to begin their three and one-half years of ministry. That's the good news!"

Squeezing his hand tightly, Jami agreed, "That's amazing! What a miracle, these are two of our famous Jewish people from the past!"

"Wait a minute," Lisa cautioned. "What's the bad news?"

"That's the 'troubling development'," he responded. "According to Revelation 11, the ministry period of these two witnesses overlaps with the first half of the dreaded 'Tribulational Period.' This means that the final seven-years of tribulation on earth must be rapidly approaching!"

"Not the 'Tribulational Period;' not already," Lisa winced, gasping for breath. "Doesn't the Bible say this is when the Antichrist attempts the final genocide of the Jews? What does that mean for us Jewish believers?"

Teary eyed, Jami pleaded, "Say it's not true Uncle Nathan, there must be a mistake. What about the Israeli national mantra, 'Yad Vashem?' Remember the holocaust is *never* to happen *again*!'"

Blotting back her tears, he said, "These were my exact sentiments to Gershom and Simeon. They warned us that the first half of the tribulation is a time for Israelis to get out of harm's way. This period provides Israel with a short time of peace. They called it a pseudo peace, because it's a false sense of security created by a seven-year treaty that doesn't last; it gets broken at the midpoint."

"*Oh my*,... the treaty...," Lisa mumbled.

"Yes mother, the treaty," Jami echoed. "Out with it, what do you know?"

Collecting herself, Lisa informed, "This treaty is already being negotiated!"

"What?... Are you sure?" Nathan asked.

"Yes," replied Lisa. "Prime Minister Kaufmann and E.U. President Vandenberg have been secretly hashing this out. I caught drift of it from my boss. He let it slip out before we took off on our girl's trip. After catching himself, he swore me to secrecy until the treaty is officially announced."

"Did Fleishman specify the seven-year term?" Nathan wondered.

Lisa's eyes closed as her head nodded up and down slowly. Nathan and Jami exchanged glances when suddenly Jami shuddered, "I can't believe this is happening! We return from vacation to this shock! What's next?... How much more bad news can we endure?"

"Girls..., we have to remain calm and be smart about this," Nathan advised. "We must prepare an exit strategy to get you and Tovia's family to safety. I'm thinking we need to go back to my place in Rome."

"What?... No Nathan," Jami rebuffed. "Things are getting really creepy there with all that is happening on the news at the Vatican. Remember, we couldn't leave there fast enough last time!"

"We need to get advice from Gershom and Simeon," Jami pleaded. "They will know what we should do."

Nathan agreed. "I will arrange a meeting with Tovia's family and all of us right away."

37

The Encounter between Satan and his Seed

Awaking abruptly to the sound of a thunderous noise, Hans Vandenberg swiftly moved to the side of his bed. Collecting his thoughts, he sensed something unusual in his spirit. "What was that startling noise," he pondered.

He began reflecting upon the dream he had been brusquely awoken from. "There must be a connection," he surmised. "*Hmm…let's see. I was in a verdant valley encircled by hordes of soldiers. Oddly, they were arrayed in a wide variety of uniforms. What was that all about, and what was I doing there?*"

"*Think, Hans,*" he whispered patting his cheeks intermittently. "*Why was I there? Yes…*, a white horse, I was sitting atop a magnificent white steed. I was holding an ornate bow in my right hand and wearing a spectacular crown upon my head. When I lifted up the bow, trumpets began bellowing throughout the basin and the armies proceeded to assemble into orderly ranks. They were preparing for war."

"*What war? Come on, try hard to recall Hans,*" he continued. "They were waiting for me to lead the charge somewhere… *I'm drawing a blank… What war…? What valley…? What voice…?*"

Exacerbated, he stood up and began pacing, when suddenly the thunderous noise sounded again startling him in his tracks. The sound resonated powerfully, the house shook and his soul became increasingly restless.

Racing outside, he shouted, "What's happening? Who are you?"

His pleadings were greeted with eerie silence.

Standing in utter disbelief, a gentle breeze enveloped his body.

Something magical about its embrace soothed his spirit. He had never experienced such a sudden shift in emotions.

Turning his gaze toward heaven, his countenance changed. He sensed something surrounding him. Something unexplainable was occurring; it was blissful. He felt powerful, yet peaceful at the same time.

"Divine appointment," said the stranger. "Hans, you have been prepared for such a time as this."

Turning toward the visitor, Vandenberg became intimidated by his appearance. He was tall, towering about twelve feet high. His robe was white, his shoulder length hair was black and an aura illuminated from his visage. Hans collapsed prostrate in astonishment.

Helping him up, the foreigner smiled and said, "There's no need for that."

Dwarfed standing beside him, Hans, the consummate politician, found himself at a loss for words.

"Do you know who I am?" The mystery man asked.

Stupefied, Hans silently nodded no.

"Where I come from, I have many titles," stated the alien. "Prince of the Power of the Air, Angel of Light, god of this Age and King of the Bottomless Pit, just to name a few."

"So, do you claim to be all of the above?" Hans asked.

"I do," he acknowledged. "I claim whatever title and wear whichever crown I must to maintain my throne, which is exalted above all the stars in the universe."

"You have my undivided attention," Hans admitted. "Certainly, you possess symmetry like no other, but what proof did you bring to substantiate such bold claims?"

"My thunderous sound alarms you and the stature of my presence humbles you," the newcomer humored. "Do you also seek a sign? Hmm…, let me think, what shall I show you?"

Then suddenly and without warning, Vandenberg was transported to an exceedingly high mountain. Beneath him lay all the kingdoms of the world and their splendor.

The stranger spoke, "All of these are mine! They are subservient to me and I can share them with whomever I please!"

Vandenberg pondered what it would be like to preside over these empires. "Control over economies, the environment and population growth rates. No more reliance upon the Vatican to control the masses. The cessation of diplomatic compromises with self-serving politicians. Also, an end to negotiating with Israel's unceasing demands for land and security. Finally, the creation of a utopian society."

"What are you thinking?" asked the Angel of Light. "Are you wondering where do I sign to reign over these kingdoms?"

"What world leader in his right mind wouldn't jump at the opportunity?" Vandenberg replied.

Breathing deep, Hans thought, "This can't be real. I must be dreaming."

"Han's, you're probably thinking that this is too good to be true...; *am I right?* Why can't it be true?" the stranger asked. "Millions recently vanished unexplainably, the Russian coalition was vanquished mysteriously, and apparitions have been occurring supernaturally around the globe. The world has evolved into a place where the paranormal is now the new normal. Everything has changed. People are no longer questioning if there is a god, now they are wondering which god to serve. This is where you come in."

"Me?" asked Hans.

"Yes you," he confirmed. "Why do you think you are positioned as one of the world's most prominent politicians in this new era? Do you think it's a coincidence that the E.U. emerges, while America and Russia declines? Think hard Han's! How did you rise to power so easily and unexpectedly? Reflect upon your political career. Finances came in at crucial moments, rivals were eliminated by scandals and the enemies of your past became stricken with illness, or in some cases assassinated. Do you think this was all merely happenstance?"

"What are you saying?" Han's questioned.

"You are the work of my hands," prided the extra-terrestrial. "I have seeded the life on this planet. In ages past, I called upon my minions to make mankind in my image, and you are the cream of the crop. I have coddled you since birth to reign over my realms. The time has come to set this truth in motion."

"How have you coddled me? Where were you in my troubled childhood?" Han's probed.

"When your father beat your mother into a coma, I heard your pleadings and healed her. When your father tried to brutalize you, I prevented it by causing him to have a heart attack. When you were diagnosed with brain tumors, I made them all disappear at the same time. The doctors said it was a miracle. Indeed, it was, it was my miracle for you."

"It was you that night in the hospital, wasn't it?" Han's asked. "I couldn't see you, but I felt your presence touching my head. I knew I was healed in that instant. I felt a great peace come over me. It was like the peace I felt when you breathed upon me this morning."

"Yes, and oh how I so desperately wanted to reveal myself to you then," his companion confirmed. "But, the hour had not come."

With outstretched hand, Han's said, "This must be the hour. This is why you greeted me today and enlightened me as to who you are. Oh, how I have longed for a remedy to cure the world's madness. I put no faith in religious devotion to Mary to right the wrongs of this world. I knew at some point that a true god would have to eliminate the Vatican stronghold upon the masses, but it was politically expedient to come alongside the Pope to restore calm amidst world chaos."

Smiling, the giant said, "The apparitions, miracles and healings were implemented centuries ago to only play a temporary role in preparing the minds of the masses for the ultimate great deception that is coming. Humanity was not ready in the past for the new age about to be revealed now through you my beloved seed."

"What's next, my benevolent father?" Han's asked. "Where do we go from here? I absolutely accept your offer to reign over the realms of this world."

"My son," he said, "You will need to sideline Israel temporarily, while we establish the world into ten districts. These territories will be governed independently by the kings of your choosing. In the near future, you will confirm the seven-year agreement that you are currently negotiating with Israel. During the first half of the agreement, you will establish the ten domains. In the middle of the seven years, you will call upon the ten kings to overpower the Vatican empire, at which time you will confiscate all of its wealth and holdings. Possessing the Vatican treasures and the loyalty from the ten kings, you will become enthroned as the uncontested ruler of this world. I have spoken it, now let it come into existence!"

"Yes, my lord, but what about the Jews?" Han's questioned. "We must do something about those Jews. They will never comply with your benevolent plan for this planet. They will never abandon their Jehovah mindset."

"Every last one of them must be eliminated," said the Angel of Light. "In so doing, we will prove that their Jehovah is the lesser god, in whom no one will ever trust again!"

And so it was that Satan, the Angel of Light, convinced his point man, the Antichrist, to prepare for the new age to come!

Cast of Characters

THE THOMPSON FAMILY

George Thompson	Tyler and Jami's grandfather, Martha's husband, retired Four-Star General
Martha Thompson	(a.k.a. Mimi), Tyler and Jami's grandmother
Tyler Thompson	(a.k.a. Ty), grandson of George and Martha, son of Thomas
Thomas Thompson	Son of George and Martha, Tyler and Jami's mother
Lisa Thompson	Wife of Thomas, daughter-in-law of George and Martha, and Tyler and Jami's mother
Jami Thompson	Tyler's sister, granddaughter of George and Martha
Grandma Naomi	Lisa's and Tovia's mother, Tyler's, Jami's, Bella's and Jaxon's grandmother
Tovia	Lisa's brother, Jami's uncle, Amber's husband, Bella's and Jaxon's father
Amber	Tovia's wife, Jami's aunt, Lisa's sister-in-law, Bella's and Jaxon's mother
Bella	Tovia's and Amber's daughter, Lisa's niece, Tyler's and Jami's cousin
Jaxon	Tovia's and Amber's son, Lisa's nephew, Tyler and Jami's cousin

FRIENDS AND ASSOCIATES OF THE THOMPSON FAMILY

Robert Rassmussen	(a.k.a. Razz),Best friend of George Thompson, respected eschatologist

Nathaniel Severs	Razz' best friend, President of UGIC
Jim Linton	Respected eschatologist and Bible prophecy teacher
Harold Hirsch	CEO of UGIC (Unistate Global Investments Corporation)

POLITICAL AND MILITARY LEADERS

United States

John Bachlin	President
Harold Redding	President, successor of John Bachlin
Donald Yates	Secretary of Defense
Benjamin Bernard	Federal Reserve Chairman
Paul Jordan	Lieutenant, the Watch Commander of Phoenix PD

Israel

Moshe Kaufman	Prime Minister
Eliezer Moday	President
Jacob Barak	Chief military commander of the Israel Defense Forces
Jonathan Vitow	IAF Lieutenant
Binyamin Lieberman	(a.k.a. Benny) IAF Lieutenant General
Ehud Cohen	The Temple Foundation spokesman
Avi Fleishman	Minister of the Interior

European Union

Hans Vandenberg	European Union President

Russia and China

Vladimir Ziroski	(a.k.a. Mad Vlad) Russian President
Sergei Primakov	Russian Prime Minister

Mikhail Trutnev	Russian senior advisor to Prime Minister
Alena Popov	Russian Secretary of Mikhail Trutnev
Anatoly Tarasov	Russian Ambassador to the United Nations
Li Chin	China's Ambassador to the United Nations
Hu Jintao	China's President

Middle East (Arabs and Persians)

Muktada Zakiri	Iranian President
Zamani Nikahd	spiritual mentor to Iranian President Zakiri
Ayatollah Khomani	spiritual leader of Iran
Sadegh Mousavi	President of Hamas
Ahmad Al-Masri	top General of Hamas
Neda	Sadegh Mousavi's Secretary
Karim Nazari	Al-Qaeda's new leader
Muhammad Imad Fadlallah	Secretary General of Hezbollah
Hassan Tereiri	Syrian President

RELIGIOUS LEADERS

Joseph Levin	Chief Rabbi of Israel's Chief Rabbinate Council
Aaron Edelstein	Rabbi of Israel's Chief Rabbinate Council
Vincente Romano	The Pope
Gabriel Vitalia	Senior Catholic Cardinal
Arturo Amanti	Former Catholic Bishop
Patrick Dolan	Former Catholic Archbishop
Ladd Bitterman	Protestant Pastor
Brad Walters	Protestant Pastor
Gary Hanah	Protestant Pastor

Endnotes

1   A sign of the Mahdi, the Islamic messiah, "It is clear that this man is the Mahdi who will ride the white horse and judge by the Qur'an (with justice) and with whom will be men with marks of prostration on their foreheads [Marks on their foreheads from bowing in prayer with their head to the ground five times daily]." http://www.answering-islam.org/Authors/JR/Future/ch04_the_mahdi.htm

2   A real threat was issued from an Israeli foreign minister to Syrian President Assad which can be read over the Internet as of 9/7/11 at this link: http://www.maannews.net/eng/ViewDetails.aspx?ID=259178

3   The tribulation is a term Christians often use to describe the last seven-year period on this present earth's time line. This period is characterized by the outpouring of divine judgments upon Christ-rejection humanity.

4   Revelation 8:5, 11:13, 16:18 (earthquakes); Revelation 9:13-19, Zechariah 14:12 (wars); Revelation 8:8-11 (seas, streams, and rivers).

5   Isralestine, The Ancient Blueprint of the Future Middle East, is authored by Bill Salus and is available through Amazon or Bill Salus' personal website at, www.prophecydepot.com.

6   John Bolton told a group, including the author, that the world may have to accept the fact that Iran will become a nuclear nation. He suggested the only alternative to this would be if some nation attacked Iran's nuclear program. He believed that only Israel would consider this, at the time that he spoke. This was on 9/10/11 at a banquet held in his honor in Beverly Hills, CA.

7   Genesis 14:17

8   Dr. Arnold Fruchtenbaum of Ariel Ministries identifies this in section C-6 of chapter 20 in his The Footsteps of the Messiah. John McTernan's article of August 23, 2010, regarding this subject is linked at http://johnmcternansinsights.blogspot.com/2010/08/elamiran-in-latter-days.html (accessed 12/2/2010). Sean Osborne's article of September 15, 2010, regarding this subject is linked at http://eschatologytoday.blogspot.com/2010/09/jeremiah-49-will-coalition-of-nations-html (accessed 12/2/2010).

9   2 Chronicles 29:30 informs us that Asaph was a seer at the time of King David. The Hebrew word for seer is chozeh and identified Asaph as a beholder of vision likened to a prophet.

10   Psalm 83:4

11   Psalm 83:12 indicates that motive of the Arab confederacy is to possess the Promised Land.

12   Use of these tactical nukes against the West would leave a no-alibi forensic nuclear fingerprint pointing at Russia and directly incriminate "President

Siroski," given the narrative above. The late (some say, and I believe, assassinated) General Alexander Lebed assured the US Congress and the American public via the CBS News program 60 Minutes, in September 1997, that between 84 and 100 of Russia's 250 1kT tactical nukes were missing. These tactical nuclear weapons were under the direct control of the Spetnaz GRU, according to General Lebed. (Notes to author from Sean Osborne on 6/25/11)

13   Obadiah 20a; emphasis added

14   Ezekiel 37:10 speaks of an exceedingly great army.

15   John 14:6

16   Based on the Nathaniel Benchley juvenile novel, The Off-Islanders, the movie which tells the Cold War story of the comedic chaos which ensues when the Soviet submarine accidentally runs aground near a small New England island town. Information accessed on 2/22/11 from the internet at http://en.wikipedia.org/wiki/The_Russians_Are_Coming,_the_Russians_Are_Coming

17   I Thessalonians 5:9-10, 1:10 and Revelation 3:10 (the church of Philadelphia is kept prophetically from the "hour or trial"). Many scholars associate this phrase with events in the tribulation period.

18   There is some dispute as to whether Pharoah Ramses ruled at the time of the Hebrew exodus out of Egypt. Some scholars believe he ruled subsequently and advocate that Amenhotep II was Pharoah at the time. Informaiton was accessed 5/5/2011 from the internet at: http://wiki.answers.com/Q/Was_it_really_Ramses_II_who_was_the_Pharoah_when_the_Exodus_happened

19   Isaiah 47:5 speaks of a Queen of Kingdoms, or Lady of Kingdoms in some Bible translations.

20   Luke 1:46-50

21   "Queen of Heaven" is another title used by Mary visionaries for the Lady of All Nations. More explanations are given in the commentary section.

22   Matthew 6:9-15. After this manner therefore pray ye: Our Father, which art in heaven, Hallowed be thy name. Thy kingdom come, Thy will be done in earth, as it is in heaven. Give us this day our daily bread. And forgive us our debts, as we forgive our debtors. And lead us not into temptation, but deliver us from evil; For thine is the kingdom, and the power, and the glory, forever. Amen. For it ye forgive men their trespasses, your heavenly Father will also forgive you: But if ye forgive not men their trespasses, neither will your Father forgive your trespasses. (KJV)

23   Oskar Schindler (28 April 1908 - 9 October 1974) was an ethnic German industrialist born in Moravia. He is credited with saving almost 1,200 Jews during the Holocaust by employing them in his enamelware and ammunitions factories, which were located in what is now Poland and the Czech Republic, respectively. Internet accessed 5/11/2011 at http://en.wiki.org/wiki/Oskar_Schindler

24   The "Message of Fatima" is available on the Internet as of 9/4/16 at this website: http://www.vatican.va/roman_curia/congregations/cfaith/documents/rc_con_cfaith_doc_20000626_message-fatima_en.html

25   Tanakh is the name used in Judaism for the canon of the Hebrew Bible. It includes the – The Torah ("Teaching", also known as the Five Books of Moses), Nevi'im ("Prophets") and Ketuyim ("Writings"). The Jewish Tanakh is the equivalent of the Christian Hebrew Old Testament

26   Jahannam is the word for Hell in Islam

27   Joel 2:28 and Acts 2:17 informs that in the last days that old men will dream dreams and young men will see visions.

28   1 Peter 1:7-9

29   Revelation 7:9 informs that all nations, tribes, peoples, and tongues are benefited by the ministry of the 144,000 witnesses.

30   Pogroms are defined as "The organized killing of many helpless people usually because of their race or religion by the Merriam Webster dictionary at this website: http://www.merriam-webster.com/dictionary/pogrom.

31   Information about the Griffon Vultures obtained over the Internet on 1/3/12 at this website: http://en.wikipedia.org/wiki/Griffon_Vulture Information about carnivores animals of Israel was obtained on the Internet on 1/3/12 at this website: http://www.listofcountriesoftheworld.com/is-animals.html

32   Information about carnivores animals of Israel was obtained on the Internet on 1/3/12 at this website: http://www.listofcountriesoftheworld.com/is-animals.html

33   Based upon Surah 3:40 in the Koran, which says: And remember the angel's words to Mary. He said: "Allah has chosen you. He has made you pure and exalted you above all women. Diary, be obedient to your Lord; bow down and worship with the worshippers."

34   The message of the third secret at Fatima is on this website: http://www.vatican.va/roman_curia/congregations/cfaith/documents/rc_con_cfaith_doc_20000626_message-fatima_en.html

35   Research taken from Revelation Road page 224, and is duly footnoted to have been gathered from Dr. Ron Rhodes book, Northern Storm Rising.

36   S.O.S. is sometimes translated as "save our souls" or "save our ship."

37   Africanized Bees - The Africanized Bee is a descendant from 26 Tanzanian queen bees accidentally released from a lab in Brazil. The Biologist working with the bees was trying to develop a strain better adapted to tropical and subtropical conditions. Instead of more productive bees, he ended up with a strain of extremely defensive bees. The released queens gave rise to what is commonly called the Africanized Bee. They have since spread throughout the

Americas. One sting from an Africanized bee is no worse than a sting from the common honey bee. It hurts but is rarely fatal. Unfortunately, the Africanized bees attack in swarms. Their victims may be stung thousands of times. That many stings can and does kill. Information gathered on 7/28/12 from this Internet site - http://www.squidoo.com/dangerous-bugs#module17098722

38   For more information on Mary of Agreda visit these two websites: https://en.wikipedia.org/wiki/Mary_of_Jesus_of_Ágreda / http://www.traditionalcatholicpublishing.com/n-city.html

39   Mary of Agreda quote is taken from the book by Thomas W. Petrisko called, "Call of the Ages," Santa Barbara, CA, Queenship Publishing, 1995, p. 449.

40   Quote from the book, "For the Soul of the Family," by Thomas W. Petrisko, Santa Barbara, California, Queenship Publishing, 1996, page 92.

41   The quotes of the Nostra Aetate were taken from the Internet on August 15, 2012 at this link http://www.vatican.va/archive/hist_councils/ii_vatican_council/documents/vat-ii_decl_19651028_nostra-aetate_en.html

42   St. Thomas Aquinas quote taken from the Internet on 10/20/16 from this website: http://www.catholictradition.org/Mary/mary18a.htm

43   St. Peter Chyrsologus quote taken from Internet on 10/20/16 from this website: http://www.catholictradition.org/Mary/mary18a.htm. As the Dr. of Homilies - http://www.dailycatholic.org/dec4doc.htm

44   Pope Gregory XVI quote from (Encyclical, Summo Jugiter), was taken on 10/20/16 from this website: http://catholicism.org/eens-popes.html

45   St. Bonaventure quotes taken on 10/20/16 from these websites: http://www.catholictradition.org/Mary/mary18a.htm, http://www.catholicgallery.org/quotes/quotes-about-mary-2/

46   The sign of peace is a ritual that is normally performed at a Catholic Mass. Read more about it at this website under the subtitle, "CDWDS Circular Letter on the Ritual Expression of the Gift of Peace at Mass." The website is: http://www.usccb.org/about/divine-worship/newsletter/upload/newsletter-2014-07-and-08.pdf

47   The Intinction is the administration of the sacrament of Communion by dipping bread in wine and giving both together to the communicant.

48   Portions of this section, beginning with the word, "Many," was quoted from the book Message in Heaven by Jim Tetlow on pages 238-239. The quotes originated from, John Leary, Prepare for the Great Tribulation and the Era of Peace, Volume 7, Santa Barbara, CA. Queens Publishing, 1997, pp 8,57,58. Message from "Jesus" to John Leary.

49   The Temple Institutes website is: http://www.templeinstitute.org/

Resource References

For more important research information, I highly recommend the following sources.

Queen of All: The Marian apparitions' plan to unite all religions under the Roman Catholic Church, by Jim Tetlow, Roger Oakland and Brad Myers

Messages from Heaven: A Biblical Examination Of The Queen Of Heaven's Messages In The End Times, by Jim Tetlow and Brad Myers

The Coming Global Transformation; An End Times Audio Presentation 3-CD Set, by Jim Tetlow and Brad Myers

The Coming Global Transformation; An End Tmes Audio Presentation Kindle Edition, by Jim Tetlow, Brad Myers and Bill Salus

Made in the USA
Columbia, SC
27 March 2024